W9-BWW-393

They are . . .

THE ROSE HUNTERS

Three adventurous Highlanders bound by a code of honor to aid a family of headstrong women whenever fate or one of the ladies beckons. . . .

This is the story of Charlotte Nash, who confronts the most dangerous Rose Hunter, blackguard Dand Ross, in a high-stakes game of passion.

"A triumph for readers."
—*Midwest Book Review* on *My Seduction*

"Simply superb."
—*Booklist* on *My Pleasure*

Acclaim for
Award-winning Author
Connie Brockway
and Her Rose Hunters Novels

My Seduction

"A fabulous love story . . . wicked, tender, playful, and sumptuous. . . . Too wonderful to resist."
—*New York Times* best-selling author Lisa Kleypas

"A well-crafted engaging read."   —*Publishers Weekly*

"Passionate and entertaining . . . with an abundance of romance, mystery, and virile Scotsmen in kilts. What's not to love?"
—America Online's Romance Fiction Forum

My Pleasure

"Utterly delicious, sexy, and fast moving."
—*New York Times* best-selling author Eloisa James

"This is why people read romance novels. . . . An exceptionally good read."

—All About Romance

"Exciting, romantic, and deeply emotional, with a poignancy and sensuality unmatched this season, Brockway's tale is a pleasure to read."
—*Romantic Times*, Top Pick!

ALSO BY CONNIE BROCKWAY

My Pleasure

My Seduction

Once Upon a Pillow
(with Christina Dodd)

CONNIE BROCKWAY

My Surrender

POCKET BOOKS

New York   London   Toronto   Sydney

The sale of this book without its cover is unauthorized. If you purchased this book without a cover, you should be aware that it was reported to the publisher as "unsold and destroyed." Neither the author nor the publisher has received payment for the sale of this "stripped book."

This book is a work of fiction. Names, characters, places and incidents are products of the author's imagination or are used fictitiously. Any resemblance to actual events or locales or persons, living or dead, is entirely coincidental.

An *Original* Publication of POCKET BOOKS

POCKET BOOKS, a division of Simon & Schuster, Inc.
1230 Avenue of the Americas, New York, NY 10020

Copyright © 2005 by Connie Brockway

All rights reserved, including the right to reproduce this book or portions thereof in any form whatsoever. For information address Pocket Books, 1230 Avenue of the Americas, New York, NY 10020

ISBN: 0-7434-6324-2

First Pocket Books printing May 2005

10 9 8 7 6 5 4 3 2 1

POCKET and colophon are registered trademarks of Simon & Schuster, Inc.

Cover art and stepback art by Alan Ayers
Hand lettering by Ron Zinn

Manufactured in the United States of America

For information regarding special discounts for bulk purchases, please contact Simon & Schuster Special Sales at 1-800-456-6798 or business@simonandschuster.com

This one is for the Buckhorn Biergartners,

Who, in my heart, have remained forever young.

PROLOGUE

St. Bride's Abbey, January 1804

*The wedding celebration
of Christian MacNeill and
Katherine Nash Blackburn*

OUTSIDE THE CHAPEL, Charlotte crossed to St. Bride's cloister walk and rubbed her hands briskly up and down her bare arms. It was bloody cold in Scotland in January and if the shawl her sister Helena had been chasing her about with all afternoon hadn't completely destroyed the lines of her new gown, she might have actually donned it, despite the jarring way the russet color clashed with her dress's soft blue.

She wasn't exactly sure why she had felt a sudden need to leave the wedding celebration. Her other sister, Kate, and her brawny soldier were so deuced happy, their future assured, the past forgotten, all's well that ends well, and how much more well could something end than that two handsome, intelligent, and worthy people find one another after years of struggle?

Nothing! Except . . . except . . . Charlotte felt as if she were reading a fairy tale's happy ending. Though

Kate had found her knight-in-shining-armor and Charlotte was delighted for her happiness, she suspected her own ending would be nothing like Kate's.

Their father had died three years ago when she was sixteen, and with his death the family she'd known had died, too. Within a year, her mother was dead and her sisters, anxious—no, desperate—to give Charlotte all the "advantages" they'd had as the daughters of well-to-do gentry, somehow scraped together enough money to ship her forthwith off to one of London's most prestigious boarding schools for young ladies, urging her to make "valuable" connections. Finally, Charlotte grasped what must have been abundantly clear to any casual observer: She was a burden. A beloved albatross. A speculative venture—nay, drain—that showed no hints of ever giving fair return on the investment. *Unless* she made good use of those "connections."

As soon as she understood her situation, Charlotte, nobody's fool, accepted it. Wasting little time on grieving for the past, she determined to live up to her sisters' expectations and used her newly discovered adaptability to do so. She'd always been a very pragmatic child; now she became a coolly unsentimental one.

Thus, within six months of their mother's death, all the Nash girls were gainfully, if not always happily, employed: serene and lovely Helena as a companion to a terrible old biddy; dark, passionate Kate, teaching the pianoforte to merchants' daughters; and Charlotte, as boon companion to Margaret Welton, the only daughter of a vastly wealthy, vastly kindhearted, and disastrously ramshackle baron and his equally derelict wife.

The Weltons asked nothing of Charlotte other than that she accept the gifts and dresses they bestowed in abundance upon her, comport herself in a manner that made even their scapegrace offspring look well behaved by comparison, and be unremittingly uncritical.

It was pleasant work if one could get it, Charlotte thought wryly as she headed down the cloister walk toward the door standing ajar at its far end. All she had to do was amuse, be pleasant, and agree to whatever pudding-headed schemes her friend Margaret came up with. She'd become a shameless hoyden, a romp, and a coquette of some renown. Except . . . more and more lately, she feared that "shameless hoyden" was the only role anyone—most notably the Weltons would ever require her to perform and, worse, someday she might be satisfied with it herself.

She wished for something more for herself. She wasn't certain what, she only knew that it wasn't the same as her sisters. She had little empathy for Kate's single-minded determination to recoup her lost security—security she'd found with her brawny Highlander and wealth to match in some smuggler's cave. She wasn't a romantic like Helena, wanting only to be loved for her true self. Charlotte smiled with a touch of asperity. In truth she wasn't at all certain who her "true self" was. A bonbon? A scapegrace? A delightful article? Probably a bit of all these roles and bored with all of them, too. There had to be more to being alive than simply filling space.

She peeked inside the doorway to some sort of library, two facing walls covered with overstuffed bookcases that towered nearly to the ceiling. She smiled. She loved books and one of her regrets over her current situation was that books, or any kind of reading material other than the Tattersall sales sheets, were in scant supply in the Welton household. She slipped inside, her gaze gliding hungrily over the embossed leather spines as she wandered past the great scarred table that sat squarely in the middle of the room.

A straight-backed chair had been pulled out haphazardly at one side as if its occupant had left in a hurry without bothering to resituate it properly. A newly printed map of the Continent was spread out across several untidy stacks of paper covered over with little chicken scratches of ink. A single sheet poked out from underneath, just enough for Charlotte to see that it was written in French.

Charlotte stilled, outrage sprouting with the dark flower of suspicion. Why was the abbott, Father Tarkin—and presumably it was the abbot's room she was in since she could not conceive of any other monk at St. Bride's being important enough to command his own library—corresponding with someone in France? *England was at war with France.* She moved closer.

Her father's name leapt out at her: Roderick Nash. She shoved aside the map, snatching up the letter and trying to decipher—

"Miss Nash?"

Charlotte wheeled around, the paper trembling in her hand as she confronted Father Tarkin. Any embarrassment she might have felt at being caught going through his belongings fell away before her righteous anger. *She* was not the one consorting with the enemy! *She* was not the one with a potentially incriminating letter in her possession!

"Why is my father's name on this letter?" she demanded.

Father Tarkin approached and angled his head to see what she held, his expression of mild curiosity fading into one of sadness.

"Ah! This is from a man greatly indebted to your father. He writes to remind me of the sacrifices your father, as well as others, made that he might continue his current endeavors. See?" He reached around her and gently underlined a series of words with one long, bony finger.

"Respectfully, Father Abbot, I remind you of what you well know," he translated softly, *"that all great enterprises require great sacrifices. Those required of me, which seem to trouble your conscience so much of late, are nothing compared to those made by others. Recall the sacrifice made by Colonel Roderick Nash as well as other unnamed men and women who have given their lives that I might continue my work—"*

Abruptly, the abbot broke off, smiling apologetically at Charlotte. "The rest does not concern you, child."

"Continue my work." Three years ago, her father had willingly traded himself to the French in exchange for

three Scottish lads he hadn't even known who were being held imprisoned in LeMons dungeon as spies. By nightfall that same day, he'd been executed. She'd always assumed that with the three survivors' return to England whatever plot they'd contrived at had ended.

The realization that someone was carrying on the work the Scots had begun in France years ago hit Charlotte with a near physical force. And fast upon that realization came another; she wasn't surprised to learn that this sharp-eyed, gentle-faced abbot was part of it. All the young men involved had come from St. Bride's, had they not?

"I am not a child, Father," Charlotte responded with a gravity few who knew her would have suspected her capable of. "And if my father died for some 'work' the writer alludes to, then I must disagree. It does concern me."

The abbot shook his head. "Only in the most peripheral manner."

Charlotte scowled, uncertain why she could not leave it alone, but the words the abbot had translated, so rife with intention, so full of the power of the writer's convictions, hummed through her thoughts like a siren's song, bringing to mind the tragic circumstances of her father's death and its immediate aftermath.

By all reckoning her father's sacrifice had been a selfless act of nobility. But it had always pricked at Charlotte that his sacrifice had not meant more, that his life had been traded for a *failed* conspiracy. And now, here was proof that perhaps the mission these young men had undertaken still lived, that her father's sacrifice had allowed important work to continue. Certainly the letter suggested as much.

She suddenly wished, fervently, that she, too, could do something that would honor her father's sacrifice.

"I can help." The words hung in the hushed quiet of the abbot's library.

"My dear child, I cannot begin to understand your meaning—"

"I can be of use if you will only let me." Her soft statement stopped whatever the abbot had been about to say. She met his gaze. His brow furrowed.

"What is it you think you know, Miss Nash?" he finally asked and with an oddly courtly motion, indicated that she take the straight-backed chair.

She was too tense to sit. "Whatever those Scottish lads had been sent to France to do remains to be done. I want to help. I need to help."

The abbot did not deny her supposition, he only tilted his head. "And why do you need to help?"

"To make my life count. To give meaning to my father's death. To make his sacrifice worthwhile."

The abbot's expression grew troubled. "You do not feel saving three young men's lives carried meaning enough?"

"No."

Father Tarkin's silvery brows rose at that, surprise and hurt in the gaze fastened on her.

"No," she repeated firmly, thinking of the man who'd written so movingly of her father's sacrifice, certain that he would understand. "Not when it could mean so much more. If someone in France has been allowed to continue his work these past three years because of my father's sacrifice, then I want to help him to succeed. I owe it to my father's memory. I owe it to my country." She saw Father Terkin's hesitation and cast about, seeking some means of making him understand. *"I owe it to myself."*

They stood staring at each other, locked in silent communication. His gaze never wavered from hers.

"There may be something . . ." he trailed off pensively, his fingers tapping lightly against the table separating them.

"Anything."

"Occasionally," he began slowly, "messengers arrive in London with information that needs to be passed on. They often travel a great distance and o'er many circuitous routes to do so and it is often difficult to estimate when they will arrive or where.

"People who wish to know what information these messengers carry, people whose aims are in direct opposition to ours, scour the city searching for the person who receives this information and then organizes our friends in London. The recipient must, therefore, take care never to stay too long in one place, to move his lodgings frequently, and draw no undue attention to himself in doing so."

He waited and Charlotte understood his silence as a test to see if she was quick enough to catch the implications of his words.

"I imagine," she said carefully, "that because the recipient moves about so often and because he never knows when to expect the courier, it makes arranging a meeting between the two difficult."

The abbot nodded. She'd passed. "Last year the courier from France never was able to deliver the information he had specifically come here to relate. His time was short before he would be missed in France and the recipient had taken new quarters."

"But," Charlotte continued, "an intermediary, someone whom both men could easily find, would expedite the situation. *Especially* if the person who acted as intermediary was someone no one would suspect of being involved," she continued. "Someone young and frivolous, with no political or religious ties, an accessible person who is always in the public eye at some fête or gala or reception or other where she might be approached easily without arousing suspicion."

"She?"

"Me," Charlotte said. "I would be the perfect candidate for that position, Father Abbot. I enjoy a freedom very few young ladies can claim, I move in a variety of circles, I can go when and where I please without causing comment." Her lips quirked. "Well, without causing comments with which I am not already familiar."

The abbot turned away from her, his head bowed in thought, his gnarled hands clasped behind his back as he moved toward the far bookcase. She watched him, holding her breath.

She hadn't realized until the opportunity to do

something for her father's cause presented itself how important it was to her. The abbot mustn't refuse her. Whether he judged her as the fashionable, mischievous young fribble the world knew or the hard-minded and determined woman she understood herself to be, only the next few minutes would answer.

"It needn't be particularly dangerous," he murmured to himself.

She waited.

He looked at her over his shoulder, his seamed face troubled. "You would only need to remember a few addresses, repeat them in passing in a crowded room."

She nodded eagerly.

"Our little band is very small—you would be approached only two or three times a year at most."

"I understand."

He turned, facing her fully. "But not *particularly* dangerous and *not* dangerous are hardly the same things. There would be some risk involved."

"I am willing to take it."

"But am I willing to bequeath it?"

She answered for him. "Yes."

He thought for long minutes and Charlotte let him, knowing that to push now would be a mistake. Finally, he issued a deep sigh. "All right, Miss Nash. All right."

A smile blossomed on Charlotte's lips. "Thank you."

"No, my child. Don't thank me. I tread a thin line and my conscience already pricks." He sighed again and reached up toward a thick, heavily embossed volume on a shelf above his head. "But as it's agreed that you shall act as go-between, you may as well meet one of my agents. The author of this letter."

He yanked down hard on the book, and Charlotte's eyes widened as, with a small whooshing sound, a section of the bookshelf swung open on a hidden set of hinges, revealing a corridor lit by a single lantern.

"Come!" the abbot called.

Charlotte's heart pattered. She was about to meet the man who had stood fast for so long, who carried out the plan begun so many years ago. A man with conviction and deep, undivided loyalties. Already in her mind he was a hero, noble, worthy, though doubtless the years of secretiveness and danger had made him wary and stern—

"No need to bellow, Father." A young man emerged from the gloom. Overlong, dusty brown hair framed a lean face and hard jaw stubbled with a dark beard that almost hid the wicked-looking scar on his left cheek. A smear of dirt traversed a strong brown throat disappearing beneath a grimy shirt. His coat was loose and threadbare at the cuffs but no looser than the disreputable trousers that hung from a flat, narrow belly. A smile flashed in his tanned face.

"This is . . . Dand Ross," Father Tarkin said, watching her closely.

She wouldn't have recognized him as one of the three young Scotsmen who had come to her family's house three years ago. But then, who could see anyone else when Ramsey Munro with his dark angel looks was in the same room? Added to which, the young man who'd stood in her York drawing room had only just come from nearly two years in a French prison.

This man was straighter, leaner, more *wicked* looking. Their eyes met, the smile froze on his face, and something fluttered in her chest, like wings beating madly against her rib cage. Spontaneously, she stepped forward, her lips opening, to smile? to welcome?—

Something flickered in the smoky depths of his gaze.

"Well, what have we here?" he asked in a thick, lazy burr. "I didn't realize ye were takin' in female orphans now, Father. But clearly 'tis so, otherwise why would she be wearing clothing two sizes too small and so threadbare that one can see through them?"

So much for heroes, Charlotte thought.

France, late autumn 1788

"Must I go with Mister Johnstone, ma'am?" the boy asked, regarding his English tutor. There was no fear in his voice just as there was no real hope that he could dissuade his mother from her plan, but Jeremy Johnstone gave him credit for trying.

"Yes. The arrangements have been made." Not a hint of motherly feeling entered the voice of the lady in the velvet gown. She pressed the boy's shoulder, her gaze above his head locked with Jeremy's. "He's a bright boy. Older than his years. He will not encumber you."

That she was nervous and anxious to have the bargain

struck and the boy away was clear from the manner in which she kept looking over her shoulder.

"I will guard him with my life, ma'am. I am honored you put such faith in me." Jeremy bowed low over the exalted lady's hand. He'd never been this close to her. Since his arrival in France three years before to undertake the education of her small, unassuming-looking son, their interaction had always come through intermediaries in the great household.

He studied her surreptitiously, trying to find some resemblance between mother and son, but could find little. Her features were rounded and pretty, yet her expression was invested with a steely resolve that had not yet found its heir in the boy.

He was a good boy, quick-witted and a natural mimic. Already he spoke English without a trace of his native accent. Jeremy not only liked him but admired him, too, for the strength of spirit within him. His unquestioning resilience in the face of so much upheaval touched Jeremy deeply.

Jeremy suspected that this upheaval—Grenoble had exploded in riots only a few weeks before—accounted for why the great lady had decided to send her only son to friends in Scotland until matters in France resolved themselves. While Jeremy knew the boy would do as his parent requested without complaint, he could not discount the misery in the lad's face. He was being taken from everything and everyone he knew, and Jeremy felt for him. "Ahem."

The lady lifted her gaze from her son and regarded him coldly. "What is it, Master Johnstone?"

"Perhaps this is not necessary, milady? Surely the king—"

"*The king is a fool and his wife a greater one. This will not end well, and if His Highness refuses to see what to my eyes is abundantly clear, then I shall not sacrifice my child to his blindness. No. The boy goes to Scotland.*"

"*Yes, ma'am.*" *Jeremy bowed deeply.*

The lady made an impatient motion with her hand and one of her servants hovering in the background snapped forward with a heavy velvet purse. This she took and in turn offered to Jeremy. "*The money should provide amply enough for both of you. Inside is a letter to my friends, asking them to give my son sanctuary. I am entrusting it to you and ask that you deliver it with my son upon your arrival.*" *For the first time, an expression of doubt wrinkled her smooth brow.* "*I wish I had time to notify them of my plans but . . . the situation becomes precarious. I dare not delay.*"

She bent down, bringing her face level with the youngster's. He returned her gaze unwaveringly. She touched his shoulder, and Jeremy could see by the slight canting of his body how the lad wanted to throw his arms around her. He did not, though. He stood silently.

"*Do not forget who you are, my son. Do not ever forget what you are or what is expected of you.*"

"*No, ma'am,*" *he promised solemnly.* "*I won't.*"

1

"LA, MR. FOX, if your eyes occasionally strayed above my neckline you might find it easier to guess what I am miming during the game," Charlotte said archly. The redheaded young man, heir to a merchant's vast fortune and as of last Wednesday owning a suspiciously acquired baronetcy, colored violently.

Charlotte took no pity. The bran-faced upstart had been staring at her bosom since he'd arrived in the company of the young people she'd invited to her town house for games and refreshments—her first "at home" since she had taken possession of the fashionable Mayfair address, a scandalous move since she intended to live as a spinster. Alone.

As Lady Welton was chaperoning the occasion, it was all perfectly respectable—even though the baroness had fallen asleep in a patch of sunlight hours before. At least, Charlotte amended with a nod to her conscience, it was *supposed* to have been respectable. But then nothing she ever did seemed to turn out quite as respectably as her lineage, lofty associations (she was, after all, the sister-in-law of Ramsey Munro, marquis of Cottrell, as well as the renowned Colonel Christian MacNeill) and delightful manners would suggest.

And that, Charlotte fully appreciated, was a great deal of her appeal. Within Charlotte's charmed circle, things could be said that one daren't utter elsewhere, a few steps of the notorious waltz might be demonstrated, the ladies' gowns were more fashionable and less substantial, laughter came more freely, and the verbal ripostes that most unmarried young girls didn't dare serve their potential suitors Charlotte doled out regularly to hers. Thus, Charlotte's set-down of the goggle-eyed Mr. Robinson brokered as many giggles among the females as guffaws from the males.

"Sorry. Don't know what I was thinkin'," Mr. Robinson sputtered.

"I don't think *thought* entered much into it, do you?" Charlotte asked sweetly, giving rise to another round of scandalized laughter. "Come, my friend, let us practice looking at a lady's face . . . no, no, no! Not my lips—the whole of my face. See? Two brows, a pair of oddly colored eyes, an inconsequential nose, a rather too decisive chin. Ah! There. Bravo!"

The young ladies and gentlemen, acknowledged by all to be by far the fastest set of unmarried young people in the ton, clapped appreciatively and Mr. Robinson, as determined to be one of them as he was to charm Miss Nash, found the self-confidence to laugh at himself, bowing in turn to her and the rest of the company.

The byplay ended, her guests began taking turns at charades again and Charlotte, realizing that the punch bowl was growing woefully low, popped out into the corridor to find a maid. She had gotten no further than the kitchen door when a masculine voice hailed her in breathless tones.

Knowing all too well what would follow, she turned around. But it was not Mr. Robinson. It was Lord LeFoy. Tall, sandy-haired Lord LeFoy. Well, here was a surprise. She'd thought he had all but offered for the Henley girl.

"Miss Nash," he breathed, coming toward her with his hands outstretched. She waited politely. His hands, finding none waiting to secure, fell to his sides.

"Yes?"

"I must have a moment of your time."

"Yes."

"Alone."

She glanced tellingly around the short corridor. "Yes."

He frowned. Apparently this was not going as he'd hoped. Poor Lord LeFoy. Things seldom did where she and gentlemen were concerned. At least, for the gentlemen.

"You had something you wished to impart of a private nature?" she prompted.

"Yes," he said, nodding eagerly. "Yes. I . . . I . . ."

"Yes?"

"I adore you!"

"Ah."

He reached down and grabbed one of her hands, snatching it to his lips and pressing an ardent kiss to the gloved surface. "I am your slave. Ask me anything, anything, and I shall do it. I am yours to command. I worship you, you angel, you devil!"

"Like Lucifer?" she asked, letting her hand lie like a dead thing in his. Really, to encourage him would be too cruel, and she already had a bit too much of a reputation for heartlessness. Added to which, she rather liked the Henleys. They would be relieved of a great deal of worry with the marriage settlement Lord LeFoy's father would offer.

"Eh?" Lord LeFoy blinked owlishly.

"Angel and devil. If I have my catechism correct, only one being qualifies on both counts and that is Lucifer."

"Ah. Yes. No. I meant that you *are* an angel but that your angelicness bedevils me." He seemed quite pleased with this explanation. "You must be mine!"

"Oh, dear. Are you declaring yourself, Lord LeFoy? Because I would rather think not, if you wouldn't mind. I like you, you see. And I should lead you a merry chase if we were to wed." At his blank expression she gave a little sigh.

"Allow me to enumerate my shortcomings," she said kindly. "I haven't it in me to be faithful. I detest jealousy and possessiveness in any degree and should react strongly and in a possibly scandalous fashion if presented with either. I should think I would be deuced expensive to keep. Added to which I have no desire now, or in the near future, to produce offspring." She smiled pleasantly.

Lord LeFoy's round eyes grew rounder. She could almost see Reason trying to assert itself in that beleaguered expression. But then Reason was not a man's strong suit when he had decided he must have something.

"I don't care. I adore you!"

"Of course you do," she answered, patting the hand still clutching hers. "The point isn't what you *feel*. It is what is *best*. I should hate for your adoration to turn to misery. I dislike being around miserable people. They are tiresome. And it *would* turn to misery. Your father . . . ? " She laughed at the thought of the lecherous Earl of Mallestrough as her father-in-law. "I suspect I should have to lock the bedroom door against him whenever you left the house. Not a very winning prescription for matrimonial harmony, now is it?"

At the mention of his father, Lord LeFoy went quite still. At least he respected her enough not to challenge her estimation of his sire.

"No, no," she said. "We are far better off as we are now with you adoring me and me wallowing in it. Very romantic. And more civil, too, because this way neither your adoration nor my wallowing in it need interfere with our lives. You will wed Maura Henley, who will make a lovely bride and a fine mother for your children and who will never throw your things from her room or cause a scene at Almacks. You shall be very happy. Except that for my vanity's sake, might you occasionally be gentleman enough to sigh wistfully when we meet in public so that I might happily hear it?"

"You would make a scene at *Almack's*?" he breathed in horrified wonder.

"Oh, I should think eventually it will become inevitable, don't you?" she asked sweetly, tilting her head.

He dropped her hand. "Begad, yes. You would. You *will*."

"Now, before some of the others decide that this little conversation amounts to your having compromised me, you had best return while I see to the punch bowl," she said brightly.

He gulped, turned, hesitated, and turned back. "Ah. Thank you, Miss Nash. You are a very . . . levelheaded woman."

She leaned forward and whispered, "Don't tell anyone."

Lord Lefoy nodded, just as eager to leave as he had been to press his suit five minutes ago, and all but trotted back to the parlor, leaving Charlotte to raise her eyes heavenward with a mumbled word of thanks.

She had no sooner begun down the corridor once more when her maid, a pert, sharp-eyed girl named Lizette, appeared. "I beg your pardon, Miss Nash, but there's a . . . man here that insists on seeing you."

A man. Not a gentleman. And not a tradesman or Lizette would have dealt with him herself. Charlotte's curiosity was piqued.

"Who is this man?"

"He says he's a thief taker, Miss Nash, and come with

word of some jewels he's recovered." Lizette's pretty, round face scrunched in consternation as she scoured her mind for memory of missing jewels. She wouldn't find any. Probably because Charlotte wasn't missing any jewels. Charlotte's heart began beating faster and a shiver ran along her skin.

"Where is he?"

"I didn't know where to put him, so I put him in the morning room, miss."

"Very well," Charlotte said. "Please explain to my guests that I may be a while."

Without waiting to see that her orders were obeyed, Charlotte followed the hall to the morning room and entered.

Her heart was still racing.

"Thief taker?" Amused, Charlotte slowly circled her favorite chair where Dand Ross slouched, legs straight out, his shoddy boot heels crossed on the clean surface of her favorite inlaid table. His unannounced appearance filled her with excitement. Not that she would tell him that. He would preen, or worse, be amused. And it was only because he always brought with him an air of tantalizing danger that she reacted thus.

She hadn't known she would find danger so . . . appealing when she'd entered Dand Ross's shadowy world. But she could not deny it, any more than she could resist it. Though she was loath to let Dand know the degree to which she looked forward to his unheralded arrivals.

She tapped one perfectly manicured nail pensively

against her lips as if pondering a conundrum before leaning forward and sniffing delicately. Her face alit with sudden inspiration. "I have it . . . Lizette misheard you. You must have said *rat* taker!"

He looked up at her through thick chocolate brown lashes. "You know, Lottie, me love," he said thoughtfully, "they are actually *wearing* bodices in Paris these days instead of just admitting to the concept."

His gaze fell on her daring décolletage before lifting to meet hers. She returned it calmly. If he expected to raise a blush in her cheeks, he was doomed to disappointment. More men than she could easily count had ogled her not-all-that-bountiful bounty without so much as warming her cheeks.

Besides, in the years since they'd met and in dozens of meetings since, he had sometimes teased her with a feigned sexual interest, but he had never acted on his bold words. He was the consummate professional: detached, cynical, uninvolved.

She studied him as he tipped a glass of claret into his mouth. The years had broadened him and lengthened him and hardened him, too, but he still had that loose-knit, damn-your-eyes sort of grace one saw in the more successful tomcats.

Dusky brown hair, hooded smoky brown eyes, a lean face with a wide mouth and thin lips and a square jaw that currently hid beneath a thick beard along with a piratical scar. Though he cheerfully admitted that mark had been the result of falling off a ladder while stealing apples and not the dueling wound she had once imagined.

She wasn't certain she believed him. She wasn't certain of what she really knew about Dand and what he wanted her to believe she knew. He kept his own counsel, his feelings—if he had any—well hidden.

"Really?" she drawled sweetly. "Well, we *are* at war and there *are* embargos on and I consider it my duty to see that my dressmaker doesn't stress the economy overmuch by any extravagant use of material."

"Such patriotism, Charlotte," he rejoined dryly. "I am struck dumb by your sacrifices. Or should I say sacrifice in the singular? It doesn't look as if you are denying yourself too much in the way of creature comforts."

His ironic gaze traveled about the exquisitely decorated sitting room, touching on the slate blue walls accented by the clean lines of white painted woodwork and on to the furniture: the settees with their beautifully fluted legs upholstered in bishop's blue watered silk, the open-backed chairs carved into elegant lyres, the pillows and cushions fitted in expensive jonquil-colored brocade. At a japanned side table his perusal checked on a riot of yellow roses and waxy white gardenias that spilled from an enormous Chinese urn.

"Are those yellow roses?"

"You recognize them."

"Oh, yes." His voice was quiet. "I nourished them with my blood. Where did you get them?"

"They came from the plant you and your companions gave us so many years ago. I brought cuttings with me from York. First to the Welton's town house and now here," she said, "to remind me of the good old days. You should see the sensation I cause when I dress them in my hair or use them to decorate what I think of—apparently erroneously—as my bodice." She grinned. "I *do* so like causing a sensation. Besides, they suit the décor," she added, surveying the room with satisfaction.

"New address. New paint. New furniture," Dand was murmuring as he too, looked around. "One must ask oneself: Is it quite respectable, though? A young woman living alone?"

"Oh, I don't think so," she answered glibly. "But then . . . what do I care for respectability when it only ties my hands and prevents me from being as useful to you and your associates as I am here, alone?"

"So practical, Lottie. You've become rather a tough little article, haven't you?"

"I should like to think so."

"I know you would," he said with a lazy smile. "How many hearts have you broken this week, cruel little Miss Nash?"

"Hearts?" She pondered. "None. Pride? A few."

"Poor bastards." He set the goblet by his feet and tipped his chair back, balancing on the back legs and crossing his hands across the hard, flat plane of his belly.

After all these months, she still could not get over the wonder that *he* was one of England's premier secret agents. It seemed so improbable. Disreputable, devious, and dangerous—she couldn't believe that her first impression of him emerging from the shadows in Father Tarkin's library had been so off the mark.

There had been an instance then, before a word had even been spoken between them, when their eyes had met and her breath and heart had stilled. Time had disappeared and she'd felt she could live there, held forever in his bright, fierce gaze. Except then he *had* spoken—dismissing her, dismissing that instant of communion. Ah, well. It was all fantastical anyway. There were no sacred bonds, no deeper union. There was purpose and duty. And that was more than enough to anchor a life.

"Still. *Something* must have prompted your change of address," Dand persisted. "What happened, Lottie? Did you finally perpetrate some social crime even the Baron and Lady Welton couldn't overlook? Did you wear diamonds before noon? Don the same gown twice in a month?" he asked. "Tell me. What did you do that made the Weltons hide the front door keys so you couldn't run tame about their house?"

"Nothing at all. It is simply that Maggie Welton had the audacity to get married," she answered airily. "And her husband, poor creature that he is, refused to invite me to live with them. Can you imagine the gall?"

Dand grinned. "How inconsiderate."

"Exactly," she agreed primly. "Yet, employing that delicacy of feeling which others," her gaze skewered him, "must only imagine, I deduced that now was the most reasonable time to leave my dear friends the Weltons and set up my own establishment. Happily, with the funds Kate and Christian conferred upon me, I am well able to do so."

Dand's gaze swept up her new gown, pausing on the Kashmiri shawl about her shoulders and the pearl bobs swinging gently from her ears. "The settlement must have been more generous than I realized."

She smiled noncommittally. He had no idea.

"Speaking of your inheritance, what news do you have of Colonel and Mrs. MacNeill?" Dand asked. "And the beautiful Helena and equally beautiful Ram, of course?"

At the mention of her oldest sister, the new marchioness of Cottrell, Charlotte hesitated. Helena's last letter had been short, her effort not to criticize or question Charlotte's outré behavior apparent in every line. At least Charlotte could be thankful that her other sister, Kate, attached to her husband's regiment in far-off lands, heard little of the gossip that blistered Helena's ears.

"Not much," she said. "Helena and Ramsey are preparing to set sail from Jamaica where Ram has been dismantling one of the old marquis's plantations. They should be in London within the month. Kate and Christian are on the Continent."

"And do they all still think I am a murderer?"

The query caught Charlotte off guard. She hadn't realized Dand cared what his former companions thought of him. Caring what others thought of one only led to sleepless nights and muddied one's focus. She had learned that lesson from Dand. Too many nights she had lain awake wondering what risks he undertook in returning to France or what dangers he had come fresh from when he arrived at her door, until, to keep herself from going mad with the terrifying images her brain conjured, she forced herself not to think of him at all.

Yet here he was, asking after the other Rose Hunters. It was unexpected. It hinted at a heart beating in concert with the rest of humanity, prey to all manner of weaknesses and foibles. She had always thought Dand Ross well-nigh impervious to any such thing. *Well, now.*

"I don't know. They don't confide in me. Please recall that as a fribble of the highest order I am much more interested in my own assorted schemes and bumble broths to give a thought to anyone else."

"You sound a little bitter," he said.

Was she? She hoped not. She would hate to think she condemned her sisters for believing she was as shallow as she'd led them to believe. Yet . . . an unreasonable part of her sometimes wished they believed in her good character, despite all evidence to the contrary. "Not really," she answered obliquely. "Actually, I try to emulate you, Dand."

He cocked his head. "How so?"

"Worldly, street-smart," she listed off his qualities. "Without remorse or an inconvenient conscience or attachments of any kind and thus having no need to make explanations to anyone."

"And how have you arrived at this rather unflattering estimation of my character?" he asked, clearly amused.

"I don't think it unflattering at all," she said in genuine surprise. "It seems most practical."

"Really?" he asked, his eyes narrowed with amusement but also speculation. "Again, what makes you think this of me?"

"Well, your two best friends, who happen to be my brothers-in-law, thought you had betrayed them to the French, killed the guard who was to have provided the evidence of your perfidy, and sought to murder them but was stopped in this pursuit only because my sister Helena managed to drive a sword into your side a moment before you, disguised as vicar, intended to skewer her with your own."

"Such a graphic account, Charlotte. Perhaps you should write one of those overheated Gothic novels that are all the rage?"

She ignored him. "And yet, here you are, unconcerned and placid as a plate of pike despite all the nasty suspicions surrounding you. How ever do you manage?"

"I take comfort in knowing that I did not do any of the aforementioned things. I do, indeed, have a conscience, Lottie. And while it is hardly spotless, I acquit myself of charges of attempting to murder my onetime companions. Besides, Father Tarkin would vouch for me."

"Ah, but you have been away from St. Bride's for a long time. People change." She moved behind his chair, looking down at the rumpled hair streaked with gold. "How do *I* know you are innocent?"

His gaze tracked her watchfully.

"*I* never saw the man who claimed to be Vicar Tawster," she continued. "Only Helena can identify him. All *I* know is that you remain intent on not revealing yourself to your former companions. Or my sister. Perhaps there is a reason."

He didn't bother to reply. His collarless shirt lay opened, pulled askew so that she could see his shoulder, tanned and smoothly capped with muscle. A few inches over would be the infamous rose brand. Though she had never seen it, both of her sisters had told her of the souvenir the torturer at the LeMons dungeon had branded into their husbands' and Dand Ross's hides.

She bent down, bringing her lips to within inches of his ear. He smelled clean, of soap and camphor. He didn't even bother looking around. He took entirely too much for granted. No man of the ton had ever taken her for granted. And yet Dand Ross did. A wicked impulse arose within her.

"Added to which," she whispered in his ear, "you didn't appear in London for many months after the episode with Helena and the sword. Perhaps you retired to France to recover from your wound? Perhaps," she leaned over his shoulder, "you carry the mark . . . here!"

Her hand darted down, pressing low on his side. Before she realized what he was doing he seized her wrist, holding her hand hostage against his ribs a second before jerking her over his shoulder and toppling into his lap. She looked up, startled, into a face dark and suddenly alien, her offending hand held in a steel grip well away from his body.

A glimmer of fear shivered through her. She hadn't realized he was so strong or could move so fast. Or that he could look at her with such a hard expression.

Abruptly, she began to struggle. He controlled her with humiliating ease, the heat from his body seeping into her in every inappropriate place, setting her skin afire and bringing to life her long-forgotten ability to blush. He didn't even notice.

"Do you really think I am a murderer?" His low voice had lost all trace of amusement. "And if so, do you really want to play this game with *me*?"

2

CHARLOTTE SHRANK IN DAND'S EMBRACE, for the first time feeling truly frightened of him. No one had ever manhandled her before. Ever. She kept her face averted, so that he would not see how he'd shaken her. "Dand . . . ? "

At once, his hold loosened. "And that, my girl, will teach you to lay violent hands on another."

She had laid violent hands on *him*? She told herself that fear alone accounted for the trembling in her chest, the sudden difficulty she had drawing a breath, and that he would not respect her if he suspected that something as simple as a snarl and an intimate touch could affect her so. "It was hardly violent."

"I suspect that depends on one's perspective. Violence is anything that threatens, you know."

She didn't understand. She shifted, aware of how hard his body was, of how hard the arms that still held her were and of his heart beating against her. It felt as though a thousand little needles were lightly pricking every part of her skin that came in contact with him. Yet, now that her fear had subsided, she felt . . . safe? Yes. Protected.

It had been a long time since she had felt that someone actively stood between her and whatever threatened her. It was nice, however illusory. Though she didn't doubt Dand would dutifully intervene if he thought she was in danger, he was seldom in London and thus seldom in a position to protect her. She would, as she had for years, have to protect herself.

But she could relish a few moments of illusion. There was nothing wrong in that, was there?

She let her head fall back against his shoulder, looking up into his brown eyes, oblique and fathomless. Despite his scurrilous clothing, his body was clean, his hair healthy and shiny. His upper lip was bowed, his lower lip firm but curved. A sensualist would have lips like his. "I don't really think you are a murderer."

"Your faith comforts me no end. Now, off with you before you put a crease in my trousers," he ordered in an odd, rough voice, lifting her to her feet.

She backed away feeling rejected and, feeling foolish

for feeling so, she hunted for something to say that would cover her discomfort. "Why *don't* you tell Ram and Kit you aren't their traitor?" she asked. "Father Tarkin would not have any objection."

"Because I've worked far too long and made far too many—" He stopped abruptly before continuing in a voice made purposefully careless. "If Kit and Ramsey discovered I'd stayed the course, as it were, there would be nothing for it but that they must come hieing back, guns blazing and swords drawn, to aid me whether I require it or not. Terrible glory mongers. Always have been."

Charlotte was not deceived. "You're protecting them."

"No," Dand answered. "I am protecting what I, what *we*, have worked so long to accomplish. I have no desire to spend the rest of my days mucking about in French stables and garrisons, charming though they are."

He pushed himself to his feet and brushed past her, heading for the window overlooking the little park across the street. When he spoke his words again took her by surprise. "You've cut your hair."

She touched her short cap of feathery red curls. "Yes. What of it?"

"It's a bold look. Wanton."

"Wanton?" She laughed at the prudish word on Dand Ross's lips. "Oh, I don't think it quite wanton. Perhaps a bit artful."

"And that is the effect you are striving for? Artful?"

He didn't turn as he spoke but continued looking out the window. "The abbot will be disturbed."

"The abbot doesn't have so many agents willing to do his bidding that he can be choosey about those who do. And I give satisfaction. You can't deny that."

"So you have repeatedly told me and, I fear, the abbot," he answered. "Am I to presume that these new trappings will somehow let you make yourself even useful to Mother Church?"

"And England," she added.

"And being *artful* is how you have managed to finagle your way from what was to have been a simple intermediary to your current status as a full-blown intelligencer?"

"It only makes sense, doesn't it? The more I became part of a certain fast set, the more information I came across. The more I knew, the easier it was to acquire additional information." She frowned. "Why do you sound so disapproving?"

"Do I sound disapproving?" he asked with a smile that didn't quite reach his eyes. "I'd only meant to relate my concern for your welfare. You see, there is this matter of a vow I made to your family, something to do with an eternal obligation, throwing myself into the jaws of death to save your lovely hide should the need arise.

"But as I have an inordinate affection for my own life, poor though it be, I thought perhaps merely shaking a warning finger at you before you actually dove into peril might suffice. Saving damsels is such a deuced time-consuming venture, don't you see?"

She preened. "Do you really think my hide is lovely?"

"You know it is," he replied matter-of-factly. " 'Twould be a sorry waste to see it turned into a worm's meal. No. I won't have it. You are the only Nash left who hasn't a full-time bodyguard sleeping in her bed. If you die, I shall count it a personal failure." He paused. "I suppose I *could* marry you."

He waited and when she only raised one of her coppery brows at him, nodded. "No? Of course not. You'd be a fool. And you are most decidedly not a fool, are you, Lottie?"

He did not wait for her answer but half turned from her. "So, there is nothing for it but that you must live without my protecting you twenty-four hours a day."

She laughed. "Don't worry, Dand. I won't be plunging into peril, nor do I intend to be turned into a feast for the maggots. And, tempting as it is to throw you a yellow rose and demand you fulfill your vow to do whatever I ask by marrying me just to see you squirm, I won't.

"I only listen, Dand. And carry what information I gather to those who can best utilize it."

"Oh-ho." Dand sucked in a low whistle of comprehension. "Not simply Father Tarkin anymore but now 'those who can best utilize it.' You aren't working for someone besides the abbot, are you?"

She'd known she would have to tell him sooner or

later. "Yes," she said. "You've said so yourself many times, 'war makes strange bedfellows.' The Church and the British government's motives might not be the same, but their goals are."

His lip twitched at one corner. "How did he talk you into serving two masters, Charlotte? Or was there little *talking* involved?" His gaze grew flat and cold. "Who is he?"

Charlotte frowned. "Who is who?"

"The English government agent you are feeding." Dand's ready smile grew thinner, sharper, a little wolfish.

"It isn't a 'he,' it is a 'she.'" Charlotte plunged ahead. "Ginny Mulgrew."

There was no reason he should recognize her name; he wasn't often in London and then only for a few days—though lately his appearances had been more frequent and of longer durations. Was it . . . a woman who drew him to London so oft of late? She ignored the little pinpricks of anger the thought occasioned.

She was being ridiculous. He had never talked of any woman, in any manner. Certainly he had never indicated he had feelings for a woman. Though, she realized, it was unlikely he would have confided in her if he had.

She waited. The hardness slowly dissipated from his expression. His gaze narrowed thoughtfully. "I see. And how did you meet Miss Mulgrew?"

"*Mrs.* Mulgrew. Her husband is a baronet but they are estranged and have been for years."

"And how did you meet Mrs. Mulgrew?"

"I had heard from a mutual acquaintance that she was making inquiries about a person whom I also considered of interest. I asked that this person introduce us." The simple explanation neglected to inform him how close she'd come to social suicide with that request. Because Ginny Mulgrew was a courtesan. No need for Dand to know that, however.

"Mrs. Mulgrew has been extremely helpful. She is as committed as you or I to Napoleon's downfall."

"Brava," Dand said, but clearly his thoughts had slipped elsewhere. "I commend the lady's patriotism. It had just better not interfere with my goal."

"Goal?" The simple word alerted her. "You aren't here to relay a message, are you? You're here with some more important purpose."

He did not deny it.

"Tell me. I may be able to help."

Dand raked his hand through his hair and nodded. "A letter has been stolen. Its contents could destroy a proposed alliance that might see an end to Napoleon's military expansion on the Continent."

"A letter?" Charlotte repeated, all else forgotten. "A letter in a specially sealed cylinder stolen from Paris?"

"Yes." His hand fell to his side. "How did you know?"

"Because it is here. Or rather the man who says he has possession of it is here, in London."

Dand was across the room in five great strides, grabbing her arm and pulling her toward the settee. He pushed her down and sat beside her. "Tell me everything," he demanded. "Who is this man?"

"Comte Maurice St. Lyon, a French loyalist, or so he claims. He has been living in England for several years. He is enormously wealthy, a connoisseur, and an art collector. Though no one seems to know the source of his wealth, he is extremely well connected.

"We know he has contacted several foreign dignitaries, as well as people without official rank or title but who nonetheless hold enormous power, hinting that he is in possession of a sealed letter that was detoured from an 'interesting' destination. He has invited them to his castle where, three weeks hence, they will have the opportunity to bid on it."

Dand leaned back in the settee. "Bloody hell." He steepled his hands before his lips and fell silent for a long moment. "Where is Comte St. Lyon now?"

"Preparing to leave for his castle, forty miles northwest of Sterling. The place is a fortress. He has hired a veritable army of men to patrol the grounds and building. The land it sits on is barren and uninhabited except for a drover's village some miles south. Everyone in the vicinity is known to St. Lyon. A newcomer would be remarked. And dispatched," she explained, anticipating his asking whether a fox had been set amongst the hens.

"Why doesn't someone simply eliminate the man?" Dand asked with such cold callousness Charlotte felt a shiver of her earlier fear. Not that Ginny Mulgrew hadn't thought of the same thing, she reminded herself.

"Because he made it clear that should any harm befall him the letter would be opened and made public."

"Steal the letter?" Dand suggested but in such a tone that it was clear he understood that this most obvious solution would already have been explored.

"No one knows where it is. On two separate occasions, the best cracksmen in London have attempted to gain entry to his town house. Both men are now dead." She managed to say this without revealing the distress she had felt over the discovery of their bodies.

"Servants?"

"All handpicked by St. Lyon. All men and women he brought with him from France. All loyal or so afraid of him that no bribe can entice them to risk his vengeance."

Charlotte could almost see various schemes and plans taking form and being dismissed in the narrowing of Dand's eyes, the slight furrowing of his brow, and the frustration in the tightening of his jaw.

"Damnation! I have to return to France within a fortnight." His hand fisted against his knee "I take it the abbot has been informed?"

"Yes. A messenger pigeon was dispatched but he hasn't answered. The bird may have been lost. But do not worry," Charlotte said softly, "the matter is well in hand."

At this, Dand's brows shot up. "Oh? *Who* has the matter well in hand?"

"Ginny Mulgrew. She and those with whom she is allied have devised a plan to steal the cylinder back."

Dand stood up. "What plan?"

"A few weeks ago I introduced her to the comte—"

"You?" Dand interrupted. "How do you know this comte?"

She shot him a terse glance. "Come, Dand. You must know my reputation. I am exactly the sort of high-spirited romp a man of St. Lyon's ilk would find interesting. I told you he is well connected." She didn't see any need to tell him that the comte had picked her out for even more special attentions until he had discovered her brother-in-law was the powerful new marquis of Cottrell. "How I know him is of no consequence. What is important is that Ginny Mulgrew has been invited to the castle. As his mistress. And there she shall steal the cylinder."

She met his gaze with practiced aloofness, waiting for him to comment on her association with the courtesan. He did not.

"How will she accomplish this, if the place is so well guarded?"

"The comte does not think highly of my gender. He considers us volatile, mercenary, emotional, and hen-witted. Any threat a woman poses—and he does allow that women might be used as tools, but only by men—could only be negligible.

"Ginny will be watched but not to the degree she warrants. Added to which, we have studied blueprints of the castle that the comte does not know exist. Indeed, we know of secret passages and priests' holes of which he is completely unaware. It may take a few days, but Ginny *will* find the letter. She has found many things before that were meant to have stayed hidden."

"And your involvement?"

"Mine?" she asked. "I'm not involved at all."

For a long moment their gazes held.

"Let's keep it that way, shall we?"

3

Jermyn Street, Piccadilly
July 15, 1806

THE EARLY EVENING AIR WAS STILL, warm, and heavy. The man standing in the shadows of St. James' churchyard's ancient trees loosened the stock about his throat, his gaze riveted on the discreet but elegant door of the town house across the street. He'd wasted enough time waiting for the courtesan within to place herself in a vulnerable situation. Time was running out. He would have to act soon. Force the issue.

He forced a deep breath into his lungs, releasing it slowly as his active imagination picked through a score of possibilities, searching for the best solution to his quandary. Who should he be when he set his plan in motion? A constable? An old woman? A ragman? A soldier?

The faces of all those he had pretended to be tumbled like patterns in a kaleidoscope through his imagination, swirling and blurring until he could no longer see his own features superimposed upon the masks and caricatures he'd created over the years. Knowing who he was, who he *really* was, was the only thing that mattered.

A little frisson of panic danced along his nerve endings. His hands fisted into balls, the nails digging into his flesh. With an effort he forced himself to relax.

There was only one way to make sure he remembered who he was. He must go back to the beginning and retrieve the identity he'd misplaced along the way.

And *she* would help him.

A thin smile flashed across his shadowed features. How ironic that Charlotte Nash should be the key to his redemption, his return from the dead, his phoenixlike rise from the ashes. How ironic and yet how perfectly fitting. Sometimes, when he saw her, spoke to her, he lost himself in her odd, lovely eyes, forgot what it was he sought. She was really most unique. Most fascinating. A man, a normal decent man, might fall in love with a woman like her.

But he wasn't that man.

The evening shadows had deepened, softening the first fine lines appearing at the corners of Ginny Mulgrew's magnificent eyes. She tilted her head, closely examining her image in the mirror, wondering if now was the time to have her staff replace the expensive candelabras and chandeliers in her house with new ones, ones that held fewer candles and thus would shed less light. She made this assessment without sentiment or regret, evaluating the situation with the cold practicality of a general devising a military campaign.

A courtesan is ever conscious of such details.

Tonight it was especially important that she be in rare fine looks. At this evening's opera, she would accept the Comte St. Lyon's invitation to join him for his "house party" at his estate in Scotland.

She tilted her chin, searching for signs of sagging. If she found any, she would forthwith adopt necklaces and chokers though, until now, her flawless décolletage had needed no ornamentation. But at thirty-six years of age, such bold confidence might not be warranted.

She pulled a long, artfully curled tress of hair free of its equally artfully unwinding coiffure and fingered it thoughtfully. Still glossy and plentiful, still owning that rich and distinct auburn hue to which so many toasts had been drunk in so many gentlemen's clubs. Her skin was still clear and fine grained. Only her hands betrayed the advent of middle years, a little thin now that they had lost some of the youthful padding that once covered the slender bones and sinews. She would wear gloves from now on. Lace or doeskin.

Ginny Mulgrew was a most practical woman. She understood to a nicety that her beauty paid the rent as well as gained her entrée into the fringes of the society from which her husband had attempted to exclude her.

Her husband. The thought of the odious creature brought a bitter twist to her lips. He would not divorce her no matter how many times she pleaded with him to do so, no matter how she behaved, no matter how many men, some of whom even belonged to his own club, had enjoyed her favors. Knowing how much she desired to be free of him, he refused.

It was his punishment to her for not being able to bear him children.

Well, at least she had the pleasure of knowing they both suffered.

She hadn't set out to be a courtesan. It had taken five years of banishment to an impecunious existence in a derelict castle in Ireland to help make that decision. No, she hadn't set out to be a whore, any more than she had set out to be a spy.

But when one of her early lovers, a man highly placed in those little known offices that manage such things, suggested she might be of service to her king—and make a tidy sum of money in doing so—she had willingly agreed. She hadn't done it for the money. She had done so, she supposed with that clear self-scrutiny that was characteristic of her, as a means of assuaging her distaste for what and who she had become.

A soft knock at the door preceded the entrance of the tall, blond footman, Finn. "Pardon, ma'am, but there's a gentleman downstairs requesting a moment of your time."

This was hardly new. Gentlemen were always requesting a moment of Ginny's time . . . and a great deal more. But the absence of a calling card and something in the footman's disapproving expression piqued her curiosity as well as aroused some slight alarm. The feeling that a malevolent gaze studied her from hidden places, that her movements were being carefully observed, had grown over the last few days.

Of course, a spy always thought such things.

"Who is it, Finn?"

"He would not say."

One of those. Some aristocrat with an overblown sense of his own importance who would not be caught dead visiting her home without hiding under a cloak of anonymity. She was well past the stage where she needed to pander to such vanity. She had a bit of her own left to tend. "Tell him I'm not at home."

"I did," Finn replied, startling Ginny. If Finn had tried to send him off without even informing her of his presence, he must be scurrilous indeed. Scurrilous sorts interested Ginny. As well, if he was her hidden watcher, it would be best if she knew his face.

"Show him in," she said. She rose, looking over the room for a more flattering setting, ever awake to the possibility that the gentleman—scurrilous or not—might be worth the trouble. She chose the rose-colored chaise, reclining on her side, her naked feet curled beneath her. Gentlemen thought naked feet extremely naughty.

A tap on the door, a throaty bid of "come," and Finn reappeared, announcing, "Mr. Ross, ma'am."

Ginny's first thought was that the man *was* scurrilous, dressed roughly, his boots scarred and his disheveled hair framing a face darkened by a beard. Her second thought was that Finn, if he discarded this man as unworthy of her attention, had no taste.

The man was tall, broad-shouldered and lean, almost rangy, moving with careless fluidity as he entered. His expression was neutral, his mouth firm and mobile, but the lamplight exposed a sardonic glint in his tawny brown eyes and a scar lurking beneath the beard. She judged him to be somewhere in his late twenties. A very nice age for a man.

"That will be all, Finn," she nodded to the footman.

"Thank you for seeing me, Mrs. Mulgrew." A faint accent. Scottish?

"You're welcome, Mr. Ross," she said. "Won't you be seated?"

"Thank you." He sank carelessly down in a chair set at right angles to the chaise. The loose-fitting trousers stretched over his thighs, revealing hard, well-muscled legs. His strong-looking hands curled lightly over the carved ends of the arm. The tanned skin bore a fretwork of little pale scars. They'd been roughly used at one time.

The smile fell from Ginny's lips. "Who are you?"

His smile disappeared, too. The impression of carelessness, as she'd suspected, was a lie. "I am a friend of Miss Charlotte Nash."

"A friend," she repeated flatly, allowing no hint of

her sudden apprehension to show in her face. Instead, she let her gaze travel over him with humiliating skepticism.

"Yes," he replied as he subjected her low décolletage, nearly transparent gown, and unbound tresses to a similar scrutiny. "Apparently Miss Nash has a habit of collecting . . ." He paused tellingly. "Shall we say, *unusual* friends?"

The riposte brokered an unwilling smile. "Touché."

This, Ginny decided, must be the man she'd heard about this afternoon, the man who'd been seeking information about her but whose identity she hadn't been able to ascertain. She hadn't expected him to look so rough. Uncivilized.

How would someone like him come to be associated with Charlotte?

Her hand slipped under the pillow beside her, brushing the pearl-inlaid butt of the primed pistol she kept there at all times. "You've had a busy afternoon, Mr. Ross."

He regarded her questioningly.

"I have heard from several sources that you have been inquiring after me. And not those sources who generally smooth the way for an introduction between myself and my gentleman friends. N'est-ce pas?"

"I believe so, yes."

"Hence, I am predisposed to believe that you are one of our Charlotte's papist associates—working in the same vein as myself but from a different approach, if you will."

"Same vein?"

"As a spy," she replied concisely.

A flicker in his eyes. "If you are a spy, Mrs. Mulgrew, you are not very discreet," he murmured. "What if I was a French agent?"

"Then you chose the wrong men to query," she stated baldly, "and would be dead by now. The men you questioned have allegiances to my friends. They would not have answered your questions without being at least certain of what you are not.

"Now, shall we dispense with the verbal fencing and get on with the business at hand?" At his silence, she continued. "Why were you asking about me?"

"As I have said, I am a friend of Miss Nash."

"What of Charlotte?" she asked.

"I am afraid you may have involved 'our Charlotte' in some machinations that could possibly bring harm to her. I am here so that you might convince me otherwise." Though he spoke in mild tones, a little shiver of apprehension ran up Ginny's spine, causing her hand to curl around the butt of the hidden pistol.

"Such concern for her welfare," she said, smiling a little wistfully and darting a provocative glance at him. " 'Struth, I envy Miss Nash her 'friends.' "

He wasn't having it. He met her coquettish gaze without a trace of budding interest.

"Are you her brother? Cousin? Uncle?" she continued. "Who are you that her welfare is your concern? And I will not consider 'friend' a satisfactory answer."

"It may have to be," he replied. "Suffice to say, I am committed to her well-being."

It came to her then, spurred on by memories of the rumors and tales surrounding Ramsey Munro, the marquis of Cottrell, and Colonel Christian MacNeill. The Rose Hunters, they'd called themselves, young men imprisoned in France for plotting the overthrow of Napoleon's government but captured before they could implement their plan. Their lives had been forfeit until Charlotte's father, Colonel Nash, had traded his life for theirs. By way of reparation, they had sworn to protect and serve Nash's widow and orphaned daughters.

She scoured her memory for further details. The young men had been betrayed in a French prison by someone within their own circle, whether one of their own or someone from the abbey where they had been raised no one was certain. A few years later, the unnamed traitor had made attempts on first MacNeill's and then Cottrell's life where, during this last attempt, Charlotte's sister Helena had stabbed him. He had disappeared after that. It had been assumed he'd died of his wound.

It also had been assumed that the man Helena had stabbed as the traitor and murderer and this man were one and the same. Dand Ross.

Ginny's shiver of apprehension became a surge of fear.

"You're him," she said softly. Her index finger curled around the trigger. "The last Rose Hunter."

He said nothing. He looked utterly relaxed. Except for his eyes.

The only thing that kept Ginny from taking out the pistol and shooting him at once was the realization that of all the people who had speculated and mused and come to the conclusion that Andrew Ross was the only person who could possibly be the traitor and murderer, Charlotte alone had withheld comment.

Which was, now that Ginny thought of it, rather odd. Because she knew Dand Ross was not dead? Or because she knew he was not culpable? Or both?

Charlotte, Charlotte, she thought, *what secrets have you been keeping from me?*

But of course, if this Dand was a papist spy, Charlotte would be obligated to keep both his identity and his existence a secret. Apparently Charlotte was very good at keeping secrets.

"Well, Mr. Ross, how can I reassure you regarding our mutual friend?"

"Explain to me Miss Nash's part in the plan she outlined to me, the plan involving the Comte St. Lyon's house party."

Ginny smothered her start of surprise.

"What exactly has Charlotte told you, that naughty child?" The indulgent tone she'd hoped for failed her. Where exactly did that 'child's' allegiance lie?

"I know that you are seeking the retrieval of a letter currently held by the Comte St. Lyon. I know he is planning to auction it off and that you are going to steal it. All I want to know is what role you have assigned Miss Nash."

"None."

At his skeptical expression she shrugged. "She provides a bit of divertissement, is all. She is so deliciously ingenuous. People are continually trying to trump her by blurting out the most indiscreet things. Added to which she has a talent for knowing a variety of diverse people with, shall we say, diverse skills?"

"Like architects."

She nodded. " 'Twas Charlotte who found the gentleman with the blueprints to St. Lyon's castle. She heard an old dowager advising another to have the garderobes in her family castle restored by the same fellow who had done such a wondrous job on the Comte St. Lyon's newly acquired castle.

"So, you see, our Charlotte, for all her youth and seeming flightiness, is extremely useful. Not to mention courageous and—"

"I would just as soon her courage was never brought into question," he cut in. "That is exactly why I am here. To impress upon you how *very* much I desire that her courage not be called into question. In fact, I insist on it."

She met his gaze wide-eyed. "I don't see why it should be. At least not in the present situation. There. I have eased your fears. Now, ease mine," she said. "Who are you? And please, do me the courtesy of assuming I have some intelligence."

"I never doubted it," he said suavely. "As you already

concluded, we share, at least for the present, a similar goal."

"Then we should work in concert with one another," she suggested.

He shook his head. "I must return to France soon. There are matters which I must attend to before I can—" He broke off. "I would stay, if I could, if only to see that you keep your word regarding Miss Nash's safety."

She dimpled prettily, using all of her wiles to disarm him. "How can I convince you? Your own contact, the man to whom she gives your letters and who organizes your network here in London, gives his blessing to her involvement with me."

"My contact?"

She allowed herself a small, victorious smile. He was not the only one with sensitive information. "Yes. Toussaint."

At his expression, she straightened. "You didn't know?"

Dand gave her a flat look of disdain. "I never asked. I need only know that I have a contact. Not who he is. I have discovered that not knowing those things which others would exercise extremely unpleasant means to find out is the only certain way to avoiding revealing them. Should one be . . . *pressed.*"

She understood the terrible implications and her respect for him grew. She glanced again at the little scars on the backs of his fingers. He had been tortured in France.

"How do you know of Toussaint?" he asked.

"Oh, not from Charlotte. I assure you. We discovered him quite by accident. One of the pigeons he uses to communicate with the abbey fell beneath an archer's arrow. The archer, a minor functionary for the secretary for Alien Affairs, thought the message the bird carried odd enough to bring to his employer's attention and thus," she shrugged modestly, "to ours. Toussaint probably doesn't even know we have him identified."

"But he knows of Charlotte's role in your network and sanctions it?" Dand asked, watching her intently.

"Yes. If not directly, by tacit consent. Charlotte's role has grown beyond what I imagine you believe it to be. She has become a vital part of a network. *My* network. I believe that had Toussaint forbidden her to act on England's behalf, she would have done so anyway. Perhaps you ought to take a lesson from him?"

"Ah. But then, Toussaint's goals and mine may not be the same," he said.

"I thought as an agent of Rome your goal was to restore the monarchy to France and with it the Roman Church with all its former rights and privileges?" she said with weighty significance. A little flicker of appreciation danced in his warm brown eyes. He really was a most attractive man.

"That is part of it. There is . . . a personal element, too." He clasped the arms of the chair and pushed himself to his feet. She tilted her head back to maintain eye contact with him. "Can you pull this off, do you think?"

She nodded.

"How certain are you?"

She frowned, irritably. "I cannot guarantee anything, but I am confident of every aspect of the plan."

"Tell me of St. Lyon."

She could not think of any reason to refuse. "St. Lyon is a collector. Of art. Of wine. Of old books. And most especially, of women.

"He acquires lovers like some men acquire snuff-boxes. The harder they are to add to his collection, the more he must have them. No particular woman incites his passion; it is the chase, the challenge of taking her from another man's protection that excites him. He *must* have what is denied him."

"And you do not think a man of such appetites poses a threat to Miss Nash?"

"Charlotte stands in no danger from the comte." She did not add that had circumstances been different, this might not have been so.

She looked up. Too late, she realized Dand had read her concern in her face. She saw the suspicion on his face and hurried to reassure him. "The comte would *never* risk society's censure by pursuing a well-connected virgin. He values his position amongst the ton far too much to endanger it by indulging in an infatuation. *If* he was to develop one."

His eyes narrowed. He moved away from where she reclined against the silk pillows. "Besides," she added in a throaty purr, "the comte's attentions have already been fixed elsewhere. As you already know, he has invited me to be his 'special' guest at the castle."

He studied her with an insultingly clinical eye. She swung her legs over the edge of the chaise and rose, going to him and laying her hand on his chest imploringly. "It is imperative that this letter the comte has stolen never see the light of day. We have credible information that the contents could incriminate several extremely high ranking officials in a foreign government currently pondering whether to aid or hinder England's efforts—officials who are extremely sympathetic to our cause. This letter could destroy them."

"You really are amazingly indiscreet," he murmured.

She gazed up at him, trying to fathom his thoughts. If he failed to win her trust, he would be dead before he reached the front door. Or would her footman, Finn? She would rather not find out. "Do you understand?"

"Of course, I understand," he said, suddenly impatient. "Which is why I have to return to France to reassure those who sent that letter before fear sends them fleeing the country and the game is up."

So *that* is who he was! The agent best known as Rousse, though he had a myriad of identities and aliases, was the architect of some of the most delicate secret alliances in Europe. Ginny stared at him with new respect.

"Which is why, before I go, I need your promise that Miss Nash's involvement in this plot ends now. Here." His eyes narrowed. "You would not consider dragging her along in your wake to provide—how did you put it?—a divertissement while you search?"

Actually, Ginny had considered such a ploy but decided that it would be odd for her to bring along a rival. The comte was no fool. And she could not afford to provoke even the slightest suspicion.

"Believe me, Mr. Ross, I have no *desire* to put Charlotte in harm's way—"

He moved so quickly she didn't have time to dive for the pistol she'd left beneath the pillow. One minute he was standing relaxed a few feet away, the next he loomed over her, his hand about her throat. Tight. She grabbed his wrist, struggling unsuccessfully to free herself. His thumb pressed deeply at a point beneath her jaw. Little sparks of light rimmed her vision.

"I see I have failed to make my point," he said. "Let me clarify my position. I do not care what you *desire* to do. I have done many things I have not particularly *desired* to do. I only care about how you act. I do not want Miss Nash endangered. *Do you understand?*" His voice was perfectly calm, perfectly cold.

She let her hands drop, nodding as she stared into his eyes. Then, as abruptly as he'd taken hold of her, she was free. He stepped back and inclined his head in a bow that, while it did not mock her, in no way apologized. "Good. I bid you good evening, Mrs. Mulgrew."

The coast of northern Scotland
Early winter, 1788

"There's a light on the shore!" The midshipman hollered above the roar of the storm.

"Bonfire or lantern?"

Jeremy, huddled with the boy in the lugger's forecabin, heard the captain bellow from topside.

The screech and crash of swinging booms and groaning wood drowned out the midshipman's panicked reply and Jeremy clutched the boy closer, trying to master his own terror.

The ship suddenly tipped, pitching Jeremy and the boy down the steeply inclined floor of the cabin until it suddenly shot up beneath them and then dashed them down again with bone-shattering force. Above, a man screamed. The captain swore viciously.

A storm had pounced upon them just as they'd come in sight of the Scottish coast. Trying to outrace the black churning clouds, the captain had turned south, away from the port of Wick. But the storm had chased them down with the savage intentness of a wolf overtaking its prey and now tossed the small lugger about savagely.

Suddenly the hatch above jerked wide open and water poured in as the captain looked down, his face taut and strained. "We're heading in! Whether to wreckers or our salvation, I do not know!" he shouted at them. "Make ready!" He slammed the hatch shut.

"What does he mean?" the boy asked. His face was white and his small body shaking violently, but he hadn't cried, and only the boy's courage saved Jeremy from succumbing and sobbing himself.

"Wreckers," Jeremy said, looking about for some ballast to which he and the boy could cling. "Men who set fires to lure boats into the rocky shores where they will be smashed to bits.

Then they scavenge the shores for loot and kill any survivors who could carry tales!"

The boy swallowed.

"Can you swim?" Jeremy asked, finding a length of heavy rope.

"Yes."

"Good." He spied a small wine cask and ripped the cork from it, upending the contents onto the floor while the boy watched him with round-eyed amazement. With numb fingers he laced the heavy rope through the brass handles on its side and recorked the cask.

"Come here. Good boy," Jeremy said, lashing the rope around the boy's waist and trying to tie a knot. "If it is wreckers and the boat comes apart, try to hold on. And if you make it to the shore safely, hide!"

"Can you swim?" the boy suddenly asked.

"No."

The boy stared and then with a violent sound clawed at Jeremy's hands. "Then you must tie yourself to the barrel!

"Don't be a fool, lad," Jeremy said, hating the sob that broke his voice. "You have to survive. I have a sacred trust from your mother. I said I would do everything in my power to see you safely to Scotland and, by God, I shall."

"No!" the boy shouted, fighting him furiously and Jeremy, God help him, slapped his small face hard, grabbing his narrow shoulders and shaking him violently as the ship listed and lurched drunkenly.

"Listen to me!" he shouted. "I count myself a man of honor. What honor would I have if you died and I survived?

No, do not ask me to forfeit that thing that makes me worthy in my own eyes. I would not ask it of you!" he said fiercely.

"But, sir—" The boy's face was terrible with conflict, with pride, and with terror. And honest devotion. Until that moment, Jeremy had never realized that the boy had feelings for him.

Jeremy's heart lurched. He tried valiantly for a smile, softening his grip on the tight, shuddering little shoulders. "Besides, lad, this is but a precaution. Even if it is wreckers, I might find my way to shore yet. So do this for me."

The boy's eyes pressed closed a second and when he opened them he fixed his gaze on the rope Jeremy was trying to tie, swatting aside his hands and doing the knot himself, his lips quivering, tears spilling from his downcast eyes.

Crack!

The ship rolled and pitched, the prow shooting up as it hit something, sending the pair of them plummeting down the cabin amid a hail of tumbling furniture and luggage and books. The sound of splintering wood and screaming men blended with the howling wind.

So that was it, then. A great calm overtook Jeremy. Silently, he hauled up the boy strapped to the empty cask and stumbled with him up the steep inclined floor of the cabin while the ship groaned and screamed. He clambered atop the overturned desk and shoved open the hatch, grabbing the slight boy round the waist and pitching him up into the darkness outside amidst a torrent of rain and wind. He seized the boy's hand as a wave washed over the shattered hull and a sudden realization caught him by the throat. He had not given the boy his mother's purse or the letter to those who were to receive him. There was no time and the boy didn't even know to whom he was going!

He tried to scream above the din and screech of shattering timbers. "Find Ros—"

A monstrous wave broke over the sinking ship, sending torrents of bitterly cold water streaming down the open hatch. For a precious few seconds he held the boy's hand against the mighty force.

A second later the hatch collapsed.

4

The Haymarket Theatre, London
July 17, 1806

"WHAT A CRUSH. Such a terrible bore, don't you agree, Miss Nash?" Some young Pink of the Ton whose name escaped Charlotte stood posed at the railing of the Weltons' private box, his drawl matching his well-practiced ennui.

Charlotte nodded, her mouth curving coquettishly, though in truth, she barely heard him. All evening she'd been distracted by the fact that on his visit to her three nights ago Dand hadn't given her a message to pass to Toussaint. Since that was his sole reason for being in London, he would be coming back to do so and soon. Tonight?

A crowded box at a popular opera would be an excellent place to do so. He might appear at any second, as an attendant, an usher, or even a raggedy beggar on the steps to the opera house. She would give him a penny, she thought, if this last proved the case. She smiled at the thought.

"La, here comes St. Lyon and begad if he ain't bringin' that prime bit o—" the Pink of the Ton broke off abruptly. "Er, he has Mrs. Mulgrew with him."

The Comte St. Lyon sauntered into the box, Ginny Mulgrew at his side. Suavely, he bowed toward Lady Welton and greeted the baron. He was a handsome man, Charlotte thought, no one could argue otherwise. A little above middle height, slender and straight with the heavy Gallic features that somehow only the French can wear with urbanity. Dark, smooth hair swept back from a wide, furrowed forehead. A broad yet elegantly shaped nose separated dark, liquid eyes. He caught her studying him and with a self-satisfied smile approached.

The Pink inclined his head, his gaze sliding indecisively toward Ginny. "Comte," he said. "Ah . . . ma'am."

Ginny ignored him, making her way to the balcony rail overlooking the crush below. The comte cut him directly, too, thereby ending the boy's miserable uncertainty of whether or not he ought to address a demirep in front of a lady. Mumbling a word of good-bye, the Pink slunk off, leaving Charlotte alone with the comte.

"How delightful to see you again, Miss Nash," he said.

Falling effortlessly into the role she'd played for so many years, Charlotte's brows rose, at once winsome and arch. "La, Comte! We meet so often I begin to fear you will find me most commonplace."

"Never," the comte declared. Though exquisitely polite, the very manner in which he refused to allow his gaze to stray from her face made Charlotte aware of her daring décolletage and her filmy silver lamé gown.

She resisted the impulse to draw her shawl up from where it gracefully draped her arms and cover herself. Instead, she laughed lightly, snapping open her fan and setting the silk and lace panels fluttering delicately over her bosom.

"No, I insist 'tis true," she protested. "And I hereby swear off any entertainments where we might meet so that you will be forced to consider me frightfully exclusive."

"Please, dear Miss Nash, do not deprive yourself of any pleasures on my account," the comte said. "It is most unnecessary as, alas, tomorrow I leave your fair city."

Charlotte arranged her features into a believable approximation of dismay. "But whatever for, sir?" she asked. "And might I be so bold as to ask where you are going?"

"Being bold suits you, Miss Nash," the comte replied.

Charlotte answered by fanning a bit faster, as if he'd set her pulse racing. Oh, she was quite good at this.

"As to why and where," the comte continued, " 'tis a dreary responsibility. I am promised to host some of my former compatriots at my castle in Scotland. They are new to these shores and feel the need to rest before they begin their lives in England's most illustrious city."

A city the comte would see overrun with Napoleon's soldiers if the price was right, Charlotte thought. "How kind you are, Comte. But how cruel of your guests to arrive during the height of the season, depriving us of your company!"

"I would that I could forgo it, Miss Nash. Still, 'tis not so great a hardship. The castle has been completely refitted and refurnished and is quite the seat of luxury. You must come and visit me there someday. Indeed, promise me you will."

"That would be most pleasant," Charlotte said, tipping her head winsomely while wishing him to the devil. "Don't you agree, Mrs. Mulgrew?"

Ginny, returned from her perusal of the pits, had remained uncharacteristically silent throughout the exchange. "Yes. Wonderful."

Around them, the Weltons' others guests adjusted gloves, fanned themselves languidly in a futile attempt to cool the stuffy atmosphere, and in general prepared to depart. Few made any attempt to speak to the comte, none to his guest. Neither circumstance appeared to worry the comte.

"Did you enjoy the opera, Miss Nash?" he asked.

"Oh, I always enjoy a spectacle," Charlotte responded with a glance across the packed opera house to the private boxes stacked up the ruby- and gilt-plastered walls like fantastical swallows' nests. Inside each of these aeries, the Beau Monde turned avid faces toward the Weltons' box.

She could almost hear them: "That girl is chasing a bad end." "Havey-cavey sort of creature, the bane of the marchioness of Cottrell's existence, I fear." "Whatever are the Weltons thinking to invite a demirep into their box? Are they *trying* to ruin their young friend Miss Nash?" and, most tellingly, "I fear Miss Nash needs no accomplice in that matter."

"Oh my." The comte had caught her wry glance at the curiosity seekers. He bent his sleek head toward her. "I hope I haven't provoked any undue speculation?"

"I am certain not," Charlotte said dryly. The comte, exquisite in a midnight blue jacket, white silk stock, and yellow waistcoat knew well enough it wasn't his presence that caused the ripple of scandalized gossip. It was Ginny's.

Her head high, her auburn hair gleaming beneath the raised houselights, Ginny looked around with bland imperiousness. Her gown, a rose-colored silk crepe ablaze with little crystal embroidered florets, put to shame any attempts to rival it. Her skin gleamed with the sheen only a powder of abalone dust could impart and her lips, reddened with currants, held the hint of a smile. Yet, for all her beauty, she stood alone, a little circle having opened up around her, separating her from the rest of the revelers in the Weltons' box. If she noticed, she certainly didn't appear to care.

"What of you, Mrs. Mulgrew? Did you enjoy the opera this evening?" Charlotte asked.

"Excuse me, Miss Nash. I wasn't attending. You were saying . . . ?" At Ginny's response, the comte turned and held out his hand. Without hesitation, Ginny slipped her own into it. His expression was triumphant.

Why, that is why he has come here, Charlotte realized. He knew that the Weltons were the only members of the ton oblivious enough, or simply unconcerned enough, to receive him and Ginny into their private box and he wanted everyone of consequence to see Ginny and know that he had won her from her former situation as Lord Denney's mistress. He has brought her here specifically to show her off as his latest acquisition.

Acquisition. The reality of what Ginny was about to do struck Charlotte all at once. Ginny was going to become the comte's mistress. She was going to share his bed. He had *purchased* that privilege.

Charlotte struggled to maintain a neutral expression, unable to quell a rush of revulsion and hating herself for the unworthy feeling. Always before when they had discussed this plan, Ginny had seemed so matter-of-fact about the intimate aspects of it, so completely at ease with the proposal, that Charlotte had unwittingly adopted her attitude—easy to do, she now discovered, when the thing had been theoretical.

But seeing the comte's avid expression and Ginny's cool sufferance, Charlotte found it far harder to support. Forcefully, she reminded herself of the many people, young soldiers and shop workers, mothers and grandfathers and children, who may well depend for their futures, perhaps even their lives, on Ginny's willingness to barter her body for an invitation to St. Lyon's castle.

Ginny was looking past Charlotte, a trace of anxiety discernible in the stiffness of her posture. The comte had turned to trade a few words with Lord Welton, a small melon of a man notable primarily for being even more in the dark than his wife, and Charlotte took the opportunity to edge closer to the courtesan.

"You look nervous. Has something gone wrong?" she asked in a low voice. "Do you find that you cannot do this, after all? Such a sacrifice—"

"Sacrifice?" Ginny cut her off with a soft whisper. "You are glorifying me, Lottie, and I will not have it. This is what I do. This is who I am. And I have no apologies to make for either."

"But—"

"Nothing is wrong except that I wish the comte had not brought me here," she continued in a low voice. "But a gentleman must crow, I suppose. I just wish he had found another fence post to do it from." Her dark eyes flickered anxiously about the opera house as though she was searching for someone. "I have had the unnerving sensation of late that I am being—" She broke off, her expression tense and a little angry.

"Being what?"

"Never mind. I am being fanciful is all," Ginny whispered impatiently, visibly wanting to be done with the conversation. "Now, go and speak to some of those young men slathering behind you before one of them slips in a pool of his own drool."

The sharp tone, clearly meant to bite, was out of character. "There *is* something else. Something you are—"

"Come along, Charlotte."

Surprised by the abrupt bellow, Charlotte spun around.

" 'Tis past time we left," the baroness, Lady Welton, announced from her seat near the balcony, her soft, pleasant face pinched with unhappiness, her large, wide-set eyes darting from Charlotte to Ginny. The reason for her misery was clear. She was forcing herself to protect Charlotte from an unseemly influence—that influence being Ginny Mulgrew—and the role was alien to her.

Lady Welton hated what she termed "vulgar scenes" with their attendant recriminations, accusations, and hurt feelings. Which went a long way to explaining the benign neglect with which she had raised her children, as well as the myriad overlooked pranks and larks her offspring had got up to, and away with, with such regularity.

Unfortunately, though Lady Welton was excellent at winking at those things she did not want to know about, not even her amazing negligence could overlook a known courtesan whispering into the ear of the girl the baroness took every opportunity to tell Society was like a daughter to her. Not that, in Lady Welton's own mind, a casual friendship—and its attendant interesting conversations—with a courtesan was anything but sensible.

She only wished she'd had the foresight to have made such a practical acquaintance before she'd married Lord Welton. A few "interesting conversations" would have saved everybody a great deal of embarrassment. And time. But Charlotte should be having that conversation in the hallway, or an anteroom, or some other place out of sight of her, so that when people pointed accusing fingers—and people *always* pointed accusing fingers—Lady Welton could say with perfect honesty that she had no knowledge of anything untoward, and thus not be held accountable.

But Charlotte was in plain sight of her and they *were* whispering, quite possibly about those "fascinating things," and thus Something Had To Be Done. Worse, *she* would have to do it.

"There's too much of a crush in here what with all these young men crowding in. A body can't breathe proper." Lady Welton glared accusingly at the coterie of Charlotte's admirers who'd swarmed into the box as soon as the curtain had been drawn.

"Not yet, ma'am," one of the young bucks protested.

"No sense going out now. You'll just end up standing in another crush waiting for a hack."

"That's right," another added. "Best to sit in a crush than stand in one."

Such sound reasoning found a sympathetic ear in Lady Welton. She hated to stand in crushes. "All right then. We wait."

"Milord." The comte, attending this little byplay, turned to Lord Welton. "My carriage is waiting across the street. Can I offer you its use?"

"Eh? Oh!" The baron's pink face alit with relief. "That would be—"

"Impossible," Lady Welton blurted out.

The baron turned, blinking at his wife who had risen to her feet, clucking like a hen whose chick was about to run after a fox. "Impossible?" he echoed bewilderedly.

"Yes." She gave a decidedly unsubtle jerk of her head in Ginny's direction. Charlotte felt a blush rise in her cheeks for her friend. Not that Ginny looked humiliated. She looked bored.

"Yes," repeated Lady Welton firmly. "I want a negus punch before we go and we don't want to keep the comte waiting. In fact, I insist he *not* wait."

"Oh." The baron turned with a sigh, long experience having taught him the futility of arguing with his spouse. "Someone get me wife a punch."

The comte accepted his defeat graciously, inclining his head before offering his arm to Ginny. "We will bid you good evening then. Lady Welton. Welton." His dark eyes slid to Charlotte. "Miss Nash?"

As soon as they left, Lady Welton snapped her fan shut and rearranged her shawl about her dimpled arms. "Well then. Let's go. No sense being the last in line."

"But, my dear, I just sent young Farley for a negus," the baron said.

"Then young Farley can drink it," Lady Welton answered, securing Charlotte's arm firmly in her own and wading into the group of young men still milling about in the box.

"I don't understand," the baron said plaintively, trailing after them.

"Oh, Alfred," Lady Welton said with the air of a great instructor bestowing a kernel of wisdom on a pupil of suspect capabilities. " 'Tis one thing to allow a woman like Mrs. Mulgrew into one's box when a great many other scapegraces and rattle-pates are already littering it," here the scapegraces glared accusingly at the rattle-pates and vice versa, "and quite another to voluntarily accept her company in a closed carriage."

And, having educated her husband on this fine point of etiquette, she elbowed young Farley, on his way through the door with the requested negus, out of her way and sailed into the crowds in the hall beyond, her husband struggling to follow.

They emerged onto Catherine Street and into a crowd of other patrons of the arts, the gentlemen trying frantically—and with limited success—to wave down a hack while their wives and daughters milled disgruntledly beneath the brightly lit portico. London's omnipresent fog had begun rolling inland from the

Thames, blanketing those on the curb and obliterating everything more than a few yards away.

Across the street, a cacophony of voices and noise issued from the indistinct outlines of the private broughams and hacks, the phantom shapes of horses and other figures. From within the blanketed depths rose the sound of spectral vendors hawking roasted nuts; little ghostly street sweepers bleating the cost of their services, ladies chattering and gentlemen shouting while the jangle and squeak of harnesses, the clatter of shifting hooves, and the rumble of carriages on cobblestone underscored it all. A driver yelled for someone to mind their step, the snap of a whip preceded a horse whinnying in reproach, and a man swore viciously as he stumbled in the murk.

At the corner of the opera house the bilious globe of a streetlight hung above a little clutch of Fashionable Impures putting on display wares currently being offered. They simpered and smiled, dimpled and cast flirtatious glances at the young beaus and dandies, bucks, and swells that swaggered slowly amongst them with the air of diners selecting their next course.

Charlotte caught a glimpse of Ginny a little farther up the boulevard, her head bent in conversation with the comte. She nodded briefly and he disappeared between the two carriages jockeying for position in front of them, emerging on the far side to be swallowed by the fog.

"We will be here for hours," Lady Welton stated petulantly. Behind them Charlotte's little mill of admirers had dispersed, seeking their own means of travel to the next party, the next gaming hell, the next entertainment.

"We could walk a bit down the street where the traffic eases up," Charlotte said.

Lady Welton looked at her as if she'd grown another head. "Why?"

"So we won't have to wait so long?" Charlotte suggested.

"Nothing better to do. Can't say I look forward to the Neebler fête. Do you? Course, you don't. Tight-fisted and uncongenial, the lot of them. They'll pawn off a few bits of mutton and a smattering of prawns for refreshments and for our trouble we shall be obliged to listen to the old windsack's daughter screech while the wife pounds on the pianoforte. No. Better to wait." She lifted her hand, waving her kerchief at her husband, who was puffing and huffing his way down the line of carriages looking for an unclaimed hire.

"Welton, a chair, please!"

"But m'dear," he called back, "where am I to find a chair?"

"Well, really, Welton," Lady Welton replied with fond irritation, "if I knew that, I wouldn't be asking you to find me one, would I?"

"Quite right," Welton muttered and quit the search for a cab, going instead to look for a chair for his wife.

"Welton is a dear," Lady Welton said comfortably, patting Charlotte's arm.

"Mrs. Mulgrew." From somewhere across the street a male voice rose above the din. "If you would?"

Charlotte glanced toward Ginny. The courtesan frowned, a look of impatience on her pretty face at being asked to cross the crowded avenue, before daintily lifting her skirts and stepping off the curb onto the slick cobblestones. She disappeared between the carriages.

"Ah!" At Lady Welton's expression of pleasure, Charlotte turned back in time to see Lord Welton leading two stalwart-looking workmen lugging between them a marble bench pilfered from heaven knew where. "One can always count on Wel—"

"Look out!"

The warning rang out over the crowds. In the sudden pocket of silence Charlotte heard the mad scrabble of runaway horses' hooves ringing against the cobblestones, the rumble of wheels over the road, and the thunder of a vehicle passing by and—a cry, a horrible thud!

Then the sound of the racing vehicle retreating as swiftly as it had appeared. The silence was broken by the sound of rushing feet and anxious voices raised in alarm.

"She's hurt! She's hurt! Someone get a quack! Hurry!"

"Oh!" cried Lady Welton softly, her hand covering her lips. "Some poor woman must have been struck. I hope I do not know her . . ."

A terrible premonition seized Charlotte.

"Charlotte, my dear! Where are you going? You cannot—"

Whatever else Lady Welton said was lost as Charlotte dashed into the street, searching for the woman who'd fallen beneath the runaway horses' hooves. A little crowd had gathered a short way down the avenue. Charlotte pushed her way through them, praying that she would not find—

"No!"

Ginny Mulgrew lay on her side, her leg bent beneath her at an impossible angle. Already the stagnant pools of water collecting between the cobbles had soaked into her beautiful gown. A hoof print was ground deeply into the material a few inches from her hip. Her face was white, her eyes closed.

Charlotte dropped down beside her, insensible to the hard stone beneath her knees. Gingerly, she wiped a heavy strand of hair from Ginny's brow. A thin line of blood seeped from a cut beneath it.

Charlotte looked up into the ring of concerned faces. "We have to get her out of the street! And find a doctor. Now!" she commanded.

An anxious-looking gentleman in a green waistcoat snapped his fingers at two liveried servants craning their necks to see. "Find some means of conveying the woman," he demanded. "Quickly!" At once they went to do his bidding.

Comte St. Lyon appeared at Charlotte's side, his expression startled. "What happened?"

"Some damn coxscomb lost control of his cattle,"

the gentleman said. "Ran the poor woman down. Bloody green-headed fool!"

"My God," St. Lyon whispered. "Will she be all right?"

"We won't know until she's been seen," Charlotte replied tightly. "And she can't be seen here, in the street."

The two servants emerged from the crowd, carrying a broad bench between them. "Carefully now."

Gingerly they lifted Ginny to the bench. Their efforts, careful though they were, brought her to instant, painful consciousness. A cry of anguish broke from her throat.

"It's all right," Charlotte said soothingly. "We're taking you out of here."

"To where?" the gentleman in the green waistcoat asked anxiously.

"My home," St. Lyon answered.

"No," Ginny whispered, her eyes, great pools of agony, fixed on Charlotte. "Please."

"My house," Charlotte said in a tone that brooked no argument. "I'll stay with her. I can better look after her than you, comte."

St. Lyon did not argue. He stood up. "I'll get my barouche," he said and hurried back across the street.

"Lottie." The thin voice was barely audible, the syllables pressed out with great effort from between Ginny's lips. "Promise."

"Quiet, dear—"

"Lottie!" she gasped, her gaze wild. "You must promise me."

"Yes, yes," Charlotte cooed, trying to calm her. "Of course. Anything."

Ginny shook her head, her face stricken. "You have to understand, Lottie. You must let *no one* dissuade you. You must go to St. Lyon's castle in my place!"

5

Culholland Square, Mayfair
July 18, 1806

"YOU MUST SOMEHOW CONVINCE both men to fall in with our plans," Ginny whispered hoarsely to Charlotte. Her color was still ashen and pain had etched tiny lines at the corner of her lips. But though her eyes were dilated with the drugs the physician had left her, she seemed lucid.

"Yes," Charlotte assured her, settling the light coverlet more comfortably around Ginny's slender figure, careful not to jar the leg cocooned in cotton batting and strapped between two wooden staves.

"Drink this," Charlotte urged, placing a cup of beef tea in Ginny's hands. "You must keep up your strength."

Ginny jerked her head impatiently. "Can Ross be trusted?"

"Yes." Charlotte set down the cup. "I tell you again, his trustworthiness is without question. And his dedication is equal to either yours or mine."

"I do not doubt his dedication. I only doubt where it lies," Ginny muttered. She squeezed her eyes shut, fighting off a stab of pain as well as the mind-numbing influence of the drugs she had taken just before Charlotte's arrival. "You said earlier you'd had a message from your . . . other associate."

"Yes," Charlotte said, frowning at the memory of the short note that had arrived a few hours ago. "He wishes to speak with me this afternoon."

"Oh?"

"We have only met twice before," Charlotte explained, her expression shaded with puzzlement. "He is in a uniquely powerful position and it is imperative that his identity remains a secret. Until a few months ago I had never seen him properly. We always rendezvoused late at night and he kept to the shadows of whatever place we arranged to meet and even then had me leave the messages beneath a stone or in an urn as he watched from afar, then later he would retrieve them."

"A most cautious man," Ginny said. "Why change now?"

"I don't know. I suspect he has heard of your accident and wishes to know how it affects our plan."

"Then you'd best go," Ginny said and her eyelids fluttered shut.

Charlotte wrapped the rough cloak more closely about her, glad that, despite its malodorous scent, she had borrowed it from her astonished scullery maid. Even the plainest gown in her wardrobe would have stood out like a beacon in this dingy sidestreet of Drury Lane. The driver of the hired hack, fearing not only for his cattle but himself, had refused to go any farther into the rookery, depositing her at the end of the alley with a grudging promise to wait a half hour before leaving.

She could not blame him. Though the day was bright and the air mild, the stench rising from the open gutters running on either side of the deeply rutted road nearly overpowered her. Tipping with drunken disregard for symmetry, the rookery buildings loomed over her, sprouting larger overhead like dark seeping mushrooms, the windows boarded over to avoid the taxes on them, rackety stairs leading to the mean little apartments above. Far below bands of silent, bellicose youths slouched in the doors of subterranean taverns and exhausted-looking men trudged past vacant-eyed women cradling earthenware jugs and listless, raggedy children.

Charlotte looked about for some signpost. There was none. No indication that she was in the London she knew at all. She spied a woman sitting on the top step leading down to yet another public house, a half-naked toddler perched on her knee sucking his thumb.

"I'm looking for Sparrow Lane. Number Twelve," she said. "Can you tell me where it is?"

The woman's gaze fell on the tan calfskin half boots Charlotte's cloak could not hide. "Fer tuppence."

"Here's a farthing."

The woman's hand shot up, snagging the coin. "There." She jerked her head back over her shoulder. "Standing right in front of it, ye be."

"Thank you." Charlotte climbed the steps to the indicated door, looking up at the tilting rooflines. Were the messenger pigeons Toussaint used to communicate with Father Tarkin in Scotland up there?

She rapped sharply on the door. She did not have to wait long. The door swung open and a hard-looking man stood before her. "Miss Nash. I am so grateful that you have come. Please." He stepped aside.

She ducked her head under the low lintel emerging into a windowless room lit by a single lantern. Inside, it was stiflingly hot and dark, the single window having been boarded up. Still, she was greatly relieved to see that it was more tolerable than the outside of the building suggested. True, the floor rolled beneath her feet and the walls bore several large cracks but someone had recently scrubbed it well, for the unmistakable scent of lye stung her eyes and filled her nose.

"Won't you be seated?" Toussaint said, a hint of French accent in his voice.

Charlotte shrugged the simple cloak from her shoulders and sat down on the edge of the chair, studying the soldier-monk who'd summoned her. When she'd met him some months ago her first impression was that he was older than he looked. His brown hair was only lightly touched with gray at the temples and his face, though weathered, possessed a firm jaw and strong throat.

Her second impression had been that he would make a most uncomfortable sort of monk. She could almost feel the hum of purpose driving him. He moved with staccato precision, as though only the greatest of efforts kept his movements in check. Even his hands, at his sides, closed and opened like the mouth of a beached fish. She was certain he was unaware of the spastic motion. But it wasn't only this ill-contained energy. Though his mouth wore a smile, the keen eyes boring into her were merciless. His quick assessing gaze stopped abruptly at her modest neckline.

"Is that . . . could that be one of the yellow roses from St. Bride's?" Disapproval invested his voice. "One of those that the boys brought your family?"

"Yes," she answered. She'd forgotten she'd pinned it to her bodice this morning. "I suppose you think that dreadfully sentimental?"

"Sentiment can destroy a person. Or a cause. Be careful." His pensive expression faded. "Thank you for coming. The news regarding Mrs. Mulgrew is most distressing. Most alarming.

"This tragedy may well hold far-reaching repercussions. Ones we may not be able to counter or offset. We cannot afford to lose that letter," he said in a hollow voice. "Tell me the extent of her injuries. Tell me if Mrs. Mulgrew might recover sufficiently to go north at some later date."

He sounded desperate.

"I am afraid I cannot do that. There is no chance she will recover sufficiently to go forth with the plan as proposed."

He released a hiss of breath and his eyelids fell shut. He opened his eyes and seeing Charlotte's expression, rose to his feet, looking down at her. "I cannot overstate the importance of this letter. It is not only the sender who stands in grave danger should his identity be revealed and it is not only his nation which shall feel Napoleon's wrath upon discovering his betrayal. The papal city, too, will suffer. More priests, so recently allowed to return to their dioceses, will suffer."

"Sir?"

He leaned over her, his fierce gaze compelling her to understand. "Napoleon and the Pope are at odds. Each month Napoleon's greed and mania for power swells. He has begun to resent the pope's refusal to join his embargo against Britain. If this letter is revealed to have been bound for the papal offices and opened . . ." He shook his head. "It will be the excuse Napoleon has been looking for to break all ties with the Church and declare the pope his enemy.

"You see now why I am so distraught. I never approved of Mrs. Mulgrew's plan, but only a fool could

not see it stood the best chance of succeeding in re-
trieving that letter. Now . . ." He gestured in the manner of someone throwing something away and turned,
his shoulders so tightly bunched she could see them
shivering. "We *must* retrieve that letter. No matter
what the sacrifice. No matter who makes the sacrifice.
We must. We *must!*"

He looked around at her and she realized he was
holding his breath, his emotions so strong a little drop
of foam had developed in the corner of his mouth. His
eyes pleaded with her for understanding. His hands
twitched.

"I understand," Charlotte said, a little revolted, a
great deal moved by his dedication and his moral
quandary. "Completely. And I must admit that I am relieved that we are in accord with one another on this
subject."

The monk straightened, turning to face her completely. "What do you mean?"

"I *intend* to go in Mrs. Mulgrew's place."

His eyes grew round with amazement. His mouth
fell open a fraction of an inch and snapped shut.
"What? I should forbid it," he whispered.

The monk was being disingenuous.

"Brother Toussaint," she said mildly, "that is why
you asked for this meeting, is it not? To ask me if an alternative might be found to take Mrs. Mulgrew's place?
And who would that alternative be if not me?"

His eyes widened with offense. "I . . . I wasn't certain . . . That is, I hadn't thought you would—"

She took pity on him. "You do not *want* me to do this. I understand. I'm not too keen on it myself. But you knew that I was the only viable substitute. It's unworthy of you to pretend otherwise.

"Please," she continued before he could renew his protest, "allow me to finish. You had made the difficult decision to suggest this but then, when I arrived, you were struck anew by how very young I am, how inexperienced in the ways of the world. So you thought better of your original, impossible decision. But your original impulse was not wrong."

He did not attempt any further remonstration, instead saying, "But how can you hope to carry off such an impersonation?" His face lit with sudden inspiration. "I can—"

"You needn't *do* anything, Brother Toussaint," she reassured him. "I will impose on Dand Ross to aid me."

"Dand? Here? Now?" She had the impression she had utterly flummoxed him. He blinked, as though trying to clear his vision. "My God . . . it *is* Providence then," he murmured, his hand forming the sign of the cross above his heart. "It was meant to be."

"I suspect Providence has little to do with the comings and goings of Dand Ross," Charlotte said dryly. "He came to report the missing letter. A fact with which we were already acquainted. He must return to France in a few weeks. But by then, I shall no longer need his aid."

"Is he coming here? To see me?" Toussaint asked.

"No." Charlotte shook her head. "He doesn't even know you are his contact."

Toussaint smiled apologetically. "No. Of course not. I . . . It is just that . . . I helped mold him, you know." This last was said with touching pride.

Charlotte regarded him with sharpening interest. "What was he like?" She could not resist asking. "As a boy?"

"Dand?" Toussaint mused a moment, lost in some reverie he found pleasant, for a gentle smile curved his lips. "Limb of Satan, the monks called him. Always doing what he oughtn't, sneaking out of the dormitory to go adventuring, inciting the other lads to get up to some misadventure or other and then as glib as the devil in wiggling his way out of the proceedings when they were caught. The old herbalist Brother Fidelis used to say that God made the switch for boys like Dand Ross."

Aye. She could well believe that. "And the other lads?" she prompted.

Toussaint smiled, and for the first time, Charlotte saw a hint of warmth in his chill gaze. "Ram was just as refined and tempered as a lad as he is a man. And Kit," he frowned, "as strong in his convictions as he was in body."

"There was a fourth," Charlotte said, "the one who was killed in France."

"Douglas Stewart." Toussaint nodded, his face filled with inexpressible sorrow.

"Kit said once that Douglas was their core. The glue that bound them together. He must have been quite extraordinary."

Toussaint frowned, as though searching his mind for an image to fit the word. "Extraordinary? I don't know. He was a bright enough boy. As athletic as some, not as athletic as others. High-minded. Earnest. But earnestness hardly qualified one to be a fit leader."

Charlotte had never heard either Ram or Kit express any sentiment about Douglas Stewart that wasn't steeped in reverence. She was fascinated. "I don't understand."

"Well, Ram had address and poise. Kit had strength and determination."

"And Dand?"

"Dand was the brightest. And he had charm. But a darker side, too, that even the best of them must find enticing. Douglas had . . . nothing." Whatever momentary mood had held Toussaint abruptly disappeared. "Enough. It is over and done and hardly matters anymore. What *does* matter is that you say Dand is willing to assist you in your plan? In what manner?"

At this, heat climbed into Charlotte's cheeks and she was glad of the relative darkness in the steamy little room. "Brother Toussaint," she said, "your conscience is troubled enough as it is. Let us not test it any further, shall we? Be content that Dand's assistance will bring me no harm and will go far to establishing my credibility as the sort of woman the comte will feel he can safely compromise."

Toussaint's brows pulled together in a scowl. "My child—"

"*Credibility*, Brother Toussaint, not authenticity."

6

∞∞∞

Northern Scotland
Christmas 1788

"I DIDN'T SAVE yer from getting yer throat slit only to see ye shot by the militia. It don't matter what Geoff says, I seen the redcoats meself marching up the great north road." *The bull-shouldered, grizzle-haired man stretched on his tiptoes and peered over the thick hedge lining this portion of the road. Seeing nothing, he dropped flat to his feet and turned around, regarding the boy with an ambivalent expression.*

"*Time to cut bait and run, and I ain't runnin' too fast or too far with a lad taggin' along. It's been a bonny treat bein' yer guide and companion, young sir, but time to part ways.*" *He squinted down nearsightedly, his broken jaw pulling his* lips into a perpetual grimace. But after nearly a month in Trevor's company, the boy recognized the expression as being as close to affection as a thief, smuggler, and very possibly murderer, was likely to achieve.

"Yer a fair dab hand with a pick and lock and might keep that in mind fer the future. But not yet. Lads as young and tender as you—" He broke off, shaking his head. "Yer fate wouldn't be much to yer likin' on the road. Nah. Better ye go to St. Bride's Abbey than take yer chances out here. Abbott come along here from town every other Wednesday. He'll be along soon."

"I don't want to go to an abbey."

The man nodded. " 'Course ye don't. But ye got nowhere else to go and the Father Abbot ain't bad as men of God go, and there's others like ye at the abbey, too. Orphans."

The boy didn't say a word.

"Ye know," Trevor said thoughtfully. "Ye could tell me who ye are and I could maybe find some folks what might be lookin' fer ye."

"I've told you," the boy said with an elaborate sigh, "I'm a lost son of the House of Bourbon, but since your friends drowned everyone who knows my true identity and left me without a penny or a voucher to support my claim. I'm likely to stay lost for a good while yet."

"Cheeky bastard," Trevor chortled. "That's what saved ye, ye know. Ye made Black Sam laugh with yer tall tales of noblemen and palaces and he decided to spare ye. As fer who ye are—well, if ye thought there might be someone ye could make yer way to, I 'spect ye'd do it without me."

"You've been decent to me, Trevor," the lad said. "Thank you for not killing me."

Trevor stared at him again and sighed. "Like me own son might have been. Clever hands and stubborn as a sinner with a prayer. Right good company, too.

"Now, I ain't sayin' I'm a clever man. But I know a few things and I'm giving the gift of them to you, lad. Ye can take 'em or spit on 'em fer all I care after ye hear 'em, but hear 'em ye will. So here it be. It don't matter who ye were before ye washed up on them rocks I found ye hid in. Whoever ye were in France died on that shore."

The boy nodded. If he felt any animosity toward the men—including Trevor—who had been responsible for the death of his once-illustrious future—as well as his companions—he kept it well hidden.

"Don't be a fool, lad. World has too many of 'em as is. Be smart. Ye can spend yer days cryin' fer what ye want or ye take what ye can get. Ye have a bonny tongue in yer head and a winning way when ye've a mind. Make good use of those things what no sea can drown nor smuggler steal. Keep them skills I taught ye fresh. Ye—"

The sound of a horse whinnying stopped Trevor midsentence. He crouched down behind the hedge, his hand hard on the boy's shoulder. "That's the abbot's carriage. Go on. Get out into the road and wave him down."

"But—"

"Fer the love of God, lad," Trevor said in exasperation. "I done one good thing in me life when I took ye off that shore. Now, let me do two. Who knows, maybe it'll be enough to let me slip through the gates come Judgment Day."

The boy grinned broadly. "Oh, I rather I doubt it," then, without a backward glance, he scrambled into the dirt road and hailed the approaching carriage.

Culholland Square, Mayfair
July 18, 1806

"Don't be absurd!" Dand declared, standing over Charlotte as she sat calmly embroidering violets on a new pillow sham.

Her butler had shown him in to the little walled garden. True to her supposition, Dand had returned this morning with a note for Toussaint. True to her expectation, he had not been happy about what she had then told him about their change of plans.

But she had not expected his reaction to be so strong nor to so alter his demeanor. Indeed, she hardly recognized in this stranger the cocksure and imperturbable rogue she'd thought she'd known. His normal ironically amused expression had turned into a forbidding one and his stance was wide-legged and combative.

"I am not being absurd," she replied evenly. "Stop acting like some overprotective *big brother.*"

"Oh, I can assure you," he said in a low velvety voice that was all the more unnerving for its softness, "my emotions right now are far from brotherly."

She swallowed, refusing to be intimidated. "If you would remind yourself that we have a goal to accomplish, this would be a great deal easier on all of us."

"No," he said roughly. "There is no way this could be easy. There is no way this is going to be anything but ridiculous. A harebrained scheme bred of one feverish mind and one romantic imagination. I leave it to you to claim whichever role you deem best suits you and leave the other to Mrs. Mulgrew."

"You cannot really accuse me of being a romantic?" Charlotte asked in quelling tones.

"I wouldn't have said so yesterday, but your present intentions leave little room for any other interpretation. You have decided to be a heroine."

"Not I," Charlotte said tightly. "Fate."

"Fate or Mrs. Mulgrew?" Dand asked suspiciously. "Where *is* the accident-prone Mrs. Mulgrew, by the way?"

She shook her head in bemusement. "It is a source of continuing amazement to me that you were raised amongst a Benedictine order of monks, an order known for their hospitality and sympathetic treatment of the ill and injured."

"I slept through the lessons on charity. Now. Again. Where is she?"

"If you must know, she is upstairs in bed." She braced herself. One . . . two . . .

"Dear God!" He closed his eyes, struggling to marshal the expletive she could almost see forming on his lips. Though why he should bother now, when he'd already treated her to an impressive inventory of profanity, she could not think.

"Tell me, Lottie," he said through barely moving

lips, "did the notion of living as a social outcast just one day seem so appealing you could not conceive of any other lifestyle? Or was the decay of your reasoning a slower process?"

She carefully placed the embroidery hoop beside her. "You don't have to be insulting."

"Yes. I do. Especially when faced with such wrong-headedness, errant self-destructiveness!" he shouted.

"Stop bellowing. The servants will hear. Ginny is here because the accident caused her leg to be fractured in several places," she explained, waiting for him to show some sign of remorse for his lack of sympathy. There was none. She tried again.

"She may well never walk properly again. If she survives at all, that is." Not a flicker of compassion. "She is in *extreme* discomfort. The doctor has dosed her with something to alleviate the pain, but she is unable to care for herself. *That* is why she is here."

"*That* is why one has servants."

"No," she stated succinctly. "That is why one has friends. And I do count Ginny as a friend. As well as an associate. As should you."

"I neither know nor do I trust Mrs. Mulgrew. She and I work for different masters. It is a rare person who can serve two." He paused for a telling second. "Which means, I suppose, I must compliment you on your talents in this area."

She smiled sweetly. "You can't shame me into doing what you want, Dand. Or giving up what I want."

"Damn it!"

"Now, then," she went on calmly, "I suggest we discuss our current situation and how we can salvage the original plan to reacquire that letter."

"My God," he muttered to himself, a study in frustration as he raked his hair back with his hands. "She can't even say the word 'steal' and yet she is determined to—no." He shook his head, glaring at her. "No."

"Yes," she stated just as firmly. "And would you *please* have a seat?"

He glared harder. She leaned forward, her voice softening. "Please, Dand. Sit. We can discuss this rationally, calmly. I am not a fool. You have never treated me as one before."

"You have never acted like one before."

She sank back in her seat, her hand moving dismissively toward him. "Fine. Rant," she said in the tone of a governess exhausted by her charge's temper tantrum. "When you are done, we will discuss this."

He stared at her, outmaneuvered by her patronization. "Suit yourself," he capitulated gracelessly and flung himself down in the wicker chair beside her. "Speak."

Oh, she hated him in this mood: imperious, superior, unapproachable. But she needed him. *They* needed him. Their plan hinged on acquiring his aid.

She edged forward off the chair, dropping lightly to her knees on the thick, lush grass before him. He looked down at her with a flicker of surprise. Resolutely, she covered his hands with hers and at once felt the restrained tension in them.

His fingerpads were callused and rough, but fine, gilt-tipped hairs lightly covered the backs of his wrists and fingers. The men of her acquaintance had naked hands, white as tallow and as soft. Not Dand Ross. His hands were strong, lean, and intensely masculine. Everything about him was virile and aggressively male. Male, she reminded herself. And in the art of making males do what she wanted them to do, she was an acknowledged expert.

"Dand," she said quietly, "you know better than I what is at stake."

His lip lifted in a sneer and he turned his hand over, grabbing her wrist and yanking her forward so that she fell against his lap. Startled, she looked up. His gaze burned down at her. "*Don't*. Do *not* try your lady wiles on me." His voice was tight with warning. "I'm not a gentleman. I won't react the way a gentleman would."

She pulled back, but rather than let her go, he hauled her to her feet, only releasing her when she was upright. She backed away uncertainly as if faced with a pet hound that had suddenly bared his teeth at her. Twice now he'd frightened her with unexpected reactions. She'd thought she knew him. She might be very, very wrong.

Abruptly, the anger left his gaze, leaving only frustration. "There is another way. There must be some other means of getting into the castle," he muttered.

And suddenly, the sting of tears started in her eyes, and she was angry. Angry at the situation, angry at the damn carriage, angry at Dand for having the effrontery to argue with her when she was willing to do this.

It wasn't what she would have chosen for herself. How dare he treat her as though she had given no more deliberation to this than she would to which gown to wear? My God, he acted as though she was going into this with reckless abandon, like she thought it was some sort of lark. She tugged her hands from his clasp and stood up, eyes flashing.

"What then?" she demanded.

"I haven't thought of it yet. But I will."

"Lovely," she clipped out. "But, for the nonce, until your formidable intellect has devised a better solution, what say we implement the one plan we *do* have? Which means that St. Lyon needs to invite *me* to his castle in Ginny's stead."

"Why should he do that?" He met her sharp tone. "I know. Perhaps you can take out an advert in the *Times* declaring that you are currently taking applications for the position of your protector and offer a special rate to St. Lyon?"

"Don't be vulgar."

"Loath though I am to offend your delicate sensibilities, may I point out that being a Cyprian *is* vulgar?" he ground out.

"This isn't solving anything. I am fully aware it will not be an easy pretense to pull off," she allowed, moving cautiously toward the point of this interview, "but we've devised a stratagem."

"I am beyond eager to hear it."

She ignored him. "Early tomorrow St. Lyon leaves for his castle, there to await his guests who, coming as they are from many different places, shall be arriving in trickles over the next month. St. Lyon will be bored, restless. A week or so hence Ginny shall write to him and offer him my company in her place."

"And you do not think St. Lyon will find it odd that you are suddenly being offered to him like a basket of apples?" he asked with heavy sarcasm. "Besides, aside from the obvious absurdity of anyone thinking you would suddenly embark on a career as a courtesan, I wouldn't mark St. Lyon as the sort of man who allows another to pick his mistresses for him.

"And even if he did, a man in St. Lyon's situation must ask himself why his would-be mistress would offer a substitute when by doing so she is robbing herself of a potentially wealthy protector."

Charlotte took a deep breath. He would not like the solutions she had to his objections. "The problem of why Ginny would offer a substitute is not as great a difficulty as you would suspect," she said. "Apparently becoming a procuress is the next obvious step in the career path Ginny has chosen." Her attempt at drollery was lost on him. His agate colored eyes, once so warm, were now flat and cold as river stones.

She attempted a smile. "St. Lyon will accept me as a substitute because . . . because he has . . . shown some interest in me in the past."

She'd been wrong. He hadn't used up his vocabulary of descriptive expletives. At least she assumed they were expletives from the tone in which he delivered them. Abruptly he surged to his feet, startling her so much that she scrambled back.

He glared at her. It must be more difficult than she'd realized for him to allow her to rush into danger when he'd sworn to keep her safe. Her heart turned in her chest, but then she steeled herself against softening. Everyone made sacrifices. Everyone compromised. If the need was great enough.

"Dand, there *is* no one else," she said, taking a step toward him. "Our group of conspirators is very small and there are scant few women amongst us. Scant being two, Ginny and I.

"Even if there were another woman, one who St. Lyon found desirable, one who could be trusted, who knows the plans of the castle and understands what she is looking for, St. Lyon would never allow a stranger into his fortress at such a time. He will be suspicious of anyone he does not know—"

"Exactly!" Dand seized on her last sentence. "St. Lyon will be suspicious of *anything* untoward, anything out of the ordinary. And what could be more out of the ordinary than that you suddenly decide to accept him as a lover when you could have any man in the ton for your husband?"

She smiled wanly at this gross exaggeration.

"It will never work. Besides," he went on, turning

and walking away from her. "St. Lyon would never risk his position in society by ruining a peer's virginal sister-in-law."

She took a deep breath. "He won't be risking anything."

He stopped, his back to her. "Why is that?"

"Because by then I shall be a Fallen Woman."

"*What?*" He turned around.

"By the time St. Lyon gets Ginny's letter all society will be abuzz with the story of my fall from grace. He is a creature of the ton, Dand. His friends in London are bound to write often, keeping him apprised of all the latest *on dits*. Which is why I need your help."

She closed the small distance between them, her skirts brushing the yellow rosebush and sending a shower of petals swirling to the grass. She reached out hesitantly. He stared at her approaching hand as though it were unsheathed steel but did not move. Tentatively, she placed her palm on his chest. He was warm, so alive. So masculine. "I need you to be my seducer," she whispered.

He stared at her for a long moment, his shock apparent in the slight widening of his eyes, the manner in which his dark brows snapped together before he muttered, "You're mad. Are you sure it wasn't you and not Mrs. Mulgrew who got run over by that horse?"

She edged closer, lifting her face, willing him to meet her gaze. "Dand. There is no one else I can ask. You only have to *appear* to be my lover. Stay late at my house. Go to a few public functions. Look smitten.

"Just think," she gave him a puckish smile, "you will be the instrument of my downfall. Most men would find that a rather choice role."

Abruptly he stepped away, breaking contact with her. He would not be cajoled. "*Stop* trying to handle me. I am not one of your wet-nosed pups."

No. He was not. He was entirely unlike any man she knew. Had ever known. She'd been wrong to try to manipulate him. She had more respect for him than that. Her hands fell to her sides and her coquettish smile evaporated. "This plan will work."

"Oh, yes. It sounds entirely plausible. You jettison your reputation and your future because you are overcome with passion for some nameless tramp."

"No one in London knows who you are. I'll have it put out that I knew you in York, that we were childhood sweethearts or some such thing, but then you bought a commission. You have just sold it and returned and upon being reunited with you after all these years I threw caution to the wind and took you as my lover.

"Anyone who knows my reputation will believe that," she said dryly. "Then in a week or so, we will part company. I shall pretend to have come to my senses, too late to save my reputation, but not too late to realize that life as the wife of an impecunious ex-captain of the Light Guards is not to my liking. Again, this will surprise no one.

"I will then let it fall in a few well-placed ears that my good friend Ginny Mulgrew has helped me determine my options and convinced me that my best course lies in following her example and procuring a wealthy protector. St. Lyon."

"Wake me, please," he implored the sky above.

"Stop that!" This was not a plan she wanted. It was simply the only plan they had.

"I won't be party to such madness." He turned, but she would not let him go. She darted around in the front of him, her hand pushing hard against his chest, stopping him.

"Yes, you will," she said. "Because you know how many lives might . . . *can* be saved if I can find this letter. Just as you know how many lives might be destroyed if I don't."

"It will never work."

"It may not," she conceded. "But we have to try. *I* have to try. And if it fails . . . well, at least I will know it was not because I valued my reputation over the lives of hundreds, perhaps thousands of innocent people. Dand . . ." The sunlight shimmered in her eyes, making it hard to see his face, read his expression. "How could I live with myself if I didn't make an attempt to get that letter? How could you live with yourself if you didn't help me?"

"How can I live with myself if I do?" His voice was low, poisoned. He lifted his hand, his fingertips hovering inches above her cheek, tracing a line in the air as if he were caressing her.

"You will have to. Just as I will."

His hand fell to his side.

"Besides, I may not have to become St. Lyon's mistress," she offered hopefully. "He might take a dislike to me. Or he might discover that I am far too fastidious for his tastes. Or too mercenary. I am only going there as his *potential* mistress, Dand. It isn't a fait accompli." She prayed this last was true. It was to this faint hope she'd clung since she'd made her decision. "Help me."

"You don't have a bloody clue what you're asking of me, do you?" he muttered, his heart beating thickly beneath her palm.

"The oath? The Rose Hunters' sacred vow of seeing to the well-being of all the Nash women?" He must help her. She turned around, trying to find the words to convince him and spied a single yellow bloom drooping forlornly from the end of a tremulous branch. She bent over, plucked it, and rose, holding the flower out to him.

"You swore you would do whatever was asked of you. I'm asking you to help me."

"I did not vow to aid in your destruction," he said fiercely, refusing to even glance at the bloom nestled in the palm of her hand.

"I know. But I would trade your vow to protect me for your aid in saving the lives of a multitude."

A shudder coursed through him and his jaw clenched. She picked up his fisted hand and pried open the long fingers, carefully placing the rose within it and then, just as carefully folding his fingers back over it. "I think it a rather good trade," she jested weakly, praying he would accept. "Please, Dand."

With a curse, he crushed the blameless bloom he held and jerked his hand free from hers. He was always pulling away from her, she realized, and she was always finding some excuse to touch him. "How?"

Quickly, while he was willing to listen, she outlined the plan she and Ginny had devised during the long hours before dawn.

"You'll have to take a false name. Too many people recognize the name Dand Ross from Helena's encounter last year. Then, come and go as if my home were your own. Act like a lover." She shrugged, smiling a little. "Pretend to ruin me."

He did not return her smile. "Make no mistake, Lottie. Whatever I do, the world will never know it as pretense," he said with chill sobriety. "You will have to live with the results of this masquerade for the rest of your life.

"In the end, even should you succeed and the war is won and Napoleon defeated, there will never be a public disclosure explaining your motives and your noble goal. There will be no celebration, no gala hero's reception for you. The papers will not write a retraction of the condemnation that will seep into every society column. No one will say 'thank you.'

"Whispers will continue to follow you. Shoulders will continue to be turned. Ladies will cross the street to avoid meeting you and young Turks will cross the street *to* meet you. In the eyes of the world, you *will* be ruined."

"I understand." She had some inkling of what the future may well hold. She'd seen something of the life Ginny led. "Will you help me?"

He stared into her resolute face for a long, silent moment before finally grinding out, "Damn it all to hell! All right."

"Thank you." Her body relaxed.

"All right," he repeated again. "But only until I can devise another plan. Is that understood?"

"Entirely," she breathed. "Believe me, there is nothing I desire more than for you to come up with an alternative."

He looked her over with thinning lips. "St. Lyon leaves for Scotland tomorrow?"

"Yes."

"Then you must be compromised soon, yes?"

"As soon as possible," she agreed.

"Where are you going tomorrow evening?" he asked and then, with something near bitterness, "You are, I assume, going somewhere?"

"Yes," she said. "I had planned on attending a subscription ball at the Argyll Rooms."

"Excellent. A public venue." He frowned thoughtfully. "I daresay I should be able to scrape up something."

She tilted her head inquiringly. "For what?"

His eyes glittered with a hard light she was quite unused to seeing in their warm, brown depths. "Why, for the opening performance of *The Ruin of Miss Charlotte Nash.*"

He strode toward the south part of the city. Tension set the broad shoulders and lined the lean visage, making those who would approach fall back before his approach. He ignored the increasing poverty of the area through which he traveled, moving heedless of any danger amongst the rookeries that lurked like poor relations at the backside of the fashionable districts.

Chance and misfortune had him ensnared, trapped him by circumstance and wretched necessity. This wasn't part of his plan. This merry-mouthed slip of a girl whose dancing eyes and saucy tongue hid a resolve as tenacious as his own, a dauntless heart that equaled his in cool and unflinching determination. She was not supposed to play an active role in these next few weeks. Damn, but she was making things difficult for him.

It was his own bloody fault, of course. He should have realized that she would be a problem from the first moment he'd set eyes on her. She wasn't beautiful like the blond Helena. Nor handsome like dark Kate, but she was more fascinating, with her devil-may-care eyes, vibrant cinnamon curls, vivacious manner, and audacious mouth—a creature of sensuality as well as intelligence.

He should have stayed away from her, but he'd grown soft over the last year or so. Too many near misses with the Dark Summoner, he suspected, made him want to savor life before he entertained death. He closed his eyes, shaking his head, nearly laughing because it was so absurd. So divinely ridiculous.

He wouldn't let it matter. Nothing before had ever forced him to deviate from his agenda, not Father Tarkin, not his "brothers," not this Nash girl. Charlotte. *Nothing*.

Fate had set him on this road years before, *decades* before. The same road that had led him to St. Bride's, the same road that had led him to those fateful associations with the others, the same road upon whose length he had honed his skills with sword and fist and mind. And as he, better than anyone knew, you cannot go back again.

So he would go forward, even if it killed him. He would use the tools presented to him to complete the task he had set before himself years earlier. He might admire Charlotte Elizabeth Nash. He damn well wanted her. He could even—*no.*

He wasn't going to let emotions stand in his way. He would find a way to make this work.

He always had.

7

∞∞∞

The Argyll Ballrooms, London
July 19, 1806

CHARLOTTE PAUSED on the threshold of the Argyll Rooms fighting uncharacteristic nervousness. Inside, candlelight ricocheted off a hundred mirrors, throwing light like confetti, sparkling on diamante-spangled bodices and winking in diamond stickpins, glossing ropes of pearls and gleaming in pomaded hair and shining satin waistcoats, here picking out the tip of a tongue surreptitiously wetting lips, there catching the glimmer of white teeth.

She knew these people. She'd met many on her arrival in this great city five years before when she'd been unofficially launched into society by her surrogate family, the Weltons. Like the Weltons, most of those in attendance tonight were kindly if slightly ramshackle types, no more likely to judge their fellow than themselves. There was Lady Partridge, concern over which sweetmeat to eat puckering her heart-shaped mouth, the perpetually befogged Mrs. Hal Verson, and sweet, handsome Lord Beau Winkel.

But there were less friendly faces, too: Hecuba Montaigne White, once the toast of London and known as "Hundreds Hecuba" for her myriad liaisons, newly in the throes of a "miraculous religious conversion" and looking for others to follow her example; Countess Juliette Kettle, her onetime schoolmate; George Ravenscroft, whom she'd once sent packing for being fresh; and Lord Bylespot, who had given her a far deeper understanding of "fresh" and to whom she'd given an even greater understanding of "no."

Those were the people she'd always been wary of alienating, those who with a word could annihilate a woman's social status and condemn her to life on the other side of the line separating Society from the rest of the civilized world. They roosted like carrion eaters about the edges of the ballroom, waiting for some social misstep or careless word to fall from unsuspecting lips that they might swoop in and pick the transgressor's bones clean.

Well, tonight they would have a feast. If all went according to plan, by midnight she would be well on her way to being a Fallen Woman. The news should reach Comte St. Lyon within a week and while she had understood and accepted the consequences of this evening on her own behalf, she could not help imagining her sisters' anguish and shock when they heard of this night's events.

Yet, what other choice was there?

Once more she glanced toward Juliette Kettle, her gaze roving the crowd, scavenging for some misdemeanor to snack on. *Bon appétit*, Juliette, she thought and, taking a deep breath, stepped through the door into the ballroom, her head high, a coquettish smile on her lips.

Within minutes she was surrounded by admirers, both men she knew and others tugging at the sleeves of their companions to beg for an introduction. She enjoined the game as the expert she knew herself to be, smiling prettily, casting sidelong glances like lures amongst the stream of men and reeling them in with a toss of her head, a winsome trill of laughter, a playful tap of her folded fan. Within a very short time the ivory ribs of that same fan were scribbled over with the names of men to whom she had promised a dance.

She flirted with an abandon she had never before employed, ignoring female friends, knowing that tomorrow they would thank their stars she had passed them by. Already little whispers, like an ill wind amongst dead leaves, rustled beneath the current of conversation and music.

As the rustle of gossip grew, so did her tension. *When would he come?* Where *was* he? And finally, would *anyone* believe she found him attractive?

Oh, she had no doubt that if a face alone could tempt a woman to her downfall, Dand's would more than suffice. But she was no ordinary woman; she was the construction known as Charlotte Nash. *That* creature was known not only for her fast conversation and daring escapades, but also for her unerring sense of style and her discrimination in regard to the men with whom she danced or allowed to take her in to dine. No one would credit she was attracted to a man in an ill-fitting or dodgy waistcoat or, heaven forbid it, one sporting a *beard*.

"I believe this is my dance, Miss Nash?" A young lieutenant who had been introduced to her at an art exhibition last week appeared at her side.

She glanced down at her fan. Ah, yes. Albright, Matthew. "So, it is!"

Gaily, she took his arm and let him lead her into the line of dancers. He handled her gingerly, reverently, his gloved hand barely touching hers. "You are charming. Splendid!"

"Thank you," she answered automatically. "You are too kind."

Charming. His admiration, so candid and clean, produced an unanticipated frisson of distress. After this evening, would ever another man find her simply "charming"? Or would the appellations hitherto attached to her name be ones no man would tolerate being associated with his daughter or sister, let alone his wife?

"No. I am not kind. I speak the truth. I have never known anyone like you. You are so exciting, so fascinating, so—"

"Provoking," a male voice purred from behind her. "You little baggage."

She spun around. A tall, broad-shouldered man stood before her in exquisitely tailored evening dress: dark blue coat, snowy white waistcoat, and an equally snowy white cravat arranged in the most wonderful folds and pinned by a single topaz. Brilliant amber-colored eyes glittered from a sun-dark visage. Glossy brown hair lay in carefully clipped precision about his neck. A hard, square jaw scraped as smooth as marble exposed a pale crescent-shaped scar on one lean cheek. His wide, well-shaped mouth wore a mocking smile.

Dand? *Dand!* And looking amazingly like a gentleman. Almost like an aristocrat, except for the sun-darkened skin and that wicked scar.

Relief washed through her.

"You promised me this dance," he said to her.

"I say, sir, you are mistaken." Albright, unhappy at this turn of affairs, stepped forward and pointed at the fan in Charlotte's hand. "You need only look to see that my name is writ upon her fan. Not yours."

"Is it?" Dand asked, his gaze moving reluctantly from Charlotte to the young lieutenant. With a smile at Albright that just missed being friendly, he casually wrested the fan from Charlotte's clasp and just as casually crumpled it into a ball. He dropped the mangled mess to the floor.

"Alas, Miss Nash has lost her fan. But I am certain she will now recall that I, and not you, have claim of this dance. And the next." His gaze returned to Charlotte. "And the next. And the one after that. You do remember, don't you, Lottie?"

The pet name fell on her ears like a caress, warm and intimate. Her heart pattered in her chest. One side of his mouth climbed in a rakish smile that stated he knew the effect he'd had on her heartbeat. It was an act, she reminded herself. This is what he did. This is who he was. This is how he survived. By acting a role. As did she.

She had never given him proper credit for being such a good actor. She must remember to commend him.

"She wouldn't dance so many times with one partner!" declared Albright, ruddy faced. "You are insulting a lady, sir. And as a gentleman, I demand satisfaction."

Dand raised his brow at Albright, his expression

lazily interested. A tomcat, Charlotte thought breathlessly, playing with a mouse.

"Before you do something your father will regret—assuming, that is, that your father holds you in affection—why don't we ask the lady if she feels insulted?" He cocked a dark brow at her. "Well, Miss Nash?"

There would be no going back from her answer. She hesitated, on the cusp of irrevocably altering her state in society.

"Lottie?" Dand's voice was gentle, as though he understood exactly what she sacrificed here. It gave her strength. She smiled apologetically at Albright.

"I fear I had forgotten that this gentlemen has claim of this dance. And those following it."

The lieutenant stared at her, a dark stain mounting his downy cheeks, insulted and aggrieved. He had set her on a pedestal and now she had plummeted from it, and he was angry at her for betraying his image of her. She understood.

"I'm sorry," she said.

"I see," he said stiffly. He bowed toward Dand. "I wish you joy of her."

His choice of words caused the blood to drain from Charlotte's face. Albright turned, but Dand's hand shot out, nabbing his arm and spinning him back around.

"I don't think I heard you properly, son," Dand said, his voice light but his eyes narrowed dangerously. "For your sake, I hope not."

The young officer scowled, self-preservation warring with pride. Impulsively, Charlotte laid her hand on

Dand's arm. This was ridiculous. How could he harm this young man for accepting as truth what they had purposely led him to believe? She didn't want the boy hurt. She had enough to trouble her conscience. "Sir . . ."

He ignored her. "I repeat, *what* did you say?"

Self-preservation won. The boy's eyes fell away. "I wish you joy of the evening," he muttered and swung around again, stomping away through the crush of dancers. Charlotte watched him go, imagining the interested questions that would greet him and his condemning replies.

"I'm sorry."

She looked back. Dand was regarding her gravely.

"Not on my account, I hope," she said lightly. "We have achieved what we set out to achieve. My reputation is in shreds."

"Not yet." With unexpected gentleness, he secured her hand and with a wry, challenging tilt of his head, pulled her into his arms and began to dance.

He was unexpectedly adept, a natural grace to his movements as he guided her down the long line of dancers that made up the country set. He didn't speak, though when the steps of the lively dance brought them together, he watched her face with an intentness that any spectator could not fail to note. Like a real lover, hungry and yearning . . .

Of course, he was just doing what his role demanded, but one could almost imagine that honest emotion begat that torrid gaze . . . She gave herself a little mental shake. She didn't know what was wrong with her, entertaining such maggoty notions. It must be all the people, the kaleidoscope of colors, the over-loud music, the scent of heavy perfume rising thick as the mist on the Thames from heated shoulders and flushed throats and glistening bosoms. 'Twas small wonder she felt light-headed.

"You look all at sixes and sevens, my dear," Dand said as he led her down the line.

"With some reason," she answered, finding the reason a second later. "You ruined my fan. A very nice fan, too."

"I'll buy you another," he answered, catching hold of her hands and swinging her lightly to the outside of the figure. "Besides, you must allow it provided a nice spectacle for our audience. Very manly of me, laying territorial claims and all that."

"By breaking a perfectly good fan?" she asked doubtfully, as he set his hand lightly on her waist.

He laughed, bringing several heads swinging about. "Indeed, yes. The boy appreciated at once that if I risked breaking your fan I must be *very* sure of your affection. But I don't expect you to understand. Women always miss the subtlety of such byplay."

His nonsense returned her humor to her. "You are right," she answered. "Far too subtle. I would have better understood your territorial claim had you thrown me over your shoulder and carried me from the room."

He didn't answer. Possessively, he pulled her closer than was proper, reminding her forcibly of how large he was, how strong. His hooded lids slipped over his eyes and his mouth curved in a slow enigmatic smile that made her feel flushed and unnerved. Drat him for being so adept at this role. For making her feel *jeune fille* and skittish and uncertain when she was not any of these things.

The dance ended, but he held on to her hand, drawing startled, offended looks from those nearby. And when the orchestra began another tune, he did not wait or ask permission, but pulled her back into his arms. This time the orchestra played a cotillion, an intricate French import that society still considered a little fast. Within minutes she realized that he was more than an adept dancer, he was superb.

"Where did you learn to dance?" she asked. "I cannot imagine there were many opportunities at the abbey."

"Not at all. Brother Fidelis is marvelously light on his feet."

Charlotte laughed at the image of the rotund monk she'd met at St. Bride's executing a minuet. Dand's gaze fell hungrily on her mouth. Very nice touch. He looked exactly like a lover would. "No, tell me truly."

"One picks up things here and there," he replied, wresting his gaze from her mouth. In a few seconds his expression became shuttered, his thoughts clearly traveling elsewhere as the steps necessitated they take other partners for a short while.

"What is wrong?" she asked, when the dance returned them to their original set.

"Nothing," he said. "It is just—"

He abruptly stopped dancing, clasping her firmly around the wrist and pulling her out of the line. Wordlessly, he headed for the pair of French doors standing open at the end of the ballroom. Other dancers hastened out of their way, their heads swinging to follow their departure.

Dand led her through the open doors onto the bright, moonlit flagstones beyond. Two older gentlemen stood in intermittent conversation at the far end of the small walled garden, their voices drifting toward them in the clear night air. They were discussing the latest embargos.

"What are you doing?" she asked in a low voice as he stopped, his hand still warm and heavy against the small of her back.

"You suggested it yourself." He sounded a bit tested, as though he was trying to convince himself of something.

"Pray, illuminate me," she said. "What are you talking about?"

"Why spend the night dancing as I attempt to scowl down every one of your poor swains when we could far more easily and effectively secure the desired result?"

"I don't understand." She tilted her head back, searching his shadowed face for some explanation. For a few intense seconds, he stared down at her, but then he suddenly dropped back a step. His hand fell away.

"God." He raked his hair back, ruining his carefully groomed locks and turning himself once more into the disheveled, slightly disreputable blackguard she knew so well. "I can't believe anyone could think you could succeed in this. This is madness."

His irritation struck a spark. "It may be madness, but madness is, I believe, our only option," she retorted. "Now did you drag me out here to bolster my confidence or do you have something more to say?"

He regarded her with a tightening jaw. "No."

"Then what are we doing out here? It is not dark, you know. People can see us quite clearly. And several are looking."

"That is precisely why we are out here," he said grimly. "That and this."

And without warning he caught her up in his arms, crushing her ruthlessly to him, his mouth descending on hers in a bruising kiss.

No one had ever kissed her like this before. He owned not a whit of the finesse or refined skills with which most of her more sophisticated suitors kissed her. He was a brute. No cajoling caress, no sweet entreating, no wanting supplication. Instead, he mounted a sensual assault, catching her off guard with the devastating confidence with which he took her mouth.

He pulled her closer, ignoring all proprieties; hip to hip, thigh to thigh, belly to belly, his mouth intent, hot, and open over hers. His hand slipped up the back of her neck, spearing through the careful arrangement of curls and ribbons, laying havoc to all her careful artifice, spilling the short curls from their ribbons and pulling her head back, making her mouth more accessible to him. God help her, she did not resist.

She hadn't been prepared for this. Nothing in her education as the ton's most darling and daring coquette had prepared her for this. Her arms reacted without volition, lashing about his neck as her mouth opened ecstatically beneath his, her heart leaping in her chest as he strained against her, over her, deepening the demanding kiss.

She sighed against his open mouth and his warm, damp tongue immediately swept deep inside her own. Thoughts tore loose from her mind, shredded on the talons of sharpening desire. Her eyelids drifted shut and her hands clutched with increasing weakness on the broad shoulders bent over her.

The world swirled, desire fast thickening into need. Her legs buckled then, and he caught her, pulling her up, sliding her body along his hard, tensile form, his mouth torn from hers. Thoughts clamored to be heard above the sensual seas she drowned in. Faintly, she heard the heated spurts of her own breathing, felt the galloping rhythm of her heartbeat. He made a sound, masculine and low in his throat, bending his head close again, his eyes luminous and heated in the twilight, ready to begin the sensual assault anew.

She wasn't. She couldn't. It was too much and she was not ready. She pushed against him, her arms stiff. He released her at once.

Uncertainly, she looked up into his face. His expres-

sion was shuttered, but his chest rose and fell deeply beneath her flat palm and she read in the thick beat of his
heart a different reaction. One not quite so detached.

"You're supposed to be carried away by passion, not
look as though you were attempting to avert a rape, my
dear," he murmured in a low, caustic voice. He looked
tellingly at the hand pushing ineffectively against him.

A wave of heat surged up her throat and she snatched
her hand back.

"Better," he whispered, bending his head and licking
a path down the long line of her neck. Fine tremors
raked her body. "Don't worry. I won't kiss you again. A
few more moments acquiescent in my arms and I think
we can close the curtain on our performance."

Performance. His mouth stopped at the base of her
throat, his tongue lapping gently against the pulse
beating frantically at the hollow there. The tremors
turned into quakes.

"Easy, Lottie," he whispered in his dark, passion-
rimmed voice. "It isn't so much after all."

But it was, she knew. It was.

"My dear, you have done it!" Ginny exclaimed as Charlotte entered the bedroom. At Ginny's request, the
maid had brought word the moment Charlotte returned. The courtesan pushed herself up on the pile of
pillows behind her, her face animated for the first time
since her accident. "You are ruined! 'Tis marvelous.
And so quickly and efficiently brought about. Truly
marvelous!"

"How did you know?" Charlotte asked.

"Lord Skelton was here an hour earlier." Ginny chuckled. "He must have left the Argyll Rooms on a dead run to carry the news to me. Such devotion! 'Struth, I may owe him a kiss!"

"What did he say?"

"He wanted to be the first to inform me of the most wicked, most delicious *on dit* to have passed through society in a decade. That *on dit* being that my young angel of mercy has been compromised!"

She leaned forward, her beautiful slanted eyes gleaming. "Did Ross really ravish you right there in the garden?"

" 'Ravish' is decidedly overstating the situation," Charlotte replied, trying desperately for an urbane tone as she willed her legs not to give way beneath her. She sank down on the foot of Ginny's bed.

That was it then. She was ruined. Except her weak limbs had far less to do with the knowledge of her downfall than with the man who'd caused it. She had been kissed many times, by many men. None of them had ever affected her like this, leaving her breathless and mossy-headed, her pulse skittering like hail on the windowpane, her stomach hollow and her joints liquid. She must be coming down with something.

She forced herself to meet Ginny's overbright, overly knowing gaze. "How gratifying for Lord Skelton. I assume you verified his 'worst fears'?"

"Only after much hand-wringing and having secured innumerable vows of secrecy from him which he duly gave and which means that by now"—she glanced at the clock, which showed one o'clock in the morning—"Everyone, including the Lord Mayor's second gardener, has heard about it."

She patted the cushion beside her. "Come sit down and tell me all."

Reluctantly, Charlotte pulled the soft chamois gloves through her fingers, unwilling to stay longer, wanting to be alone, to think. But also, she feared, to remember. "There's not much to tell and I am exhausted beyond belief."

"That, my girl, is definitely a lie," Ginny said, her arched brow tipping upward. "Come. Tell me."

"He chased off young Lieutenant Albright, commandeered me for two dances, dragged me out into the garden, making care that we should be appropriately framed by the doorway, and kissed me."

"And you?"

"I kissed him back. Enthusiastically."

"Good girl. This needn't all be unpleasant work. And then?"

"Then he hustled me across the entire crowded ballroom, threw his greatcoat over my shoulders, and lifted me bodily into a hired chaise, which he then entered himself, calling out loudly for the driver to take us to my home."

"Perfect!" Ginny approved. "And then?"

"Then, two blocks later, he rapped on the carriage ceiling, bade the driver to stop, got out, and wished me a good evening."

"Oh?" Ginny sounded disappointed. "That's all?"

"That's all except that he mentioned his intention of taking me for a drive in Hyde Park tomorrow during the fashionable hour in order, so he said, to cement my infamy in the minds of any who hadn't quite tumbled to the obvious yet." She didn't tell Ginny how Dand had looked during that short carriage ride, his face obscured by the shadows as he sat slouched in the far corner of the dark carriage interior, silently vibrating with palpable tension.

"Excellent. I can see he has thought the entire process out to an admirable degree. I begin to think I approve of Mr. Ross. Tell me, how did he look?"

"Look?"

"Yes," Ginny said. "Was he as uncouth looking as"— she cleared her throat—"as you have always said he was? Or had he adopted a bit of town bronze?"

"Oh, he was most bronzed. And while his actions were decidedly uncivilized, he looked perfectly well maintained."

"Even more excellent!" Ginny cried. "The news shall travel so fast it may even overtake St. Lyon on his way north. But to make sure, I must pen him a letter tonight and let drop that I am very much afraid that my headstrong young friend Miss Nash has gotten herself in a most difficult situation."

The man pushed through a crowd gathered around a boy hawking newspapers by calling out bits about Napoleon's latest exploits, barely aware of the jostling crowd. He had to concentrate. The board had changed within the last twenty-four hours. Luckily he was adept at accommodating change.

But . . . God help him, he hadn't realized that he would be so affected. That he would find it so difficult. Even now emotion threatened to overwhelm him.

He swallowed hard, feeling the grip of his old mania upon him and looking quickly, spied a wretched little yard, black at this late hour and empty. Head low, he stumbled into the inky darkness—his breathing ragged, his throat constricting—and dug in his great-coat for the penknife he carried there. Then, with a sense of shame and relief, he peeled off his glove and splayed his fingers wide. No more visible scars. Not anymore. Once this was over and he took his rightful place in Society, he would no longer need to . . . perform this abomination upon himself.

He pulled the thin, lethally pointed blade out of its malachite case and stared down at the silvery tip lying so sweetly, perfectly honed in the palm of his hand and tried to find the wherewithal to resist its glittering al-lure.

His head fell back against the brick wall, all the emotions within him fighting each other, pride and despair and anger and . . . yes, *love*, twisting and twisting and twisting his heart, his very soul!

With a soft cry of self-disgust he plunged the tip of the blade into the tender flesh between his index and middle finger, hissing at the piquant, the brain-clearing pain. Lovely pain, like acid eating away the guilt and doubt and horror, leaving nothing behind but exquisite . . . pure . . . pain.

Slowly, calm returned. His humor returned. His sense of perspective was restored. His mental acuity, always keen, seemed sharper. He felt the world a more lucid place. Carelessly, he slipped the blade back in its sheath, his thoughts already having turned to the night's events and the various problems they posed. He thought about the girl and he thought about the whore and he thought about the man known as Dand Ross.

Of course. Of course. Why hadn't he seen it before? It would all work out splendidly. Even better than he'd originally planned. It was almost, indeed, as if God meant it to be.

Perhaps he did.

8

Culholland Square, Mayfair
July 20, 1806

"Miss Nash! Miss Nash!" Lizette, Charlotte's maid, did not even bother to knock on the door. She simply burst into the room, eyes wild and mouth agape.

Charlotte struggled upright in her bed, alarmed. "What is it, Lizzie? What ever is wrong?"

The maid flew to the bedroom windows, snapping open the heavy brocade draperies and filling the room with bright sunlight. She spun around, her hand to her chest.

"There is a man downstairs in the front hall! He showed up in a fancy carriage ten minutes ago demanding that the butler let him in. But when he told him that you were not receiving, he came in anyway! He's down there now and told me to tell you to *hurry*!"

"He told you what?" She blinked to clear her eyes. She hadn't slept much the night before. Humiliation kept her wide awake until the wee hours of the morning. And not mortification based on the fact that she'd ruined herself in Society, but humiliation founded solely on her inability to hide her physical reaction to Dand Ross's unexpected amatory expertise.

"Who is he?"

"I don't rightly know, ma'am! A nabob, I'm thinking. He's brown as an East Indian but dressed like a toff, tricked out neat as a pin, and speaks a treat. Only not a gentleman. 'Cause what gentleman would act in such a manner? None!"

Dand was here? Charlotte thought in confusion. He'd said he was coming for her in the afternoon.

She glanced at the ormolu clock sitting on the fireplace mantle. It showed nine o'clock. An ungodly hour to be calling unless something momentous had happened.

She scooted out of the big, soft bed, thrusting her arms through the diaphanous jonquil silk dressing gown that Lizette, bless her anticipation, held out for her, then hastened out the door.

"Shall I send for the footmen?" Lizette asked, scurrying after her.

"No!" Charlotte called over her shoulder as she hurried down the stairway on bare feet. Something must be amiss. Otherwise why would Dand insist that she hurry? She dashed down the steps and along the landing above the hallway—

"Someone go tell the wench not to waste time primping." Dand's voice, bored, imperious, swollen with masculine indulgence and flavored with a subtly foreign accent, brought her up short. "A fellow wants to see what manner of ride he's buying under all the rigging, eh?"

That brought her up short. She looked down over the balustrade into the front hall. Dand stood in the center of the parquetry floor, leaning lightly on a silver-headed walking cane as he looked about with casual interest.

He didn't look overset. He looked quite comfortable. This was all wrong. She was a seasoned veteran of a hundred flirtations. She was a mistress of titillation. She was the incomparable, the unattainable, the provocative Miss Charlotte Nash. He was a . . . a . . . rat catcher!

But a handsome rat catcher. Deuced handsome. There was no denying it. His navy blue coat stretched across his broad shoulders without a single crease marring its perfectly tailored surface. Buff-colored trousers hugged muscular thighs while black Hessian boots that gleamed with a mirrorlike finish encased his calves.

"What are you doing here?" she called down from where she hung over the rail.

He looked up. His eyes alit with pleasure. "Ah, Lottie! And looking most fetching. I declare myself inordinately pleased. Indeed, I am!"

The sardonic gleam in his eyes made her uncomfortably aware of her dishabille, her short curls tousled from the bed and her face probably pallid after her fitful night's sleep. For a pert coquette and heartbreaker of the highest order, she was at a decided disadvantage. "What are you doing here?"

"Well, since I have taken over the payments, I decided I'd rather avail myself of your winsome company than add the expense of a hotel room to our arrangement." He'd definitely adopted a slight French accent.

"Our *arrangement*?" she echoed. "What the devil do you—"

"Mind the children, Lottie," Dand replied in a low voice, his gaze traveling over her shoulder.

Turning her head, Charlotte followed his gaze. Behind her, Lizette hovered in wide-eyed, titillated amazement.

"And . . ." she heard Dand murmur.

She looked down into the hallway. The footmen, Brian and Curtis, stood below, flanking the front door, their expressions similarly bewildered and astonished, ready to act at her first word. She leaned further out and saw the cook, her head poking out from behind the green baize door leading to the kitchen, nodding as if all her worst suspicions had finally been confirmed. Even the tweenie, her dustbin still clutched in her hand, had crept out of the front parlor to see what was going on.

Oh, dear. Oh, my.

A soft sound escaped her lips.

Dand clucked his tongue sympathetically. "Ah, my poor darling. I didn't mean for your maid to wake you. But the silly chit would not listen to reason." He tilted his head as though a thought had just occurred to him.

"Why, Lottie," he said, in a gently scolding tone, "you didn't inform your staff about me, did you? Naughty girl. No wonder everyone looks so green about the gills. Tell them to be about their business, why don't you?"

He looked around at the servants, his gaze very level, a warning in its dark depths. "Or shall I?"

"No. No." She hesitated. What tone did one take when one was all but announcing to one's staff that one had become a Loose Woman? He'd caught her entirely unprepared. It wasn't fair. She would have to improvise. Something casual and haughty and polished . . . "All of you, go away. Go to work. Just *go!*"

Dand smiled apologetically at her startled staff. "She desires a moment alone with me."

"Go!"

Her staff went, scurrying away with the alacrity of beetles under a bright light. A few seconds later the only evidence left of their onetime presence was the gentle swinging of the green baize door.

Dand grinned up at her. "That went well, I thought."

"Did you?" she asked coolly. "I bow to your doubt-less greater expertise. Now, again and for the last time, what the blazes do you think you are doing?"

"Tch, tch, such language. You know, Lottie, the most exclusive birds of paradise are known for being genteel in public and otherwise in private. I am much afraid, my dear, that you have it quite reversed."

"Dand—"

"Just trying to offer what advice I can," he said lightly, balancing his cane on his shoulder and starting up the stairs toward her. His movements caused her to back up. He couldn't possibly mean to come into her bedroom! There were some lines even she had never crossed. This was one of them and she reacted instinctively.

"Stop. Stop right there!" she commanded. He halted halfway up the stairs, regarding her in puzzlement. "You. You wait in the . . . in the dining room!"

"You know for such a tough little piece of work, you are amazingly provincial—"

She didn't linger to hear more but spun on her heels and marched down the landing and to her room. Quickly, she shed her nightdress and dashed water in her face before scrubbing at her teeth with a bristle brush and hurriedly donning a prim and extremely modest gown of plum-striped ivory batiste.

What was the meaning of this? Clearly, he came

here intent upon lending verisimilitude to their act. But *exactly* how far did he intend to go to solidify her shattered reputation? She wasn't sure of anything other than that it might be farther than she would like to go. *Was afraid to go*, her imagination whispered as the memory of their passionate embrace stole upon her, leaving flutters in her stomach. Enough. Sweeping her short mass of ringlets back from her face with a black velvet ribbon and having regained her aplomb, she went to face Dand.

"Where is he?" she asked the footman.

"Monsieur Rousse is in the dining room, ma'am."

Monsieur Rousse? He really had gone mad.

She found Dand settled comfortably at the head of her dining table, spooning a bit of egg onto a piece of toast. Upon her entrance, he waved his silver fork over his plate. "Your cook makes the most amazing eggs, Lottie! Claims scallions does the magic."

She ignored this, moving gracefully toward the table. She was worldly too, and it was time that he remembered it. "At the risk of redundancy," she said tightly, "what are you doing here? And when did you adopt a French—"

He cut her short with a brief, telling gesture and reached for the coffee pot, pouring out a thin stream of black, steaming liquid into his cup. "The French custom of drinking coffee in the morning?" he interjected smoothly, casting a warning glance at the doorway and thus alerting her to his suspicions that they were being eavesdropped upon. "Because I am French."

He smiled sunnily, making Charlotte wonder for a second if he was, indeed, partially French. He certainly spoke the language as a native. And not the rough patois of the commoner, but the silky buff of the aristocrat. But no. That was nonsense. He was a Scottish orphan, playacting.

"You ought to eat," Dand went on comfortably. "Curtis!"

At once the door leading to the kitchen swung open and her youngest footman entered. Dand was right; the servants were listening in. "Sir?"

"Miss Nash requires sustenance. Egg?" His brows rose inquiringly, and his gaze traveled over her slender body in insolent assessment. "Two eggs. And toast."

This was too much. She was not a broodmare he won in a bet and come to see if she was worth keeping. She was *supposed* to be his mistress. Mistresses were treated by their aristocratic lovers with a great deal of charm and adulation. Or so she'd heard.

Seeing the storm gathering in her eyes, he went on. "*And* honey. Clearly she requires sweetening."

Curtis, well-trained footman that he was, managed to excise his budding smile, but he could not hide the unabashed twinkle in his eye. "At once, sir."

"And no more hovering about the door," Dand added as an afterthought.

"I meant no disrespect, sir. Only hoping to provide as prompt service as possible, sir."

"I am certain. But I shall take it greatly amiss should

I ever discover anyone listening at doors. You might mention this to the staff."

"Of course, sir."

As soon as Curtis left, Dand settled back in the chair. *"Now* we can speak."

"Oh, thank you," Charlotte said sarcastically, pulling out the chair at the opposite end of the long table.

"My dear," he said as she prepared to be seated, "I have done what I could to make us private, but if you insist on sitting twelve feet away, I daresay it will not take an ear to the door to hear our conversation."

He was right. But he needn't look so smug. She had, she could see, a great deal of catching up to do before she regained an equal footing with Dand. She had given away far too much during last night's kiss. But that was last night and this was this morning, and she had remembered who she was and who she must be if she was to succeed in her masquerade.

With a gracious nod, she walked toward him. He rose and pulled out a chair for her, which she accepted.

"Now," she said, motioning him to be seated, "please. Speak. First, why the French surname?"

"While I liked your notion of introducing me as your onetime neighbor's lurking lad, I decided it would be too easy to disprove," he answered. "Your father, my dear, was once a man of some means and your childhood home was in one of York's most exclusive neighborhoods. I am sure there are others in London today who once shared that same neighborhood and who could say with frightening surety just who inhabited which house on each and every street."

"And your pretending to be French helps us how?"

"A French émigré," he corrected. "Andre Rousse who, with his family, once shared a glorious season in Bristol after escaping the dire goings-on in my poor papa's native country. There happy chance led to our fateful meeting." He paused in his recitation and fixed her with a brightly inquiring look. "Do you ever think our meeting was fateful, Lottie? I do. At any rate, our families met.

"I am sure you appreciate the brilliance of this fable, do you not? Should anyone find it odd you never mentioned me, well, one doesn't mention one's French affiliations these days unless absolutely necessary, does one?"

She had to concede his plan had merit. "I suppose that makes sense."

" 'Struth, you shall turn my head with such flattery."

She almost smiled. She placed her chin in her hand and tipped her head. "But why are you *here*, Dand?"

He popped another forkful of egg in his mouth. "I should think what I am doing here is self-evident. I have come to lend verisimilitude to my role of your protector."

"That can be done quite well without your presence in my home at this ungodly hour."

"I disagree. Oh, yes, we set a number of tongues wagging last night. But as far as the ton is concerned, you are simply compromised. Indeed, most of them are probably waiting for an announcement in the *Times*. Especially old St. Lyon, knowing who you are and, more importantly, who your brother-in-law is.

"I mean, really Lottie, what is more likely, your imminent engagement or your imminent entrance into the world of the demirep?

"Pleasant though the task would doubtless prove, I could spend *weeks* kissing you on every street corner and at every public venue in London before it finally became apparent that there was *not* going to be any announcement in the *Times* and that you were *not* simply compromised but well and truly ruined. And then, and only then, would the cautious St. Lyon be drawn into your trap—by then your ruin coming far too late to be any use to me." He smiled blandly. "I meant 'us.'

"No. St. Lyon must be convinced, as you so properly pointed out last night, as swiftly and emphatically as possible."

He took a sip of coffee. "And what more emphatic means of erasing any doubt as to your state than for me to take up residence here? Besides, no rumors are so swift or clarion as those spread by one's own staff."

He meant to live here? She stared, straightened slowly, her mouth forming an "O" of shock. Until this moment she hadn't realized he meant to take the charade so far. Yes, a few early breakfasts, some late evening visits, unchaperoned certainly but . . . *live here*?

"But . . . but . . ." she sputtered. "I don't . . . I mean, I thought if there was some chance that afterward we might . . . that if some doubt could be left as to my, er," she fumbled around for a delicate way of saying what needed to be said, "my . . . *state.*"

"Oh. You mean you'd hoped you might find some room to wiggle out of being labeled a courtesan?" he supplied sympathetically.

What had happened to the angry, nearly impossible to convince Scotsman? The man who'd sworn and raged at her for even suggesting that she assume the guise of a lady bird? He'd disappeared. Someone had exchanged him for this doppelganger with his fine clothes and elegant insouciance.

"I am afraid we must all learn to live with the choices we make, Lottie," he said with that same loathsome kindliness.

"Why have you changed? Why are you suddenly so amenable to this plan?"

"I went back to my rooms. I thought about it." His gaze became shuttered. "I thought about what I would be willing to do to achieve what I set out to achieve and accepted that I would do anything necessary, accept any risk or sacrifice, to see my way to the end of this enterprise."

She regarded him dolefully, wishing she hadn't been quite so persuasive. At the same time she realized how absurd she was being.

"Come, Lottie," Dand said, his gaze softening, becoming once more familiar, amused, ironic. "Yours isn't the only sacrifice, you know. As soon as your brother-in-law Munro hears of this, he shall chase me to the ends of the earth in order to poke me full of holes with his sword. And your other brother-in-law, the re-doubtable Kit?" He laughed. "He won't rest until he's had the pleasure of breaking every bone in my body."

"Not once they are made to understand the whys and wherefores of the situation," she said. "Besides, they won't even know it is you."

His gaze sharpened, but his voice remained light, "One can but hope—"

A sound in the passage brought his head swinging round at the same moment he grabbed her wrist, yanking her from her seat and into his lap.

"Ah!"

He had just time to clamp her firmly around the waist and whisper, "Play along!" when the door swung open and Curtis appeared bearing a domed silver plate. The footman stopped, eyes rounding as he saw where his mistress sat.

"Put it here, Curtis," Dand said casually, his hand traveling a slow possessive path up Charlotte's back while Curtis went brick red. She forced herself to take a breath. She could do this. She could.

"There's a lad. Now, sweetling, are you certain I must feed you?"

It was a good thing she'd turned her head, for her footman would have been amazed to read on her lips a word she suspected she oughtn't even know.

Dand's brown eyes lit with unfeigned delight. "Ah! She's come over shy! How . . . delectable. Leave the plate and begone, Curtis. I have a little wooing to do!"

She heard the plate clatter on the table top and a few

seconds later the door swing shut. With an angry sound, she pushed at Dand's chest, trying to scramble out of his lap, but his arms held her firmly in place.

"Just what did you hope to accomplish with that little byplay, besides embarrassing . . . poor Curtis?" she demanded indignantly, mostly indignantly because held thus she could not help but be aware of his musculature, the easy strength of his arms, the scent of him. Even through linen and wool, the heat of his warm body, masculine and utterly unique in her experience, was hopelessly distracting.

"The servants, Lottie. They are our most important audience in this ruse. They must carry stories and to do so, they must have stories to carry. I suggest we feed their store of tales as often as possible."

She answered his nonsense by attempting to rise. He would not let her. Instead, he laughed. "Who would have thought it? The rakish, rompish, *disastrous* Miss Nash, a prude?"

His lips drew close to her ear and whispered, "Don't go all soft and girlish on me now, little heartbreaker!"

The little warm puff of his breath summoned the ghost of last night's yearning. "I am not soft. I am not a prude. I am a hoyden, a coquette, a romp, and a flirt," she announced, her pride stung, her body humming with awareness. "I most decidedly am not a prude."

"Then stop acting like one. Stay." His arm shifted, pulling her back, forcing her to relax against him. The ghost took on substance, became a renewed craving.

"Stay," he repeated in an odd voice. "Familiarize yourself with me, my body, my touch."

It made sense. Perfect sense. As long as he didn't know of the desire whispering like black rain through her veins, drugging and euphoric. Too potent to be ignored. Too real to be denied. Her arms, still looped in a rigid circle around his neck, began to loosen. Her body began to melt into him as though her very flesh softened in response to his hardness, needing to absorb, accommodate, cleave—

No! Even if she and Dand hadn't been . . . comrades? Co-conspirators? Everything in her life's experience clamored for her to be on her best defense. And that meant being absolutely honest with herself.

To Dand this was all a great game, and London and Paris and everything in between was a chessboard on which everyone was a piece to be moved, manipulated, used for his ultimate goal. But she wasn't Dand. She couldn't see everything quite so objectively. The question now was, was she good enough an actress to keep hidden her reaction to him?

She would have to be.

"All right."

"It's not a death sentence, you know," he whispered. Did his lips brush the outer curve of her ear? She shivered. "Besides, as you so cleverly pointed out to me, it is only for a short time."

She turned, looking up and into his eyes. They were as clear as amber glass, honeyed and warm, wrinkled at the corners with the wry amusement she knew so well.

"In a few weeks, two at the most," he continued, "we shall enact an equally public and equally passionate disaffection wherein I dismiss you from my life and you, scorned and ruined beyond hope, slink back to our sordid love nest to make what repairs you can of your pitiful life."

He'd deliberately made it sound like the most overwrought and overheated sort of novel. She could not help but laugh, relieved when he dispensed with the tomfoolery with her ear. Or so she told herself.

"How odious!"

He nodded serenely. "Tragic."

"That will never do."

He wasn't attending. He'd burrowed his nose into the curls at the nape of her neck. She froze. He inhaled deeply, extravagantly.

No. No. She was not a simpering little milquetoast miss, swooning over a man's attentions.

"What is that fragrance?"

"Jasmine." She had to remember to breathe.

"Pretty." His breath sent warm eddies trickling down her spine and set her nerve endings quivering. She bit hard on the tender lining of her lower lip. She wasn't going to be distracted that easily—and where had he learned this trick, anyway?

"I have a better idea of how to end our faux association," she said, pulling away from him and trying to sound unaffected. "*I* shall dismiss *you*. And in the throes of an agony and despair too great to contemplate, you shall then hurl yourself off London Bridge." She hesitated, sensing that this might be going a bit far. "Or take the next boat to Egypt."

"No, no," he corrected gently, refusing to release her and nuzzling her neck anew. Little tremors of pleasure sifted over her skin. "You see, if *I* dismiss *you*, then your subsequent decision to take another lover soon afterward can be logically attributed to the fact that in your misery you are seeking to recapture with another those moments of sublime pleasure and happiness you found with me."

"I beg to point out how disastrous such an impression would be to my mission," she returned politely, turning abruptly in his embrace and thus bringing her lips dangerously close to his. His gaze dropped to her mouth, feasted on it.

"Why is that?" His lips parted a fraction. His head angled as if he was about to—

"Because," she squeaked. She tried again. "Because no man—especially St. Lyon—would willingly measure himself against a previous lover, especially one he has been led to believe is superior."

Dand frowned, but his gaze remained fixed on her mouth. Was there a bit of something on it? Delicately, she made an exploratory swipe of her tongue along her lower lip. Dand's pupils blossomed with darkness. His chest, which had been rising and falling with such deliberate cadence beneath her, stilled.

"No," she said, trying to find her footing in the face of his riveted attention, even though she suspected it was feigned. "It will be far better if I give you the old

heave-ho, in which case St. Lyon will be bound to believe that my experience with you was so dismal that
upon its dissolution I at once set out to seek reassur-
ances that it need not always be so." She smiled sweetly,
leaning in and cupping his jaw in her palm. His beard
was like the finest sandpaper, but his skin was warm.
"N'est-ce pas?"

"We can decide on the particulars later." He looked
distracted. A little . . . befogged. He pulled back
abruptly and rose to his feet, lifting her as he did so and
setting her to his side as easily as if she were a child.
"For now, where would you like me to have my things
brought?"

"What? Oh." She felt a little light-headed. Too little
sleep, too many sensations. "You shall not have much
room," she said. "So don't go moving a lot of things in
here."

"I don't have a lot of *things*," he replied.

Of this she had no doubt, but his admission brought
to mind something that had been niggling at the back
of her mind since last night. "Where *did* you come by
these clothes and the ones you wore last night? And
how came you to look so well groomed in so short a
time?"

"Oh. That. Easy enough. I simply nipped over to
Munro's town house and borrowed a few things from
his wardrobe. We always were of a similar build." He
leaned back in the chair. "I'm glad to see what with the
good life he's been leading he hasn't run to fat."

"You broke into the marquis of Cottrell's home and

stole his clothing?" she asked, unable to keep the admiration from her expression.

He shrugged with elaborate modesty. "Well, I *am* a spy, Lottie."

"And," she motioned toward his perfectly clipped head of hair, his smoothly shaved jaw, the intricate folds of his cravat, "the rest?"

"The ladies on Barrow Street were most obliging."

A little white hot spurt of some unidentifiable but extremely unpleasant emotion rippled through her.

"You won't be needing their ministrations in the future."

One brow shot up inquiringly.

"Now that you are . . . otherwise engaged, it would never do to have you seen coming and going out of low brothels."

"They weren't low," he replied with a hint of a smile.

"I don't care!" She composed herself. "You mustn't be seen coming out of any brothel or house of pleasure. At all."

"I wouldn't be seen."

"You won't risk it," she said through grated teeth.

"Can you tie a cravat, then?"

She'd never had occasion to try, but she wasn't about to tell him this and risk having him shoring off to some doxy's eager hands. "Of course I can."

He tilted his head, studying her with notable skepticism. "And you learned this . . . ?"

She smiled secretively. Let him think what he would.

"I see," he said shortly then, with an offhand smile,

"I had best find out what the driver has done with Ram's clothing. I should hate to bring into question your much vaunted discrimination by appearing in Hyde Park this afternoon in anything less than sartorial."

"You're enjoying this, aren't you?" she asked.

"Why, yes," he answered. "I am rather."

9

St. Bride's Abbey
October 1792

"You stay with me awhile," *Brother Toussaint told the lad with the impertinent tongue. "The rest of you are dismissed."*

The other four boys, Ramsey, Douglas, John, and Christian, set down their wooden practice swords and with reluctant backward glances at Dand Ross, straggled out of the empty stables, clearly wondering what Dand had done now. But if the boy felt any unwillingness to be separated from his friends, he showed none.

He waited with practiced patience, scuffing his toe at an ant that crawled by. Something in that guileless countenance troubled Toussaint. Was it something in the way the lad moved? Nothing like the Munro boy's predatory grace, but a quality one noted only when he walked away, his spine straightening, his shoulders squaring with a sort of imperial authority. Where had the boy learned to walk like that, and, more interestingly, why did he go to pains to hide it?

Or maybe it was the watchfulness that hid behind the puckish glint of his eyes? Whatever it was, something about the boy reminded Toussaint of death and disdain, guillotines and bloodied ermine robes. But if his suspicions were correct that meant that one of the most exalted families in France had mislaid their scion in a Highland abbey. What were chances of that?

Then why did something in Toussaint insist Dand Ross was so much more than the Scottish orphan he and Father Tarkin claimed him to be? Were the rumors true? he wondered. Sometimes at night, in the throes of a nightmare, did Dand Ross cry out in French?

"They don't know you at all, do they? The rest of them?" he mused aloud, thoughtfully rubbing his hand over his head.

The boy blinked at him, perfectly guileless, which itself was a lie; the boy was slippery and filled with worldly knowledge. "Aye, Brother," the youngster replied glibly. "They know me right well, I'd say. Enough to call me the devil's own."

"And are you?"

"Nah," the lad said with a cheeky grin. "Father Tarkin wouldn't have no demon in his flock now, would he?"

"I don't suppose he would," the onetime captain in Louis X's Royalist guard answered, his deeply seamed face troubled. The opponents of the Royalists would go to great lengths to

wipe out any pretenders to the French throne. How much money could one get for the information that St. Bride's harbored a member of the royal family? A great deal.

The abbot had specifically asked Toussaint to watch this one, to do what he could to refine him because, Father Tarkin had told him, he thought Dand Ross had potential. But potential for what? Toussaint wondered.

He tilted his head, studying the innocent face. Nothing there but an entirely likeable young rapscallion. Except . . . the eyes, which held his gaze so winningly, held too much amusement, too much awareness for one so very young.

"How long have you been here, Andrew?"

"They call me Dand, sir."

"How long?"

The boy shrugged and pulled at his collar, looking about uncomfortably, just a boy hoping to find the answer that would release him from an adult's unwelcome questioning. "Don't know. Close to three years, I'd guess. Father Tarkin must have it in a book somewhere. Why?"

Toussaint smiled narrowly. A child did not question his elders. Especially his ecclesiastic elders. "Do you like the switch, Dand Ross?"

"No, sir." There was a grim little bite in his quick response. So ho! The boy disliked authority, did he? No surprise there. He was the most likely of the quartet to find trouble, to do what he'd been especially bid not to do.

"Then mind your tongue, boy."

"Aye."

"You have been here longer than any of the other boys I have been asked to train."

Dand pondered this a few seconds, though Toussaint had the notion he knew to the day when each boy had arrived and under what circumstances. "Except for Dougie Stewart. He was here afore me."

Toussaint already knew this, of course. He had made it his business to find out as much as he could about these five boys Tarkin wanted taught the martial arts. It seemed a very odd directive for an abbot to make.

Christian MacNeill and Ramsey Munro's histories were easy enough to trace. Douglas Stewart had arrived as the only survivor of the epidemic that had destroyed his family. John Glass had been sent from his uncle's home after his newly made widow decided that her obligations to house and feed her husband's relatives did not extend to nephews.

Only Dand Ross seemed to come from nowhere, having been found on the road by Father Tarkin. The boy had established himself as a rascal but an amiably aloof one. As was only natural, scuffles broke out in the dormitory that determined the dormitory's pecking order, but none ever involved Dand Ross. He stood separate, the well-liked outsider, a bit of trouble incarnate waiting to be indulged.

Until Christian MacNeill had arrived. And then, strangely, all the parts that had been needed to make a complete whole seemed to have found one another. Douglas and Dand and Ramsey and Kit, the four individuals had overnight coalesced into a brotherhood.

"Is that all, Brother Toussaint?" Dand asked, glancing longingly at the door.

"Almost, boy. Where did you come from? Where were you before you came to St. Bride's?"

The boy's face twisted in exasperation. "I dunno. Here and there. I don't remember any town names. But they were far away."

"Your parents?"

"Got none. I've been on me own forever," he said.

"I see. One last question. The other boys. You are all so close."

"Aye. They're like my own brothers," Dand said staunchly.

"Brothers can sometimes encourage each other to antics and feats of bravery that may be dangerous or foolhardy."

Dand waited.

"For their own good, if I were to ask you to report to me their conversations and deeds, would you?"

"No, Brother Toussaint, I would not." He spoke without hesitation.

"Not even if I threatened you with punishment?"

Dand smiled then. It was a most grown-up smile. Most disconcerting in that thin, impish face. "If you did that, I might agree."

"I see." So the boy's loyalty was not so deep after all. Perhaps his potential was not so formidable as Father Tarkin—

"But then," Dand added with an unmistakable glint in his soft, brown eyes, "I might only tell you what I thought you wanted to hear."

Toussaint regarded him with shock.

Then again, maybe Dand Ross would end up being even more formidable than any of them had imagined.

*   *   *

Hyde Park, London
Afternoon, July 19, 1806

The afternoon was bright, and the air warm and the park filled with members of the ton enjoying the fine weather. Charlotte felt particularly stylish in a gown of cream batiste sprigged with tiny green leaves. Stylish and self-assured.

"Good Lord, Lottie," Dand said with an air of patient frustration, "you are as stiff as a bishop's mitre. Whatever has gotten into you, my girl?"

All right. *Mostly* self-assured. But only because she was unused to being shown off as a piece of property and she hadn't mastered the knack of it yet.

Dand held the rented horses' reins in one hand, expertly guiding them at a leisurely pace along Hyde Park's most popular boulevard. His free arm lay across the back of the carriage seat, not quite touching her, but from any spectator's vantage declaring his uncontested ownership. No one had ever "owned" her before. Was it any wonder that she was a trifle tense?

And he had the gall to ask what was wrong.

Compounding her unease was the lowering notion that she amused him. Each time he looked at her she saw the humor lurking behind the pretended warmth, the flicker of some thought he would not share. Worse, no matter what her misgivings, it did not do one whit to dampen her reaction to him.

Each time he touched her, no matter how insignificant or unintentional, cascades of pleasure raced along the surface of her skin. Each time he spoke she was required to look at him and thus see the contours of his lips and recall how they had felt moving over her own.

"Nothing is wrong with me," she declared, knowing she sounded even stiffer than her posture. "Whatever would be the matter with me? I am fine."

"I am relieved to hear it. Perhaps my concern stems from the fact that you don't much present the aspect of a lady so smitten with desire that she is willing to throw away her good name to be with a man. And that is why we are here, is it not? To satisfy Mrs. Mulgrew's doubtless well-intentioned instructions to convince society you are run amuck with uncontrolled passion?

"It would help if you did not continue to shy away every time I look at you or touch you." His smile became complacent and predatory at the same time. "And I will be looking at you. And touching you. So, do be a good sport and try to fall in with the spirit of the thing."

"Unconvincing, am I?" She rose to the implicit challenge. *This* game she felt confident in playing. Even with Dand. "Might I suggest that you are unfamiliar with how a *lady* comports herself in such a situation? Doubtless your experience with barmaids and their ilk have led you to believe that unless a woman is wriggling in your lap she isn't displaying the proper enthusiasm for your manly charms."

His eyes sparkled appreciatively. "I confess, being but an insecure and conceited male, I do require rather obvious indications that my efforts are appreciated."

Bedamned, she thought admiringly, but he was a good sport! "Piffle."

"Truly, I am delighted there is an easy explanation for your rigidity for I had begun to suspect that . . ." he trailed off, shrugging.

"Suspect what?"

He shook his head, expertly turning the coach onto a smaller though still well-traveled lane. "It doesn't bear comment."

"No," she said, determined to find out what he'd suspected. "I insist."

"Well," he said reluctantly, "I had begun to suspect you were all aflutter because of our kiss last night and are sitting there anticipating another with all manner of maidenly trepidation."

Fire scalded her throat and clawed its way up into her cheeks. By heavens, she was blushing! She hadn't blushed in years.

She kept her gaze fixed on a sycamore tree farther down the lane. "Kiss?" she repeated in a determinedly bored voice. "What kiss? Was there a kiss?"

"Yes," he answered calmly. "In the Argyll gardens. I kissed you."

"Oh. *That* kiss. I'd nearly forgotten. I was so tired by the end of the evening, you understand."

"As I assumed." He nodded. "I see now how ridiculous I was being. But then, that only goes to prove how misleading a lack of expertise can be."

At that, her head snapped around. He gazed blithely ahead. *"Lack of expertise?"*

"Yes," he answered easily. "I thought since you are clearly so unfamiliar with kissing, it may have disconcerted you."

"I am not unfamiliar with kissing!" she declared. "I have been kissed many times. Many, many times. Men are *always* kissing me."

He frowned, his brows drawing together in an expression of unquestionable pity. "Oh, my dear," he said in a low voice, "I am so sorry."

"*What?*" she demanded. "*Why?*"

How *dare* he think her inexperienced? she thought, giving scant pause to the notion that most young women, particularly those who *were* experienced, would very likely rather be thought not to be. How *dare* he judge her wanting?

And how *dare* he drive without gloves? His hands, fingers twined in the leather reins, were calloused and rough enough. Sunlight glinted on the light smattering of gold-tinted hairs on their backs and wrists. Was the rest of him covered with that same glinting—? *No.* She would not wonder. She would only think that hands like that, masculine, strong, and hirsute, ought to be decently gloved. Clearly, he hadn't any idea of what a gentleman did, how a gentleman acted. *Or* how a gentleman kissed.

"Why do you say that?" she repeated.

He glanced around and, seeing no one in the immediate vicinity, pulled the carriage off the path beneath the shelter of a tall, tricolored beech. There, he wrapped the reins loosely around the brake and turned to her, a grave expression on his lean, handsome face. "I didn't mean to insult you."

"You didn't insult me," she snapped.

"It is only that, well, from your tepid response to my kiss, I concluded that you were rather green at it, you see."

Tepid? He called *that* tepid? She recalled all too clearly that she'd nearly crawled up his body in her effort to prolong the experience. What, she would like to know, would he call "eager"?

"But now . . ."

" 'Now' what?" she demanded.

"I am mortified that my gender has given such a poor account of itself, the evidence being that your previous experiences have been so obviously brief and forgettable."

"They weren't forgettable," she denied hotly. "They were very nice."

"Nice." He gave a delicate shudder—putting her much in mind of her brother-in-law Ram when he was most disgusted with something. " 'Nice' isn't the experience one is striving for when engaged in a passionate embrace. In fact, in the lexicon of passion 'nice' is a condemnation, an embarrassment. In short, a failure."

He was regarding her like a kindly tutor. A light breeze ruffled his freshly shorn hair. His razor had scraped the side of his throat. The raw mark made him look both vulnerable and strong, a contradiction that caused all sorts of odd, sensual bursts to go off in her stomach.

"There is *nothing* wrong with 'nice,' " she declared firmly. "One doesn't have to abandon oneself to one's baser nature, to feel agitated and harassed and fraught with unseemly sensations in order to declare a kiss a triumph."

He grinned wickedly. "Well, yes, actually one does."

She turned away. "It is no use discussing this with you. You clearly have a completely different perspective than I. One taken from a very low angle, I might add."

He laughed. "Oh, you'd be surprised at the little bonuses we at the lower end of the social spectrum enjoy. Alas, it's not a clean profession you've chosen to simulate, Lottie, me luv. And a kiss, a proper kiss, is a wet and heated, straining and urgent, affair."

"It sounds exhausting," she intoned coolly before adding the ultimate condemnation. "And messy."

"Aye, that it is." His burr, notably absent during his impersonation of her French lover, had returned, whiskey smooth and velvety soft. "A successful kiss clouds the thoughts of the clearest mind, makes fools of principles, wreaks havoc with intention, destroys all sense of self-preservation and substitutes yearning in its stead."

"I can't imagine why anyone would fancy such a thing," she said primly. He answered with a wolfish smile.

"That is what I was afraid of. You'll have to trust me in this, Lottie. There is something wondrous in being held captive by sensation, in losing control and giving rein to passion and instinct. In passionate surrender, one finds the ultimate freedom."

His words awoke a surge of longing and teased the adventuress in her soul into breathless anticipation.

He tapped her playfully on the nose, breaking the hypnotic spell his words had cast over her. "Now, despite your personal preferences in the matter, your current attitude will never do. You simply don't have the aura of a woman in the midst of a dangerous liaison. Luckily, we can remedy that."

"What do you mean?" she asked suspiciously.

"What your former partners failed to supply, I can provide."

"And what would that be?" she asked tartly.

"Experience. An experience that will decidedly not be 'nice.' "

Her breath caught in her throat.

The corner of his mouth rose in a lopsided smile and he lifted the hand lying along the back of the carriage, his thumb skating just above the corner of her mouth. "What about it, Lottie? Ready to get a little messy?" His voice was low, suggestive, and irresistible.

"No."

"What? Not even for God and country? Where is the tough, worldly temptress you claimed to be?" He was laughing at her. Charlotte hated being laughed at. No, that was not entirely correct. She was generally accounted a woman well able to laugh at her own follies. It was having Dand Ross laugh at her that she hated.

She hesitated. Perhaps she did need a patina of . . .

whatever it was Dand thought she so sorely lacked. Perhaps . . . for the right reason . . .

"All right."

She'd surprised him. It was clear he hadn't expected her to acquiesce.

A thought occurred to her. It was as tempting as Dand's wicked suggestion. *She might teach Dand a thing or two, too.*

"What would you like me to do?" she asked serenely.

"Relax." His thumb swept gently along her lower lip. "This isn't the Inquisition, you know. And just because we are aiming for something other than 'nice,' doesn't mean it will be unpleasant."

"Promises, promises," she murmured, eyeing him from beneath her lashes while remarking with satisfaction the tiniest start in his expression.

For a short while there she'd forgotten who she was: Charlotte Nash, Society's most coming chit, as fly to the time of day as a woman twice her age, a fluent temptress, a naughty wench, and an acknowledged heartbreaker. But now she'd remembered and she would make Dand remember, too, and if he hadn't ever known her reputation was warranted, well, he would soon enough.

He leaned forward and brushed his mouth gently over hers. It was a kiss quite unlike last night's fevered entanglement, so soft a bit of down might have imparted as much pressure, so brief, a whispered word lingered longer. Yet, for all its brevity and lightness, it instantly teased to life a thousand rich sensations along the curve of her lip.

Oh, my.

He drew back and looked down. He smiled.

"I don't believe I have ever kissed a sacrificial virgin before. Will you require oil afterward, do you think, for the pyre?"

She followed his gaze. Her hands were clamped tightly in her lap. This would never do. She had been about to reestablish her reputation as a hoyden and a romp, not dissolve into breathless anticipation after one little kiss. *He* was the one who was supposed to dissolve.

"I am being tepid again." She managed to say with nothing more than mild regret. "Please. Let me have another go. I swear I will muster some enthusiasm." She brightened at his look of amazement. "I am by all accounts a fine actress. But tell me," she furrowed her brow in consternation, "just how much appreciation ought one evince for a gentleman's efforts?"

His look of surprise disappeared. Whatever momentary advantage she'd gained, vanished. He sank back against the carriage seat, seeming to give her query all due consideration. She couldn't completely refrain from smiling.

Lud, but she adored playing with Dand Ross! There was no more worthy an opponent.

He scratched his chin with the edge of his thumb, squinting up at the sky. "As loath as I am to admit it," he finally said, "we males are deplorably easy to control. Our self-esteem is transported or destroyed with the tiniest gesture. A well-timed sigh will make a man your slave, while a frown can cast him into an inferno of self-doubt."

"I rather fancy making you my slave, Dand," she said in a husky undertone.

He bent his head modestly. "Well, I was speaking more or less in general. Not all men are so predisposed."

"You, for instance? Being a superior specimen?" she asked.

Again the modest smile. "Superior? Perhaps less susceptible. But, by all means, if you wish to test your skills, do have a go."

"I believe I shall."

With a confidence she was far from feeling, she leaned toward him and reached up, cupping his hard jaw in her palm. He hadn't shaved since the morning and the stubble of his beard against her soft palm was uniquely, distinctly, and potently masculine.

"I prefer a freshly shaven man," she lied, fanning her fingers lightly open over his scarred cheek, her fingertips playing delicately over the silky sandpaper. He turned his head, deliberately rubbing his cheek into her hand, like a great tawny cat. "Smooth and civilized. But I approve the scent of your cologne. Sandalwood is my favorite of those gentlemen use."

With a little thrill she realized that in spite of the amiable expression frozen on his face, his eyes had darkened and his breathing had grown a little *too* even.

He shook his head and she noted for the first time, more by touch than sight, the slight cleft in his chin. "A mistake, that. No man wants to be told his lady has been in close enough proximity to another to note and approve his scent. No matter how innocent the reason."

"Oh," she said naughtily, "there is nothing all that innocent about it. My brother-in-law is a most handsome man."

"Damn his pretty face anyway," Dand said, and in spite of the smooth smile, there was a little tightness around his eyes. "Do you think you might get on with the kissing and enslaving bit? I have a lunch appointment."

She laughed. He could say what he liked, she'd seen the little flare of hunger in his gaze. He was not, after all, unsusceptible.

"As you wish," she purred. She shifted closer, closer . . . Her eyes locked on his. No sound but the susurration of their mingled breath disturbed the air. Boldly, she swept her index finger against his lower lip. Again. This time running the tip along the sleek inner lining.

He caught it between his teeth and wet the sensitive tip with his tongue.

She shivered. No one had ever done such a thing to her! 'Twas beyond bold. Beyond imagining. Sensation shot straight from that touch to the core of her, flooding her body with electrifying awareness, filling her low in the loins with a liquid fire.

His eyes narrowed, the lids partially shielding his rich, brown eyes, shadowing them with a thicket of gold-tipped lash, making them darker and more luminous. Like a night predator's. An amused night predator.

He released her fingertip. "*Breathe*, Lottie, m'love! We haven't even gotten to the kiss, yet! Perhaps we should postpone this little contest for some later time, when you have had a chance to study the field and can bring a bit more artillery to the battlegrounds, as it were?"

More artillery? With an effort she swallowed the heated retort rising to her lips, but then his words sparked an association in her thoughts: battles, weaponry, her brother-in-law trying to teach her a few of the more rudimentary skills of swordsmanship one dreary afternoon.

She raised one brow. "On the contrary. I haven't even entered the field yet."

"Really?" His smile was onerously self-satisfied. He thought he'd chased away her confidence.

She leaned forward, spreading her hands flat against his chest and resting her weight against him. She tilted her face up to his and had the satisfaction of feeling his muscles contract beneath her palm.

"*Whatever you do, let it always be done . . . calmly,*" she silently recited Ram's first lesson. Dand's gaze rested watchfully on her.

"*And without Precipitation.*" Her lips touched his.

"*But still with all Vigor—*" She pressed her mouth more fully over his, tilting her head to make a seamless contact, canting forward so that her breasts, tingling with expectancy, cushioned themselves against him.

Her hands slid down the hard contours of his chest and slipped beneath his open jacket. The silk waistcoat could not mask the rigid corrugation of rib, the taut waist, the flat belly. He was so tight, she thought breathlessly, all of him as solid as stone.

He smelled of sandalwood soap and sun-heated starched linen, and he tasted of coffee and his lips were warm and firm. She deepened the kiss, wrapping her arms about his waist beneath his jacket, willing him to react, to demonstrate some evidence that the sensations rippling through her were shared.

He *was* reacting. She felt his body grow harder, his muscles straining, a thick new presence urgent against her hip.

"*Breathe,*" she murmured his own words against his mouth in a triumphant haze of sensuality. She uncoiled her arms from around him.

She thought he would surely end their kiss now, shown up, beaten at the game he'd challenged her to play. She should have known better. He obliged, pulling her back into his embrace, stealing her breath back from her, drawing it in as though trying to winnow her very spirit away.

She turned her head, but he caught her face between his hands. His tongue reached into her mouth, not quickly, like a thief, but slowly. His palm eased round the back of her head and his other arm dipped low and circled around her back.

She should never have accepted the challenge . . . She should . . .

Heat flushes rippled through her, tingling in the fingers clinging desperately to the edge of his jacket, mounting in her cheeks, swelling her breasts with a heaviness she didn't recognize.

Without warning, he dragged her onto his lap, his tongue languidly exploring the heated recesses of her mouth, taunting her to taste him, feel him, *engage* him. She surrendered with a rush of longing that made her head swim.

Her tongue found his, tangling wet and urgent in an open-mouthed kiss. Her hand pushed beneath his jacket and climbed his broad back until she found his muscle-capped shoulders. She clung to him, absorbing the heat of him. He shifted her unresistingly on his lap, tipping her until she lay back. He bent over her, her head cradled against his shoulder. She could feel that most alien part of him even more distinctly now, a demanding masculine reminder of where this sport led, how it must end.

"Dear God," she thought she heard him mutter. "Not much more, Lottie. I beg you."

She wanted to stay, feasting on the sensations provided by his body and mouth and arms. But his words reminded her of who she was—Charlotte Nash, a coquette of the most notable degree—and who he was—Dand Ross, not her suitor. Not her lover. They were playing a game and another game within that one and both of them knew it.

She broke away from the kiss, searching for the right tone, the perfect degree of casualness, the lilt of triumph, the sardonic flavor of mockery so he would not know how much she was affected.

" 'Beg,' Dand? Then I may enlist you on the spot as my newest slave?" she demanded, wanting all the while to throw herself back into his arms.

His expression showed no emotion. Without a word, he scooped her up and deposited her lightly back on the passenger side of the carriage before unwrapping the reins from around the brake post.

Only then did she notice the other carriages, moving with suspect leisure away from where they'd parked, their owners either red-faced and avoiding her glance or meeting it with a satyrlike interest.

What a spectacle they'd provided! What entertainment! How could she have failed to notice? Had Dand? Had his husky plea for mercy been more playacting? His body's reaction nothing more than that: a physical reaction to physical stimulus?

"I trust my performance passed muster this time?" she asked, somehow managing a light, cavalier tone.

That brought his head around. "Performance."

"Yes. Certainly our audience appreciated it." Her hand flashed out in an encompassing gesture toward the other carriages. He looked around, his expression unmoved and uninterested. Of course, he had known they were there. Of course.

"I thought I did exceedingly well," she went on in a hard, bright voice. "Indeed, I insist you apologize to my former tutors in the amorous arts."

"Well?" Why must she insist on hearing him confirm her suspicion and why did her voice choose that instant to quaver? She swallowed, tilted her chin proudly. "Should I count you amongst the enslaved? Why won't you answer me?"

Rather than speak, he reached out and gently tucked a curl of hair that had come loose behind her ear. "What are you doing?" she asked.

"I told you you'd get a little messy, Lottie," he said.

Curiously, he watched her flounce up the stairs to the front door, chin high and shoulders square. It didn't look as though she had any intention of checking her headlong march. Indeed, he doubted she was even aware she was about to collide face first with the door. He winced at the thought and was about to further offend her by shouting for her to mind where she was going when the front door was miraculously snatched open and, without the slightest check in her stride, she sailed through it and disappeared from view.

Curtis, who'd apparently been standing at attention at the front door and had seen his mistress's arrival—as well as her state—met Dand's gaze with one of resigned and universal male understanding before quietly closing the door.

Dand snapped the reins lightly across the rumps of the matched pair of gray geldings. He supposed he oughtn't have teased her so ruthlessly, but she was so deliciously ripe for teasing and he could never quite resist tweaking Miss Charlotte Nash's nose. Besides, she had been taking her role as Society's premier heartbreaker entirely too seriously. She went about town acting brazen and hoydenish with an earnestness that was actually quite touching. He smiled.

She was . . . amazing. An amazing amalgamation of pride and practicality, audacity and modesty, hard-hearted pragmatist and sentimental idealist, woman and girl. Her mouth was as sweet as nectar and her kiss as fiery as red peppercorns, her touch both electrifying and soothing, her sighs yielding and conquering.

His smile dissolved.

Now, just what the hell was he going to do about it?

10

∞∞∞

Partridge Hall, St. James Square
July 22, 1806

"OH, SHE IS SURELY RUINED BEYOND REPAIR!" The countess Juliette Kettle intoned as she popped a morsel of pickled pork belly into her mouth. Her dining companion on her right, Lord Beau Winkel, puckered his brow unhappily. He rather liked Charlotte Nash. She was damn good company as well as a fetching little article.

On his right the Baroness Welton leaned over her plate and glowered across him at the countess. "I shouldn't be the least surprised if there wasn't an announcement in the *Times* within the week."

"La!" The countess sucked a bit of grease off her fingertip. "A bit late in the game for that, isn't it?"

"Perhaps for some," Lady Welton said frostily, her plump cheeks pink, "But for the Marquis of Cottrell's sister, exceptions would doubtless be made by all but the most stiff-rumped prigs or those without any aspirations to move in the very best of circles."

As a returning salvo, it was a definite success. The countess was a well-known and rabid social climber, ambitious to join those in Society who had hitherto withheld their invitations from her. "There are some things which cannot be overcome because one is fortunate in one's associations," the countess returned stiffly.

"Love can overcome a great deal, Countess," Lady Welton said.

"Love?" This came from the dining companion sitting opposite Lady Welton, an immaculately turned out sprig of the ton by the name of Rawsett, a recent and late arrival to the season's festivities, having just finished a prolonged tour of the Americas.

Lady Welton regarded him coolly. "Certainly you have heard the word, young man?"

The little cockscomb bit back a superior smile. "On more occasions than I care to recall, my dear lady. I am just surprised that you would use the term to describe the goings-on between Miss Nash and her . . . admirer."

"Oh, I don't know," Mrs. Hal Verson, seated on Rawsett's left said wistfully, a faraway look in her pansy brown eyes. "Have you seen them together? I did. At the lending library Wednesday. The manner in which he looks at her . . . It takes one's breath away. And she, when he does not note it, watches him with a sort of bittersweet anguish."

"Does she?" Rawsett mused. "And here her reputation insists she does not own the sort of tender sentiment one associates with young ladies of her breeding."

"Her reputation is well earned." The words fell like stones into the conversation. It was Lord Bylespot, who'd once made suggestions to Charlotte Nash that she'd forcefully—and painfully—refuted and was now forced to witness her accept from another man. At twenty-eight his blond good looks were already much damaged by drink. He stared sullenly down at his plate and without another word, tossed back the entire contents of his wineglass. "And whatever notoriety she earns with this latest escapade will be just as well deserved."

The other diners traded uncomfortable glances. Lord Bylespot had a nasty tongue and a grudging nature. More importantly, on occasion, he had been known to gain the prince's ear. If he decided that Charlotte Nash was beyond the pale . . . Well, she had best gather those sympathetic to her if she hoped to weather the current straits into which she'd flung herself.

Culholland Square, Mayfair
July 24, 1806

"And, lest you think this is the end of it, I give you fair warning that your queen is about to follow your cleric to his untimely end," Charlotte crowed. She had nestled herself into the corner of the settee she shared with Dand, her legs stretched out and her feet on his lap. She folded forward at the waist and with a jaunty flick of her hand, tipped over Dand's white bishop.

From the other end of the settee, Dand frowned down at the chessboard laid out on the small table between them, his long fingers carelessly kneading Charlotte's tender left foot.

"For a chit who pleaded with me to rub her feet because they hurt from all her cavorting about on the dance floor the previous evening, you are not very gracious in your triumph," he remarked, studying the board.

In reply she crept her right foot up the hard plane of Dand's belly, trying to dig her toes into his stomach. It was like trying to dig them into flagstone.

"Stop that," he said distractedly, swatting away her foot.

She started to reply, but he pressed the heel of his hand into the arch of her foot, massaging deeply, and all she could manage was a purr. Meeting his original challenge that she learn to accept his touch without startling or blushing had proven an easy task to accomplish, she mused in a haze of enjoyment. Perhaps, too easy?

It had been eight days since Ginny's accident and five since Dand had taken up residence in the back bedroom. With each passing day she found herself seeking out those light touches and soft caresses he employed with such devastating effect. Caresses, she reminded herself, that he performed for public entertainment. She mustn't forget that they were an act and not real.

If only she could say the same of her own reaction. But she couldn't. She knew full well the disastrous manner in which her heart accelerated in anticipation of his lingering glance, the gentle stroke of his finger on the inside of her wrist, or the heart-stopping instances when he brushed the curls back from her brow as if it was the most natural thing in the world.

"You think me undone," he said, his gaze narrowing on the board. "You think you have unmanned me."

"Unwomaned you, actually," she corrected.

His gaze flashed up to hers for an instance and then, with a grin she could not help but answer, he returned to his contemplation of the board. And *that* was another problem; perhaps a greater one. The more time she spent in his company, the more time she wanted with him.

Even when they weren't in public and he wasn't watching her with that loverlike intensity—lover-*like*, she must keep reminding herself—he still excited her, challenged her, provoked and amused her. She looked forward to these moments when they were alone, out of sight of their audience, closeted together. Sometimes when he looked at her then, she saw something more in his considering gaze than irony or amusement. Something he went to pains to hide. But he couldn't. Not entirely. She'd seen the same look in too many men's eyes not to know what it was. Desire.

No man's ardor had ever frightened her before. But Dand Ross's unvoiced and unacknowledged desire did. And not in an entirely unpleasant way. It was electrifying. If Charlotte had learned one thing in her short life, it was to enjoy the moment, because the next might hold something far from pleasant. A father might die or a mother, a sibling might send one to live amongst strangers, and one's future might depend on one's ability to please strangers . . .

She embraced that doctrine now, creeping her foot lower down on his stomach. At once she felt the muscle contract beneath the arch of her foot. A muscle shivered above his upper lip, but other than that he gave no sign that he felt anything. Tentatively, she rubbed her heel against the rough wool of his trousers, low on his belly.

His gaze shot up to meet hers, a warning in their dark depth. Her breath stopped. "Watch out, Charlotte. Even a dog on a chain will choke itself to get at the bait if it's tempting enough."

"Well, I daresay it's a good thing he's been chained,

then," she said, little alarms going off in her mind, alarms that she chose to ignore. "In order to prevent any such attacks."

"Sometimes chains break," he said in a low voice, his gaze holding hers.

"It's luck we're just playacting, isn't it?" she asked and waited breathlessly for his answer.

He didn't answer.

"Isn't it?" she insisted.

In answer he only smiled and reached down, removing her foot from his lap and casually repositioning a rook on the chessboard.

He was teasing her. Well, she could do *that*, too. Leaning back in her chair, she raised her arms overhead, stretching extravagantly. "Give up, Dand," she purred.

"Never," he answered, his eyes trained on the field of battle. "You see, you have underestimated the lengths I might go to in order to protect my lady."

He picked up his knight and pondered a few seconds before dangling it above a black square. If he took that move, his knight would be aligned in such a manner that she could not capture his queen, as had been her intent. But the move also opened his last remaining bishop to annihilation by her pawn and placed his king in jeopardy.

"A bold move."

"But perhaps necessary." His lazy gaze rose, trapping hers. His voice had softened to no more than a murmur. "I must ask myself what am I willing to do to see her secure and how many men I am willing to lose in the process. And finally, ultimately, how will my choice effect the outcome of the game?"

He rolled the knight between his fingers, tilting his head and regarding her searchingly. "Tell me, Lottie. What do you think? Should I abandon my darling girl, or should I play the smart game and let her be sacrificed?"

Something in his voice made her shiver, something in his regard grew dark and alien.

"I don't know either," he whispered and at that moment the sound of footsteps in the hallway outside broke the odd moment.

At once, he reached down the length of the settee, grabbed her by the waist and pulled her into his lap. Just as quickly, she put her arms around his neck, mussing his hair as if they had spent hours in a prolonged and impassioned embrace. The door swung open and Ginny tottered in on her crutches, Curtis hovering behind her.

"Why, Mrs. Mulgrew, what a surprise," Dand said, making no move to release Charlotte.

"A chair, if you please!" Ginny barked, with a sharp gesture that sent the footman scurrying in, pulling out a chair, and waiting while she teetered over and sank down as gracefully as her splinted limb would allow.

Ginny waited until Curtis had retired from the room, before turning her gaze upon them and seeing them still so entangled, rolled her eyes in open exasperation.

"I could hear you two mumbling about queens and

bishops halfway down the hall, so *do* dispense with the torrid embrace. I am unimpressed," she said coolly. *"And* unconvinced."

Charlotte squirmed. Dand held her tight.

"I think you could let me go now," she said.

"Good heavens, Charlotte, did you not just hear Mrs. Mulgrew? We are unconvincing in the role of lovers. We must strive to remedy that, for practice, so they say, makes perfect," he said, negligently caressing the downy skin on the nape of her neck. "Besides, I like you on my lap. In my arms."

She wished he hadn't said that. Because she believed him. And she really wished he wouldn't do that. It was hard to think when she wanted to lie back in his broad arms and let him do all the wicked things she had hitherto only sampled. Things she imagined late at night when all the formidable barricades she erected to keep reality and playacting separated fell apart for those few minutes before sleep overtook her only to be carefully reconstructed upon waking the next day.

"Apparently you require more than 'practice,' " Ginny said coldly.

Her words caught Charlotte by surprise.

As far as she could tell, their plan was going well. Why, already the invitations usually overflowing the hall table had been cut in half, a clear sign that her notoriety was well on its way to being established. Soon no one would want her at their home. Such success! she thought wryly. Who could ask for more?

Ginny should be beaming, not snapping at them.

Dand idly rubbed between her shoulder blades, his cheek burnishing the curls at the crown of her head. A seemingly tender gesture that had a not-so-innocent effect on her, stoking the warm sensations their earlier wordplay had aroused into a hotter fire. Any moment now and she would be purring. Her head would fall into the lee of his neck and shoulder and she would will him to look down at her as she lifted—

"Mrs. Mulgrew seems overset," Dand whispered into her hair and then, to Ginny, "Should you be up?"

"I am leaving this afternoon," Ginny intoned brusquely.

"Surely that is not wise," Charlotte said, rousing herself from the cloud of pleasure-spiked lassitude into which she'd sunk. "You are still weak and you might yet be taken with a fever. I cannot afford—"

"You cannot *afford* to have me here, acting like some sort of farcical doyenne," Ginny cut in coldly. "People may take it into their idiotic pates that I am playing the part of chaperone. Yes, yes, I know it is absurd, but the public *is* absurd especially when it comes to slandering those whom it wants to extol, or"—she paused tellingly—"the sister-in-law of those whom they fear. And you, my dear Charlotte, are both. And you are not helping the matters what with the way you treat Ross."

"I don't understand."

"Clearly," Ginny said, sniffing. "What are all these blushes and sidelong glances I hear tell so much about from the servants in this house and my acquaintances outside? You are supposed to be a woman in *lust*, not love!"

"And you," she glared at Dand, "had best stop acting the lovesick swain and start acting like an overly possessive lover. My God, man! You said you must return to France and soon. In that time you must cement in Society's imagination your uncontested right to Charlotte's time and then effect a very public, very dramatic break with her."

Dand regarded her. "You have been pulling the strings in this little puppetry show thus far, Mrs. Mulgrew and we have obliged. *I* have obliged. I should be careful, however, that you don't get caught in your own devices."

Though his expression was amiable enough, a threat lurked in his level gaze that gave Charlotte pause. Once more, Charlotte found herself wondering just what Dand Ross was capable of doing in pursuit of his goal. She suspected it was more than she realized. Worse, rather than cause her to withdraw, his untapped capacity for danger only made him more fascinating. Ginny visibly tensed. "I know what I am about. I thought you did, too." She turned back to Charlotte. "Or did you forget?"

"Of course not," Charlotte replied, though in truth the days had passed so quickly she had let slip to the back of her mind that the climax of this little play was to take place soon. And then . . .

"I will strive not to disappoint," she heard Dand say.

"You may return to your home with an easy mind. *If* you still own such a capacity."

It sounded like a dismissal, an imperial one, and amazingly, Ginny seemed to heed it as such. What was going on here? Currents were sweeping along beneath the surface of this meeting, currents Charlotte had not suspected or been warned about, currents that suggested they had a prior knowledge of one another.

"Good," Ginny answered, rising to her feet. "As for my capacity for ease, I am certain it matches your own." Her gaze skewered him.

Charlotte, still in Dand's embrace, felt his arms tighten fractionally as Ginny stumped from the room.

"Dand? Dangerous to me?" Charlotte asked with a smile. "I think you are mistaken, Ginny. Perhaps to an enemy he might be, but not to me. I am his . . . comrade."

Charlotte had followed the courtesan up to her bedchamber and asked her point-blank about the undercurrents she'd sensed between Dand and Ginny. The celebrated beauty leaned back on the pile of pillows and sighed. She had made some negligible comment about Dand having visited her early on in their deception to make certain that Charlotte was not a cat's-paw in this game.

That is all she would say—other than to end with a worried warning that Dand Ross might not be what he appeared to be. In fact, he might be dangerous. Charlotte neglected to tell Ginny that she already knew that.

"But he wouldn't hurt me," she avowed stubbornly. "He's as faithful as a hound."

"Let me tell you about hounds, Charlotte," Ginny said. "My father kept lion hounds when we lived in Alexandria. I was fond of one in particular, a huge amiable-looking creature that I begged my father to let me make a pet.

"He agreed, of course, why wouldn't he? Jabari was the most gentle, docile, and slothful of beasts. Content to sleep on my bed and let me dress him in the maid's scarves. He used to eat Turkish delight from my hand, carefully licking each of my fingers afterward."

Charlotte smiled.

"Then, one day, my father decided I was old enough to go on a lion hunt. It was terrible. And thrilling. After hours on the veldt, the hounds cornered a great lion who'd been raiding the local tribe's cattle herd. One after another the dogs darted in at the beast and one after another were driven back yelping, shredded by the lion's claws and torn by its fangs until finally one hound flung himself like a spear at the creature, locking his jaws around the beast's throat.

"Though savaged, the hound would not let go until the lion went down, his windpipe crushed in the hound's jaws."

Charlotte felt herself blanch at this brutal depiction.

"It was only afterward, as the men tended the dog's many wounds that my father pointed out that the dog who'd entered the fray with such single-minded ferocity was my own gentle Jabari. I had never seen that part of him, so savage, so relentless, so lethal. It frightened me to think that an animal with such a capacity for violence had slept at the foot of my bed each night."

Charlotte shivered. "I imagined you stopped letting him sleep in your room after that."

Ginny laughed. "Good Lord, no."

"Why," Charlotte asked in surprise, "if he frightened you so?"

"Because I was his mistress. *I* had control of all that magnificent savagery. Do you understand the sense of power that gave me? The heady, delicious *power* of it? Indeed, he slept at my side for the rest of his life." She paused, her expression wry. "But *I* never slept quite so easily thereafter."

"Is there a lesson in this tale, Ginny?" Charlotte asked, aware her tone was a little brittle. The courtesan's words too closely echoed her earlier realization: that Dand's capacity for ruthlessness acted upon her as a potent stimulant.

"Yes," she answered, with a lift of her exquisitely plucked brows. "Be careful you know what sleeps in your bed, Charlotte."

St. Bride's Abbey
August 1793

"How I envy you boys!" Brother Fidelis, who had brought the four lads their midday meal—biscuits, cheese, and beer—in a pail, paused at the entrance to the walled garden and looked

around with obvious enjoyment. "To spend your days amid such beauty!"

Legend had it that long ago a crusader had brought back a yellow rose from his journeys in the Far East and given the unique bloom to St. Bride's in thanks for the abbot having sheltered the knight's family during the plague. The abbot had built this walled garden especially as a showcase for that rose, the only yellow one in all of the British Isles. But time and politics had diminished the Catholic population of the Highlands until there was no manpower to spare for the tending of flowers when other tasks were so urgently required. Until the current abbot, Father Tarkin, had turned the small abbey into a sort of orphanage for the grandsons and daughters of the few Catholic Scots left after the rebellion of Forty-five and Prince Charles's last aborted attempt to regain the Scottish crown. The father abbot had seen in the abandoned rose garden a perfect place for rowdy and undisciplined boys to use up their unfocused energy and learn obedience.

The rose garden had become the special project for the four rowdiest, strongest, and most likely to find trouble: Douglas, Kit, Ram, and Dand, the latter climbing out of the trench he was digging to grin wickedly at the benevolent and rotund monk. "Don't deny yourself on my account, Brother Fidelis!" he called to the still beaming monk. "You can take my place anytime you've a mind!"

Brother Fidelis did not take offense. Brother Fidelis never took offense. Now, had Dand served such sass to the other master gardener, the crabbed and sour herbalist Brother Martin, he would have been rubbing ointment on his scrawny behind for a week. But Brother Fidelis just wagged *his finger at Dand and said, "Someday you'll appreciate what you're doing here."*

"And what exactly is that?" Douglas, grunting under a bale of hay with which he was to mulch the transplants, paused to ask the monk.

"Making something beautiful. All those who come here seeking solace and comfort need only look here, walk amongst these paths to be reminded of God's great love."

Douglas cocked his head. "You really like the roses, don't you, Brother?"

Brother Fidelis smiled. "I love them. Now back to work with you," he said and ducked out through the garden wall's only door.

Ram Munro heaved the heavy rock back in place atop the collapsed wall surrounding the well. He stepped back, wiping the sweat from his brow with the back of his sleeve and looking around. All around them the roses bloomed with careless effort, making a mockery of the four teenage boys who toiled so that they might thrive.

"What do you think, Dand?" Ram called panting to what he could see of him. Dand had dropped once more into the trench on the other side of the wicker fence separating him from Ram. Now the rhythmic appearance of a shovel rising and falling above the top-woven wicker was the only visual sign of him. "Will we ever tame this masterpiece, do you think?"

"What masterpiece?" came Dand's grunted reply. The shovel didn't stop swinging.

" 'Tis no masterpiece!" Douglas, having dumped his bale of straw, leapt atop the half-tumbled rim of the garden well.

He snapped the branch from a scrub elder and wheeled around brandishing it. " 'Tis a dragon and I am Tristan come to slay it!"

"And I am Galahad!" Ram proclaimed, picking up another branch and pointing it at Douglas.

"Why not just be King Arthur himself?" Dand called out from within his hole.

"Because he never got to go anywhere!" Douglas explained, swinging his branch at Ram, who countered prettily and returned the favor. Douglas laughed delightedly. "He had to send others on his quests. I will go on my own quests, thank you very much! And have . . ."—his makeshift sword banged against Ram's—"my own adventures . . ."—another swing and another clatter of wood—"and win my own glory. And this . . . "—he paused to sweep his free arm out in a gesture encompassing the whole garden—"shall be my proving ground."

"What do you mean?" Kit demanded from where he bent some little distance away, straining to pull a massive root from where it had embedded itself in the wall separating the rose garden from the rest of the abbey. Even at fifteen years, his shoulders were as broad as most men's.

"I think this is one of those tasks," Douglas said, "that is meant to prepare you for your way in life."

Dand's head popped up over the wicker fence. "Well then, I can stop digging."

"Why's that?" Ram asked suspiciously. Dand Ross never had a thoughtful answer for anything.

"Because I can say with the utmost conviction that I am as well qualified to dig ditches now as ever I will be."

Douglas grinned and with a sigh tossed down his sword-branch, leaping lightly to the ground, his play ended. "There are greater things awaiting you than digging ditches, Dand Ross. Never you forget it."

"Aye," Dand whispered softly as he watched the boy amble away, "I never doubted it."

11

∞∞∞

A castle on the Scottish moors
July 27, 1806

"A CELEBRATED BEAUTY, of impeccable if somewhat less than illustrious breeding, has taken a lover. Some Frenchie," the Englishman, a buffle-headed Pink of the Ton named Lord Rawsett, realizing his faux pas, coughed. "I mean a Frenchman."

"Of the old regime, no doubt," his host, Maurice St. Lyon, said. Luckily for Rawsett, the comte was too preoccupied with this interesting bit of information to take exception to the slur on his nationality. Besides, having lived amongst the English since the revolution, he was used to bad manners.

"No doubt." Rawsett nodded. He stripped off his

multi-caped greatcoat and tossed it into the waiting arms of the footman. True to his scandal-mongering nature, Rawsett had bleated out his most impressive bit of gossip as soon as he'd crossed the threshold of the castle and spotted his host. Now he turned, sucking in a little whistle of appreciation.

"Not bad for a castle, St. Lyon, m'dear. Not bad at all." He looked around, taking in the thick Oriental carpet, the heavy tapestries lining the freshly chinked walls, the shining parquetry floors, and the gleaming, newly installed glass in the windows.

"You should see the place I was raised," Rawsett said. "No plumbing. No heating. No Society."

And of the three, St. Lyon guessed, Rawsett would miss Society most. The man was the consummate rubbish merchant. A pattern St. Lyon had noted amongst the sons of country gentry who'd flown their dodgy ancestral manses for the bright lights of Society. Once there, they seldom willingly went back to their country estates. From what St. Lyon could gather from the pretentious nobody, so it had been with Rawsett.

"I have had all the most modern conveniences installed and every creature comfort provided for," he said. "I hate being discommoded as much as you, Rawsett, m'dear."

"And you have certainly staffed yourself well, too." Rawsett wiggled his fingers at the discreetly silent pairs of footmen standing by the entrance and at two large windows, men chosen for loyalty and fighting abilities rather than the usual well-turned leg and Apollonian good looks. "Must cost you a bleeding fortune. But then, one can't have too many servants, eh?"

"Not when one suspects his home has been targeted for theft," St. Lyon answered. Twice in London he had apprehended thieves sent to steal the letter. Unfortunately, they had been hirelings, kept in the dark as to their employers' identities and thus no amount of persuasion had elicited any useful information. He would give much to know the names of those who worked against him—not only so that he could cut out the threat at its source, but also because he could then sell that information for a great deal of money.

"I trust your journey was not over-strenuous?" he asked Rawsett.

The young man's mouth pursed with annoyance. "One can only expect such when traveling in these savage parts." He gave a delicate little shudder. "But for you, dear St. Lyon, I willingly gave up the bright lights and fine company of the season. I know you appreciate my sacrifice, especially because the fascinating transgression I just mentioned was unfolding as I left."

"Oh, I do!" St. Lyon enthused.

Rawsett, with his dandified and overly scented curls brushed forward over his pale forehead and wearing one of dozens of pairs of chicken-skin gloves dyed to match a preponderance of waistcoats in every conceivable hue, was a complete tulip. But a useful one. And unexpectedly shrewd.

Indeed, it had been Rawsett who'd brought him the letter he was planning to auction. The citified turnip had come upon a "dying old Froggie Royalist" during his travels in the Italian states—the Grand Tour being closed to him—and had been pressed into returning the gentleman's personal effects to his relative in Rome.

True to what St. Lyon knew of Rawsett's character, the self-involved ass had forgotten his promise until he'd been introduced to St. Lyon upon his return to London earlier this spring. With that enormous ethnocentricity for which the English are well noted, Rawsett had decided that one Froggie was as good as another and prepared to deliver the dead man's things into St. Lyon's hands.

But when St. Lyon had recognized the Royalist's name, something in his manner tumbled Rawsett to the fact that he held something more interesting than a few "Frenchie love letters and such." Nipped by curiosity and greed, he'd decided to examine the dead man's possession before giving them into St. Lyon's care. One of them had been a little cylinder and its accompanying and extremely suggestive letter. Rawsett knew then that he had Something of Value.

But then, just as St. Lyon was preparing to relieve Rawsett of his burden—and consequently his life, too—the English tulip had evinced an unexpectedly astute streak and, realizing that he was in no position to achieve the full value of his find, suggested that he and St. Lyon enter into a partnership, asking for his share a very reasonable percentage of what St. Lyon knew would prove a fortune. Not being a particularly bloodthirsty man, simply a businessman, St. Lyon had agreed. Besides, gentry, even country gentry such as Rawsett, were generally eventually missed. Rawsett had other uses, too. He seemed to know everything about everyone.

"Ah, yes. The celebrated beauty. Anyone I know?"

Rawsett pulled a face and looked about, as if afraid of being overheard. "Oh, I should think so," he intoned heavily.

"And she is?"

Rawsett inhaled and expelled the name on a heated rush of breath. "Miss Charlotte Nash!"

"Miss Nash?" St. Lyon echoed, amazed. True, Ginny Mulgrew had hinted in her letters that the vivacious young Charlotte had been over-testing Society's indulgence of late, but he would never have guessed this, from a gently bred lady!

"Yes." The pomaded fop could not contain a trill of delighted laughter. "So young. But so hot-blooded. One should have seen it coming, I suspect. Well," he leaned forward confidingly. "Actually, I did."

"Do you have this Frenchman's name?" St. Lyon asked, interested.

Rawsett, having spied an errant thread hanging from his coat sleeve and having abandoned gossip for sartorial adjustment, looked up with a characteristically blank stare. "Name?"

"Yes," St. Lyon said patiently. "Of Miss Nash's lover."

"Oh. Oh, yes. I do. Rousse. Andre Rousse."

"It can't be," the comte murmured.

Rawsett screwed up his face in earnest concentration before answering. "No. I am certain I have it right because I recall the name rhymed with chartreuse and that had been the color of the waistcoat I was ordering from my tailor when Skelton came in—to order the most heinously ill-considered jacket. I swear, the man has no sense of style whatsoever—and revealed"—he paused—"all."

Then, with a meow of distaste, he set his index finger alongside his nose. "Man's a terrible gossip."

"And Lord Skelton expressly told you that Andre Rousse was Miss Nash's lover?"

"Not only lover," Rawsett said with ill-concealed eagerness, "but her protector. He has taken over the payments on her house and makes free use of the *front door*!"

Could it be? St. Lyon wondered. The name Rousse had many associations for him. The older ones were clearly discountable, but more recent ones might prove interesting.

Those men St. Lyon remained in contact with in France had, in their missives, infrequently mentioned an agent of nebulous affiliations who on occasion had interfered with, and on others had aided, those dedicated to the restoration of the monarchy. His name had been Rousse. It could not be that this was the same man who had plucked the fruit that St. Lyon himself had so often been tempted to steal.

"And you say this is a new . . . friendship?"

"Far as I can tell, the man just arrived in town a fortnight ago and straight off is seen kissing Miss Nash in public and entering and leaving her house at very interesting hours of the day."

"Servants' gossip," St. Lyon suggested.

"No, this comes from several reliable witnesses. Members of the ton."

Perhaps Charlotte Nash *had* taken a lover, whoever he was, damn him for his insolence, St. Lyon thought. St. Lyon could have seduced the little cat, but he was far more circumspect. He'd had to be. But once this Monsieur Rousse left . . . Well, now that the fruit had been plucked, there was nothing to prevent it from passing to other hands. And that, he thought with an inner sigh, might be a while yet.

He still awaited the arrival of three more well-financed "guests," and given the difficulties of traveling from afar across a continent now divided by war on almost every front, it would be another few weeks before they appeared and the bidding could finally commence. In the meantime, he had to keep a diverse and not always amenable group busy enough so that they did not kill one another. He might have employed Rawsett in that capacity for a while. The fool was amusing, Alas, he had another, much more important, mission for his cohort.

Poor Rawsett, he would be unhappy to be told he must leave again, St. Lyon thought, tucking his hand companionably through Rawsett's arm and drawing him toward the great hall. Perhaps he wouldn't tell him until tomorrow.

"Tell me, Rawsett, are there any wenches down at the crossroads tavern worthy of—how does one put this delicately?—*serving* their betters?"

Rawsett, beaming at having his sophisticated partner ask *his* opinion on the merits of rustic lady birds, rubbed his hands together and prepared to expound.

St. Bride's Abbey
Autumn 1794

Dand Ross squatted down, hands on his knees as he peered up into Douglas's bruised face. He let out a low, appreciative whistle. "Now what, I'm asking myself, could a noble lad like Dougie Stewart have done to raise the ire of the eternally persecuted John Glass?"

Douglas moved his jaw experimentally before spitting out a gob of blood onto the stable floor. "You're an idiot, Dand."

"Will you wipe the blood off your face, Doug? The sight of it is makin' my stomach do all sorts of unpleasant things," Dand said, reaching into his pocket and extracting a raggedy kerchief. He tossed it to his friend, who mopped at his lip. The damage wasn't as bad as initial evidence would have it. He would sport a bruised eye and a fat lip, but the cut was shallow and his teeth were all intact. "Why were they on you like that, Douglas?"

"John heard Ram and me talking about the brotherhood of the rose. He wanted to take the vow."

Dand's expression twisted in comical confusion. "That bit of theater in the garden last month, you mean? When you had us stab our thumbs with the rose thorns, clamp hands, and bleed all over one another as we pledged eternal allegiance one to another? You took a beating over that bit of nonsense?"

"It isn't nonsense to me, Dand," Douglas said quietly. His gaze was intent, piercing. "Or Ram. Or Kit."

"All right, Doug," Dand finally said. "Why didn't you let him say the words? They were just words, after all. You would have saved yourself a good thrashing."

At this, Douglas blinked. "They weren't just words, Dand. Don't you understand that? It was a promise. It was a vow. It was . . . sacred in a way. I wasn't going to cheapen it by letting John Glass make a mockery of it. He wouldn't die for you. He wouldn't die for anyone. If I let him make the vow, it would cheapen it for all of us. Don't you see that? It would mean nothing. Don't you take anything seriously?"

Dand leaned forward, resting his elbows on his knees, his hands dangling between. "They're just words, Doug. Not worth taking a beating over."

"Are you saying you wouldn't have done the same as I?"

Dand laughed, just as genuine in his disbelief as Douglas. "No, Doug. I wouldn't."

"Then I pity you, Dand Ross, I truly do," Douglas said. His face was tight and unhappy. He headed for the stable door, fully intending to leave Dand behind. But then he stopped as if he could not, despite his better instincts. "I love you, Dand. But I despair of you, I truly do," he said.

"No more than I do you," Dand whispered, jumping to the ground and following him.

12

~∞∞~

"MA'AM?" Lizette's head popped around the bedroom door. Caught in yet another reverie where Dand kissed her in between bouts of declaring himself her devoted slave, Charlotte guiltily dropped the yellow rosebud she'd idly been twirling between her fingers and swung around.

"Yes, Lizette?" Charlotte said.

"Lady Welton is downstairs and would like a few moments of your time."

"Lady Welton?" Charlotte repeated with pleasure. It had been days since she had heard from her onetime benefactress. She had begun to worry that something was amiss in the Welton household and decided that one of the boys must be cutting up rough or perhaps Maggie had decided to return early from her trip abroad with her new husband. "By all means, show her into the front parlor and offer her some refreshment. Tell her I shall be down directly."

With delighted anticipation, Charlotte brushed her short curls and threaded a ribbon around her throat before hurrying downstairs. She entered the room with her hands held out in welcome. "Lady Welton! How wonderful to see you!"

The older woman, dressed in a notably subdued fashion, rose and awkwardly took Charlotte's outstretched hands in hers, squeezing tightly as her gaze swept Charlotte from the top of her well-coiffed head to the dainty kidskin slippers peeping from beneath the hem of her white Swiss-dotted gown.

"You don't look like a soiled dove," Lady Welton blurted out.

"A what?" Charlotte's pleasure vanished. She shouldn't be surprised. Indeed, she should have realized that no outrage committed by a Welton offspring could have accounted for Lady Welton's long absence. Perhaps, somewhere deep within, she had.

Now, Lady Welton's gaze darted anxiously about the room as if looking for some sign of an ongoing bacchanal. Then, with a fastidiousness Charlotte had never before witnessed, she perched her rounded little rump gingerly on the edge of the divan and surveyed Charlotte with a mixture of mystification and sorrow.

"You know, Lottie. A . . . Woman of Easy Virtue."

If this hadn't been so obviously distressful for her former benefactress, Charlotte might have laughed. Thank God, Lizette arrived at that moment with a tray. She arranged the decanter of iced lemonade and glasses on the table before Charlotte, bobbed a curtsy, and left. Gratefully, Charlotte took the moments provided to prepare for this interview. If Lady Welton's opening salvo was any indication, this meeting could only prove a most painful one.

Baroness Welton had come for a purpose. Just what that purpose was remained to be seen, but already Charlotte suspected it boded little good for the girl who'd once been sheltered in the Welton home. But for the creature she and Dand Ross had created, a budding Cyprian who would enter St. Lyon's castle and steal a volatile missive, it would doubtless amount to a victory. She must cling to that.

It really was too bad her heart would not allow her to enjoy her triumph.

"What does a Woman of Easy Virtue look like?" she asked, pouring out the bittersweet liquid.

Lady Welton, forgetting for a moment her discomfort, squinted thoughtfully. "Abandoned. Blowsy. Feverish and . . . unpleasantly hungry."

"Good Lord!" Charlotte murmured, a little repelled. "Well, perhaps I am made of a different metal?"

"I hope not," Lady Welton answered.

Charlotte regarded her in surprise. "Why is that?"

"Because the alternative is that you have not entered into this improper liaison because of passion but because of . . . money." Lady Welton said the last word as if it fouled her mouth.

"Those are my only choices?" She tried to sound

offhand, but Lady Welton, the misery clear in her blue eyes, was far too dear for Charlotte to fully disguise her own distress.

"No." Lady Welton held out her hand and at once, without considering that a hard-hearted trollop would ignore such a gesture, Charlotte reached out and took it. Lady Welton's hand trembled.

"I understand you, Lottie," she said. "I know you. You are so like me, unwilling to let the ponderous pronouncements of Society tell you what to do or who to know or how to act. I know you are high-spirited and flirtatious and perhaps a little too often at the mercy of your impulses."

Impulsive. How little this dear woman understood her. Everything she did sprang from a focused and predetermined plan. Everything except her reaction to Dand Ross. She was the least impulsive woman she knew.

"I know how a young man can turn one's head and make any sacrifice seem worth a few minutes in"—she swallowed—"his embrace. Especially if he is handsome. Especially if he exerts . . . untoward pressure in gaining a hold over you."

Dear God, Charlotte realized, Lady Welton was asking if Dand had seduced her against her will!

"Lady Welton, I am not—"

Lady Welton's hand darted up and covered Charlotte's lips, silencing her. "Please, Charlotte. *Think*.

"You have only to tell me you are not willingly adopting this . . . life, that you regret your situation, and I shall find a way to make this right. Welton, for all his havey-cavey ways, is not without influence and I shall do everything in my power to see that you . . . do not suffer overmuch from this . . . misstep."

Slowly, she lowered her hand, covering Charlotte's and squeezing tightly. "Please." She was desperate for reassurance, so wounded. So betrayed. "I do not know how to explain to Maggie. I do not know what to say to Welton. Please. We love you, Lottie."

Pain swept through Charlotte, shaking her to the core. She could not speak. She had accepted that there would be distress and anguish she must bear, had never fooled herself that her life after this venture was ended would ever be anything but difficult. And she had, of course, considered her sisters' unhappiness, telling herself that whatever hurt they endured would be assuaged with time and their husbands' love and support.

But she had never appreciated that what she was doing would so profoundly affect those others who loved her, admirers and schoolmates and friends. Certainly she must count Lady Welton amongst them.

How could she hurt so many? How could she hurt Lady Welton, who had never shown her anything but kindness, who had sheltered her and cosseted her, treating her like a daughter of the house rather than the penniless hanger-on that she knew herself to have been?

What choice did she have?

"I am sorry, Lady Welton," she managed, her lips rigid with her determination to keep her smile in place. "But I am quite satisfied with my present situation."

Lady Welton's hand fell away. "I do not believe it. You . . . you cannot understand what this means, child. You will be an outcast. You *are* an outcast."

Charlotte forced a lilt to her voice. "There *are* societies besides the ton."

Lady Welton shook her head. "No, my dear. Not for you there aren't.

"Do not fool yourself by telling yourself such lies. You were raised amongst a certain set. You were raised to a certain manner, to have certain expectations of your life and your future.

"You are used to being lauded and courted and celebrated. To going wherever you wish with the certainty that you will be welcomed when you arrive. To meeting people who do not turn from you on the streets, but greet you with admiration and affection. To dining with friends who want nothing of you save your company.

"Charlotte, we have always been blunt, you and I. I will be blunt now. Is *this* woman, this Mrs. Mulgrew, the sort of person with whom you wish to spend the remainder of your years? Are you content with the company she represents, the women she knows who must, because of their circumstances, always stand aside for their betters? Do you want to spend every moment henceforth knowing that you are being assessed like a piece of cattle by disreputable and dissolute men?"

Charlotte turned her head, afraid that she would break down in tears and Lady Welton would misread her distress and send for the militia to wrest her from Dand's evil clutches.

"Lud, Lady Welton," she managed in a rush, "you seem to know an inordinate amount about the life of a lady bird."

The earnest light abruptly died in Lady Welton's expression, leaving her looking suddenly fragile and injured. "You are being deliberately hurtful," she said softly. "I would not have thought you capable of such. Indeed, I do not know you."

Charlotte looked up, chin high. She had not played the role of self-involved bon vivant for so many years only to have her skills fail her at the first inconvenient stab of conscience.

"I daresay," she said carelessly. "And I suspect that is really the reason for this visit, is it not?"

"What?" Lady Welton asked, confused.

"So that you might tell me directly that you can no longer know me," Charlotte said. "Most decent of you. Most honorable. Pray, consider yourself to have fulfilled whatever obligation you feel you have toward me."

"That is unfair." Lady Welton's hands twisted in her lap, her expression as wounded as that of a lapdog that had been kicked.

"It is," Charlotte agreed before she could stop herself. "But you know you really have no choice but to agree with my assessment, don't you? You *can* no longer know me," Charlotte said in a far softer, gentler voice than she'd intended. "I understand."

Tears welled up in Lady Welton's eyes. Tears of sorrow. But also relief. "I wish there was some other way. I wish—"

The door to the morning room swung open and Dand, immaculate in Ram Munro's purloined garments, stood in the doorway, his gaze possessive and protective. A lie. Everything about this whole sordid ordeal was a lie. His ardency, her lost virtue, their relationship, his past—even down to his damn clothing. She returned his gaze knowing she was not doing a good job of masking her misery. She bit her trembling lip.

His gaze narrowed, tautness hardening his features and then he was coming into the room, straight toward where Lady Welton sat dabbing at her eyes with the handkerchief she always kept tucked in her bodice.

"Lottie, me love," he said with a devilish grin. "You didn't tell me we had company!"

He *couldn't* expect her to introduce him to Lady Welton. It would be the highest insult to the poor woman. Charlotte would not do it. She wouldn't!

As though scalded by his words and afraid that Charlotte, or at least this alien creature she'd once known as Charlotte, would do just that, Lady Welton stumbled to her feet. Then, head held high, tears streaming unchecked down her powdered cheeks, she chugged wordlessly past Dand and disappeared into the hall. A moment later they heard the front door shut.

Charlotte tried. She tried as hard as she could to find her easy cavalier manner, the trick of insincerity and casualness. She looked up, lifting one brow as she gazed into Dand's tanned, angular face.

"Well, that went rather well, I thought," she said.

And then he was pulling her up and into his arms,

holding her close, his hand cradling her head against his broad shoulder.

And she broke down and wept.

13

∞∞

Jermyn Street, Piccadilly
July 30, 1806

Two DAYS LATER, Ginny looked up from leafing through the fashion magazines piled around her divan and upon seeing her young friend, at once put aside her contraband editions of *La Belle Assemblée*. Charlotte looked unwell.

Though she lacked the classic beauty of her sisters, Charlotte had always possessed something more, a vivacity and élan that invested her countenance with an irresistible appeal. But that animation was missing now. Violet shadows encircled her gold-flecked eyes and strain made her mouth pale and vulnerable.

With a sense of foreboding, Ginny closed the magazine on her lap, dispensing with the customary greeting and saying instead, "What is wrong, Charlotte? Where is Mr. Ross?"

Had the blackguard finally introduced Charlotte to the ways of the flesh and proved to be an ill-suited guide for that first expedition? Had he been unkind? Ungentle? Anger hummed through Ginny's veins.

"He is otherwise occupied."

Ginny studied Charlotte closely. No. *That* was not the problem. His name would have awakened much more of a reaction had it been. She cleared a space beside her and motioned for Charlotte to sit. With a wan smile, Charlotte complied.

"Tell me what has you looking so dour, my dear. Is it that you fear for this enterprise because of my blunt words last week? You don't hold my harsh tone and ill-chosen words against me, my dear?" Ginny entreated. "I was thinking only of what was best for our enterprise."

She had not quite realized how much she valued Charlotte's company—the companionship of a woman of her own class, with an education similar to hers, who has seen things and known people she had once seen and known.

"Besides," she went on brightly, "perhaps my words facilitated a needed impetus, for in the last few days you have pulled this masquerade off marvelously well, Lottie.

"Though I must admit to my own small part in that," she dimpled. "A few coins in the palm of your well-paid staff convinced them to be far more forthcoming in spreading word of the goings-on in your love nest. All of Society is abuzz with talk of your indiscretions."

Indiscretions. The word came out flat.

"Yes," Ginny hurried on. "Society can speak of little else."

"My indiscretions are a triumph, in fact."

"Yes." With a frown, Ginny reached for the china pot sitting on the table beside her. "Let me pour you a cup of chocolate. You look undone, my darling."

Charlotte did not reply.

"What brings you here?"

"I came because I want to know some things. I *need* to know some things."

Calmly, Ginny poured out a stream of steaming dark liquid into one of the exquisite little porcelain cups. "Of course. What is it you want to know, Lottie? What has you so at sixes and sevens?"

Charlotte fixed Ginny with a direct gaze. "Was it hard on your family?"

The stream of chocolate stopped. "Was what hard on my family?"

"When they realized the lifestyle you had adopted. What was their reaction?"

Ah. So that was what this was about. Pity tugged at Ginny's well-armored heart. Well, she supposed she ought to have expected this. A thing was so much easier done in conjecture than reality. But it was far too late to go back now. All she could offer this ridiculous, gallant innocent were some lies to soothe the transition from Diamond of the First Water to Pariah of the Highest Order.

"I don't have much family to speak of. A younger sister," who hadn't spoken to her in a decade, "an uncle," likewise, "and a few cousins here and there. They were not pleased, but eventually they learned to accept that over which they had no control." By cutting off all but the barest contact with her.

She finished pouring the chocolate, hoping Charlotte did not notice the deliberation with which she did so while she searched for the right things to say. "The aristocracy is well used to scandal, Lottie. You will be a nine-day wonder. Everyone will be agog only until the next bumble broth catches their attention."

"So as soon as another's ruin is effected, I shall be forgotten." Charlotte's tone was dry.

Perhaps she owed the girl the truth. "Forgotten but never forgiven.

"Some of your family, depending on the degree of affection they hold for you, will do what they can to ease your way. But for their children's sake, they will not be able to publicly receive you in their homes. At least those in town."

A tremble shook Charlotte's slender figure, but her gaze remained steady, her voice calm as she said, "I see."

"If you find yourself a powerful enough lover, and an ardent one, he might force your company upon his acquaintances—his male acquaintances. And some of their wives might be pressed into receiving you at some of the less elite gatherings. But by and large, you will forever be outside of the circle in which you once moved."

Ginny half expected anger, tears, a messy scene of

reproach and accusation. Charlotte surprised her. Though she grew pale, she only nodded. "Thank you for your candor."

Charlotte's calm acceptance made Ginny feel small and guilty. They were feelings she loathed and thus instinctively struck out against. "I suppose you do not feel you were adequately warned," she said shortly.

Charlotte's smile broke Ginny's heart. "You are wrong."

Ginny closed her eyes, hating the emotions she had long thought herself rid of—self-recriminations and guilt. They bubbled up within her, unchecked and undeniable, forcing her to consider what she, in her ambition and determination to do what she deemed right, had done. What right had she ever had to embroil this . . . this girl in her world, condemning Charlotte to her own fate?

"There is an alternative," she heard herself say. "You can leave London. But you would have to do so at once.

"You can go to your brother-in-law, the marquis. You will never again enjoy the prestige and admiration you once did, but you might recover some portion of it. Even the most straitlaced matron might be made to accept that you made an error, a youthful peccadillo, if you are seen to adequately—and publicly—regret it by hiding yourself away on the marquis's country estate for a few years. In time, you might return to Society."

Ginny could not tell if the girl heard her. She looked faraway, gazing into a future Ginny could only imagine.

"I love my sisters," she murmured. "I have dear friends who my actions have put in untenable positions."

"I know."

"I dislike having them suffer on my account, because of the affection they bear me."

"I understand."

Charlotte shook her head, as if trying to clear her thoughts. She bit her lip and passed a trembling hand wearily over her face. "I do not know," she whispered to herself. "I do not know."

Ginny reached out and gently touched her arm.

With a tired smile, Charlotte stood up, her chocolate cooling untouched in its porcelain cup. "Thank you, Ginny. I must go."

"But," Ginny asked, "what will you do?"

"Yet another thing that I do not know," she answered quietly and without another word left.

She had never assumed taking Ginny's place as St. Lyon's mistress would be easy, but she hadn't realized it would cost so much. And, fool that she was, she had never fully appreciated that it wasn't just her and her sisters who would have to pay the price.

No one, least of all she, had bothered to ask whether others were willing to pay the price required for her to become publicly disgraced. No, she had kept that choice for herself. The knowledge had haunted her since Lady Welton's visit, plunging her into an abyss of doubt and self-recrimination. She hadn't left her room in two days, pleading a headache as she tried to navigate her way to an answer. Finally, desperately, she had sought Ginny's advice. The courtesan's answer only left Charlotte wondering whether she had the right to continue on with her masquerade or the right to refuse the alternative Ginny had suggested. She still did not know.

She pulled off her gloves, setting them beside the silver slaver that had once held a dozen invitations a day but now held but a single letter. Sightlessly, she picked it up and carried it to the morning room, her mind on the day at the abbey two years ago when she had embarked on her exciting career.

It had seemed so noble then, so glorious, a great masquerade for the good of England undertaken in her father's memory. What would he say if he knew what she had become . . . at least, what the world thought she had become? Would he be proud if he knew the reasons for her actions? Or would he only be amazed and dismayed?

Had she done only what her wild heart had wanted? Were her motives dross or fine? And most importantly, did her motives matter?

She entered the morning room, dropping her shawl on a chair as she passed. Distracted, she picked up the ivory letter opener and slit the wax seal from the envelope. Without much interest, she opened the letter. Upon seeing that it was from Kate, her heart lurched.

She read:

Dearest Charlotte,

I am sorry not to have written in so great a while, but the regiment's need to move with all haste has denied me those free hours which I have generally set aside for correspondence. It has been a trying month, little sister. We lost several of the regiment last week in unexpected skirmishes. Poor Lt. McHenry lost his arm and he newly wed with a wife at home. But I console myself with the knowledge that at least he will be returning to her. Which leads me to the only bit of happy news I can impart:

Kit has been called back and we will be returning to London by the end of the month! How I wish it could be for good. But it is only to report and confer with his superiors. Unless this war ends soon, we shall be returning forthwith to the Continent. Oh, Lottie. I want so desperately for this awful conflict to be done!

How glad I am that you are safely in England, my darling, and lest you fret over my safety, I make haste to assure you that the officers' wives are kept well away from the field of battle at all times. But though I am safe, and Kit takes as much care as he can to shelter me from this wretched business, one cannot ever be so far away that one is safe from the knowledge of what occurs on the battlefield.

There is so much destruction. So much waste. So many lives ended and so many more destroyed and not only our soldiers', Lottie, but also our enemies'—for when one sees a man bloodied and in agony, one cannot help but feel pity for his state no matter which side of the conflict he is on! But even more grievously still, it is heartbreaking to see the effect war has upon the lives of the people who live here, unwilling spectators, a captive audience to the barbarism of war.

So many of the fields that we pass stand unharvested and untended. The barns are empty, their stores stolen or confiscated. Those who can flee before us do, and those who cannot stay to bear witness to the horrors.

God did not mean men to kill one another. He has set within each of us a revulsion of the act that these soldiers must find some means of circumventing in order to do what needs to be done. But it wounds them so, Lottie. I know, for I have seen the aftermath of "glorious battle." I have walked amongst the tents late at night and heard them crying.

It is my worst fear that their nightmares will not end when, God willing, they return home but will plague them for the rest of their lives. It is a terrible thing we ask of civilized men, Lottie, to engage in killing one another.

I only wish that I could do something to bring about a finish to this war. I would do anything! Anything! But what can I do except support my dear Kit and hold the hands of the wounded and dying? And pray to the Good Lord that this fighting ends, that this war is resolved quickly. Every day so much is lost—for all people. It must end. Pray God, it ends, Lottie. For all our sakes.

Your loving sister,
Kate

Carefully, Charlotte folded the letter, calm returning to her for the first time since Lady Welton's visit two days ago.

"Miss Nash? Can I get you anything?"

Charlotte looked up to find Lizette standing in the doorway, regarding her with a worried expression. It was an expression she had grown used to in the past forty-eight hours, hours when she had declined Dand's company and every suggestion that they go out and set Society's tongues wagging faster still. Hours when she had shut herself away—uncertain what she would tell him when he demanded to know what was wrong.

Well, she would soon ease Lizette's mind. And Dand's. She was done with hand-wringing and second-guessing her course of action. Kate's letter had reminded her that she was in the unique position to do something other than *pray* for an end to this war.

"Yes, Lizette," she said with a smile. "You can set out my gold tissue dress. I am going out this evening. And when Monsieur Rousse returns, you must inform him that we have a play to attend tonight and that I insist he be present for the curtain fall on the first act."

Lizette's pert features bloomed into a smile at the saucy tone Charlotte employed. "Yes, ma'am!" she said, bobbing a curtsy.

14

〰〰〰

"AND SO OUR PLAY DRAWS TO ITS CLOSE," Dand said as the rented carriage rumbled toward the Countess Hamstead's mansion.

The invitation had been sent and accepted well before Charlotte's fall from grace, and as Countess Hamstead herself enjoyed a somewhat checkered past, she had made no attempt to disown the invitation. Or perhaps she had assumed that Charlotte still possessed enough nicety of feeling to prevent her from embarrassing both her hostess and herself by arriving.

Alas, Countess Hamstead, Charlotte thought, your rout provides simply too perfect a stage to pass up.

She shifted and the paste diamonds she'd borrowed from Ginny glimmered in the murky light, the deep inky blue velvet of her cape dissolving into the shadows while her bosom glowed as pale as a dove's breast above the daring décolletage.

She felt calm, composed, sure of herself. No nerves. No unease. Just a tiny bit of impatience that the next act be finished. In the opposite corner from where she sat, Dand silently lounged. After tonight, they would part ways. He would go back to France and she . . . to Scotland.

The carriage rocked to a halt, caught in the crush of traffic moving at a snail's pace along the boulevard leading to the Hamstead mansion. He was silent for a long moment, even his gloved hands, white against the severe darkness of his evening dress, were motionless where they rested on the silver top of his walking stick. She sensed his ease slip away. She could almost feel the intensity of his gaze.

"Are you quite ready for this evening?" he asked as the carriage started up again.

"I am," she replied. "And you?"

"Oh, most definitely. Though I still don't see why I have to be the one to be given the old heave-ho."

He was offering her a distraction, she realized. Gladly she took it. "We have discussed this at length. St. Lyon must think I am not some pitiful young girl, but an unsentimental opportunist. One looking for a richer and more generous protector."

"I suppose it makes sense. But I warn you that my masculine pride may never fully recover from the insult you intend to deal it tonight."

"And I make haste to reassure you that it is not the weight you carry in your breeches but the one you carry in your purse that will be called into question."

"Dear me, Lottie." Dand drew back, shocked. "How exceedingly gamy."

"Wasn't it, though?" she replied complacently. "I have been practicing such lines all evening. Ginny has been sharing the most delicious insights with me."

"I should hate to imagine," he said dryly.

"There is no sense in ruining myself in a halfhearted sort of way. *I* shall ruin myself with panache." She smiled and hoped she at least looked gallant. She would like to end this conversation with Dand secure in the belief that she could carry off her part in tonight's performance with aplomb. "Or at least humor."

"How I will miss you, Lottie," he murmured. "I have truly enjoyed these days together."

"As have I," Charlotte returned graciously so that he would not suspect the full extent of the truth she had just uttered. Those hours they had spent closeted together meant a great deal more to her than she was willing to admit. Even to herself. And those hours when their roles required him to flirt with her, to touch her, she would miss even more.

Dand's endearments made her limbs weak. Dand's ardent gazes made her pulse race. Dand's whisper-light caresses made her catch her breath. And Dand's kiss . . . ? Enough to make a more foolish girl, a greener girl, a more romantic girl than she, lay awake at night and wonder where such kisses ultimately led and despair that she would never find out.

Luckily, she was not that girl.

Still, she thought with an abrupt return of the irreverence and audacity she had rediscovered upon reading Kate's letter, what with all the sacrifices she had been making of late, she ought to have a safe-conduct to the head of the queue when the time came for her to stand at the Pearly Gates.

The carriage drew to a halt. She pulled back the curtain and stared up at the flight of broad marble steps leading to the open double doors brilliantly lit at their top. Footmen stood in a line on either side of the doorway, receiving the guests that flowed like a spangled river up from the street.

"This . . . is insanity," Dand uttered softly. Even in the darkness she could make out his crooked smile.

"So you've repeatedly told me," she said but without rancor. They were too far along now to cry off and they both knew it.

"It was not supposed to happen," he murmured. "Madness."

"Mad horse," Charlotte corrected, thinking of the carriage that had struck down Ginny and so profoundly altered her own destiny. "I wonder what spooked it? There is undoubtedly a lesson there: The best laid plans can be laid to waste because of a scrap of paper, a boy's peashooter, or a slinking cat."

"Yes." Dand's voice trailed off. There was a long moment of silence and then with exaggerated gallantry, he said, "Whilst I have the opportunity to do so, let me commend you on your performance these last few weeks."

He sounded like an admiring fellow professional applauding his cohort's performance before the closing night's final act. "Thank you. And I, yours. And now, I suppose we'd best get on with it?"

"Yes."

Neither of them moved.

"Lottie."

"Yes?"

"You know I am to return to France in a few days."

"Yes. Pray, be careful."

"Yes, yes." He brushed away her worries, "But . . . what I wanted to say is . . . You know that after tonight I can't come to the house. And if we chance upon one another in some public place, you must give me the cut direct."

"I understand. Having decided my future lay elsewhere, no looking back over my shoulder."

"Exactly." She saw the flash of his white teeth and her heart turned over. "So this is the last time we will talk for a while."

A great while. And when they saw one another again everything would have changed.

"But," he went on, "if you should need me in the next few days, I'll have taken rooms in Bedford Square. Afterward, at any time afterward, you have only to contact Father Tarkin in order to find me. He will know how to reach me."

His concern touched her and she covered her emotions with a bright smile and a little shake of her head. "Should I send a yellow rose, too? If it's in season, that is?"

When he didn't reply, she reached out and lightly touched his hand. "Oh, Dand. Let us be done with your oath so you can cease looking all grimly resolved and spending heaven knows how many of your future years waiting in dread anticipation for the arrival of a flower."

She sat back, smiling gallantly. "Here then is my official word: I, Charlotte Nash, hereby release you from your pledge."

"It is not for you to release me, Lottie," he said, his quiet voice filling the darkness. "Only my heart can judge when I have paid my debt."

"Poor heart," she whispered.

"Constant though, pitiful thing," he agreed and suddenly leaned forward reaching across the short distance separating them and touched her cheek lightly with the very tips of his fingers.

Damn him anyway! She told him so often that he had to wear gloves. He always forgot and now the electricity of his bare touch set her eyelids drifting shut on a wave of longing.

"Darlin' Lottie," he murmured softly, "if ever you have need of me, call for me and I will come to you." His fingers skated down her cheek to the side of her neck and curled lightly behind, combing through the short curls at the nape of her neck to cup her head. He drew closer, his breath was soft with the scent of brandy and warm in the closed carriage and she heard her heartbeat because she'd stopped breathing.

"Should you require anything of me, anything at all, no night will be too dark, no road too long, no ocean wide enough, nor any king's army great enough, to keep me from doing your bidding or dying in the attempt."

Her heart leapt at the suddenly vibrant tones, the dark power of his words and she wanted—my Lord, how she *desired!*—to believe there was something more than honor here. Something deeper than sheer, obstinate nobility.

His mouth touched hers, a bittersweet kiss unlike any they'd shared, gentle and yearning and just as he lifted his hands to capture her face between them and deepen it, the carriage rattled to a halt and swayed as the driver jumped to the ground. Reluctantly he released her and sank back in his seat, his eyes gleaming in the semidarkness.

"And," he said in a low, throbbing voice as the door swung open, "I will need no bloody rose to guide me to you."

"Told her she'd be making a spectacle of herself," Monsieur Andre Rousse declared loudly, but to whom it was unclear. Several near him turned at his loud, slightly slurred declaration.

"Can only believe that's what she wants. And what is that, you might ask yourself?" he snarled, his wild-eyed gaze riveted on the object of his treatise. "I'll tell you. Any woman who appears in public in such a state of undress does so in anticipation of hanging from more men's necks than a secondhand cravat!"

Not since the great actors Sarah Siddons and John

Kemble had last appeared together on the stage over two decades earlier had the ton enjoyed such a spectacle. A hush fell over the crush that had formed in the foyer leading to the Hamstead dining tables. Heads swiveled, lips stilled, breaths held.

The tall, handsome Frenchman, Monsieur Rousse, having spied his paramour, Charlotte Nash, bellowed the words at her as she stood flirtatiously tapping her folded fan against the chest of a besotted-looking knight. Upon hearing the vile accusation, the lady turned as pale as her gold tissue gown—which honesty compelled any objective viewer to admit was fashioned in such a manner as to leave little to the imagination as to what charms lay beneath the thin gauze. Derisive dames would later scathingly declare that the gown had been moistened to better cling to what all must admit was indeed a spectacular figure.

Slowly, the ginger-haired vixen turned and leveled her catlike eyes on the man all Society assumed was her lover. "A secondhand cravat? Yet another thing you can ill afford, Rousse?"

The push toward the doors ceased altogether. The current scene had been building all evening. Monsieur Rousse—whom nobody knew, yet everyone knew *of*— had entered with Charlotte Nash on his arm, ignoring the titters of amazement and hisses of disapproval that followed. Miss Nash had abandoned him at once, and he had proceeded to drink himself into a state one old general had admiringly admitted would have seen him—and he a three-bottle man—on his face.

Contrarily, Miss Nash contented herself by flirting in the most outrageous manner possible with any man who did not shun her company, which, several wise old matrons pointed out, was a far greater number than various wives, mothers, and sweethearts would have liked.

Rousse had watched her sport with a black-eyed glare as he tipped glass after glass of port down his throat, ignoring the come-hither glances from the more adventurous matrons who in their midnight confession or hastily scribbled journals admitted to understanding—in a purely conjectural sense—why someone as flighty and passionate as Charlotte Nash had ruined herself upon him.

But when Charlotte leaned forward and whispered something that caused a moon-eyed youngster, and heir to a vast and vastly vulgar trade, to go scarlet with pleasure, Rousse had stormed across the room and snatched her away, pulling her into a small closet. For the next ten moments pacifying murmurs and sporadic roars of outrage could be heard from its interior. However, whatever balm Miss Nash had used to attempt to soothe her beastly lover had apparently failed. He emerged from the closet with a curse on his lips and the devil in his eye. A few minutes later Miss Nash appeared, sighing with annoyance before returning to her winsome ways.

That had been two hours ago.

Now, with a savage sound, Rousse was pushing his way through the throng with the apparent intent of doing bodily harm to Miss Nash's person! He got to within a dozen feet of the girl who stood with an imperious look of disdain before several gentlemen, fearing the worst, laid hold of him.

He thrashed angrily in their grip. "Let me go. Release me, you devils! Unless you poor wretches are in her thrall, too!"

"Let him go," drawled Miss Nash with a derisive flick of her hand. "He will never leave until he has made an exhibition of himself."

Reluctantly, the gentlemen released Rousse's arms. His fine eyes lost their wild glare and he moved past the last few people separating him from his quarry until he stood before her, shuddering with emotion.

"Yes, Rousse?" she inquired in a bored voice. "What further remonstrations must you make? Pray be quick about it, though. A quadrille is forming, and I do love a quadrille."

"You are cruel."

"If refusing to perpetuate an uncomfortable delusion is cruel, then I confess my guilt."

"Heartless trollop! I would have worshipped you!"

A little smile tilted her lips. "Then I have saved your soul from certain sacrilege and you should be thanking me for bidding you adieu. And I *am,*" she continued in stony tones, "bidding you adieu."

And with that she started to turn away. But by now Rousse was in the throes of an agony one could only guess at and fervently hope never to have to endure. His face was terrible—wretched and despairing and furious. He seized her arm as she passed. Without a hitch, she swung around. The sound of her gloved palm striking his cheek resonated over the mesmerized crowd.

He dropped her arm, stunned, drunk, mortified.

"And now that you have humiliated us both, perhaps you would be good enough to leave?" Her voice had lost its chill indifference. For the first time, she sounded overset. Her eyes gleamed with what might have been tears.

For a long moment they stood staring at one another, emotions playing across Miss Nash's face that no one, not even the most opinionated termagant, could interpret. And then with a bow—quite a good bow for one so well in the boughs—Rousse made an elegant leg and whispered softly, "Your servant, ma'am. Your slave."

And while Miss Nash stayed on until the wee, wee hour and danced, tongues began to wag, whispers following her as closely as her shadow.

"*She all but declared he could not keep her in a style she wanted.*"

"*Just as she all but declared that she was looking for someone who could.*"

"*I always thought her too forward.*"

"*But this forward? I know her sister, the marchioness of Cottrell. She will be devastated.*"

"*Probably not. She would know to expect such a thing. Unlike my poor naïve son, Jeff.*"

"*Or my innocent nephew Carl.*"

"*And my unsuspecting husband.*"

15

∞∞∞

WAITING WAS THE HARDEST PART, Charlotte decided
four days later as she listlessly threaded another skein
of blue silk through the eye of a needle. She had studied
the blueprints of St. Lyon's castle renovations for so
many hours she could have made copies to scale from
memory. She knew to within a foot where every window and every servants' hall led, which closets were
deep enough to hide in, which doors led to stairwells
and which panels hid priests' holes. After that . . . she
filled the hours.

She was sick of needlework, tired of reading, fed up
with her own company and the only other person she
cared to talk to was ensconced in some Bedford Square
apartment putting on a fine show as her cast-off lover—
or so Ginny informed her. He was drinking, gaming,
and wenching—at least she assumed he was wenching—while she embroidered *pillow shams*!

It wasn't fair. Oh, she had invitations. Invitations to
go on carriage rides in the country, take the night air at

public pleasure gardens, or dine tête-à-tête with a number of wealthy gentlemen. She was so bored she'd almost accepted the last such invitation she'd received from a rising politician. At least the conversation might prove interesting. But then the conversation was unlikely to be about politics, wasn't it?

So she sat. And played whist with Ginny during the courtesan's daily visit, and tapped her fingers as she stared out her window at the little square across the road and thought about Dand. And wanted to be with Dand. And practiced a few of his more colorful words.

She took a deep breath. This was getting her nowhere. She must think of other things. For instance, by now St. Lyon would have received Ginny's letter and presumably answered it. What if he didn't take the bait? No. She refused to believe it. She would not allow herself to think along such disastrous lines.

So, since she didn't allow herself to dwell on Dand and his despicable dalliances, and she dare not consider the unimaginable—that all she had done had been for naught—she was left scant little to think about other than . . . than . . . pillow shams.

Blowing out her cheeks, Charlotte set aside her embroidery and wandered disconsolately toward the candy box an admirer had sent her. Already half a dozen little gold tissue nests stood relieved of their almond paste creations. No wonder, she thought sardonically, so many of the soiled doves pointed out to her at the opera houses were plump little pigeons.

She had just picked up a little marzipan rose when

the door to the parlor burst open. Ginny stood framed within, balancing atop yet another elegantly wrought pair of crutches. Her pretty face was vivid with ill-suppressed excitement and she was waving a piece of paper like a flag at the king's birthday.

"It's come! Your invitation!" she breathed, clomping into the room, pivoting neatly on one crutch and with the other slamming the door shut. "I arrived at the same time as the messenger and took it upon myself to pay the postage. I know his hand, Charlotte. 'Tis from St. Lyon!"

She swung across the room, her crutches banging loudly against the floor, and thrust the letter at Charlotte. "Read!"

Charlotte took the paper and without bothering to find an opener, slipped her finger beneath the seal. Proud that her hand did not shake, she snapped the folded sheet open and read.

So that was it, then. She took a deep breath. Another.

"What does he say?" Ginny demanded. Wordlessly, Charlotte handed her the letter.

Dear Miss Nash,

How aggrieved I was to hear of the nefarious and distasteful attentions to which you have been subjected of late. I flatter myself to think that I might know something of what you are experiencing, having myself been cast out from all I once knew and then finding myself in a different, though I hasten to say not necessarily inferior, situation.

It can be most distressing, especially if one does not have friends nearby upon whom one can rely to offer not only support and sympathy, but also companionship and gaiety, in order to remind one that life, with all its rich and ample rewards, continues to be an adventure for those bold enough to accept its challenges. Please, I beg you, let me offer you the use of my castle and my friendship during this unsettling time.

Unless you send word otherwise to my driver Jeffries, I shall send my carriage for you on Saturday morning with the intention of conveying you to my castle.

With the most ardent hope that you will accept my offer and eagerly anticipating the pleasure of your charming company,

Maurice, Comte St. Lyon

Ginny looked up, her expression a little amazed. "That's it, then. We've done it, Charlotte. He's sending his carriage for you tomorrow."

"So soon?" Charlotte murmured.

"Well, my dear, it only proves his ardor. You ought to be flattered."

"Yes," she said. "I should be." She squared her shoulders, as if physically assuming a burden, but when her gaze met Ginny's it was lucid and uncompromising.

"Now, the hard part is done and the simple matter of finding the letter and replacing it with a fake remains," she said. "Oh, and I suppose I shall have to make myself agreeable, too, in order to hold St. Lyon's attention.

And yet not so agreeable that he cannot bear to be apart from me for those hours I will need to search."

She smiled—a new smile, harder and tighter. "I shall simply have to find some means of suppressing my colossal magnetism."

Ginny was not having it. The courtesan knew Charlotte too well. Her dark eyes narrowed with pity. But pity is not what Charlotte needed now. She needed strength.

"As soon as you find that letter," Ginny said, "you must contrive an excuse to leave immediately."

"In the nick of time, you mean?" Charlotte could not help the dry cut to her retort. There likely would be no nick of time and they both knew it.

Ginny turned her head, chewing at her lower lip. "He's . . . a considerate lover, Lottie," she said in a low voice. "He is kind during . . . during intimacy."

Kind? the word caught Charlotte by the throat.

She didn't want St. Lyon's *kindness*. Regardless of what "kindness" St. Lyon showed her body, there could be no possible way in which he could become more "intimate" with her than Dand. She had spent weeks playing at being in love with Dand Ross, while falling in love with him in truth, refusing to think of another in his place, of another man touching her.

She knew every variation of the color in Dand's eyes, from the warm amberine color of melted toffee to near black of burnt coffee. She knew every scar that etched his hands, the way his brows crooked up an instant before he smiled; the lazy way he moved; his careless grace; his idle strength, the purpose prowling beneath his lassitude.

She understood the keen intellect that hid beneath casual curiosity, the hard realist that held sway over the easygoing rogue. She knew the way he tasted. She knew the way he smelled. She had but to close her eyes and every sense she possessed conspired to construct his image in perfect detail.

How could she be more intimate with anyone? Only with the physical act of making love.

The answer fell upon her with terrible weight and with it a stunning realization.

Because she was still a virgin, St. Lyon would be able to tell she hadn't been intimate with anyone.

The room was stuffy and overheated, but since the rain was driving against the window from the east, he had little choice but to keep it shut. Outside the night sky was black and dense and thick with the promise of a greater storm to come.

With an irritation he seldom felt, he yanked his shirt from his torso and tossed it to a chair and then lay down on the narrow bed that came with the apartment. He crossed his boots at the ankle and laced his fingers behind his head and contemplated a spider industriously weaving a web directly overhead. There was a portent in that spider's machinations, he thought with a return of dark humor.

Had everything in the last six years been part of God's plan to bring him to his knees?

Probably.

In spite of every effort, he'd been unable to extradite his life from being so tightly bound to Charlotte Nash's. He smiled in the darkness. Damn the little hoyden, anyway. He had thought that by playing an accommodating scoundrel, he could keep a surreptitious eye on her while deftly keeping her out of the other threads that comprised the fabric of his life. It only made it worse. It only made her trust him. She had let herself relax with him, did not bother to put up defenses, to guard herself.

Dear God, if she knew the extent of the self-restraint with which he'd met her shattering little caresses; if she understood the physical pain he'd endured under the scourge of her familiarities, her kisses and sighs; the self-control he'd practiced in not responding fully to those innocent provocations—she wouldn't have shared the same room with him, let alone the same house!

He didn't just want her; he wanted her *entirely*. He closed his eyes tightly, his jaw muscles working in frustration and anger. He should have been able to eschew these entanglements, this desire, this—

Love, he thought bitterly.

He didn't have much time. The worst possible end to this farce would play out if he was caught on these shores by Ram—a disaster second only to the problem presented should Kit MacNeill find him here. He had to be away by the time both or either man returned to England and his sources told him that would be soon.

And then . . . ? Then he couldn't come back until the final curtain was set to be drawn.

He would *not* be distracted by the thought of Charlotte waiting for an invitation from St. Lyon. The comte was a practical man. A wary man. Even if he did send for Charlotte, the odds were greatly in favor of his waiting to do so until after the auction of the letter. By then the impetus that forced her to his bed would be gone. But what if the comte—

No. He had to leave. It was imperative. He could not stay and keep Charlotte from St. Lyon, no matter how much his heart insisted he do just that. There were things for which he had worked half his lifetime. People, perhaps hundreds of people, depended on the success of his mission and he would not forfeit their lives because he'd fallen in love with Charlotte Nash.

"Monsieur Rousse?" The maid who served the apartments he'd rented knocked at the door. "Message for you, sir."

He supposed he should put on his shirt so as not to offend the girl, but he was hot and sticky and the girl had probably seen a great deal more interesting things in her short life than a man branded with a rose. He swung his legs over the bed, got up, and opened the door.

"Yes? The message?" he asked curtly.

The girl dropped the note into his outstretched palm, bobbing a quick curtsy and hurrying away, leaving him to retreat back into his room.

He wasn't surprised by the arrival of a note. He was still collecting information in London from various sources, most of whom preferred the anonymity provided by a letter rather than risk exposure by seeking him out for a face-to-face interview. Still, the quality of the paper was better than his correspondents usually employed.

He broke open the seal and at once the elegant feminine hand leapt out at him, the signature discreet, with only a few flourishes, far less elaborate than would have expected from so extravagant an owner as Charlotte Nash.

"Please. Come tonight."

Stuffing the tails of his shirt in his trousers, he took the stairs down to the front hall two at a time, snatching up his coat before plunging into the rain.

St. Bride's Abbey
Spring 1799

"No one must know where you are going. None of the other lads, nor any of the monks. As far as they are concerned, you have decided you have had enough of the monastic life and are heading out to experience the fleshpots of Edinborough." Father Tarkin paused before each of the young men standing straight-backed before him. He looked into each pair of eyes with a deep, probing stare. *"No one will find any reason to doubt the story. The four of you lads have been living in each other's pockets close to a decade."*

Kit MacNeill hesitated. *"What of John Glass?"*

"What of him?" Father Tarkin asked.

"He knows something is up. He's been pestering Douglas with questions about where we go after matins and why Ram is so intent on perfecting his French accent."

"And what have you told him, Douglas?" Father Tarkin turned his attention to the brown-haired young man at the end.

"I told him we're planning to fly some evening, to turn our backs on the abbey and make a name for ourselves in the world." Douglas grinned. He was excited, Dand could see, eager to undertake the mission that Father Tarkin, Brother Toussaint, and the mysterious visitor from France had formulated. "And that's not far from the truth, is it?"

"Not if things go as I pray they do," Father Tarkin said. "In which case no one will ever know who you are. Just like now." His eyes touched upon and held Dand's gaze for a telling instant that the other lads did not seem to notice.

He had taken the old wrecker's advice to heart those many years ago when Father Tarkin had picked him up off the side of the road. It had been years before he'd admitted to the canny abbot the name of the family he'd been born into. Of course, by then it had hardly mattered. His immediate family was all dead, and those who would be interested in knowing his whereabouts would have been hard-pressed to find him. Added to which, there was no proof—none—that he was who he knew himself to be.

Except, he hadn't forgotten. He'd never forgotten. He never would.

"I know who I am." Beside him Douglas spoke with quiet assurance. "And I know these men beside me. I don't need know their lineage to know their quality."

Father Tarkin looked at him approvingly and gave a slight nod. "Well said, Douglas."

"I only hope it proves true," muttered Brother Toussaint, dividing his doubtful gaze between the four young men. "Kit's too impetuous. Ram is too silky for his own good, Douglas needs to rid himself of the notion that he's on some noble mission, and Dand . . ." He shook his head. "I don't know what he's thinking. But then I never have."

"Dand doesn't know what Dand is thinking half the time," Douglas said, clamping his hand on Dand's shoulder and breaking the tension. "Luckily for him there are three of us to lend him some thoughts when he runs out."

The others broke into laughter. Even Toussaint gave an unwilling smile.

"Don't worry, Brother," Douglas said more soberly. "We'll do you proud. I swear it."

16

∞∞∞

Culholland Square, Mayfair
August 3, 1806

CHARLOTTE SAT ON THE HALLWAY BENCH directly across from the standing clock, listening to the falling rain. A single wall sconce bathed the corridor in a honeyed glow, muting the rich colors of the Oriental runner and steeping the bouquet of yellow roses on the hall table to tea-colored umber.

She trained her gaze on the front door, waiting for a shadowy form to coalesce on the other side of the narrow sidelight. She heard the clock's mechanism slip and whir and slowly toll out ten deep chimes.

An hour ago she had substantially finished packing her bags. Forty-five minutes ago she had sent her message to Dand. Thirty minutes ago she had dismissed the staff for the evening. They had needed no encouragement to accept their mistress's charity and quickly, lest she change her mind. Fifteen minutes ago she had come down here.

The punishing bang of the brass knocker caught her by surprise. She leapt to her feet, moving swiftly to the door and unlatching the lock. She opened the door. Dand Ross towered over her, his head bare and dripping with rain, his great coat unbuttoned, his shirt soaked, and his eyes dark as the night sky.

He was startled at finding her opening the door. His gaze traveled over her shoulder, searching behind her for her staff. His mouth, generally so ready to smile, was tight-lipped, his expression intent.

"What is wrong? Where are the servants? What has happened?"

Now that he was here, moving deftly past her into the dimly lit hallway, the confidence with which she'd written that note vanished.

"Nothing is wrong," she said, twining her fingers tightly together. "I gave the servants the evening to do with as they would. As for what has happened . . ."

He turned and waited, water dripping from his shabby greatcoat, a puddle forming under him and spreading across the marble parquetry floor. He'd rid himself of Ram's finery, she realized. He wore his old clothes, patched and ill-fitting.

"St. Lyon has written, extending an invitation to me to visit him in his castle."

His body tensed. "When?"

"His coach is coming . . . the morning after next," she lied, unwilling to invest this encounter with unnecessary haste.

He took one step toward her and stopped as if checked by a leash. *"In two days?"*

"Yes," she answered softly.

His brow dipped in a fierce scowl, and his lips parted on something like a snarl. "I'll be damned."

"I believe that is my role," she said, trying to win some humor from the situation. "Unless I eventually repent my wicked ways, which I shall surely do."

"Don't."

She turned her back on him, using the excuse of shutting the door to master a kaleidoscope of reactions: joy, fear, guilt, *desire*. She heard him shedding his great-coat, felt him move close behind her. He reached beneath her chin and urged her head around so that she looked at him over her shoulder. His face was composed, but his eyes . . . there was unplumbed darkness in his gaze. Always before she had seen the wry glint of humor, the patina of indolence. Why had she never noticed the depths beneath the gleam?

Gently, he cupped her cheek. With a soft sigh, she closed her eyes. He didn't make a sound, not a single breath from the lips so close to the wispy curls at her temple. The rest of her body pirouetted toward him, like a flower seeking the course of the afternoon sun. She felt his other hand, the fingers gliding beneath the silken curls at the nape of her neck, palming the back of her head.

"Why did you send for me, Lottie?" The hands so gingerly holding her face, shivered.

She opened her eyes. Her heart raced in equal parts fear and apprehension and anticipation. "I want you to make love to me, Dand."

He caught his breath. "Why?"

Because you were my first hero, and you still are.

There was truth and there was such a thing as too much truth. "I am a virgin," she said simply and waited.

It did not take him long to understand her meaning. His hands abruptly dropped away from her face. He fell back a step, as if he'd been struck. His expression was stunned, disbelieving. "My God."

Flames rushed to her cheeks. "I can't go to St. Lyon as a virgin." As an excuse it was a damn good one. No, better than an excuse. It was the truth, but it was only part of the truth, the greater part being that she wanted him to be the man who introduced her to the mysteries between men and women.

He half turned from her, his gaze searching the ceiling, the walls, looking anywhere but at her. "And you have decided to grant me the honor of relieving you of your maidenhead?" He spoke with astonished and bitter restraint.

"Who else?" she asked softly. "Who else should I ask? Where else should I go? To a stranger?"

Her words vanquished the feral curl of his lip, the deadly glint in his eye. With a sound like a laugh but terrible, he shook his head. "No. You should not go to a stranger." He crashed his fist into the wall in front of him. "No." The plaster exploded beneath his knuckles. "No."

"Dand!"

He stopped, flattening his palms against the wall, his head hanging below his shoulders. The wet material of his shirt stretched across his broad back, every muscle delineated, tense and rigid. "A moment, my dear," he said in a voice beleaguered. "A moment."

"I am sorry, Dand," she said. She had known he would find this . . . hard. What she asked him went against every code of honor a gentleman lived by. Yet she could not explain to him the truth, that she loved him, that she wanted him with a hunger that needed no facile reasoning, no excuses to follow the dictates of her heart.

But she had to be careful. He would never allow her to go to St. Lyon if he suspected she loved him. It wouldn't matter whether he returned her feelings or not—and she had no reason to believe he did. He only allowed her to go now because he believed she was as inured to sentiment as himself, as coolly detached from softer emotions as he was. Why would he think differently? Until recently, she had thought so herself. But looking at him here, now, his broad back tense and virile, his long arms pushing at the wall, she felt the leap of desire.

"Please, Dand. It is just that it would be so much more . . . comfortable for me because," *I love you*, "I trust you."

"You trust me?" He echoed in a dazed voice. His back muscles bunched. With a curse, he pushed himself away from the wall and straightened. "You trust me."

"I do. I think most highly of you, too, and that makes a difference to me in this . . . endeavor."

He turned. His gaze locked on hers. He looked older in the shadows, dangerous, unpredictable. A little shiver, half of trepidation, half of excitement, raced through her. "High praise, indeed. And not unwarranted, surely? Because who else but Dand Ross would take a lady's maidenhead and send her forthwith off to another's bed, having rid her of the inconvenience?" His gaze grew black. "You're right. I can't think of another."

"Dand." She reached out and captured his hand, lifting it to her face and rested her cheek against it. "Neither of us would have this play out in such a way had we a choice. I know that."

She turned her head and pressed her lips against his palm. His head drew back, his eyelids dipped and his nostrils flared.

"I know you are not indifferent to me. I have . . . felt you. And you must know for all my protests, I like your kisses very much." Such tepid words for such a vibrant longing.

"Dear God, Lottie," he whispered. "How am I to do the right thing when you say things like that to me?"

"This *is* the right thing," she answered earnestly, willing him to do this. "This is what I want. What you've *made* me want. I lie awake at night and chase after every sensation you've awoken with your touch, your glance, your kiss. And I know that with all the fakery and masquerading, this at least is not counterfeit. Not on my behalf." *Because I love you.* "And not on yours. I know because I know you."

"Do you?" he whispered, his tone raw.

"Yes. So please make lo—"

She never got a chance to finish. He pulled her roughly to him, his mouth finding hers. In answer, she lashed her arms around his neck.

He was wet and cool, the rainwater drenching him, soaking through her thin silk night rail. His arms shook, his body trembled, and they were falling to their knees on the carpeted floor. She clung, needing him, wanting him, yielding against him as he lavished kisses against her eyes and temples, searing a fiery trail along her jaw and down the downy softness of her neck, plunging his hands into her thick curls holding her still for his questing mouth, as if he could not have enough, as if he was afraid she would leave him starving.

"I won't. I can't," he muttered thickly against the soft white flesh rising above the gauzy décolletage. "God, Lottie. *Think* what you are asking me to do!"

He pushed away from her, holding her shoulders in a grip too tight. He shook his head, his upper lip twitching in a snarl with his fierce attempt to master himself. Master this moment.

"There," he panted, looking down at her with wild eyes, his voice filled with tortured humor. "You once asked me if you'd succeeded in making me your slave. Well, be satisfied with this: You've brought me to my knees. But don't ask more. I *cannot* do this. Don't ask it of me."

She stared up at him, her mouth alive and lush from his kiss, her body tingling with craving. She would die if he left her in this state. She had to find some means to convince him to forgo his honor, his sense of right and wrong, his obligation to her father's memory.

"Am I to abandon our plan then? Or find another who will accommodate me? I will. I vow it. You once told me you would do anything, risk anything, to achieve your goal. Credit me with the same resolve. I will not give up now, so close to the goal."

"It might not even work!" he ground out. "You might lose everything, give away everything, even the right to experience this first time with someone you love, all for *nothing*. Don't you understand? There has never been more than a chance for this to succeed."

"It's a chance I must take," she said. "*We* must take. Because it's the only one we have."

"No."

She pulled away from him, rising shakily to her feet and he thought she would go then, leaving him to search for what scraps of peace he might find in this night. But she did not. She moved down the hallway to the table and jerked a yellow rose from the vase. Like a battle-dazed soldier, she returned to where he remained on his knees. Her eyes shimmered. The rose trembled in her hand.

"No."

"You said anything." She dropped the rose at his knees. "Make love to me."

A shudder coursed through his body and then he was surging upright, scooping her up into his arms, his face set. With a sound of joy, she linked her arms around his neck, settling her head against his chest. The heavy drum of his heart pounded thickly with each measured rise and fall of his breast. Beneath the damp material his skin was hot.

He strode down the hall and climbed the darkened stairs, finding her room at the top and backing through the doorway. Her lamp, lit as she prepared for the evening, cast a nimbus of light across the pristine counterpane that covered her bed.

Carefully, he laid her down on it, easing her shoulders against the soft pillows before releasing her and sitting down beside her hip. He leaned over her, bracing his hands on either side of her face. His gaze roved hungrily over her features. "You have created for me a brighter hell than any I could imagine."

She held up her arms.

All reason, all resolution, all the years dedicated to a single purpose, died at the sight of her, washed away by the implicit honesty of that gesture. Beneath him, in the shadow he cast over her, her silky flesh glowed amidst the tumbled gauze of her gown. The flickering light made a lustrous firebrand of her reddish curls. Her eyes glittered, gold shot umber, lambent, unshadowed by question, bright with anticipation. He could not move away from her. He could not force his will to make him act.

"I thought I was lost before," he breathed. "But you have wholly undone me."

He bent, his lips grazing the soft scented flesh swelling above the low neckline. Shudders of pleasure rippled through him, disarming him with the overwhelming tenderness of his response.

Her eyelids fluttered closed and he moved up, tasting her, his tongue sweeping against her lower lip, dipping into the corner of her mouth. Her breath checked. He abandoned her lips, his mouth drifting over the point of her chin and down to the graceful column of her neck. It arched in welcome for him. For *him*. Intoxicating. A delirium of fantasies come true.

He could feel her pulse fluttering at the base of her throat and set the edge of his teeth against that vulnerability. It would be so easy to hurt her. She was so fragile. Then why did he feel like the one in imminent danger?

Her gown was damp from where it had pressed against him, making the material nearly transparent and revealing the deep rose colored nipples beneath. He brushed aside the filmy material, revealing her naked breast. She stilled and he lowered his head, nipping the lush under-curve.

"Oh . . . my!" Her hand trembled against his spine. The breathy pitch of her response caught at his heart, twisted it anew, but he did not stop. It was far too late to stop. He captured the hand fluttering so tentatively—whether on the brink of rejection or welcome he would not test—and trapped it beside her thigh. He touched his tongue against the crest of her breast. She flinched, shocked by the intimacy.

With his free hand he outlined the curve of her opposite shoulder, skimmed over the diaphanous material still covering her, down the narrow rib cage to the womanly dip of her waist and the flare of hip, along the tensed thigh to her knee. There, he pulled up the material of her gown, dragging the hem higher and higher until his knuckles brushed the satiny hollow behind her knee.

With an expertise he did not know he possessed, he untied the little satin ribbons of her stockings and with the palm of his hand rode down the perfect curve of her calf, rolling the stocking to her ankle. When he reached her foot, he pulled it off and let it drift to the floor before serving the other leg to similar treatment. Then he bent her leg at the knee, urging her to let her legs fall open for him.

She did, though the hand he still held captive fisted into a little ball of tension, and the eyes she turned to him were apprehensive and eager and wary.

He felt himself grow hotter, harder, the imperative to do as she'd asked swelling him. His body was rigid and graceless, unwieldy when he wanted to move with her effortlessly in a dance as old as time.

"Let me go," she whispered.

That was it, then. He couldn't refuse her, even though he longed to caress her, to take her, to play with her body, to get drunk on all that sweet femininity, become tangled in her arms, in her glossy curls, in the snare of scented silky flesh and smooth, tapered limbs. He straightened and released her wrist.

Her fingers rose as hesitantly as smoke in a still room, finally settling on the side of his face. She traced the crescent-shaped scar beside his mouth. "I won't leave. You do not have to force me to stay by holding me captive. I am captive without constraints. Don't you see? I want *you* to make love to me, Dand. *You.*"

"Oh, Lottie." It was all he could say. Roughly he hauled her up into his embrace, bruising her with a kiss, his hands plunging into her thick hair, rocking her, desperate and aching for what she could give him. He turned, rolling onto his back and pulling her down on top of him, taking her weight so that she lay fully on him. He spread his hand low on her back, his other hand cupping the back of her head as his mouth plundered hers.

He shifted, turning, moving her beneath him, seeking between their bodies for the edge of her gown, yanking it away from separating them and—! Lord. Skin like butterfly wings, tender with a powdery sort of silkiness and higher, crisp curls and softer flesh yet. He settled his hips into that perfect lee, his erection pushing between her legs, gasping with the exquisite sensation.

A fever was rising in him, the need to take her almost unbearable in its urgency. He gripped her shoulders, using his lips to burnish her temples and eyelids, cheek and neck, the lobe of her ears and the point of her chin, before recapturing her mouth, feasting on the little sounds she made. All his best intentions for gentleness dissolved before need, as he pulled at the gown's neckline and heard the hiss of ripping seams as he bared her to the waist. The dim light revealed her breasts, soft little rose-tipped mounds.

He slipped his arm beneath her waist, pulling her up toward him, drawing a nipple into his mouth, his tongue flat against it. Exquisite pain pooled in his groin. He molded her to him, rocking into the jointure of her thighs and heard her make a sweet sound of pleasure and fear. Benediction? Or curse? God, he could not tell anymore. It was muddled and jumbled, a black moonless night, unnavigable and empty of answers.

"Want me," he muttered roughly, licking her breast. "Desire me."

She answered as if his words had been the permission she'd waited to hear. She tore at his shirt, dragging it from his shoulders, the sound of buttons popping and skittering across the floor. With unerring deviltry, her fingers found the cursed scar on his chest. He felt the instant she recoiled, the second that passion fell before realization. With a growl, he heeled back, letting the light wash over his chest, letting her see how he'd been branded. He waited.

Charlotte had never seen anything so blatantly male. His body was so beautiful, so perfectly knit, strong and healthy. Long bulging muscles crafted the arms holding him suspended above her. His broad shoulders tapered down his rib cage, his chest carved of planes and shelves covered with dark hair that thickened in a vee, growing denser as it traveled in a line down his belly to disappear beneath the waist of his trousers.

The sight stirred the embers of her desire, painfully renewing the ache that built beneath the unfamiliar bulge pressed intimately between her legs. Need throbbed low in her belly, in her breasts, in her lips, causing a tenderness that only roughness could cure.

She knew she should be scrambling to cover herself, but all she could think was that she wanted to feel him, press her bare breasts to the hard contours of his chest. There . . . against the infamous rose brand, a pearly raised scar the size of her palm. How much it must have hurt! How much he had suffered!

She pushed herself up on her elbows and slowly, purposefully, brushed her lips against the angry scar. His chest swelled on a harsh, indrawn breath. She kissed him again, gently. His skin was hot, moist, the flesh fine-grained over the dense muscle beneath. Desire grew and held her imagination captive. Bold and lascivious thoughts skittered through her mind. Desires for things she hadn't names for, places she wanted to touch that she could not identify with words, feelings he roused in her that she wanted to rouse in him.

A man's body, she thought wonderingly, was fantastically graceful and unbelievably sensitive. She had only to blow lightly across his throat to send tremors coursing through him, only to give the lightest nip at the base of his neck for him to squeeze his eyes shut and breathe heavily through his nostrils, only to set her tongue delicately in the corner of his mouth to—

He swept her arms from under her, forcing her down into the pillows, his face taut, his eyes burning. He reached between them, pushing her legs apart, and he was there, between her legs, a thick, hard shape pushing into the most intimate softness of her body.

She stared up at him, suddenly apprehensive, her fingers digging into his shoulders. He looked so foreign to her, so hard and angry, nothing like the companionable rascal who'd teased and taunted her. He looked . . . like a man in extremity, holding on by the smallest of margins.

With a sound of capitulation, he fell forward, his face fitting into the curve of her neck, his breath harsh and heated in her ear, his hand diving beneath her hips and spreading under her buttocks, lifting her. Then . . . he was coming *into* her, pushing *inside* of her, and he was thick and large, *too* large, stretching her as he slowly thrust a portion of his body into hers. The intimacy of it shocked her more than the discomfort. She twisted, trying to pull back from the intrusion. This could not be the end promised by all those mounting tensions and flickers of deep, deep pleasure? Not this.

He would not let her go. He pulled up, bracing himself on his arms, his hips still canting forward, staring down at her through half-closed lids, his eyes black and unreadable, his jaw tight as he pushed until he'd hilted himself fully within her, buried to the root. She dared not move lest the discomfort grow, and waited anxiously, feeling betrayed by her sisters, by Ginny, and by her body, which had gone from aching anticipation to tense suspension.

He swallowed, his breathing staggered, his face covered with a fine sheen.

"Dand . . . ? "

"Yes." His breathing was like a bellows now and his torso and arms and face glistened in the low light. His gaze was hard, as penetrating as his body, just as implacable. "Yes. My God, Charlotte. You are so small. So tight."

Closing his eyes he rocked slowly against her. With him so deep inside of her, the movement pulled at her most intimate parts, tickling to life a nascent sensitivity. He retreated from her body, just a matter of a few inches, but the movement tugged against some central bud where pleasure dwelled, drawing from her the most extraordinary desire to arch against him. Pleasure pulsed at his slow reentry, the stimulation he provided quickened with his next thrust and became desire at the next.

Her muscles tightened. There was more. Her body instinctively knew it, sought it. Without knowledge, without expertise, she could only follow what instinct dictated. She wanted, she needed. He could provide.

He was too far away, braced over her on arms whose muscles quivered with each thrust. She slipped her arms around his rib cage pulling him down over her, making him look at her, his weight a welcome stimuli, vital and virile and masterful. He caught her knees and pulled her legs up over his hips. Again and again, faster, deeper, his body hard with strain, he thrust into her and with each hard penetration she heard her answering gasps and barely recognized them as her own.

Her world was reeling, each stroke of his body intensifying the liquid spiral of pleasure coiling tighter inside of her, bringing her nearer to the unexplored moment of crisis, of perfect pleasure, the culmination of desire. Exquisite. Torturous in the building anticipation. She clung to him, seeking an anchor against the careening whirlpool of sensation. She couldn't see, couldn't think, could not hear anything other than her staccato pants, his savage breathing as he took her harder, deeper. It was there . . . just out of reach . . . taunting . . . teasing . . . needing only . . .

Yes! Her body bowed, arching, straining in grateful welcome. *Yes!* Pleasure exploded like gunpowder, brilliant, shocking, and powerful. *Yes!* Tears ran down her cheeks. Laughter bubbled up in her throat. *Yes!*

Even as the astonished laughter tripped from her lips, Dand rocked back and once more came into her, his head thrown back as he breathed a shuddering sound like a prayer. He held there for one long eternity, every inch of his beautiful body shivering. And then he was sinking down, rolling to her side, catching her and folding her against him.

And while he held her and exhaustion seeped into her limbs and pleasure drugged her mind, she could not help but be glad that he did not let her go, but held her as tenderly and fiercely now as when they had moved as one and said nothing of leaving her. And so she let her thoughts drift and for one short space, pretended there would be no tomorrow.

The rain had stopped by the time Charlotte awoke, her cheek resting on the warm dense musculature of Dand's chest, his arm, heavy with sleep, wrapped about her. For a few seconds she held her breath and let herself believe that this was only the first morning of many more exactly like it, that the passion they had roused themselves to share again and again during the long and turbulent night would be repeated again, day after day, week after week, across many seasons, and through the course of many years. It was easy to do in the predawn darkness with the scent of their lovemaking still hanging heavy in the air and his body closely entwined with hers.

But then she heard the sound of heavy wheels passing on the street below her window. A bird trilled from somewhere far away and she knew that morning would not be far off.

Dand must leave before then.

She closed her eyes, rubbing her cheek against his chest.

"Lottie." He pulled her closer and she wondered how long he had been awake, how many minutes they might have shared that she'd wasted in sleep. Too late now. Far too late.

"My maid will come to me soon," she said. "You must be gone by then or the Polite World will next decide that we have reconciled."

"Put St. Lyon off for a few days," he said, his voice grim. "I just need a few days more. Say you haven't the right clothes, you need to make arrangements—"

"Dand, we haven't time. You know it as well as I. The auction could begin at any moment. I need to be there before the letter leaves Scotland with a new owner."

"A few days more—"

"May spell disaster." She rose up on her elbows, balancing her forearms on his hard belly, her fingertips resting over his heart. "Dand. I have to go."

She saw the shadows move across his face, a pale glint as if he'd bared his teeth. From deep in the house she heard a door shut. The tweenie going to clean and light the grates.

"You have to leave, Dand. Please. We can't risk St. Lyon hearing of this."

"To hell with St. Lyon." With a growl, he rolled her beneath him and with unerring aim found her mouth in a hard, desperate kiss. She responded in kind, desperate to entangle herself with the very fabric of his being, only . . . The dawn was here. Obligation and responsibility jeered at her, poisoning her pleasure until she finally broke away.

"Please," she whispered, wanting more than anything for him to stay, to make love to her again, to never leave, to never know of wars and the letters that could change the course of them. "Please."

He lifted his head. "I'll go. I'll think of something. And I'll be back this afternoon."

"When?"

"Three o'clock. Four at the latest."

"It better be afterward. Six o'clock. I'll let the staff go again."

"Six it is."

He moved away and she felt the bed dip as he sat up and groped for the clothing she'd helped him shed in their eagerness and haste. She watched him in silence as he stood up and could not help but admire the tensile strength of his silhouette, the broad shoulders tapering to the trim hips and long, muscled thighs and calves. He pulled on his clothing and looked down at her.

"You've utterly destroyed my intentions, you know," he mused quietly. She could not guess his meaning. "But I swear if there is any way in heaven or hell to do so, I'll make this all come right. Watch for me this evening, Lottie."

"Yes."

He started to go but then, as if proof against a terrible foreboding, swung back around, dipping low and lifting her up to meet his questing lips. She answered him with more passion than she'd intended, wrapping her arms around his neck and kissing him back with all the hopeless longing in her heart. Finally, he released her and eased her down, with almost courtly care, tucked the cotton sheet about her before straightening.

"Until evening," he murmured and like a ghost dissolved into the lightening gloom, only the quiet catch of the doorway leading into the still black hall alerting her to the fact that he had indeed gone.

And only then did she allow herself to reply, as tears overflowed her lids and ran down her cheeks. "Goodbye," she whispered.

17

◇◇◇◇

THEY COULDN'T SEE *the sky, but the weather always had a way of finding even the deepest pits of the LeMons castle dungeon. In the winter the cold whistled down the shafts and stairwells numbing fingers and toes: in the summer, the darkness baked with a humid fetidness. And now, in spring, the rain seeped down the mold-blackened dungeon walls, pooling on the uneven flooring.*

Dand squatted next to the wall, his head lolling forward, his back pressed against the damp stone. They'd taken Douglas away early yesterday, before dawn. Kit had been returned at the same time, staggering in, clutching a blood-soaked rag over that hideous disfiguring brand. A rose, he'd gasped, grimacing as Ram had swabbed the burned tissue with a bit of brandy he'd bribed from one of the guards.

Anytime now and they would come back and then they would take either him or Ram. And question them as they had Kit.

They'd asked him who had aided them on their journey, whom they had contacted at Malmaison, which of Napoleon's guards were loyal and which secret Royalists. Kit hadn't told them, of course. When Kit had refused to tell them, the warden had decided to exert more pressure by burning a rose into Kit's chest.

Little did the warden know how ironic his torture had proved. They had come to France masquerading as Scottish sympathizers, ostensibly bringing Napoleon's wife Josephine a rare new rose for her collection. In reality they were to meet co-conspirators at her home, Malmaison. But they'd been found out. As a symbol of their treachery, the warden had fashioned an iron brand in the shape of a stylized rose.

How fitting that Douglas's precious brotherhood be forever marked with the symbol of their fidelity.

Dand glanced at Ram, standing a short distance off, somehow even in these squalid pits managing to emit an elegant detachment. Beside him stood Kit looking grim and exhausted, shadows carving diabolical angles in his gaunt face. If they lost too much more weight, they'd all end up looking like gargoyles, unfit for anything but scaring children.

He closed his eyes. There were more important things than personal honor. Ram understood. Kit, too. But he never had been able to make Douglas see past his childish notions of chivalry. The poor bastard really did think they were knights and this a glorious crusade. Some glory. All that was wanted was—

The sound of feet and chains dragging over rock roused him.

The barred door swung open and Douglas came in moving very carefully, uncertain of his strength. His face was blanched and stark, his eyes blinking rapidly, unseeing, his *lips moving in trembling little fits and starts. His startled gaze fell on Dand, as if he hadn't expected to see him there. He gasped and held out his hand.*

Dand struggled to his feet.

Douglas's shirt did not conceal the thick, bloodied pad on his left breast. "I . . . I wasn't . . ." His hand shook with a terrible palsy as he spoke and his face contorted. "Please. You have to know that I couldn't . . . I did not . . ."

"I know," Dand rasped, sickened. "You did not break faith. I am sure you were entirely noble, my friend. True to the end. No one would ever doubt it—"

"Time to pay the warden a little visit, monsieur," the guard who had led Douglas back to the cell announced dolefully.

"Yes," Dand said. "I expect it is."

Culholland Square, Mayfair
August 4, 1806

"What do you mean, she's gone?"

Handsome and fit as a young Greek god, Curtis was also no fool. For all his picturesque athleticism he recognized that he was no match for the angry man facing him across the threshold. The first bloody streaks of twilight pricked Monsieur Rousse's amber eyes with a devilish glow, causing the young footman to back up a step.

"She left early this morning, sir," he gulped. "A carriage came and the driver loaded her luggage—"

"Luggage?" Monsieur Rousse leapt on the word.

"Yes, sir. A great pile of luggage." Curtis glanced worriedly around at the nearby residences. So far he didn't see any interested maids looking through their sidelights, nor had any passersby paused to see what new disaster their unwanted neighbor had visited on their once respectable enclave.

Curtis liked Miss Nash. He would not want to see her prey to even greater scandal than she already was and this man, despite his hitherto easygoing nature, had been the instrument of her downfall. That he had the nerve to look as if he had every right to be here, demanding to know where she was and with whom, almost made Curtis want to test his mettle. Almost.

Instead, he asked, "Won't you come in, sir? Perhaps one of the maids knows more than I."

"Yes." Monsieur Rousse strode through the door as Curtis stood aside. "Fetch the maid Lizette."

"I am sorry, sir. I cannot. Lizette is accompanying Miss Nash."

The Frenchman froze. His face grew very still, very calm. His composure alarmed Curtis even more than his former anger. It was the eyes, Curtis thought, trying not to meet that black gaze. Humor, fierce black humor with the promise of violence, blossomed in their dark depths.

"So she lied," he said, his lips twisting in a terrible smile.

He swung around and descended the steps in a single bound, striding down the street with his greatcoat billowing behind him as his parting words were caught by the wind and sent back to the footman. "Who would have guessed it of the adorable little minx?"

And Curtis thought he had never heard foul language sound so damning as Rousse's endearment.

She had lain in his arms, let him drink the sounds of passion from her lips, shared her body with him over and over again during the course of one night seared more deeply in his soul than the brand marking his chest. And all the while she had been lying, knowing that she would be leaving, going to St. Lyon in the morning. Knowing that when he came back for her he would find her house empty, as she must have known he would because, by God, they had made love, and a lover did not relinquish his adored to another, and he was that lover. *By God*, he should be proud of the wench, she had read him so very, very well.

That had been yesterday morning, barely twenty-four hours ago. He had accomplished much in that short time, but not nearly enough. Not yet.

Well, darling, my dearest, he thought with a terrible smile as the hired hack careered through the streets, *as expertly as you played me, you do not know quite everything about me. I might yet surprise you.*

The carriage slowed as it threaded its way into the dockyards, where workers loaded and unloaded the sloops and merchant vessels still transporting cargo and sailors spilled from the subterranean doors of gin shops and taverns, taking their fill of pleasure before boarding ships or celebrating having survived another dangerous voyage. They were all dangerous journeys, these days.

The embargos and blockades Napoleon had set against England had slowed the traffic in and out of the London docks, but there were still captains with confidence in the fleetness of their ships and their own formidable seafaring skills willing to risk unfriendly waters for the right price, or the right prize. It was with one such man Dand Ross had arranged a meeting.

There was still much to consider. His plans were collapsing. Unless his network of colleagues was informed of his new strategy, things could take a terrible turn. There were important messages to be composed and sent, agreements to be reached, and all must be accomplished by the time the tide went out and he left.

With a sound of impatience, he banged on the hack ceiling, calling for the driver to halt. He opened the door and swung to the ground before the carriage had stopped. He tossed the driver his fare and in the same motion gestured at one of the linkboys that hung about the taverns looking to run errands.

"Which one is the *Mudlark*?" he asked.

The boy pointed at a small sloop with freshly painted black sides. A pair of sailors were rubbing the sheen from the paint with handfuls of sand. A wise captain, Dand thought appreciatively, did not chance the moon's light bestowing a bright kiss on his helm.

He reached into his pocket and withdrew a thick envelope. He stared at it, wavering, fighting the impetus that thundered for his attention.

He did not want this. He did not need this. He had vital matters to attend to.

When all was said and done, when images of Charlotte spent with passion, or tense and arching as he pushed into her, or wide-eyed with surprised pleasure, or drugged with postcoital lethargy filled his mind and the scent of her still clinging to his body conspired to ensnare his reason and ambush his intent, there was still the past to be reckoned with, still enemies to be found, still a place to be reclaimed in the world.

Still an old debt to pay.

He handed the letter to the boy with a few quick instructions. Then he pressed a shiny coin into the lad's grimy paw and a hissed a grim threat into a filthy little ear, because he knew boys. He knew what treachery they were capable of, and he knew exactly what words to say to make them pay attention. The boy gulped and bobbed his head emphatically, and Dand Ross headed down the gangplank toward the *Mudlark*.

18

∞∞∞

The Great North Road and Scotland
August 4 to August 9, 1806

THE JOURNEY NORTH to St. Lyon's Scottish castle was long and tedious, despite the luxurious appointments of the chaise St. Lyon had sent. Charlotte was miserable. Only the intermittent distraction provided by her maid made the trip endurable. As for Lizette, she seemed perfectly content with their situation, flirting with the muscular young outriders St. Lyon had hired to protect them from highwaymen, or chattering blithely on without stop when she wasn't.

The soft padded leather seats and tasseled velvet curtains at the windows evidently impressed the luxury-loving maid. She took full advantage of the little tufted footrests, the down-filled pillows, and cashmere lap rugs. Charlotte could almost hear Lizette's thoughts, they were so clearly reflected in her content expression: If this was coming down in the world, then a fall from grace might not be altogether undesirable.

Under normal circumstances, Charlotte would have found her maid's pragmatism amusing, but now, here, she was too preoccupied to pay much heed to Lizette. And when eventually Lizette realized Charlotte was attending very little of what she said, she demonstrated a truly wonderful ability to sleep under almost any conditions, leaving Charlotte alone with her thoughts. And uncomfortable ones they were, too . . .

The thing was . . . she could not stop *remembering*. The night she had shared with Dand filled her mind and played havoc with her resolve. She told herself that by leaving without telling him her intentions she had not so much deceived Dand as spared them both a difficult good-bye. Her stubborn heart would not believe it.

She stared out the window at the passing scenery, but each mile only led her further into a maze of self-doubt. How had he felt when he returned that evening to find her gone? But then, what would he have done had she told him that St. Lyon's carriage would take her the next morning rather than a day later? What did she expect of him?

That he would demand she marry him and to hell with St. Lyon, the letter, and all of Great Britain? *Dand?* He'd held true to his course through torture, betrayal, changing fortunes, and great personal loss. Why would he change now? Because he'd taken her maidenhead? She allowed herself a small, sad smile. He hadn't said he loved her.

Aye, he'd adored her with his body and that most eloquently. So eloquently, in fact, that she could not believe he did not feel *something* for her, something more than desire. But then, what did she know of lovemaking? she asked herself. Perhaps it was always so.

But she did not believe that, either. And she clung stubbornly to her belief that a man and a woman could not share such potent pleasure without the emotions, *both* of their emotions, being engaged. Because if she had told him she was leaving for St. Lyon's castle within a few hours and he had done nothing to prevent it or at the very least try to persuade her not to, her heart would have broken. No, far better not to test his feelings for her. At least this way she could believe what she wanted, what she *needed* to believe.

Even if Dand had consigned the rest of the world to the devil for love of her, could she really purchase her happiness with the blood of young soldiers? She feared, greatly feared, that she could and this, more than anything else, convinced her that she must do this thing, alone, while she still had the . . . the *guts*. So that if the final die was cast and no other choice presented itself, she would become St. Lyon's mistress.

Such were the thoughts that pursued Charlotte in ever-tightening circles of joy and despair, growing impatient as one day unfolded into the next. By the fifth day Charlotte was cursing St. Lyon's tender regard for her comfort. If she had been a budding Cyprian, she would have probably appreciated his care. But though she promised the driver there would be no retribution should he dispense with their leisurely gait and move more swiftly, the grizzled old Frenchman remained obstinately determined to abide by his master's wishes that the journey not tax the lady's strength. So they plodded along, starting late and stopping early at the coaching inns St. Lyon had decided were suitable as with each mile Charlotte grew more tense.

As they traveled, the landscape gradually became as bleak as her thoughts. The cultivated fields awash with summer green that surrounded London became a rolling countryside patchworked with orchards and fieldstone fences. These gave way to the moors where the land grew steadily rougher, the inclines steeper, and the sky bent closer. Pine replaced maple and birch, and hay fields gave way to high flower-spangled meadows and finally slate-covered tors naked except for a thin blanket of gray-green gorse and wine-tinted bracken. The towns grew farther apart and smaller, too, the houses more tightly clustered, as though to present a united front against the vastness beyond their borders.

Finally, near noon of the sixth day, the carriage left the main road and followed a rutted lane up a low, bare hill. There, the driver stopped and called for her to enjoy the prospect. Eagerly, both Charlotte and Lizette poked their heads out of the windows. Lizette sucked in a breath of dismay. Charlotte empathized. She imagined Lizette thinking that "falling" was not so desirable after all, if one was forced to live in a place like this. So remote. So stark. So unattractive.

A mile away in the center of a broad valley stood St. Lyon's castle. It rose straight up from the sheer side of a rocky shelf overlooking a broad, fast-moving river. Even from here she could appreciate the massive weight of the castle, the thick vines swarming the base of steel-colored stone. Narrow windows punctuated only the most upper stories. Nothing short of a catapult would breech those walls and the only egress Charlotte could see was a steeply pitched drive that led up to a massive wooden gate guarded by twin towers.

A fortress indeed. Charlotte sat back in the carriage and the driver clucked to the horses. No way in without the permission of the owner and no way out but by the same means. The open moors that surrounded the castle provided no place for concealment. The only bridge within sight spanned the river directly opposite the castle and thus within full view of the windows looking down from the very top of the crenulated guard towers. Around these twin towers the ivy crawled thicker and more abundantly, their leafy fingers almost reaching the dark casements.

They drove across the bridge and up the steep drive to the massive gates, which swung open at their arrival. Once inside, amazingly, magnificently, the forbidding aspect disappeared in the interior courtyard. Rather than the bleak cobbled quadrant of most castles, St. Lyon had developed inside a charming garden. Yew hedges clipped in fanciful shapes clustered in the corners while beds of blue and white flowers—the colors of the Bourbon kings, Charlotte realized—lined the well-raked gravel drive. In the center a marble fountain splashed amid a tangle of ivy and waiting beside this, his aquiline face relaxed into a welcoming expression, stood Maurice, Comte St. Lyon. Her soon-to-be lover.

Charlotte studied him thoughtfully. He was handsome if one preferred black curls over chestnut brown hair, or heavy Gallic features over square masculine ones, or a slender athleticism over a rangy grace. Or a wet-lipped mouth over a mouth as firm and masterful as its owner's hands were. Which she didn't.

She dug her nails deeply into the tender flesh of her palms, fighting a sudden surge of panic. St. Lyon must not suspect that she had come for any reason other than to inspect him as her potential protector. He must believe that she had no other designs on him and certainly no other reason for being here. The driver pulled the carriage to a halt and scrambled down to pull open the door and retrieve the block from inside.

Her foot had barely touched the step before St. Lyon was by her side, taking her gloved hand and assisting her to alight. Once she had emerged, he did not relinquish her hand but instead stepped back, his gaze sweeping over her from dusty kid shoes to what she feared was a sadly crumpled gown and wilted little bonnet.

Drat! A woman in search of a new lover would have stopped en route to repair her looks. She met his assessing gaze with a raised brow and a merry smile.

"I could not abide the thought of spending a moment in some rattletrap hovel when I knew a much more convivial greeting awaited me here, St. Lyon. I hope I do not disappoint you too much?"

His dark face lit appreciatively. "How could a lady as delightful as yourself disappoint anyone, Miss Nash?"

"As well spoken as ever, Comte." She dimpled in a

manner she had once overheard a gentleman describe as delectable.

St. Lyon's hand tightened perceptibly before he released hers. "Let me express my unmitigated delight in welcoming you to my abode."

"Your pleasure in receiving me can be no greater than mine at having arrived, I assure you," she said, twinkling for all she was worth.

"You are, as ever, deliciously candid." He looked beyond her shoulder to where Lizette was being handed out of the carriage by a strapping footman. "Ah, you have brought your maid. I am, for your sake, most glad. The servants here are not used to tending a lady."

He was overdoing it, Charlotte thought, though she continued to smile. All these references to assure her that in his eyes, if not the world's, she still deserved the title "lady." He bowed and stepped aside, ushering her forward. "I will have my housekeeper, Madame Paule, show you to your rooms and then, perhaps you will do me the honor of joining me in my salon prior to dining?"

Already a closeted conversation? Through a sheer act of will she kept the lightness in her voice and a smile on her lips. "And what time would that be, Comte?"

"We dine at nine o'clock. Shall I have a footman come for you at, say, eight-thirty?"

"That will be fine," she answered and nodded for Lizette.

He motioned toward the staff standing behind them, a quartet of footmen and a small, compactly made woman with a dark, almost masculine, face. She stepped forward and bobbed a quick curtsy, murmuring, "If you will follow me, ma'am?" before leading Charlotte and Lizette through an open doorway into the castle.

Inside, the impression that St. Lyon had transported a fashionable St. James mansion into the wilds of the Scottish Highlands continued. Though only a few high windows allowed in the afternoon sun, no expense had been spared in filling the great hall with light. Candles and lamps, sconces and mirrors lit even the darkest corner, setting to glow the gilt frames of the massive paintings that lined the freshly plastered walls, glinting in the silver candelabras and urns overflowing with exotic hothouse-raised fruits and flowers and adding luster to the exotic silk tapestries covering the walls. Beneath her feet, a thick Oriental carpet muted the sound of her heels as she followed the housekeeper toward the great staircase rising before them.

Silently, Madame Paule led them upstairs. At the top, they followed the minstrel's gallery that overlooked the great hall to its far end and turned, entering a corridor. Tall windows overlooking the moors pierced the left wall while the right wall contained an equal number of closed doors. The housekeeper continued to the end where she stopped and, pushing open a door on noiseless hinges, stepped aside to allow Charlotte to pass ahead of her.

It was a western room, and as such filled with soft afternoon light that set the crimson damask-clad walls glowing. Vases the height of a child filled with towering peacock feathers and gilt palm fronds flanked the cen-

tral panel of windows. Sumptuous, Charlotte thought.
One might even say decadent.

A gold-filigreed black marble mantle dressed the
fireplace next to an old-fashioned bed raised on a dais,
the heavy crimson velvet curtains surrounding it embroidered with stylized hinds and hares in gold and
royal blue. Dozens of soft pillows crowded the head of
the bed and lay invitingly on a divan covered in royal
blue brocade. A large ebony table inlaid with mother of
pearl filled the near corner, its surface overflowing with
crystal perfume bottles, jars of salves and creams, pots
of delicately dried petals and powders, and a full set of
ivory-backed brushes and combs.

It was all exquisite, lush, and impressive, but most
impressive of all was the enormous gilt mirror that
hung directly opposite the foot of the bed, the huge
surface reflecting back most of the room.

"Here is everything you might want." Madame
Paule crossed the room and indicated a gold-tasseled
silk rope. "And here is a bellpull should you need
more."

Curiously, Charlotte went to the window and looked
out. Far below the river ran sparkling and swift, disappearing into a copse of trees some distance off.

"Now I must return to my duties," Madame Paule
said. "The castle is full of guests. Gaspard will have
your luggage up directly. If there is nothing more you
require, ma'am?"

Lizette, who had puffed herself up at the Frenchwoman's subtly dismissive tones, answered. "Yes.

Mademoiselle requires a bath. A *hot* bath. And a fire. At once."

Madame Paule nodded politely though her raisin dark eyes held a touch of animosity. "But of course. I will have it seen to at once. And—"

"And where am I to sleep?" Lizette interrupted. "I don't see a closet for me."

"No, *miss*," Madame Paule said, a little purr entering her voice. "You have rooms above stairs. With the rest of the servants."

Poor Lizette. There was nothing Charlotte could do for her. How so, when there was nothing she could do for herself? The reason this bedchamber had no separate alcove for a servant was abundantly clear; a maid might interfere with late-night visits.

"Oh?" Lizette sniffed, but her cheeks looked a little rosier than usual. "Fine. You may show me later. *After* I have seen to *Mademoiselle* Nash's needs."

"Of course." The Frenchwoman inclined her head. "Your bath shall be sent up directly. And I shall have one of the footmen escort you to the dining hall," her gaze flickered toward Lizette, "and you to your bed, at half past eight. If this is convenient?"

"Yes," Charlotte answered and wished it was.

19

∞∞∞

IT WASN'T UNTIL LIZETTE STOOD BACK to admire her handiwork that the full impact of the gown Charlotte wore, with its extremely low décolletage and semitransparent material, hit the maid, rendering her momentarily speechless.

"Well?" Charlotte asked worriedly.

"You look . . . extremely . . . That is, you are . . . That gown is amazing," Lizette finally managed.

Silently, she handed Charlotte the ivory-backed mirror, a completely unnecessary courtesy. Charlotte couldn't have avoided her reflected image had she wanted to, not with that great monster of a mirror taking up half the wall. She took a little breath and turned, meeting her reflected gaze. Her eyes widened. Lizette was right, she did look amazing: amazingly brazen. Amazingly decadent. Amazingly provocative. But most of all, amazingly available.

The nearly translucent green silk fell in shimmering folds from just below the bodice hugging the very crest of her bosom, the merest scrap of satin figured over with little shimmering beads that winked in the light and caught the bullion gleams in her hazel eyes. Like moss swept by the current of a brook, the silky material slithered down her torso, revealing more than concealing the pale figure beneath. It was a courtesan's gown, Ginny's gown, quickly remade to fit Charlotte, a gown designed to entice and incite.

Charlotte's gaze traveled to her reflected face, to the glistening pink lips and soft powdered blush staining the apples of her cheeks and then to the hair threaded with a bronze ribbon that escaped to trail provocatively down the nape of her neck. Not a whit of jewelry marred the smooth expanse of her throat, collarbone, or bosom. The only other garments she wore were the long, skintight gloves that covered her from fingertip to just past the crook of her arm. The combination of nearly naked breasts and primly covered palm, wrist, and forearm was especially provocative. As Ginny had said it would be.

A discreet knock sounded on the door. She started and looked at the mantle clock. Eight-thirty. Her knees began to shake.

"I can't," she whispered. She was a coward after all.

"Ma'am?" Lizette asked, her little face puckered with confusion.

She wasn't ready. Not now, not yet. She had to put St. Lyon off, just for the night. Just one more night to accustom herself to the idea.

"I can't . . . See to the footman, Lizette. Tell him I'm

not ready. Tell him to wait. I . . . I don't like this ribbon in my hair. I prefer a feather. Or flowers."

Lizette blinked in confusion but went readily enough to the door and stepped into the hallway. Charlotte heard the sound of voices, the words, "a lady's prerogative" and "a while yet" before her maid returned, closing the door behind her. Relief swept through her.

"Sit down, Miss Charlotte. I'll make quick work of it."

"No!" Charlotte snapped, then, more quietly, "No, Lizette. You must take your time. I must eradicate the memory of my disheveled appearance when I arrived and supplant it with a far more attractive one."

She sat down on the divan.

This, Lizette understood. Like an artist who has been told to rework a masterpiece, she scowled and then, accepting the challenge, picked up a comb and brush. Twenty minutes later, having tried a black ostrich feather, a white ostrich feather, a rope of pearls, a tassel from the bed's curtain, and various ribbons, she finally smiled.

"There." She had clipped the tips from a dozen of the peacock feathers standing in the vases. These she had braided together with gold threads and woven cunningly through Charlotte's cinnamon-colored locks. The iridescent purples, greens, and bronzes winked and flirted with each turn of Charlotte's head.

"You're a genius, Lizette," Charlotte said, more thankful for the extra time than with the results of Lizette's labor, as stunning as they were. There would be no time now for a tête-à-tête with St. Lyon. She smiled, immensely revitalized by the postponement of her private meeting with him.

"Feel more the thing now, don't you, miss?" Lizette asked, nodding.

"Indeed, I do, Lizette," she answered.

The company gathered in the great hall waiting to go into dinner consisted of fifteen men and four women. The men had dressed as carefully as if they were attending Almack's Wednesday night ball while the women dressed not carefully at all but instead much in the same manner as Charlotte. In other words, like well-kept doxies. Charlotte wasted little time examining them, her attention surreptitiously fixed on St. Lyon. Would he be angry that she had already ignored his command?

He came forth as the footman announced her name, his hand stretched out in welcome, his gaze bright with appreciation. She had made a name for herself in London as being outré; fashionably, naughtily, irrepressibly—and thus forgivably—outré. She had stepped well beyond that distinction this evening.

"My dear, you are exquisite," he murmured as he raised her hands to his lips and brushed a kiss across her gloved knuckles. "But I am most sorry we did not have that little chat before dinner. And I fear you will be sor—"

"St. Lyon!" a peremptory voice interrupted whatever he had been about to say. St Lyon straightened as a powerful square of a man with a steel-colored frizz of hair chugged up to them. He was wearing some sort of military uniform with which Charlotte was unfamiliar. "I demand you introduce me to this magnificent lady at once."

"Of course, Your Grace." St. Lyon inclined his head. "May I present Miss Charlotte Nash? Miss Nash, Prince Rupreck Gulbran."

Charlotte sank into a low curtsy as the grizzled block beamed. She had no sooner rose than she was being introduced to a half dozen others, men with strange accents and diverse manners, amongst them a middle-aged nabob, a fiery Italian princeling, a plump, dew-lapped Austrian without title but the manner of a king, and a thin, elderly Spaniard with the eyes of a poet. The women did not approach her and St. Lyon made no attempt to bring them together. Nor, Charlotte noted, did they associate much with one another.

This must be the way of courtesans, Charlotte realized, never to be certain of their welcome, always wary of other women as their rivals. She frowned, trying to shake off the dark thought that this could well be her world henceforth when she heard St. Lyon saying in a measured voice, "And here, my dear, is someone with whom I believe you are already acquainted."

Puzzled, she turned around and found herself staring straight into Dand Ross's burning eyes.

"We meet again, Charlotte."

Her heart skittered in her throat and her lips parted with an involuntary welcome, a thrill of happiness suffusing her. But then she recalled herself, realizing where she was and by whom she stood, and a second later was glad she had not given away her feelings as the significance of Dand's presence hit her.

He had let her come here, prepared to become St. Lyon's mistress, without giving her the smallest hope that her sacrifice might not be necessary. He had lain with her, taken her maidenhead, and never told her that he had been granted entrée to St. Lyon's inner circle and could accomplish the task of searching for the letter himself, without her having to prostitute herself.

How long had he been planning this? Had he already found the damn letter? Was she completely redundant here?

A worse thought invaded her mind, torturous and poisonous and horrible. Perhaps this had always been his plan, to use her as a diversion while he searched. To sell her virginity for a few uninterrupted hours?

The thought broke like glass inside, cutting painfully, leaving her flushed and breathless.

"Cat got your tongue, Charlotte?" Dand asked sardonically. The French accent he'd utilized in London was more pronounced, more aristocratic. He'd dressed more somberly, too, though the cut of his coat was even more exquisite than Ram's purloined garments. His stocking was snowy and crisp, his cheeks and jaw shaved as smooth as marble.

He looked foreign, alien, and unfamiliar. The soft warmth she once found in his gaze no longer existed.

The genial expression and the relaxed smile were all gone. A stranger stood before her.

For the first time Charlotte realized how hard the angle of his jaw was, how firm and cruel his lips, how hooded his eyes. Always before, laughter and irony had masked the essential ruthlessness of that handsome face. No longer. She saw the will that directed the ready smile, his capacity for pitilessness, perhaps even cruelty. And the scar on his cheek? It had never been caused by his falling from a tree.

Ginny had been right. The man she'd taken to her bed had been feral. And hadn't he said himself that he would do whatever he deemed necessary to achieve his goal?

"Why is he here?" she heard herself demand and now Dand's lips finally formed a smile. There was nothing pleasant in it. The expression in his eyes promised dire things—as if he was the one who'd been wronged! But then, that was the role he'd assumed, the cast-off, embittered lover. How could she have forgotten? And how could she have forgotten what an accomplished actor he was?

"Monsieur Andre Rousse is an emissary for certain exalted ecclesiastical principals," St. Lyon replied, his watchful, slightly conciliatory manner making it abundantly clear that he knew the pair of them were reputed to have been lovers.

"I see." Her heart had begun pounding in her throat and her breath fell light and quick from her lips. How had he arrived here so quickly? How had he arranged an invitation? Ginny's male associates had tried every way imaginable of securing a means into this gathering, but those attending had been closely vetted and their credentials well documented.

The evidence mounted that he had planned this all for a long time, well before she had sent for him to come to her bed. He'd used her. Just as she'd used him to rid herself of her virginity—at least, just as he *thought* she'd used him. She was ridiculously grateful for having maintained that lie.

Whatever her feelings for Dand, at least she had kept some scraps of her pride intact by keeping them from him. As far as he was concerned, they were both here for the same purpose—both of them coldly and calculatingly going about the business of spying, undeterred by sentiment and unmoved by frail emotion.

So it would be. So she would be. A tough little piece of work. She did not want anything from Dand Ross other than to know whether he'd already found the letter. If not, she would search for it herself as she had planned.

There were more important matters at stake than her pride. Or her heart.

"You look overset, Charlotte," Dand murmured. "Quite pale. Are you unwell? Or is it my poor self that has you so at sixes and sevens?

"My poor darling." His lids drooped over his dark gaze. "I would leave to spare you distress, but then, I can't quite bring myself to care. I'm afraid you're rather stuck with me."

She kept mute, slaying him with her gaze. Then, lifting her chin without bothering to reply, she turned deliberately away from him and, with every appearance of indifference, publicly cut Dand dead. In spite of his virulent tone, she had understood the subtext of his little speech. He couldn't leave because he hadn't yet found the letter. At least now she knew.

St. Lyon fell into step beside her. "I am so sorry, my dear. I intended to warn you in my library beforehand."

"No matter, Comte," she assured him coolly. "Why and where and how Monsieur Rousse occupies himself does not in the least affect me."

"Does it not?" the comte mused. "And here I thought you looked a great deal affected. You are magnificent in your scorn. No, my dear," he said, shepherding her toward a punch bowl set on a table at the far end of the room, "I am afraid that you are very *much* affected. You still have strong emotions for this young man."

She waited, knowing that to protest would only corroborate his belief.

"It is, of course, only to be expected. Women cannot heed what their minds, even so interesting and strong a mind as your own, tells them when their heart speaks."

"My heart is not speaking," she said stiffly.

"Perhaps not in the vocabulary of love, but it speaks of passion nonetheless. I can read it quite clearly in your eyes, your heightened color, the stiffness of your pose. I am a master of such language, my dear." He was regarding her closely, almost eagerly, and Charlotte abruptly realized that he *wanted* her to feel something for Dand. Passion, if not affection.

Of course. Hadn't Ginny made it perfectly clear that St. Lyon took his greatest satisfaction in seducing women already intimately involved with other men? She must be careful and she must be wise, perhaps even wise enough to circumvent the role she had set out to play. Everything she knew of St. Lyon confirmed him to be an arrogant man, proud of his sexual conquests, his identity profoundly tied up with his concept of himself as irresistible to women.

If St. Lyon thought she was still fighting a potent attraction to a past lover, pride alone would keep him from taking her to his bed until he was certain she could not resist him rather than seeking to eradicate the memory of another by using him as a substitute. Indeed, he would enjoy the challenge.

And while in the process of luring her to his bed, she might have time to search the castle and find the letter without having to compromise herself.

"How perceptive of you, Comte. I don't suppose you know the receipt for some potion that could rid him from my memory?" She lifted one coppery brow.

"Ah," he said. "You regret your association with Monsieur Rousse. You wish to turn back the clock, to be given the opportunity again to make certain significant choices."

Damn. She wanted him to see her as a courtesan, not a spoiled rich girl who sobbed into her pillows at night over the loss of her maidenhead. She gave him a catlike smile. "As much as I dislike having to contradict you, my dear Comte, I am afraid you have misread me. I do not regret the *association*. I regret Rousse."

He laughed and handed her a cup of punch. "You are, as always, unexpectedly direct, Miss Nash. It is an aspect of your delightful personality I am determined to explore."

"Oh, I hope you explore a good deal more than my personality, Comte," she murmured, gazing at him over the rim of her punch glass.

He reached out, his hand low, hidden from most of the others in the room, and trailed his fingertips lingeringly along her forearm. She fought her instinctive recoil and smiled. His hand crept lower, toying with hers.

"All in due time, my dear. I am awaiting the imminent arrival of one more guest and then, a few days later, everyone will be returning to whence they came and the castle will be mine. *Ours*, if you choose to stay. I promise I shall devote my full attention to you. And I promise, when we embark upon our mutual exploration, there shall be no shadows from the past to distract us."

She'd been right in her assessment of his character! Relief swept through her, making it easy for her to smile brilliantly into the comte's dark eyes and whispered, "I shall hold you to that pledge, Comte."

20

⌇⌇⌇⌇

"WHERE IS CHARLOTTE?" Ramsey Munro, Marquis of Cottrell, asked without preamble.

Ginny Mulgrew, receiving the two unexpected visitors in her morning room, maintained her smile though the effort grew greater with each passing moment. "I cannot say, I am sure, milord. I cannot imagine why you think I would be privy to your young relation's plans."

"Because the chit has adopted you as her most current means of thumbing her nose at Society," Colonel MacNeill, rough and handsome and brawny, declared in his rich Scottish accent. "I have heard of her involvement with you from more than one source since my arrival in London."

"And I have had a similar experience in the three days since my ship docked," Munro said, adding, "So, let us dispense with your equivocations. If you had any feeling for the girl at all, you would have refused to associate with her."

What the marquis of Cottrell thought of her lack of regard for an innocent young girl was clear in the slight curl of his lip and by his autocratic tone.

"Miss Nash and I are acquainted," Ginny conceded. What else could she do? Any number of people must have fallen over themselves to inform the marquis of his sister-in-law's choice of friends. She and Charlotte had anticipated the marquis of Cottrell's interest. They had just not anticipated that it would be so soon on the heels of her having left for St. Lyon's castle. Certainly neither of them had expected the early arrival of Colonel Kit MacNeill.

Having the two scouring the city in search of Charlotte was dangerous. Both men had a reputation of getting what they wanted, through whatever means necessary, and right now they wanted to find Charlotte. Their determination to do so spoke volumes about their affection not only for their wives but for the girl herself and Ginny could not help but empathize. Her sympathy notwithstanding, she could not allow them to know where she had gone. Charlotte needed—no, after all her sacrifices she *deserved*—as much time as possible to succeed in her search.

"Baroness Welton informed us that Miss Nash took care of you in her own home during your recuperation from an accident." The huge Scots colonel strode across the room, his hands clasped tightly behind his back as though to keep them from finding Ginny's throat. "You aren't thinking of repaying the lassie's kindness by keeping her family from her?"

A little trickle of sweat ran down from Ginny's temple and was absorbed by her lace fichu. "Of course not. I wish I could help."

"Oh, I am sure you can," the marquis purred, flicking open a Limoges snuffbox and dabbing a pinch of snuff on his hand. He lifted his wrist and inhaled delicately, the dark eyes never straying from her, promising all sorts of retribution should she fail to answer to his satisfaction.

She hoped that Finn stood nearby, ready to act if she should give the signal. Though looking at the two tall, impressive-looking Scotsmen, she profoundly hoped that if her footman needed to act, he brought plenty of help. And a pistol.

The colonel swung around from where he'd been staring out the window. "You lived with Lottie. Tell me, this . . . this man she is rumored to have . . ." His face grew ruddy. "To have cohabited with, this *Monsieur Rousse*, you must know something about him."

Ginny raised her hands in a simulation of helplessness. "I do not! Charlotte said she met him when she was a girl while she and her family were visiting Bristol."

"Charlotte is *still* a girl!" MacNeill said roughly. "A stupid little girl. I cannot believe she would—Who *is* he?" he abruptly shouted, causing Ginny to shrink back in her seat. If these men ever discovered that Andre Rousse was Andrew Ross, she would not give odds of their onetime brother surviving that knowledge. She almost felt sorry for him, but then she recalled the steely resolve and easy strength of the man.

"A Frenchman," Ginny stammered. "A Royalist? I don't know! He and I did not spend much time together. He was utterly besotted of Charlotte and demanded all of her time." She swallowed, not having to feign her fright. "Most of it alone."

The marquis of Cottrell's pale face tightened at this insinuation of how Charlotte had occupied her hours. He turned away and the colonel renewed his combative stance in front of Ginny.

What a pair they were, she thought. So easily taking up the other's slack, so effortlessly working as one in their goal. The Machiavellian abbot Father Tarkin had fashioned them into a team.

"I believe that after Charlotte," she bit her lip, her glance darting away as if she could not bring herself to meet MacNeill's green glare, "sent Monsieur Rousse on his way, he took rooms in Bedford Square."

"We've been there," MacNeill said, his jaw bulging with frustration.

Cottrell had his emotions once more under his control. "To whom else have you introduced her?" he asked smoothly.

"Introduced her?"

"Please." Cottrell's handsome face twisted with derision. "Do not play coy. I do not ask what motivations could lead a woman, a woman who once had dignity and standing, into trying to ensnare a gullible girl in the same trap into which she has fallen, but I do ask that you credit me with enough intelligence not to believe your lies. You have embroiled Charlotte in your life.

You would condemn her to your fate. We"—his quick glance garnered a curt nod from MacNeill—"shall unembroil her. And you *will* help."

The blood drained from Ginny's face. She had never heard so blunt and cruel a condemnation of her and with such justification. More, she had never thought that anything any man could ever say to her would ever have the power to hurt her again. She had been wrong. Not that it mattered. She would not give Charlotte up. Not yet.

"I did not solicit Charlotte in any way. I am not a procurer. I am sorry if you do not believe me." She lifted her chin.

Cottrell studied her for a long moment. "I do believe you. But there is something more you know. Something you are keeping from us."

"I agree." MacNeill's green gaze narrowed. "And have no doubt, Mrs. Mulgrew, if I thought it would do anything but impede the speed with which we might find Charlotte, I would not hesitate to wring from you whatever knowledge it is you are holding back. But if we do not find Charlotte and quickly, I shall return and when I leave I will be satisfied that you have given me every bit of information you own."

Her heart jumped in her chest and her mouth went dry. But courage, at least, Ginny had never wanted. She drew herself up and regarded the big Scotsman haughtily. "Are you threatening me?"

It wasn't MacNeill who answered.

The marquis of Cottrell leaned forward, bringing

his beautiful black-eyed gaze on a level with hers and purred, "Mrs. Mulgrew, you can count on it."

"She was lying," Kit MacNeill said as he followed Ramsey Munro through the front door into the Cottrell mansion.

"Yes. The only question is, about what? I believed she was truly offended by the suggestion that she had acted as Charlotte's procurer—" He broke off and his jaw flexed with ill-contained emotion. "Dear God, Kit, I can scarce believe the words that have been coming from my own lips. 'Seduced. Procurer. Courtesan' and in relation to Charlotte. *Our* Charlotte. Our impetuous, wrongheaded, vivacious, and entirely honorable Charlotte. This will kill Helena." He looked at Kit and seeing the dark savagery on his friend's face, realized at once that he was not the only one who feared the injury this would cause the woman he loved. "I'm sorry, Kit. I know Kate will feel this just as deeply."

"Kate won't believe it. Nothing anyone says will ever convince her that Charlotte has opted for a life of a soiled dove. Charlotte herself could say the words, drag her latest paramour through our doors and Kate would only say that that there were things we did not understand going on beneath the outward appearance."

Ram sighed. "Yes. I know. Helena, too, has shown decided tendencies in that direction." Though, Ram conceded silently, his wife would not be as hard to convince as Kate. Kate had not spent the last three years witnessing Charlotte make a mockery of Society, her bold flirtations, or seen the company in which she traveled. Helena had.

"I'll go see Baroness Welton again. Perhaps she has remembered more about this Rousse other than that he was French and seemed to have Charlotte in some sort of spell."

"At least Charlotte sent this Rousse away," Kit said.

"And within a few days both of them disappeared? It seems unlikely that the two are unconnected." Ram closed his eyes.

"Don't think it, Ram," Kit advised, knowing the dark alleys down which his friend's thoughts had traveled. His own had been there already. What if this Rousse had taken Charlotte, had her still, or worse, had, in the time-tested way of all scorned lovers, taken the ultimate revenge and killed her? Then Rousse had best kill himself next, Kit thought savagely.

With a visible effort to rid himself of the haunting possibility, Ram opened the door beside him and motioned Kit to precede him into his library. A footman appeared in the doorway, bowing as he offered Ram a silver salver upon which rested two envelopes. Distractedly, Ram accepted them and with a nod, sent the footman away. He looked down and at once recognized the handwriting. " 'Tis from Helena."

He opened the envelope and quickly read the short letter. He met Kit's interested gaze. "They have anticipated us. Your wife and mine have gone to interview Baroness Welton again in hopes of divining some further information."

Kit allowed himself a small, dry smile. "You didn't really expect them to sit here and wait, did you?"

"No," Ram answered, turning over the second envelope. There was no inscription on the outside. He pulled out a sheet of paper. His face grew still.

"What is it?" Kit asked.

"An anonymous letter saying that Charlotte is in Scotland at the Comte St. Lyon's castle. As his 'especial guest.' "

"St. Lyon?" Kit echoed.

"A French expatriate and a womanizer of some renown," Ram replied, nodding, his expression troubled. "St. Lyon may be a debaucher, but he is extremely circumspect. He has far too great a love of Society to risk being evicted from it."

"Which means," Kit said gravely, "there is no longer any need to be circumspect where Charlotte is concerned."

"If this bloody letter is even right," Ram said with controlled ferocity. "It may be a prank or have some other purpose."

"Aye. But we can't afford to ignore it."

"No. We can't. I'll go north, you stay here and continue searching."

Kit shook his head. "Oh, no, Ram, my lad. I'll go with you. You've hired agents aplenty to search the city. If there is anything to be found, they will do so. This is the first trace we've had of Charlotte's whereabouts. I won't sit in London while you go. Besides, I will doubtless want to add my . . . *voice* to any opposition you lodge with this St. Lyon should the rumor in this letter prove true."

"All right," Ram agreed. "I leave you to inform Kate and I shall do what I can to keep Helena from following after. We shall leave at first light, agreed?"

"Agreed," Kit answered.

By now Ramsey and Christian would have gotten his letter. They would be beside themselves at the thought of their sister-in-law's situation and in their haste to save her they would race to their destruction. He only had to wait. Everything was coming together with clockwork precision. Everything he had forfeited so many, many years ago would be returned to him ten-fold. His reputation, his home, his consequence . . . his *life*.

He must not be prey to the same impetuous short-comings as the others. He must bide his time. Still, the temptation to reveal himself was immense. He closed his eyes, mastering the self-destructive impulse. He was tired. Exhausted. Even with victory so easily within sight, he had not realized what it would cost him to be near to Dand and not be able to speak.

21

~∞∞∞~

"IF YOU HAD BEEN LADY of the manor two hundred years ago, this is where your enemies would await your judgment." The comte, preceding Charlotte up the narrow spiral staircase on this, the last part of her private tour of the castle, emerged into the cold empty room at the top of the circular guard tower. He turned and offered her his hand. She took it, allowing him to assist her through the hatchway onto the dank slate floor.

"What do you think, Charlotte?" He spoke her Christian name warmly. "Would you be merciful, or would you extract the ultimate penalty . . . death?"

"It would depend on the crime," she replied, shivering at the coolness.

She looked around. Open windows faced each other at the four compass points, allowing an unconstrained panorama of the surrounding countryside. From up here she could see the road upon which they'd arrived threading across the vast empty wasteland. To the west hunched the mauve-stained silhouettes of the mountains, while directly below them the river winked and glittered in the evening sun.

"It's awe-inspiring," she said, surreptitiously looking about. This room had once been used as an interrogation chamber. The blueprints claimed a very narrow passageway built between the thick stone walls led from the ground floor up to here, ending in a peephole where an unseen witness could view an interrogated man's confession. But where? And did St. Lyon know about it?

Yesterday morning she had utilized Lizette's uncommon talent for irritating the housekeeper Madame Paule with preemptive demands and seized the opportunity to search a few of the common rooms while her watchdog was occupied. Though she had found a priests' hole concealed behind some paneling, it was empty.

Late last night, she had sneaked from her room and searched the comte's library, cursing because though she suspected she was simply going over ground Dand had already covered, she could not take that chance. Dand and she had not communicated since her arrival and the library, aside from the comte's quarters, was the most likely place for him to have hidden his letter. She had found nothing.

Now she faced her would-be paramour. "It's beautiful in a lawless, ungovernable sort way."

"Oh, it may look lawless, but I assure you it is most secure," St. Lyon commented. "Though why the builders thought anyone would want to own this patch of nothing is a mystery."

"Why did you want it?" Charlotte asked.

He shrugged. "Why the hunting, of course. Grouse in the heather and ducks on the river and that stand of forest far off to the south? Filled with deer and cunny."

At her expression he laughed. "What? Did you think I bought the place for nefarious purposes? Perhaps I use it as a den of iniquity, a prison where I spirit away young ladies?"

He clasped her wrist and pulled her gently toward the wall, pointing to a series of iron rings fixed at various heights in the stone. With a hooded gaze, he lifted her arm and pinned her wrist near one of the thick rings. "Perhaps you think I keep them chained in this tower until they succumb to my desire?"

She was prepared. She did not recoil. She congratulated herself. She met his gaze with one equally as self-assured and sophisticated. "I do not think, Comte," she answered, "that you would find such a practice at all necessary."

He eyed her a second before smiling and letting her go. "I should hope not. But you, my dear, are presenting quite a challenge."

"How so?" she asked. "I am here, am I not?"

"But so, too, is your former lover and he, my dear, could not help but put a blight upon what I'd hoped would be a blissful interlude."

She had refused to think of Dand since her arrival three days ago, avoiding every occasion that might bring her into contact with him. When she was obliged to be in the same room, she acted as if he did not exist. Unfortunately, it was only an act.

Concentrate though she tried upon the task at hand, he was ever with her. The sound of his voice across the room brought a light flush to her cheeks. Whenever she looked up she found his gaze upon her, speculative or hard, pensive or angry. He was only pretending to be the wounded, angry lover. For her it was not an act.

She longed for him at the same time as she mentally castigated him for his deception of her and cursed herself for her stupidity. He had always been forthcoming in admitting that he would do whatever was necessary to achieve his goal. Sacrifice whatever was demanded. Or whoever.

"Send him away," she demanded in the tones of a woman who is used to being indulged. "He disturbs me."

"As I said," St. Lyon replied in conciliatory tones, "he is here representing others."

"I don't understand. What do you mean about his having 'ecclesiastical associates'? He is nothing but a French émigré."

"My dear." He looked honestly surprised. "You really do not know who he is?"

"A Frenchman I met in Bristol many summers ago. A childish infatuation which I, unfortunately, did not have the common sense to recognize as such when we met again in London this summer."

"But . . . did he not say *who* he was?"

Charlotte's interest was piqued, but she evinced only slight peevishness. "No. What do you mean? I never liked guessing games. Tell me if you think I shall be impressed, who is he?"

"He is Andre Henri Rousse, cousin to the murdered Duc d'Enghein and great-grandnephew of Marie Therese of Austria."

Charlotte almost laughed. God Lord, when Dand adopted a role, he adopted an impressive one, she must give him that. But the expression on St. Lyon's face told her all she needed to know. St. Lyon, despite his recent adoption of the English values, still went in awe of his old regime. No wonder Dand had decided upon that particular alias.

"Yes, well, eightieth in line or eighth in line to a non-existent throne is all the same, is it not?" she asked in a bored voice. "Certainly his exalted position has afforded him no comfort that I can see. For all that he looks well turned out, his tailor owns him. Hasn't sixpence to scratch."

"You are truly a most practical creature," St. Lyon mused, and Charlotte feared she had misstepped.

Her role called for her to be mercenary but not so much so that St. Lyon would take a distaste of her. He must think that she desired *him* first and his pocketbook second.

"Of course," she murmured as if to herself, "I should not have noticed his lack of means had there been other compensations." She trailed off, leaving St. Lyon to imagine what particular attributes Dand lacked. "I do wish he would leave."

"There, there, my darling Charlotte. He'll only be here a few more days," St. Lyon said soothingly, as though he were dealing with a spoiled and recalcitrant child which, Charlotte had become convinced, was exactly how St. Lyon thought of women.

"No parties. No masques. No society." She pouted. "Like you, Comte, I am a woman used to a certain quality in all things. Beauty and gaiety are like bread and water to me. And there is a dearth of both here. Added to which," she fixed him with an accusing stare, "you have not been candid with me."

"How so?" The comte picked up her hands and squeezed them gently. "Come. Speak."

"You told me you were coming here to ease the transition of your fellow French expatriates and yet, except for Monsieur Rousse, I count only one other Frenchman amongst your guests."

He stilled for a telling few seconds then, "I admit it. I was not forthcoming. You have caught me out." He lifted his hands in a charmingly self-deprecating manner. "You know, of course, that I am something of a collector of rare and artistic things. Well, in the course of my collecting I occasionally come across something of a great deal of value to others. In which case I offer it to special guests at auction."

"Like Tattersall's!" she exclaimed.

He smiled with poorly masked superiority. "Yes, my

dear. Like Tattersall's. Only sometimes—how to put this delicately?—there are questions about the legalities of my selling some of these things."

"Ohh!" She regarded him in round-eyed speculation. "Such as," she looked both right and left and whispered, "jewels? *Royal* jewels? Royal *French* jewels?"

He placed a finger alongside his nose and nodded. "Just so."

The faith he put in her gullibility was truly marvelous.

"How thrilling!" she said, drawing back and twirling lightly around. "I should *love* to wear royal jewels. Think of the envy I should provoke!"

"And I would love to see you wear them. But, alas, you never would be able to appear in them in public. They are far too recognizable and to pry them from their setting would destroy much of their value. Far better to sell them and buy *new* jewels."

She schooled her features into a doubtful expression. "Hm. I suppose. But still, I must say, considering how valuable the jewels are, your composure is extraordinary. Aren't you afraid someone will try and steal them? Why there aren't even any guards about!"

He laughed. "Should the need arise, my staff have varied and diverse skills, my dear. But it shan't."

"You are very certain of yourself. *Or* your guests."

"Oh. I have no faith in my guests at all. And please, we are a little beyond your having to dredge up an approximation of shock at my comment, aren't we?"

She dimpled and laughed. "Just so!"

"Well then," he went on approvingly, "I was going to say I have no doubt that several, perhaps all of them, have at one time or another since their arrival gone poking about my private quarters, tipping over fruit bowls and peering under flowerpots. To no avail, I might add."

"Pride goeth before the fall," Charlotte gently chided.

"Oh, it's not pride, darling girl. It's a simple matter of not being able to find what isn't here. Aha! You begin to see why my insistence on waiting for our final guest. He has the . . . jewels with him."

"Really?" She blinked at him in admiration while she cursed their foul luck.

Damnation! St. Lyon had an accomplice. She must warn Dand not to hunt for the cylinder any longer. He would only put himself—their mission—at needless risk. She puckered her face. "But what if *he* steals them?"

"So little trust for one so young. It's rather charming," St. Lyon said indulgently. "Fret not, little dove." He was growing more comfortable with her by the moment, relishing his role of the worldly older man. He chucked her lightly under the chin. "My associate is not a brilliant man, but he is smart enough to know that he is incapable of orchestrating this sort of auction. Besides, he brought it to me in the first place."

"How clever. And when will this fellow arrive?"

"Oh, that will be very soon." St. Lyon said. "Punctual fellow, Rawsett."

"Rawsett?"

"Perhaps you know the name? A fribble of the highest order, but a useful fribble nonetheless. Once he has arrived"—the smile he turned on her was ripe with confidence and pleasure—"I shall hold the auction and then what happens to the jewels shall no longer be my problem. And once my business is finished, I shall devote myself to making you forget Rousse."

"Who?" Charlotte asked archly.

And St. Lyon laughed.

22

∞∞∞

Comte St. Lyon's castle, Scotland
August 12, 1806

"I ACCEPT THE WAGER, COMTE," Charlotte's gaze slid brazenly around the hazard table. "The silk stocking I am currently wearing against your thousand pounds."

The players at the other card table quieted, their hands forgotten as they heard Charlotte's declaration. Because to a man they knew that the little soiled dove who'd fluttered into their midst had, until very, very re-

cently, been a lady. Just as every one of them knew that
the man responsible for her downfall was sitting at the
very next table, his back to her back, his eyes fixed on
his cards. His visage was as cold and remote as the
mountains to the north.

It was all so unimaginably, deliciously indecent! And
in the middle of the afternoon! Who could tell what
entertainment dinner might provide?

"All's fair in love and war," the comte said, watching
her closely.

"Did you say 'love,' Comte?" The man, Rousse,
turned and threw his arm over the back of his chair, regarding Charlotte Nash with haughty disdain. Though
how any red-blooded male could look so coolly at one
so vibrantly, lusciously feminine was beyond most of
the other men's capacity to understand.

Her nutmeg-colored curls gleamed like polished
metal and the thin sheath of tallow-colored silk that
skimmed over the curving lines of her lithe young body
accentuated her peach-flushed skin. Her lips, perpetually on the brink of a knowing smile, glistened with the
succulent ripeness of youth and her eyes glowed beneath their fringe of gilt-tipped lashes. No matter that
she was not the exotic beauty her older sisters were reputed to be, her chin too sharp, her bronze shot eyes
languorous and down-turned at the corners as if she
had just risen from bed, her mouth too full and saucy.
She was naughty, coquettish, and fully awake on every
suit. Much better than beautiful.

The comte's brows rose at Rousse's unexpected interruption. "Indeed, I did, Monsieur Rousse. What of it?"

"Nothing. Except after my own recent experiences"—his dark gaze flickered briefly over Charlotte Nash's indecently clad body—"I would be remiss if I didn't warn you that the tender sentiment you have enjoined is not within a certain individual's capacity to feel."

"I am sure your concern would be appreciated were it not patently a matter of what these English call 'sour grapes,' " the comte said.

Charlotte stared past Dand, cursing him for making it all but impossible for her to drop a word in his ear about his search for the letter. Besides, if the fool did not have a care, the comte might decide the best way to win her affection would be to play knight errant to Dand's vulgar brigand. The two men were regarding each other in a manner that put her in mind of stiff-legged curs meeting over a contested patch of ground, the air roiling with masculine pride and the potential for violence.

And what good would Dand be to their mission, injured or worse? She wouldn't allow it. She'd given up far too much to see her plans ruined by petty masculine posturing.

She turned calmly back around, as if Dand hadn't spoken. "I always insist on seeing the color of the gold on the table when I play. I suspect it is the same for you gentlemen."

She stretched out her leg and slipped her satin slipper off her foot.

"My dear? Would you not prefer a more private—"

"I do not need any privacy. At least not for this." She glanced up. Every pair of masculine eyes in the room, including the comte's, were trained on her foot. Every set except Dand's. He met her gaze with a cold, warning glare. To blazes with him! Since he'd cast her into the role of diversion, she wouldn't want to disappoint him.

"I declare, I don't know what any of you gentlemen could want with this. Perhaps I should have wagered a few minutes alone in the outer closet?" She held Dand's gaze meaningfully. Around them, a dozen men blustered or cleared their throats. "Too late, gentlemen," Charlotte declared with a feline smile. "You only wanted my stocking. Next time you might consider asking for more."

She leaned over, sliding her hands beneath the hem of her skirt and finding the tops of the stocking tied with a ribbon garter just below her knee. Dand's jaw muscle tightened. A little tic moved beneath the wicked-looking scar.

Don't.

Had he actually whispered the word or did she simply want to hear it? No matter. She was wed to her role now. With a flirtatious glance around at her rapt audience she rolled the sheer embroidered bit of silk down her calf, the movement hidden by her skirts. Then, with a pert show of ankle, she pulled it free of her foot and gaily held it aloft.

Dand stood up. No one but she seemed to notice. Nor did they notice when without a word, he strode from the room as though he could no longer bear the sight of her.

She smiled. Gaily. Confidently. "Here, Comte, is my wager. If you would deal the cards?"

With an appreciative smile, the comte dealt out the three cards. Charlotte picked them up, trying to simulate interest. She had none. She did not want his money—though she knew that is precisely the appearance she must give—and she didn't care if she lost her damn stocking. The vulgarity with which she had shed it could hardly be outdone by simply losing it.

Two queens and a four of hearts. She did not even bother drawing another card, and when the comte turned over his own pair of tens and she flipped over hers and said, "I win," she felt rather that she'd lost. Still she smiled. Laughed. Dimpled and glowed with avarice and triumph and accepted the congratulations of the other men in the room and the other ladies, too, who were far less enthusiastic.

"And now, if you will excuse me, Comte? Gentlemen?" She picked up the wisp of silk lying on the table and slipped her bare foot into her shoe.

"I will leave you while I go and change for the evening. You will not disappoint me by stopping play while I am gone? I shall return anon and insist on playing until the footman announces dinner." She was rewarded by a chorus of gruff masculine assurances that while they would eagerly await her return they would indeed continue to play.

Glad to escape, Charlotte hurried into the great hall where those guests who had chosen not to play cards loitered in front of the huge open fireplace. Though they stood or sat within close proximity of one another, they still remained distinctly separate. Only a few leaned toward each other speaking in low voices. Most covertly studied their companions or stared at the fire, their expression thoughtful and assessing.

Rivalry for the coveted prize St. Lyon offered had brought them here and that same rivalry kept them apart. Which of these men worked for Napoleon? Which for the Austrians? Which followed a personal agenda or, even more likely, had business that a treaty between nations would threaten? The last two years had taught Charlotte to appreciate that in every nation—including Great Britain—lived men who profited greatly by war.

She did not waste time worrying over their various reasons for being here but looked about hoping that Dand had taken her hint and waited out here for her so that she could tell him that the letter was not yet in the castle and that he needn't risk exposure by looking for it. He was nowhere to be seen.

Mentally cursing, she hurried to her room, her nerves stretched to the breaking point. How long could she play on St. Lyon's attraction without succumbing to his increasing demands? God help her, she was not cut out for this. She could talk a good game, but when it came to the actual moment when she would lie in his arms—She closed her eyes, fighting the panic and the revulsion. It was just a physical act. She would pretend it was someone else. She would pretend, she thought bitterly, that he was—

A movement behind alerted her. She began to turn. A muscled arm snaked around her waist, jerking her back against a hard masculine chest while a broad hand clamped over her mouth.

"Quietly," Dand whispered. "St. Lyon is a jealous suitor. He has his servants watching you. Watching this room." His breath was warm, stirring the soft tendrils behind her ear, his mouth so close that when he spoke his lips brushed the side of her neck. "Will you stay quiet?"

She nodded and he uncovered her mouth though his arm stayed, locking her in intimate contact with his body. A thrill of fear ran through her. Yes, she'd had glimpses of something within him that eroded her peace of mind, little hints of a purposefulness that would stop at nothing to achieve its end, but she'd still trusted him. No more.

"If my room is being watched, how did you get in?" she asked coolly.

"The window. I should hate to mount an assault from the base of the castle, but slipping down from the room above was not too great a task for a man of my talents." His lips moved against her ear, velvety soft but firm and warm. She steeled herself against the treacherous temptation to melt in his embrace.

"There's no need to look for the letter. It isn't here."

"What?" His arm loosened. Without looking at him, she jerked away and moved casually toward the huge mirror opposite her bed. She studied her reflection with bitter satisfaction. Not a trace of the upheaval his presence caused appeared in her face. She looked unconcerned, indifferent. Good.

"He anticipated that some of his guests would search for it, perhaps even be prepared to take it by force, so he sent it away with a confederate. A man named Rawsett. He is due to arrive any day now. With the letter. So you can dispense with your nocturnal hunt."

She glanced at his image in the mirror. He was regarding her closely. "You should leave then. At once."

She laughed. "Oh, no. Too late for that, I should think. Besides, there's no saying where St. Lyon will stow the letter. You'll still need to hunt for it. I'll still be a good diversion. At least"—she tilted her head and after a second of deliberation, pulled her already dangerously low neckline a little lower—"I shall do my best."

"Diversion?"

"Yes. Once Rawsett has arrived, you shall doubtless need me to provide a further distraction. Isn't that the role you assigned me?"

"Is that what you think?" His voice was colorless, his eyes narrowed.

"What else? Oh, it was all very clever of you. I stand in awe. You manipulated me like an impresario. You knew I would not fall in with your plot in so auxiliary a role. So you allowed me to think I had a more vital one, a starring role."

She laughed again, proud of how amused she sounded, how careless. "Imagine, I actually thought your bedding me was *my* idea." She turned around, wanting to hurt him, to repay him in the same coin. "And of course, once that little hurdle had been passed, what did I have to lose?" *My heart.* "Nothing of consequence.

"So, here I am, groomed, ruined, and ready. At your service, as it were. There is one little question that has been nagging at me. Tell me, however did you manage to arrive before me?"

"A boat," he clipped out.

"I see." She smiled, nodding as if that was the only thing that had occupied her thoughts, as she delighted in seeing the flickers of fury dancing in his eyes. And then, turning in a little pirouette, "What do you think, Dand? Will I do? Am I appealing enough to keep St. Lyon occupied while you search?"

"Occupied," he said flatly. "You have *occupied* an entire room of men with your earlier exhibition, Charlotte. But have a care. St. Lyon is only mortal. If you keep provoking him as you did tonight you might find him in your bedchamber yet."

How dare he caution her? When he could have stopped her from this—had it suited his plans. "You sound jealous, Dand. One would think that you had forgotten that your role of lover is merely that: a role," she said coolly and then, "Besides, how do you know that St. Lyon hasn't already been to my bed?"

He was across the room, seizing her arms and jerking her back against him before she had finished. "You little witch, what new hell are you trying to consign me to?"

She ignored his anger. She had her own hurt to tend. "Tell me. Because I am curious, you understand. Was everything, even your initial resistance to my request that you take my maidenhead, designed to lead me here, to this place? To St. Lyon's bed?"

She could feel his physical reaction, a sudden stillness that translated into a subtle tensing of the muscular body pressed so closely against her own. Damn! Why did she have to react so strongly to him? Why could she not explain to the nerve endings flooding with visceral memory and muscles shivering in anticipation of his touch that he had *used* her.

She'd come to London green and frightened but determined to make her way without her sisters' aid. She had used her frivolity and insouciance as camouflage to mask her fear and uncertainty. At first they had been an aid, helping her find and hold a place in Society. Later she sustained the masquerade because it provided a unique opportunity to do something, to *be* something more than a coquette who would become a romp and a cipher.

But she had allowed Dand Ross past those trappings, shyly opened the door to not only who she was but how she wanted *him* to see her—as someone honorable, determined, *worthy*. Even her own sisters didn't know her so well. Not like Dand. And then—betrayal.

She didn't bother waiting for his answer. She was too

hurt, wanting only that he should feel some of the pain he'd caused her in return.

"Not that I would have resisted, mind you." Her low voice throbbed with the anger humming in her veins. "Not that I would have *questioned* you. Not that I would have protested. But you daren't take that chance, did you? You *used* me.

"Well, Dand. You, of all people, must appreciate this as well as accept it. Now *I* am using *you*. To keep St. Lyon jealous, his interest piqued and ready."

When she finished, her breasts rose and fell in agitation against the bolster of his arm, her shoulder blades pressed like knives into his chest as every fiber of her grew tight. For a long moment he was silent. She started to turn, but he kept her imprisoned facing forward, his strength as implacable as his silence.

"*Used* you," he finally said and, damn him, his voice was as cool and dark and unaffected as the night sky. "Your faith in my character is truly impressive, Charlotte. First you think that I would make . . . would bed you just to rid you of your virginity thereby lending veracity to your role. Now you think that I've manipulated you into whoring for me so that my search of the castle will be marginally less dangerous."

"Tell me I was wrong."

"Would you believe me?" he asked with terrible calm. When she didn't answer, he went on, "As I recall, when I left you it was with your request that I come to you the following afternoon. I came. You were gone."

She would not let him see the agony he'd caused her.

She wouldn't. "I wished to spare you the difficulty of that parting," she said. "I thought you would have found it hard to send your . . . mistress to another man's bed. I should have known better."

"Your consideration unmans me," he said bitterly. "What a diligent little pragmatist you are, Lottie. I never fully appreciated it before. But since we are bartering suspicions and accusations, let me remind you that you told me yourself you were allowing me into your bed, into your body, as a means of ridding yourself of that problematic maidenhead. The only difference is, *I* didn't believe you."

"You bastard." She struggled to turn in his embrace, her hand rising to strike his face. With a growl, he grabbed her wrist, wrenching it down, repositioning his hand low across her belly and pulled her forcibly back into him.

"You can't play the abused lover," she spat. "You're here. You can't deny what is plain for any fool to see. Even me. You can't take advantage of my—" She'd almost said "love," but pride stopped her. Thank God.

"But I *have* the advantage," he said, the dark liquid accent caressing her. He shifted his arm, his hand spread wide and low over her stomach, his fingertips riding just above the jut of her pubic bone, pressing in a little and causing her pulse to lurch in her throat. She let her gaze flicker down to the sight of his hand, a dark possessive imprint on the pale satin. He lowered his head against the curve of her neck.

She hissed as he nipped the rounded point of her

shoulder and soothed it with a kiss. Her joints went liquid.

"Such a valiant little patriot, Charlotte. Do you want to hear an explanation of how I came to be here? Of why I am here?"

Yes. No. What if he said things she could not bear to hear? "I am not in the least interested. Now get out of here. St. Lyon may be coming."

"You really are trying to destroy me. Well, darling, if that is to be my road, I insist we travel it together." He released her wrist, toppling her forward so that she had to catch herself with her palms flat against the mirror to keep from falling. He followed her in, his loins pressed firmly against her bottom, trapping her there. His hands clasped her waist for a second before stroking down the side of her hips to the tops of her outer thighs.

Firm, warm lips slipped languidly down the side of her neck. The touch of his tongue set a quicksilver flash of desire spearing toward her core. She took a deep breath. *Wretched, treacherous flesh*, heedless of protecting her heart.

She started sideways, but his big hands tightened, holding her in place. *"Do not move. Do not, or I swear I do not know what I will do."*

She believed him, something beyond dangerous, something hunted, lived in his voice. She shivered, still tilted forward against the mirror as he moved like a dark incubus behind her, his hands unseen below.

"You have put me through hell, my darling, my

beloved. But like that fool St. Lyon, I find I am made of dross metal where you are concerned."

Incrementally, inch by inch, he rucked up the soft, malleable fabric of her gown gathering it into his palms as the back hem rose slowly from her ankles, to her calves, to just above the back of her knees.

"What are you doing?" she gasped.

" 'Tis a little trick I learned from your demonstration this afternoon." His mouth trailed fire down between her shoulder blades. He kissed the bare skin there, his mouth was open, urgent, his tongue tasting her as he fitted her more snuggly into the lee of his hips.

The tips of his fingers, warm and calloused, brushed beneath the edge of her hem, grazing the sensitive flesh high on her thigh. Her head fell back against his shoulder. She could barely hold on to a thought. Somewhere in the last few seconds she had ceded will to sensation. Her skin prickled with an electric sense of anticipation. She felt drunk with the need for more contact.

At least she was not alone. The breath buffeting her neck and shoulder was harsher now, quicker, the hands so skillfully playing with her trembled. She should feel triumphant. She only felt desire. And that way led to the destruction he'd promised.

"Stop." Her voice sounded less like a command than a plea.

"No. Never." His sounded almost tender.

Her head fell forward between her braced arms. She was panting now, her breasts shivering with each draw of his palm following the curve of her upper thigh around to between her legs, his knee between hers, gently nudging them apart. Her eyelids slipped halfway shut as his fingers found soft, tender swells of her most feminine parts. Higher. Higher. Brushing with tantalizing lightness until her whole body shook with mortification and excitement that he would do this, play with her so, here.

He fit his hips against her, pulling her back against the erection swelling the front of his trousers. His touch lightened, barely holding her against him, making her painfully aware of his arousal and of how little he needed to do to have her spread beneath him.

"Are you trying to shame me?" Her pulse pounded in her temples, her wrists, pooling in her breast and where his fingers played with such indolent ease. "Make me say that I want you. *I want you.* There. Satisfied? You win."

His hands dropped from her as if her skin scalded him. He fell back a step and somewhere she found the strength to push herself away. She caught sight of herself in the mirror. Her hair was coming down, the short curls rampant on her neck. Her eyes were dark and luminous, her skin flushed with excitement.

Taking a deep, shaking breath, she turned to him.

"You have this wrong." His face was set, terse, his eyes pools of glittering onyx. The light caught the wicked crescent of the scar he wore on his cheek.

"You told me lies." Without volition, her quivering fingers rose and feathered a touch against the old wound.

"Many," he agreed roughly, turning his head and catching her fingertip between his teeth, licking the tip and sending a firestorm jolting through her hand and wrist and spiraling up her arm to flood her breasts and belly with heavy desire.

"What do you want?" he asked. "To know the exact degree and extent of my lies? Which one? The ones I've told you or the ones I've told myself? Do you think I *wanted* this?" His laugh was low, tormented.

"You haven't told me everything."

"I've told you nothing," he agreed again, his scent filling her head, suffusing her world, marking her. "I haven't told you that I—"

With a sound of frustration, he pulled her into him and kissed her with checked violence and, God help her, she returned his kiss, her face lifted to his, her body arching in to him. She tangled her hands in his hair, drinking in the scent of him, her tongue stirring in his mouth.

His anger and jealousy and frustration melted at the moment of her surrender. He hesitated, knowing her capitulation was only desire momentarily relinquishing that formidable, obstinate pride and knowing too that her pride would return. He understood pride. Hadn't she stripped him of his own? But he could no more relinquish her now than he could stop his heart from beating. She was his. *His*.

He lashed one arm around her waist, with the other hand undoing the line of buttons at her back. He pulled the gown down, pulled the chemise skimming the tips of her breasts down, letting the silky material sag to her waist and freeing her breasts.

Her skin was milky and satiny, like moonlight over snow. He drew his palms down over the firm, high mounds, his thumbs playing with the tight nipples as she moaned into his open mouth. He sucked gently on the tip of her tongue and released her mouth, lowering his head to take an apricot-tinted nipple. She gasped and arched back, her hands in his hair holding him tightly as he suckled, cries of pleasure shaken from her throat.

His body tightened, swelled, ached.

His hands moved down her hips, dragging the material up until he felt the satiny twin arcs of her buttocks. He slid his hand between her legs and felt her little recoil of apprehension and more, the rich dampness of her body's welcome.

She wanted him. Her arousal destroyed what little restraint he had kept. Need cut through him like a hot knife, like a fiery brand, instant and eviscerating and immediate.

He jerked at his trousers, pulling himself free of the constricting material, then caught her, one hand behind her knee, the other beneath the round, soft buttocks. He boosted her effortlessly up, her leg catching instinctively above his hip, the soft crisp curls and dewy womanhood pressed to his groin. He felt the softness slide like a warm, wet fist about the head of his erection and shuddered, pulling her closer, pushing into her.

She arched back, her other leg instinctively climbing about his other hip, until her legs locked about his waist, the movement thrusting him deep, deep within.

He forced himself to go still, his gaze feasting on the sight of her pleasure as he held her suspended in his arms, her body cleaved to his, her eyes closed.

He lifted her slightly, withdrawing, and she gasped at the sensation.

"No," she muttered, her eyes flying open to find his own hungrily watching her. The feel of his erection moving inside was alien, unbelievably exotic and stimulating, frighteningly powerful and arousing. "Do not stop. *More.*"

Nothing else existed but this. She could not master a single thought. She only wanted, needed him, desired him. He let her slide down, her breasts dragging against the rough clean linen of his shirt but this time his hips worked in counterpoint to the movement, taking a deeper ownership of her body.

Her fingers dug into his shoulders. Even beneath the linen she could feel the strain of his muscles knotting. The ache that had begun in her breasts and lips and fingertips, raced thick and hot to pool where he filled her. An ache built with each long, restrained thrust he dealt her, swelling like a wave meeting another, building in force.

Another stroke. Another thrust. Faster. Deeper. She met each one. At first tentatively, awkward in her vulnerability, anchored to the world only by his body, his power, the strength of his arms holding her, his arousal filling her, stretching her, and then with growing desperation as the welling need within her grew.

His shirt grew damp with his sweat, his eyes burned

as he stared down at her, his face muscles working with each thrust. He would have her utterly. He would take her from herself. Pleasure beat at her, thrummed in her veins, a rumble of thunder growing in her ears as the blood rushed in her body, driven on the cusp of an irresistible tidal wave. Gratification so intense it brought tears to her eyes jolted through her. Again. Again. She closed her eyes and with a sob, surrendered.

She felt him rock back then, the rhythm holding him in its grip growing faster, wilder, until with one last powerful thrust she heard his own cry of savage exultance fall heavy and triumphant in her ear as shudders racked his body. She held on to him, feeling the echo of repletion in the tremors shivering his muscles.

She collapsed then, limp, wrung of sensation, her thoughts hazy and drunk. Vaguely she was aware of him lowering her gently to her feet, of his arm supporting her as he pulled her chemise up. His mouth touched her temple, lingered. She drew a shaky breath. She must—

"Miss Nash? Miss Nash!" Madame Paule's voice called from the other side of the chamber door.

The sound instantly recalled Charlotte to reality. She stumbled away from Dand, dragging her gown closed over her breasts, her hunted gaze darting toward the door handle. Thank God, she'd locked it.

Dand uttered a low, vehement curse.

"You have to leave. Now. *Please*," she whispered urgently, her lips trembling on the verge of tears. She could not fall apart. Not now. She raised her voice, praying that it did not betray her. "One moment, Madame Paule!"

She turned to Dand, who was savagely repairing the front of his trousers. He raked his hand through his hair, damp and rumpled, his mouth twisted in a snarl.

"You have to go, Dand."

He grabbed her arm, hauling her with him toward the open window through which he'd come. Only when he was within reach of it did he release her. "I'll go. But lest you are uncertain about what that was, what *this* is," he ground out in a low, savage voice, "let me make it clear for you. You are mine. *Mine.*"

And before she could reply, he'd grabbed the upper sill of the window and swung himself up and out of the room.

23

Jermyn Street, Piccadilly
August 13, 1806

GINNY MULGREW IMPATIENTLY DRUMMED HER FINGERS against the carriage's open windowsill. Two hours ago the boy she had set to keep an eye on the Marquis of Cottrell's residence had reported that the marquis and Colonel MacNeill had ridden out on horseback. A few coins to a maid had delivered the information that the marquis had left word for his wife that he and the colonel were going to Scotland to retrieve the marchioness's sister.

Ginny had vacillated for an hour before deciding on her present course. It was time she and the abbey of St. Bride's joined forces to bring about a mutually advantageous end to her quickly unraveling plans. She would approach Toussaint—and the thought of the soldier-priest's face when he discovered that she knew all about him and his practice was the only bright spot in her day—and convince him to send word to the abbey that someone must intercept the would-be rescuers before they utterly mucked up Charlotte's mission. She knew St. Bride's to be within a day's ride of St. Lyon's castle. And there was only one road leading to that remote stronghold. It should not prove beyond the abbot's surprisingly long reach to do as she requested.

The carriage rolled to a halt and her driver, a formidable ex-pugilist named Ashford, clambered down and pulled open the door. "Here it be, ma'am," he said. "Number Twelve Sparrow Lane. And a rare rough patch of ground it be. I'm thinking I ought to go in wid ye."

"Thank you, Ashford, but no," Ginny said, climbing out and eyeing the rickety façade before her. "But if you would wait here and remain vigilant, I would be obliged."

With a doubtful expression, Ashford nodded and then took up a position by the lead horse, his arms crossed over his thick chest.

Ginny knocked at the door and waited a good few minutes before knocking again more forcefully. She frowned when there was no answer. She knew Toussaint had not relocated. She paid good money to be informed of the monk's frequent changes of address.

But then, it was a tall building and there was no saying that he wasn't on the roof with his carrier pigeons and simply did not hear her. Well, she wasn't going to stand around pounding on the door all day and she wasn't going to come back here. Besides, if he had gone elsewhere she might find a clue as to where inside.

She motioned Ashford over. "If you would open this door, please," she said and stood aside as with a mighty kick Ashford sent the cheap door exploding inward off its hinges.

"Thank you. Now, wait for me." She sailed through the still swinging door and stopped at once as a foul odor filled her lungs.

"Dear God," she muttered, anxiety pushing at the edges of her formidable self-containment. She had smelled death before.

Marshaling her courage she moved through the front hall and into the small, dark room in the back. The stench was thicker here, the scent of lye lying like a caul over it. Pulling out her lace handkerchief, she held it to her nose as she moved tentatively along the perimeters of the room. There was little furniture, a table with a lantern on it, a pair of chairs, a narrow bed, and beside it a small squat trunk.

She knew. But she had to be sure. She pulled up the clasp and opened the lid.

A man lay folded inside, the side of his head black where it had been caved in. A Bible lay open on his legs, as though someone had tossed it in as an afterthought. It was Brother Toussaint.

Choking on the stench, Ginny stumbled from the room, her broken leg screaming in protest. She barely felt it. Panic spurred her on, sending her racing into the street and calling for Ashford. But it was not the dead man that filled her with alarm.

It was Charlotte. The girl was in danger. She had been set up, manipulated into making the trip to Scotland.

Because Brother Toussaint had been dead for a long, long time. Too long. Whoever had given his blessing to Charlotte's plan to take Ginny's place as St. Lyon's paramour, it hadn't been this man.

LeMons dungeon, France
March 1800

"Did you tell him?" Douglas insisted, his fingers digging into Dand's shoulder, the blood flowing anew from the deep brand on his chest. The exposed and raw nerve endings screamed in protest and Dand's thoughts swam on a river of pain. "What did you tell him?" Douglas demanded, shaking him.

"Leave off!" Dand gasped. He was shaking all over and his stomach lurched. He was going to vomit. Sweat poured from his forehead and trailed down his face and throat, the salty perspiration adding its own special hell to the pain.

"Leave him alone, Douglas," Ram said, grabbing Douglas by the arm and hauling him away. "Can't you see? He's near done for."

"I need to know if he said anything to Gardien," Douglas said, his eyes filled with a blind sort of desperation. "If he told him who our contacts were. If he told him where we came from. If he told him anything about our plans."

"Jesu, Doug. Would you hold it against him if he did?" Kit came over, shaking his head and gently pulling the blood-soaked shirt away from Dand's chest. "The poor lad has been burned even deeper than me. There's only so much you can ask of mortal flesh."

"You're right. Of course, you're right," Douglas said, releasing his hold on Dand and sinking back, squatting on his heels, his head bobbing up and down in manic agreement. "Of course. You can't ask more of man than what he can stand, and Dand, he never thought all that much of our vows anyway. Did you, now?" He reached out and Dand was amazed to see a tear course down his dirty, thin face. "It's all right, Dand. It's all right."

With choked laughter that sent the nerve endings in his chest shrieking in protest, Dand swatted Douglas's hand away. "Oh, no, you great bloody saint," he said. "You'll not be besting me this day."

"What do you mean?"

"I didn't tell them a bloody thing."

24

Comte St. Lyon's castle, Scotland
August 14, 1806

"Miss Nash?" St. Lyon stood at the bottom of the stairs peering through the haze that crept in every evening and hung over the courtyard. Charlotte, seated with a book open but unread on her lap, reluctantly lifted her head.

Yesterday, amidst a flurry of bashful stammers and downcast glances, she had told the comte that the cool evening air aided in reducing the headaches that always accompanied this delicate time of month. Gentleman that he thought himself, he'd since indulged her desire to be alone, though she often spotted him watching her through one of the windows that looked down over the courtyard. Her relief at being able to escape her role as his potential mistress, even for a few short evening hours, was profound.

Ever since Dand and she . . . ever since *then*, she had managed to avoid any prolonged contact with the comte. Damn Dand and his possessive proclamations anyway. Nothing had changed. Everything had changed.

She no longer knew what to believe. While her mind insisted on clear-sighted objectivity, her heart told her something decidedly different. She would have thought it easy to ignore that fallible organ's whispered suggestion that not everything was as it seemed. A woman in her precarious position could not afford to disregard facts. Certainly a spy and a thief, which she was, could not risk her life on emotions born during a torrid physical encounter.

But they hadn't been born then. They had been born long before . . .

Nonsense. She had a job to do, a mission vital to the lives of countless others.

"Yes, Comte," she called back. "I was enjoying the air. So soothing. Won't you join me?"

The comte ascended the steps and made his way across the graveled drive to the marble bench. Dusk sifted fine mauve shadows over the courtyard, making colors dimmer, softer and shapes indistinct and insubstantial. Little curls of mist scattered at his approach.

"I shall never get used to how cold and wet your country is," St. Lyon declared, stopping in front of her. "In the morning, at dusk, in the cities and in the country, this perennial damp. Fogs and mists and rains. Now France, especially the southern part, where my family once ruled, is a land of sun and brilliance."

"You must miss it."

"Yes," St. Lyon said, taking a seat beside her. "But someday the wheel of power will turn again and those whom I have kept as friends will welcome my return. Until then there is beauty in this country which compensates for its climate."

He turned his gaze on her, leaving her no doubt as to his meaning. Charlotte dutifully simpered. A wolfish look appeared on his face. He leaned forward. "Are you . . . feeling any better?" he asked urgently.

"Some." She touched her stomach gingerly.

He frowned and straightened.

"The cool mist is most restorative."

"I am glad." He didn't sound glad; he sounded petulant. "I note that Monsieur Rousse is no longer troubling you with his presence."

"Thank heaven." *Where was Dand?* Though she saw him at meals, he was always seated well away from her and as she had taken herself out of the social activities, she did not see him otherwise.

"He still annoys you," St. Lyon said with satisfaction.

She nodded with every appearance of sullenness. "Excessively."

He hesitated a few seconds and then, in exaggeratedly casual tones, said, "Tell me, my dear, what do you really know about Monsieur Rousse?"

She frowned. "I know he hasn't a feather to fly with. He is French. And you tell me his family has some sort of exalted connection to the Bourbons, a claim which I find frankly suspect. Why do you ask?"

St. Lyon watched her intently as she answered. What was this all about?

"Oh, nothing. And tell me again, how was it that you met him?"

"Oh, years ago when I was just a child. His family, at least the people he was traveling with, were in Bristol at the same time as my own. We had rented a house for the summer and his, I suppose it must have been his entourage, occupied one nearby. He was quite exotic and I was quite easily impressed."

"And you met him again in London?"

"He found me," she said with sulky dignity. "Unfortunately, for a while I only saw him with the eyes of the gullible and overly romantic child I once was."

"Did he ever mention *why* he was in London?"

Every nerve in Charlotte jumped to full attention. These were more than a jealous would-be lover's questions about his competition. She lifted her chin. "He said it was because of me."

"That was the only reason he gave?"

Charlotte turned a cold gaze on St. Lyon, playing the role of overconfident beauty to the hilt. "You suggest he would need another?"

The comte, whose appreciation of the female intellect had never been great, accepted her childish pique with good grace. No, that wasn't exactly right, Charlotte realized, he accepted it with relief. What did he suspect about Dand? For clearly he suspected something. And why? Had he seen Dand on one of his hunts? Or had someone else?

He laughed indulgently. "No, no, my dear," he reassured her, taking her hand and patting it comfortingly. "You are more than enough reason for any man to make any number of arduous and dangerous journeys. I was just curious, was all. Now let me tell you something that will delight you."

Charlotte sniffed, allowing herself to be cajoled. "What?"

"My man, Rawsett, arrived this afternoon. We shall hold my little auction the day after next and then *everyone* will be leaving. Except, of course, for you and I." His gaze slipped lingeringly down her face and throat to her bosom. She half expected him to wet his lips with his tongue.

"Good!" she said and then, "When shall I meet Mister Rawsett?"

St. Lyon laughed. "You little wench. You really want to meet what Rawsett brings with him, the royal jewels." He shook his head. "I am afraid that will not be possible. No, do not ask. You aren't even supposed to know they're here! Everything is most sub-rosa. Some of these men could lose their very lives if it was known what they were here for. Royalists are notorious zealots. They would see anyone who even attempted to purchase the royal jewels as a traitor."

Charlotte gave him credit. He had given some thought to coming up with an explanation of why she couldn't play with the nonexistent gems.

"They needn't know," she suggested slyly.

"No, I dare not risk it," he chuckled. "I was most indiscreet and I know you would not like me to get into any trouble on your account. Besides, I have other jewels at my disposal that will grace that lovely throat just as well."

Dinner that evening proved a tense affair. St. Lyon's colleague, Lord Rawsett, sent his regrets with the excuse that the journey had exhausted him. The guests, having apparently been apprised of the fact that the auction was imminent, eyed each other distrustfully. When they did deign to speak with one another, they did so with ill-concealed impatience. To a man, it had become obvious that they were now doing little more than marking time.

The only exceptions were the women, who, not being privy to the importance of what was about to occur, seemed put out that the party, which had been none too lively to begin with, had further degenerated. Indeed, they had grown so bored with their tight-lipped and sullen companions that in desperation they finally turned to one another for conversation which, Charlotte was amused to see, was no different than any other group of ill-acquainted females, centering on the newest fashions and whether or not such and such a milliner was worth her fee. However, Charlotte—coming as she did from a genteel and well-heeled background and therefore having entered their profession not out of necessity but for other, unfathomable reasons—they viewed as outré and bizarre. They did not invite her to join their discussions. Nor did she have any desire to be included.

She had her own concerns.

Upon seeing her tonight, St. Lyon had apparently decided that little interlude in the courtyard was to be the precursor to a more intimate association—regardless of the time of month. As luck would have it, she was wearing the most extreme of the gowns Ginny had lent her. The delicate ivory tissue fit like a sheath of honeyed cream over her body, molding to the swells of her breasts and clinging to the dip of her waist and the slender muscles of her thighs, offering a visual repast for any gentleman willing to partake. St. Lyon partook with relish.

He sat her at his right side and spent most of the meal ignoring the gentleman on his left, whispering in her ear, his gaze sliding with heated interest over her person, his fingertips brushing her arm or her legs far too often for it to be accidental. He even insisted on feeding her little morsels from his plate, extolling his chef's talents as all the while his gaze lingered on the manner in which her mouth opened to receive the bits of fish and creamed mutton he offered her.

She played her part. She simmered and bit her lip and laughed at his sallies and endured his touch. But even though it was St. Lyon's gaze that stripped her naked, it was Dand's gaze she felt. He had been seated far down the table on the side opposite her. He wasn't eating. He had pushed his chair away from the table and slouched down in it, one arm flung along the back, his other hand idly twirling the stem of his wine-glass.

He refused to talk, too, playing the surly cast-aside lover to the hilt. Whatever comments his dinner companions made to him, he ignored. His attention, like his dark gaze, was fixed on St. Lyon. And her.

She had to find some way to tell Dand about the questions St. Lyon had asked regarding him. She must put him on guard. But with the comte's attention so firmly fixed, she could not think of how to pass word to him. Perhaps when the gentlemen retired for their after-dinner drink she might send Lizette to Dand's room. The maid had proved useful. She did not ask uncomfortable questions but did as she was bid without hesitation.

Her plan, alas, was short-lived. As soon as dinner ended, St. Lyon stood up and raised his glass. "Sirs, our time together grows short. What say we dispense with our nightly port?" His gaze flickered playfully toward Charlotte. "I, for one, have a far more pleasant pursuit to occupy my evening."

She tried to return his unctuous smile. The sound of Dand's chair banging against the wall brought her head swinging round just in time to see his broad-shouldered figure striding from the room.

"Ah. I see Monsieur Rousse is retiring now," St. Lyon said mildly. "An excellent notion."

* * *

St. Lyon would be here at any moment. She didn't
have time to waste on girlish vapors. This might be the
only chance she had to warn Dand of the comte's suspicions.

"Lizette, I need you to do something for me. Something very important," she said, starting to scrawl a
note. "As soon as I finish, I need you to take this—"

A loud knock interrupted her.

"Charlotte. It is me, St. Lyon. Let me in." His
peremptory tone brooked no delay.

Damnation. Her gaze met Lizette's anxious one.
There was no time to finish her note. She nodded at her
maid. Drying her damp palms on her skirt, she waited
as Lizette unlatched the door. St. Lyon entered, barely
glancing at the maid.

"You can go now," he told Lizette. "And you needn't
return this evening."

Bobbing a hurried curtsy and with one last worried
glance at Charlotte, Lizette fled, closing the door behind her.

Charlotte empathized. She turned her back on the
comte and began to casually unclasp her pearl ear bobs.
"I am not sure I appreciate your tone, Comte," she said
coolly. "Nor your appearance here, uninvited. We have
no relationship which should lead you to believe you
can make free with my room or make assumptions regarding how I choose to spend my time."

Out of the corner of her eye, she watched him coming toward her. He stopped directly behind her. In the
mirror she saw him take from his pocket a heavy emer-

ald pendant strung on a gold chain. "You know, it has always been your arrogance coupled with your immodesty that attracted me. So proud and so bold. But now is not the time to treat me so high-handedly."

"I might say the same." She refused to give him the satisfaction of turning. Instead she watched as he slipped the pendant around her neck. She tilted her head, coolly examining the flash of the emeralds against her white skin, as if completely indifferent.

His hand fell on her shoulder, the blunt fingers curling around the pendant, his knuckles pressing into the soft flesh of her bosom. A shiver of distaste raced through her. He bent his head and kissed her on the side of the throat. His mouth was hot and moist. She closed her eyes, preparing to endure.

"Get away from her."

Her heart leapt at the sound of Dand's voice. She swung around. Dand stood just inside the door, his stance wide, his hands curled lightly into fists at his side. Her gaze flew to St. Lyon.

With an odd smile, he slowly turned to face his adversary. "Ah, Monsieur Rousse, timely as ever."

Dand ignored him. His eyes were fixed on Charlotte. "Really, how could you think I would let another man take my place?" he asked, his tone amused and desolate. "I told you, *you are mine*. I meant it."

Amazing, terrible, so wrong in this place and at this time, yet her heart awoke with undeniable joy and swelled, filling her.

"A fool for love," St. Lyon said and brought his hands

up, applauding lightly. "And, God knows, there is no greater fool than that. Gaspard! Armand! Jacques!"

The bedroom door burst open and three huge men rushed into the room, grabbing hold of Dand's arms. He whipped around and heeled back, jamming his elbow hard into one of his attacker's chests and doubling him up. He snapped his head back, the contact of his skull against the face of the man behind him making a sickening *crack!* as blood spurted from the Frenchman's nose.

The man swore but somehow managed to seize Dand's arms, locking them behind him and twisting savagely as the third man shifted to the front of Dand and pummeled his midsection with a series of savage blows, dropping him to his knees.

It was over in a matter of seconds. The man Dand had felled staggered to his feet and with a curse, smashed his fist hard across Dand's face. He crumpled senseless in his assailants' grip.

"Comte!" Charlotte stumbled to her feet. "What is the meaning of this?"

St. Lyon, a look of horrid satisfaction on his face, glanced over at her. "Your lover, my dear, is a thief. Or rather, a would-be thief."

"I don't understand." She could not tear her gaze from Dand hanging limp in the rough clasp of St. Lyon's lackeys. He was breathing hard, his head moving as though he attempted to clear his thoughts.

"Rawsett identified him. I told you he was a well-informed man. This is not Andre Rousse. He is a thief, sent here to steal my prize. Quite a catch, though. He should be a font of interesting information. Expensive information."

"What are you going to do with him?" Charlotte demanded.

St. Lyon smiled. "Nothing that needs concern you, my dear. And for that you may be eternally grateful. But thank you for your aid in helping me secure him."

Dand raised his head. A trickle of blood fell from his broken lip. "If you think I'm a thief, St. Lyon, why didn't you just take me at dinner?"

"My guests are fretful and anxious enough as it is. And you, my cohort advised me, are most formidable. I should hate to have had you injure one of my little pigeons or scatter the rest of the flock in some spectacular sort of brawl. So I simply set you up, *mon ami*.

"Regardless what your mission here, it would take a blind man not to see how Miss Nash interfered with your concentration. My God, man." St. Lyon shook his head. "Have you *no* pride? You fairly make me blush the way you watch her. Only a man in love looks at a woman so.

"So, I decided to use this vulnerability to my advantage. I rather pawed Miss Nash throughout dinner, then came here to her room with my retainers following close, but not too close, behind. You reacted exactly as I expected you would."

Dear God, *she* had been the author of Dand's capture. Because he could not do what she and he had decided so many weeks ago must be done. He could not let her become St. Lyon's mistress, and now he stood in grave danger.

Fool! she castigated herself savagely. *Selfish, lovesick idiot!* She had actually felt joy when he had appeared. As though he was some sort of knight and she was a princess. She had *wanted* him to rescue her, to claim her for his own. And now he could well die for it and it would all be because of her.

St. Lyon turned to her. "Again, my thanks, my dear. Unfortunately, I think that I will be occupied for the rest of the evening. But then, I hope you do not think I am such a brute I would actually force myself on you? It was but an act for your friend's benefit."

She had to do something. But what? It would do Dand no good if St. Lyon suspected she loved him or even cared for him.

She walked over to where Dand stood on wobbly legs, his arms twisted at a painful angle behind him, and stopped directly before him.

"Friend?" she sneered. "He is no friend of mine." She turned as if in sudden realization. "Why, *that* is why you were asking me questions about him this afternoon!"

St. Lyon watched her closely.

"You were trying to determine if he and I were in league! Had you misunderstood my answers, or had they been less to your liking, you might have—! Because of my short association with him I might have—! *Oh!*" In a flash her hand struck out, dealing a resounding slap to Dand's face. She stayed before him, breathing heavily, hating herself.

He shook his head, as though to clear it and raised his eyes to hers, tasting the blood that sprang anew from his split lip. He smiled. "Congratulations, Lottie. You must have been wanting to do *that* for a great while."

"Take him away!" she said, whirling before anyone could see the tears stinging her eyes.

With a flick of his hand, St. Lyon motioned them to take Dand out and bowing, followed them.

25

∞∞∞

Comte St. Lyon's castle, Scotland
August 15, 1806

As THE FIRST MAUVE STAINS of dawn marked the horizon, Charlotte paced to one side of her room and back to the next. Where had they taken Dand? She thought she knew. Where better to get information than in that cold tower room where so many others over the decades had been questioned?

She had to find some way to free Dand, to find the letter, to escape. The possibility of doing any of them seemed improbable, accomplishing *all* three, impossible. She had to concentrate. Her only advantage was that St. Lyon wasn't certain whether she was an unwitting party to Dand's plot or an accomplice. Facts suggested he believed the latter.

She had tried leaving her room after St. Lyon had left last night only to have her steps dogged by a footman. She had made some paltry excuse about wanting something more to eat and found her way to the kitchen where the small staff, surrounded by the heaps of parings and carcasses and foodstuffs they'd been preparing for the next day's meal, had stared at her in gape-mouthed wonder.

Then, about half an hour ago, she had once again ventured out, only to be shadowed by Madame Paule while she went to the library and selected a book to read. If they kept watching her so closely, her chances of finding Dand or the damn letter would be bleak.

Her hands clenched in frustration as a tentative scratch at the door brought her wheeling around. "Come!"

Lizette, her bright eyes darting from side to side, slipped into the room. Charlotte's shoulders slumped. She'd forgotten her maid. Yet another responsibility. She had to get Lizette out of here unscathed, too. The girl deserved better than to be caught in the machinations into which Charlotte had thrown her. Indeed, she'd been most stalwart.

An idea occurred to Charlotte. Perhaps Lizette could serve both her own interests and Charlotte's. "Lizette, I am in trouble," she said without preamble.

"Aye, Miss Nash. I saw what Monsieur Rousse looked like when they dragged him out of here last night. The comte caught you together, did he?"

"Yes," Charlotte answered slowly, uncertain how much she ought to tell Lizette and deciding that the less the maid knew the less she could be held accountable for. "I have made a terrible mistake. I cannot tell you much, but I am being watched and I must find Monsieur Rousse before anything more happens to him."

"You love him, don't you?" Lizette asked and then, as if realizing her boldness, blushed. "Oh! I am sorry, miss. It's just that it never did sit right with me, you coming here when all the world could see you were still madly in love with Monsieur Rousse."

"It's all right, Lizette. You are quite right. The thing is this, I need your help. I need you to make some sort of commotion that will draw the footman away from the hall so that I can slip out. Can you do that, do you think? And then return to the room as though I were still here?"

"Yes, ma'am." Lizette nodded eagerly. "I know just the thing. Give me half an hour so it don't seem too convenient-like. You'll know when to bolt."

Charlotte nodded, impressed with the girl's canniness. With a quick curtsy, the maid slipped out of the room. Charlotte heard Lizette trading some flirtatious words with the hovering footman and then her footsteps retreating down the hall.

Quickly, Charlotte donned a fresh gown, a muted

plum-colored batiste that would meld with the early-morning shadows. She paced, her eyes returning again and again to the mantle clock. She knew where the staircase leading to the tower peep began, behind the fireplace in the anteroom at its base, but she wasn't certain where in the tower it ended. She had just finished going over her route in her mind when she heard a bloodcurdling scream from outside her door.

"Help! A rat! It's climbed up me skirts! Help!" Light footsteps pounded by her door, followed by more cries for help echoing down the hallway. A second later, she heard the footman call after Lizette and then the sound of him running in pursuit.

At once Charlotte ducked into the empty hall, picking up her skirts and running as swiftly as possible to the small, negligible doorway that marked the servants' staircase. She raced down them, stopping at the bottom to determine if the hallway outside was empty. It was. The staff were busy laying fires in the common rooms and setting the dining table for breakfast.

She moved quietly to the tower anteroom and stooped beneath the mantle of the empty fireplace. There. A small slit in the back indicated the hinges of a hidden door. She pushed and with a sound that filled her ears as loudly as thunder, the heavy portal pushed inward. She did not bother shutting it but slipped inside.

At once she realized the challenge she'd posed herself. Inside, it was black. The smell of mold and ancient smoke hung like a miasma in the air and a cold draft blew down from above, buffeting her cheek like death's kiss.

She shivered and edged forward, feeling with her foot. A step. She gingerly examined the dimensions with her foot. Ten inches high, six or seven deep. She stepped up again and again. Five steps, ten, a dozen. She swallowed, looking back at where the dim light from the anteroom filled the bottom of the narrow chute. Then the stairwell curved round and even that slight light was lost to her.

The wall pressed in on both sides, not much wider than the breadth of her shoulders, the outer one slanting in toward her as though the wall would at any moment collapse and trap her here in the blackness. The stairs seemed to go on forever. She ignored the tendrils of panic that clamored at the edges of her reason. She would not fail. She would not turn back—

High above she heard a voice, echoing and disembodied. Dand's. She groped along the wall, afraid of slipping, forcing herself to go slow, to be quiet, though every fiber of her being insisted she hurry.

A bar of light appeared overhead, illuminating a rectangular patch of stone. The peep. Cautiously she made her way up to it and caught her breath as she realized how large the peep was, at least a foot across. But how could that be? She would have seen it on her trip to the tower with St. Lyon.

Pressing back against the far wall, she looked out. For a second she did not understand what she was seeing and then, as she edged closer, she realized why she hadn't seen the peep earlier: It wasn't on eye level with someone standing in the room. It was above. The peep was hidden by the lintel stone capping one of the tower windows.

More confidently, she moved closer and looked down. St. Lyon sat in a chair in front of Dand, his legs crossed, his attitude resigned. Charlotte forced her gaze to Dand.

They had stripped him to the waist and chained his wrists to the iron rings embedded in the wall, his arms spread wide. The manacles had chaffed his skin raw, thin trickles of blood ran down his arms. Midnight blue bruises marked his ribs and the side of his face. But most terrible of all was the rose brand, gleaming darkly on the muscle of his left breast, a reminder that he had been here, or a place much like it, before.

"Is there anything I can do for you? I mean, short of letting you go of course," St. Lyon asked.

Dand didn't reply. Instead, he tried to shift his shoulders. The ache had settled in deeply after nearly a dozen hours, digging knuckles of pain in his back and neck. And he was damn thirsty. Every word he spoke reopened the cut on his lip.

St. Lyon sighed. "I know who you are. You're Andrew Ross. One of those *noble* orphans." He dragged the word out with a slight sneer. "Those boys who got themselves into that muddle in Malmaison. Unfortunately, you all got caught before you could be any use to the Royalists. Or your Church. Or whoever or whatever it is you were working for."

Dand glanced down at the rose brand stretched out along the muscle leading to his upper arm. "However did you guess?" His parched throat lent a deep rasp to his voice.

St. Lyon tipped his head, ceding the point. "Yes. You are rather distinctive."

Dand licked the blood from the corner of his mouth, making an effort to stand upright because his arms were getting bloody tired of holding his dead weight suspended between them. Not that St. Lyon had beaten or tortured him. But his underlings had been a little rough in escorting him up here, especially the one whose nose he'd broken. Consequently, by the time they locked him into the metal cuffs, he'd been unable to hold himself upright for a good while.

"I know why you are here."

"Pure genius," Dand managed.

"And I also know all about your companions."

Now *that* earned Dand's attention. He glanced up sharply. St. Lyon caught the involuntary movement. He smiled. "Ah, yes. I know all about your little conspiracy. The marquis of Cottrell and Colonel MacNeill are on their way here, due, I should say, to arrive soon. How did you think to get them inside the castle? Or did you think you'd only need to leave the back door open?" He chuckled.

What the hell was he talking about? Dand waited,

hoping the bastard would say something that made sense.

The comte's smile faded a little. "Although really, even for infamous Rose Hunters the hubris of thinking the three of you could take on me and my staff is a little extreme."

"I don't know who you've been chatting with, Comte," Dand croaked, "but you've been misinformed."

"I doubt that. My informant hasn't been wrong yet. Even to knowing how you would react to my appearance in Miss Nash's bedchamber."

Thank God, at least St. Lyon didn't suspect Charlotte. It took every ounce of Dand's overstretched resources not to let his relief show.

"Really, rather disillusioning, that," the comte said. "I had you marked for a man who would go to any lengths to secure his goal."

"Sorry to disappoint you."

"I *was* disappointed. Especially as the lady so clearly has no reciprocal feelings."

"Leave her out of this." Pain vanished. Plans to escape and plans to still secure that damn letter evaporated. All that was left was an instinctive need to protect Charlotte, a need so innate, so deeply rooted, he couldn't have reacted in any other way.

"I should like to . . ." St. Lyon trailed off.

Dand lifted his head, meeting the comte's gaze. "If you hurt her, in any way, to any degree, I will kill you."

The comte clucked his tongue, once more appearing

disgruntled and dismayed. "See? There is that arrogance again. So overwrought, all these dire threats and such."

"If she comes to any harm," Dand repeated softly, "you will die."

This time the comte's self-assurance did not fare so well. He sniffed, frowned, and stood up. "I am a gentleman. I have no intention of hurting her. Quite the opposite actually."

"Make certain of it," he muttered thickly.

"Yes, yes. Or you will kill me." The comte snickered. "The fact is, my friend, you are chained to a wall. You are guarded by several of my best men and even as we speak, your colleagues are riding into a trap. And finally, tomorrow, after I have finished selling the Prussian ambassador's extremely indiscreet letter to the pope—"

"I thought you hadn't read it," Dand cut in.

"I lied," the comte said calmly, then continued. "As I was saying, after I have auctioned off the letter, I shall, for a tidy sum, offer you and your companions to Napoleon's representative. I am sure he will be all atwitter to discover with whom you have been working in Paris."

"Ram and Kit aren't involved in this."

"Oh, please." The comte rose and snapped his fingers at one of the men hovering outside the door.

"I am sorry that I can't let you down from there. But you do have a reputation of being, how did he put it?, *formidable*. However, I can assuage your thirst." He turned to the guard. "Go and get Monsieur Rousse a glass of water at once."

"You are all kindness."

"I am a civilized man, Mister Ross, not a barbarian. I leave that to the *citizens.*"

"Ha!" Dand laughed. The sound rattled in his dry throat. "The citizens' acts are those of rank amateurs compared to the centuries of atrocities committed by the aristocracy."

The comte shrugged. "True enough. But at least I do not indulge in torture for the pure sport of it," his glance fell tellingly to Dand's brand, "as some of the revolutionaries have."

He seemed satisfied with this last remark, and with an impatient gesture motioned the guard out of the tower room, turning at the last moment and giving a courtly bow in Dand's direction. "I still do not know . . . Part of me wants to believe you really are Andre Rousse. Why is that, do you suppose?"

Dand snorted. "I haven't a bloody clue, Comte."

"Humph." The comte eyed him for a few more seconds and left, closing the tower door behind him.

At once Dand straightened and twisted round, managing to angle his hand in such a way that he could grasp the metal chain. He pulled as he rocked the chain back and forth, working at loosening the iron ring holding him. Earlier, when the guard had gone for dinner, he'd thought that he'd felt the slightest movement from deep within the rock.

"Dand." A voice, so soft that for a second he thought

delirium had found him, filtered across the room. "Dand!"

Charlotte. How—?

He looked up, scanning the mortared stone and saw a faint shadow move above the north window. She must have found one of the hidey holes.

"Charlotte," he said in a low, urgent voice. "Be careful. The guard will be back soon."

"I know." A pause. "What can I do?"

Brave lass. The only indication of her distress was a slight breathlessness.

"You have to find a way out of the castle," he said in a low voice. "You have to warn Kit and Ram. They are coming—"

"I heard," she broke in. "But . . . why? They aren't involved."

"Someone went to a great deal of trouble to make St. Lyon believe they *are* involved."

"But—" She broke off as she realized that how and who and why were not important now.

"Can you do this?" he asked.

"As soon as I find some way to open your manacles. Lizette can distract the guard—"

"No!" His imagination flashed through a dozen scenes of Charlotte being caught, implicated, sold alongside him and the others to Napoleon's agents. "*No.* There isn't time. This is more important and, if all goes well, Kit and Ram may well be in time to effect my rescue." He found a smile. "How much they will love that."

"I have to find a way to help you escape."

My God, was that a sob he heard? A sob for *him*? From his oh-so-hard and tough little spy?

It was almost worth being chained to this bloody wall to hear that. Almost, but not quite, because he couldn't do a bloody thing about her tears, couldn't hold her and console her and promise her all the things he wanted to promise her, had wanted to promise her for so long, far longer than he'd been willing to admit.

"You aren't going soft on me now, are you, Lottie?" he asked gently.

"Yes!" A wretched little snuffle. He could imagine her trying to smile and it tore at his guts. "*Yes*. Happy? You've brought me to this low state, Dand Ross. And I'll see you pay for it."

"Promise me," he whispered urgently.

He heard her breath catch and then her voice, low and vibrant, as though she was promising him her life, not retribution. "I do. I will. I swear it."

"Find Kit and Ram. They're the best chance we have of seeing your promise kept. Now go. Please."

She hesitated on the verge of saying something, and he prayed she would not. It would be too much like a parting gift and he had never had more to live for. But instead she only whispered, "I'll see you soon, Dand," and was gone.

26

CHARLOTTE WALKED BOLDLY down the hallway toward her bedchamber ignoring the footman-cum-guard's start of surprise. She doubted he would tell his master that she had gone missing for half an hour, particularly as nothing untoward had occurred during that time. He would be punished as well as made to look foolish at having been duped by a mere woman.

The entire St. Lyon staff, with the possible exception of Madame Paule, had a lamentable lack of appreciation for female intelligence. A fact for which Charlotte was profoundly grateful. She had an idea.

She entered the room to find Lizette holding one of Ginny's more luxurious gowns in front of her as she twirled before the huge mirror. "It's a lovely dress," she said gently.

With a guilty start, Lizette spun around. "Oh, miss! I am sorry. I didn't mean any harm! I just never had something so beautiful and I didn't think—"

"It's yours."

The maid stopped fidgeting, staring at Charlotte with round eyes. "What?"

"It's yours for helping me."

"Th-thank you, miss! I never had anyone be so generous to me before! I . . . I . . ."

"I need you to help me again, Lizette," Charlotte said. "Only this time it will be a great deal more dangerous. No, wait," she said as the maid stepped eagerly forward. "Listen carefully before you answer, Lizette.

"You don't even know what is at stake and I can't tell you. I must tell you, however, that you *could* lose your life in this endeavor. I do not think it will come to that. I would not ask this of you if I thought the peril too great, but there is still a chance and you must understand the risks.

"One last thing," she said, holding up her hand. "You needn't do this. The dress will be yours regardless. You already own my gratitude."

The little maid gave her a pert smile. "Of course I'll do what you ask, miss. I knew the risks of working for a lady with your reputation when I come to you. My dad warned me, but I wouldn't hear of nothing else.

"You see, I figure the greater the risks, the greater the rewards and sure enough, I already have a lovely new gown! Besides, frankly, miss, I don't have in mind to spend the rest of my life in service. A few nice gowns could help a girl with a plan for her future."

Dear God, Charlotte thought. And Dand thought *she* was a tough little pragmatist.

"Now, what is it you want me to do?" Lizette asked, carefully folding her new dress.

Charlotte told her.

"Still feeling unlike yourself, Miss Nash?" Comte St. Lyon asked solicitously.

Charlotte regarded him coolly. "Yes."

"I hope you are not still angry about last night? I hoped you would understand that my untoward behavior was simply a means of drawing Ross into a situation where he could be taken into custody with as little distress to my guests and as much discretion as possible."

"And what of *my* distress?" she demanded, knowing her color was high. Knowing this because she had applied the rouge herself before finding the comte after dinner. "You might have told me your plan. Or is it you don't trust me? What a foolish question. Of course you don't. Why else have you set that harridan Madame Paule to follow me and those footmen to dog my footsteps?"

"It is for your own safety, my dear."

"And from whom am I supposed to be endangered?" she asked wrapping her shawl about her shoulders. They stood in the alcove leading to the courtyard. Lanterns hung in the tree branches bobbed like fairy globes in the developing mist.

"Ross has been taken away," she said. "Are there other villains amongst your guest list, the guest list whose delicate sensibilities you are so determined to protect?"

He regarded her with an expression mixed of impatience and surprise, both stemming from her unexpected acuity. "You are correct," he finally said. "I do not altogether trust you. I dare not. What I am doing is too important to my future.

"However," he reached out and secured her hand. "I hope once this is over and we are both more certain of one of the other, you will understand and forgive me."

She snatched her hand away. "You can hope."

As she anticipated, he was growing weary of her tantrum and, as she had also anticipated, her temper was clearly relaxing his suspicions about her. A woman so at the mercy of her emotions could not possibly be a viable agent. Unless it was an act . . . But a man of such discernment, such experience with the gentle sex as Maurice St. Lyon, would always be able to tell when a woman was acting and when she was not.

"How can I make this up to you?" he asked.

"You can leave me alone. And tell your people to stop following me."

"I am sorry. I cannot do that."

She pouted, her lip trembling. "Fine! I promise to stay here in the courtyard in plain sight of whoever might care to look. But you . . . stay away from me!"

He threw up his hands. "If you insist on staying out here and catching a chill just to prove how heinous you find my company, suit yourself."

"I shall!" she said, snapping her shawl over her head

and flouncing out into the courtyard. She flung herself down on the marble bench and waited a few moments, letting the quickly thickening fog grow denser before standing up and striding to the edge of the path where the yew shrubs grew nearly as high as a man. "Comte! Are you still watching me? Answer me!"

"Yes, Miss Nash." He sounded annoyed. "I am still here."

"Well, since you enjoy watching me so much, watch this!" She reached behind her neck and snatched off the pendant he'd given her last night. She held it out toward his indistinct figure, standing under the arcade. The light caught the emerald. "Do you see what this is? It's your pendant—oh!" The emerald slipped from her fingers. She dropped down to search at her feet and a few seconds later a female figure rose, the pendant held stiffly out.

"There! You can have it back!" she called out and had the satisfaction of hearing the pendant skitter on the flagstones by his feet.

"Watch her!" he clipped out and turned, stomping away.

From where she crouched behind the yew shrub, Charlotte silently applauded Lizette's marksmanship. They'd traded places when Charlotte had dropped to the ground and her maid rose from the same place. Lizette, dressed as closely to Charlotte as the wardrobe would allow and having cut her brown locks in the same style, had been waiting behind the yews for the last forty-five minutes.

"Stay here for an hour. If St. Lyon returns, lift your nose in the air and stalk off in the opposite direction," Charlotte whispered. "Watch the river after midnight and into morning. When you see a light under the window let down the rope."

"What if you don't come back by morning?" For the first time a quaver of fear shook her maid's voice.

"I will, Lizette," Charlotte promised. With or without help, she wouldn't abandon her or Dand. She prayed that Dand was right and Ram and Kit were on their way here and that they would be able to do something. Yet even as she prayed, she could not help but ask herself what they could do even if she did find them. How could two men and a woman hope to assault the fortress St. Lyon had made of his castle? And yet the alternative, to do nothing, was untenable.

"I'll come back, Lizette," she repeated. "I swear it."

"All right, miss," Lizette said, swallowing as she bolstered her courage. "Best go."

Charlotte moved along the edge of the yew hedge on hands and knees until she came to the far corner. There she shed her gown and donned the boy's breeches and shirt Lizette had stolen from the laundry that afternoon. Then, careful to keep to the servants' hall and the corridors that ran parallel to those used by the family and guests, she made her way to the kitchen and the final phase of her plan to escape undetected from St. Lyon's castle.

*   *   *

Charlotte forced herself to roll limply, hoping that in the dark the tired kitchen boy wouldn't note that the pile of refuse and carcasses and peelings and parings and rinds and feathers he dumped from the kitchen cart behind the stables outside the castle contained a human figure.

He didn't. She waited, lying in an oozing, fragrant stew until she heard the cart wheels rumble up the steep drive and the boy's shout for the guard to open the door. It was answered by the groan of the huge portal on its ancient hinges. Then, spitting and wiping the garbage from her face, she stood up and looked around. The quarter moon was on the ebb, but its paltry light was enough to pick out the gray ribbon of road threading over the crest of the hill. It was the only road anywhere near and thus the one on which Ram and Kit must arrive.

They *had* to come. Dand's life depended on it. He couldn't die. He could not. The thought was too devastating to entertain and she thrust it from her thoughts.

She trotted along the road until her legs ached and her shins splintered in pain. Then she walked. She walked under the bright band of the Milky Way while the owls commenced their evening hunt, sifting the wind on soundless wings. She walked until her feet were blistered in their dainty slippers and the thin, delicate soles had been worn through on the gravel road.

She had been walking for four hours when she saw them. Not Ram and Kit, but a band of men marching along in a double line, twenty at least, led by two men on horseback.

She hesitated, uncertain of who they were. They did not wear red coats and she had heard tales of how well organized the bands of smugglers and highwaymen were. They hadn't seen her yet.

She scrambled down the side of the road and waited, holding her breath and so heard coming from one of the horsemen, a sophisticated voice drawl, "Thank God, Parnell kept some of the militia at his estate to deter the smugglers."

His companion on the other horse answered, "Thank God, he responded to Father Tarkin's request. I think the bastard still has a soft spot for my Kate."

It was Kit!

With a sob, she scrambled up the steeply pitched sides of the road as a familiar voice replied, "Since we are thanking the Almighty, I suppose we ought to offer up a prayer of thanks that the inimitable Mrs. Mulgrew came to her senses and revealed all in a message to the abbot."

"Yes," the deep Scottish burr grumbled. "And when I get hold of our little sister, it will be she who is thanking God that I don't throttle her. *If* I don't throttle her. And Andre Rousse shall pay, too, by God!"

She made it up to the road and stumbled out of the concealing bracken almost beneath the hooves of the horse, waving wildly. The horse shied and reared. She didn't care. She grinned up at them. "Ram! Kit!"

"What is it?" Colonel Christian MacNeill asked his brother-in-law.

Ramsey Munro, marquis of Cottrell, canted one of his elegant brows and surveyed the ragged, filthy creature gamboling beneath their horse's hooves. "Begad, Kit, I do believe it's Charlotte!"

27

∞∞∞

Comte St. Lyon's castle, Scotland
August 16, 1806

TRUE TO ST. LYON'S WORD, the guard returned with a tin of water for Dand to drink, threw it in his face, and with a satisfied grunt retreated to the other side of the tower door. Dand could not have cared less. Since Charlotte had left he had strained to hear any sound that could tell him whether she had succeeded in escaping from the castle. When the hours had passed without so much as a raised voice, he had allowed himself a smile.

Smart, devious, clever Lottie. His darling. His love. She'd escaped.

Now he stared out the window trying to decide if it was lighter in the east or not as he worked obstinately at the bolt embedded in the rock wall. He could definitely feel it grating against the stone and a little drift of dust had begun trickling from the bottom of the ring. How much longer would it take to unseat it from its ancient mooring? However long it took, he thought with a dry smile. It wasn't as if he had much else to occupy his time, though in his mind he followed Charlotte as she crested the road to the south and disappeared into the wilds.

Ram or Kit would find her. Or, if not them, eventually a croft or a drover. She would use that quick tongue and quicker mind to find her way home. And that should be enough for him. But it wasn't. Loving Charlotte had made him greedy. He wanted to be with her, to spend long years working, laughing, debating, planning, and making love with her.

He hoped that when Ram and Kit arrived they wouldn't require much of him in the way of additional aid. That Kit and Ram *were* coming was a notion to which he stubbornly clung. Absurd, when in all probability, they would all be captured and end up back in LeMons dungeon. And wouldn't that be the ultimate irony?

As he laughed, he heard a sound outside the door. The guard mumbled, a male voice replied. A familiar voice. Even though he had expected to hear it, his heart still thudded at the sound.

The door opened a few inches and stopped as if the person on the other side hesitated.

"Come in, Douglas, me lad," Dand said.

The Nash town house, York
1801

"How Dougie would have loved that," Ram Munro said, his smile even more sardonic than usual. "The vow of service to the beautiful virgins, the rose, the symbol of our fidelity, given over to their care . . . he would have swooned with delight!"

Kit MacNeill shot him a sharp, assessing glance, his heavy jaw, pared down by so many months in LeMons dungeon, bulging. "Yer not mocking the dead, are you, Ram Munro?" he asked setting a large hand on the slender young man's shoulder.

Angrily, Ram shook it off. They stood at the bottom of the drive leading to the Nash house like three barristers with different clients at a land hearing, uncertain and suspicious of one another, wanting only to each go his own separate way. And yet, most of their lives they'd been as close as brothers.

But betrayal, Dand Ross had discovered, tended to sever even the strongest ties. And these men believed that one of their number had betrayed them and those who'd depended on them, a betrayal that had resulted in the death of the best of them, their undeclared leader, Douglas Stewart.

Dand could have put their minds at ease, could have

healed the wound that cut them off from one another. But that would entail another sort of betrayal, of one who had already paid the ultimate sacrifice for his . . . weakness. So he said nothing, though it ate at his heart and played havoc with his conscience.

"What do you think, Dand?" Ram turned to him, his dark eyes narrowed thoughtfully. "You've been awful quiet. You were never quiet before. Not even in the dungeon. Not until after they took Douglas to the guillotine."

Dand gave him a flat, unfriendly look. "I told you before and I'll tell you again, one last time and that is all: I did not reveal a bloody thing to the warden nor to anyone at LeMons."

Kit spat savagely onto the dirt street, "Aye! And I've sworn the same thing! And Ram, too, for that matter! But we know that one of us is a liar, don't we?"

He wanted to say no. But because of the love he once bore Douglas Stewart, he remained mute.

"How did you know it was me?" He looked older, premature lines carved into the corners of his mouth and forehead, but then Douglas had ever been a fretter.

"What is this, Dougie?" Dand asked. "No greeting, no embrace for your long-lost brother?"

"How did you know it was me?" Douglas asked again, slowly entering the room and skirting the perimeter, his gaze darting hither and yon as if he suspected some trap, as if he did not believe the evidence of his eyes and that Dand was only pretending to be chained to the wall.

Dand shrugged. The movement set needles into the muscles of his shoulders. "Captain Watters, Reverend Tawster, Lord Rawsett—they're all anagrams for Stewart. You always loved to embellish everything."

Douglas smiled, a little bitterly. "And you never appreciated it."

"I never had the need," Dand rejoined. "A man either did a thing or he didn't. He either was noble or he wasn't."

Douglas laughed. "You never understood true nobility. You think because you didn't squeal to Gardien you were noble? You just endured pain better. Like a dumb beast."

The laughter abruptly ended. "It was your fault, you know," Douglas whispered.

"How so?"

"In the dungeon, that night they brought you back after . . . branding you. You remember?" He was very close now and he stared into Dand's eyes with terrible earnestness, a trace of the boy he'd been lingering there, still scared, still aching.

"Yes."

"I asked you if you'd told Gardien the names of our confederates and you said no. You even laughed, mocking me, saying no, you were just as good as me." Douglas tipped his head, his mouth clenching as though to hold back tears. "But I *had* told Gardien. And I looked at you as soon as you said that and . . . and I saw that *you knew it!*"

Douglas flung himself around, running his hand

through his short dyed hair. "I couldn't bear that. I *knew* you would tell the others."

"I wouldn't have."

Douglas did not hear him. "Unless you thought I had made up for it by dying." He was reliving some potent, terrible memory. "The thought of them, all knowing that I'd failed, that I'd dishonored myself when none of them had . . . the idea of them looking at me like you had . . ." He gasped as if in physical pain. "I couldn't live with it."

"But you couldn't die with it, either," Dand said coldly.

"But I did!" He snapped around, his head nodding violently and now Dand could see the madness that had seized Douglas Stewart, virulent and filled with self-hatred. "I arranged with Gardien for my own death. I told him I would tell him anything he wanted to know, any names, any bits of information, *anything*, if he would just stage my death so you would honor me!" His voice broke at the last, filled with self-pity.

Dand would have felt sorry for him then, would have given him all the sympathy he was begging for, except . . . "But that wasn't the end of your deal with Gardien."

Douglas stopped sniffling and lifted his face. His eyes were red-rimmed but assessing. "What do you mean?"

"You staged your death so we would think you died heroically, the first of us to go under the blade. *But you arranged with Gardien for us to be next.*"

Douglas's eyes narrowed.

"That was the deal, wasn't it?" Dand asked. "We were to be killed a few days later, just long enough to do justice to your glorious memory. Long enough for me to feel guilty for doubting your integrity, your nobility, and for Ram and Kit to spend their final days blessing your name.

"Quite a nice little mourning party you had planned for yourself, Douglas. Too bad Colonel Nash mucked up the works by trading himself for us."

Douglas didn't even bother to deny Dand's accusation. "Gardien couldn't resist the coup of acquiring a national hero like Nash. He betrayed me!"

Seeing the disgust in Dand's eyes, Douglas lurched forward, grabbing a handful of his hair and slamming his head back against the wall. Pain exploded in the back of Dand's skull and lights tripped across the black velvet of his vision.

"I should have been celebrated, I should have been a hero! Instead I have lived in France, making myself useful to thieves and traitors and despots. Because of you! You and Ram and Kit. Because of you three I couldn't come back."

He laughed suddenly, the sound shrill and manic. "But like Lazarus, I am about to rise from the dead. I will regain everything I once had and more."

"How?" Dand scoffed. "By killing me?"

Amazingly, a look of hurt passed over Douglas's face. "I never wanted to hurt any of you. I only tried to facilitate matters. The only time I took an active role and tried to . . . hurt Ram, that blond bitch nearly killed me.

"I spent a year recovering from that wound," he said darkly. "That's when I developed my plan. I thought about things, about why things happen, and why I had failed. And I realized it was because God wanted me to be the hero he'd intended I should have been."

From far below Dand heard a startled shout and the sound of running feet. Ram? Kit? He had to keep Douglas talking.

"What plan was that?" he asked.

"This plan," Douglas answered quietly. "For months I had been following Miss Nash, knowing that eventually one of the Rose Hunters would have to visit her, to fulfill that pledge you made. When I saw her with Ginny Mulgrew I suspected what she had become. And then you came to her and I knew for certain. You may be illusive, but your reputation is not. After that, it was all . . . providential."

"Go on," Dand said, holding Douglas's gaze as from far below the sounds of conflict grew. Douglas didn't appear to notice. He seemed to *need* to tell Dand his plan, to *need* Dand to appreciate how clever, how far-sighted he'd been.

"I killed the Frenchman that carried the letter St. Lyon now holds," Douglas recited gravely. "I gave it to St. Lyon. I killed Toussaint—please do not look like that. He never valued me—and I took his place, arranging a few meetings with Miss Nash, while in my guise as Rawsett, I encouraged St. Lyon's interest in both Mrs.

Mulgrew and Miss Nash. Then I drove Mrs. Mulgrew down in the street and sent for Charlotte Nash.

"As Touissant, I had intended to suggest that she take the whore's place. Imagine my amazement when she suggested it herself and then told me that you had fallen in with the plan?"

He turned his head slightly, the sounds of strife below having finally penetrated whatever need to confess drove him. It did appear to alarm him. "Ram!" he exclaimed tenderly. "Or Kit. They would of course put up a great fight. But even they cannot withstand the force of St. Lyon's thirty men."

Douglas was wrong. Not about the odds but about what was happening below. There were far too many voices to account for the capture of only two men, regardless of how proficient they were at fighting. Something else was happening. And he needed to keep Douglas distracted long enough for it to play out.

"Tell me, Doug lad, how will all this return you to the illustrious position you have been so wrongfully deprived of?"

If Douglas heard the sarcasm in Dand's query he ignored it. "Simple. I sent a note to Kit and Ram telling them that their sister-in-law had become the mistress of a known womanizer. At the same time I informed St. Lyon that two men in league with you were on their way here to steal the letter.

"And so they were and here they apparently are. Shortly, they will be killed. Then St. Lyon will kill you. I, in turn, shall kill St. Lyon. After which, I will retrieve the letter and hand deliver it to Father Tarkin, where I shall then reveal that having escaped the guillotine I have spent the last six years working *sub rosa* for the good of the Church. I will be hailed as a great hero."

"And the Nash sisters?" Dand asked.

The dreamy smile stayed on Douglas's lips. "Oh, I shall kill them quite soon. They've seen me and while I don't think they paid too much attention to me in my disguises, I won't take any chances."

He closed his eyes and inhaled deeply, blissfully. "And once all of you are dead, I will finally be alive again."

His face twisted, the young boy that lurked behind the man, appearing once more, lost and tortured. He squeezed his eyes shut. *"I just want to go home."*

"If we die, you'll never be alive again, Douglas. You'll never be able to go home."

Douglas's eyes snapped open. He frowned. "What do you mean?"

"You depended on us, Ram and Kit and me, to tell you who you were. Right from the beginning. If we are dead, there will be no one to tell you who you are."

"That's not true," he said, but a tremor of terror underscored his insistence.

"Certainly it is," Dand said reasonably.

"No." He shook his head violently. "I'm . . . I'm . . ."

"No one."

Douglas's lips parted, his brows bunched above the bridge of his nose.

"What do you think I have been doing all these years, Doug?"

"What?"

"Finishing what you set out to do. I took your place because you're dead."

"NO!" Douglas launched himself forward. Dand tensed, jerking sideways and felt the bolt move. Incrementally. But it moved—

Douglas's fist caught him in his damaged ribs, buckling his knees. He collapsed like a sack of wheat, his weight catching on his abused shoulders, dragging a groan from his chest. At the same time a stab of hope pierced his clouded thoughts as the bolt gave up another fraction of an inch.

"No! No! *You* aren't the leader! *You* didn't keep faith with the oath. You're *dead*!" Douglas shouted, standing over Dand, his face red, tears streaking his face, his eyes ablaze.

"Dand!!"

It was Charlotte, calling from the stairwell outside. *God, no.*

"Charlotte! Run!" he shouted, throwing himself against the chains holding him.

"It's over!" she cried, elated. He could hear her footsteps racing up the steps. "Everything is fine!"

"No! *Douglas is here!*"

It was too late. Douglas slipped to the side of the door just as Charlotte burst into the room brandishing a pistol.

"Kit and Ram and the militia have secured the castle and St. Lyon is trapped in his library!"

She understood the second she saw him that something was wrong. She spun around, raised the primed pistol, and fired.

28

∞∞∞

Comte St. Lyon's castle, Scotland
August 16, 1806

"DAMN!" CHARLOTTE EXCLAIMED. The shot went far wide, ricocheting off the wall and sending a chip of stone flying into the man's face . . . "Toussaint!"

"No, Miss Nash," said the foppishly clad man, shutting the door. "I am afraid I deceived you. My name is Douglas Stewart."

Her amazed gaze flew to Dand. His face twitched with ill-contained emotion, but his eyes remained coolly appraising.

Toussaint–Stewart smiled at Dand. "You really should have taught her how to aim a pistol."

"I'll rectify that oversight as soon as possible."

The man pursed his lips. "Hard to do from the grave."

"What is the point in killing me now, Douglas?" Dand asked, amazing Charlotte by how calm and reasonable he sounded. She did not move. She dare not draw any attention to herself.

"You heard her," Dand continued. "Ram and Kit have found some pet soldiers somewhere and taken the castle. St. Lyon's guests are doubtless flying like cunny before the hounds and St. Lyon is quite probably burning any incriminating documents he owns. Including your hero-making letter. And you are exposed."

"Only to you," Douglas said. "You die and no one knows I was here. Oh, I shall have to begin again, I grant you that. But I have waited this long, I can bide my time."

He glanced at Charlotte. "Of course, she will have to die, too. But she always *was* going to die."

"No," Dand said.

"Yes." Douglas's hand whipped out, seizing Charlotte's arm and dragging her forward. She fought, scratching and twisting, kicking at him, but he was not Dand; he did not care if he hurt her. He wrenched her arm behind her back and twisted, forcing a cry from her lips. She went limp in his grip, knowing that to fight further meant a broken arm.

"Let her go," Dand said, his quiet voice lethal.

"Not a chance," Douglas said. "You know, I actually believe you love the chit. What is this obsession you and the others have with these Nash women? Granted they're pleasing enough to look upon, but when you are pleasuring yourself, one woman is as good as the next." He frowned, a little petulant, a little offended. "How could this physical rutting take the place of what we had? What we were?"

"And what was that?" Dand asked. "A bunch of boys with wooden swords playing at being knights?"

Douglas's mouth pleated angrily and he shoved Charlotte toward Dand, one hand tight about her throat, the other still holding her wrist between her shoulder blades. She gasped in the pain.

"Then say good-bye to your beloved, Dand," he spat. Dand pitched himself forward only to be caught short by the tether of chain.

Charlotte searched about frantically, trying to find some advantage, and that is when she saw it, the little crumbles of mortar beneath the ring securing Dand's right wrist. She met his gaze and then looked directly at the ring. He gave the barest of nods.

It was poor odds. But then, they were the only odds they had.

"Please," she rasped as Douglas's hold tightened. "Let me kiss him once more. One last kiss. Please."

"Why should I grant you any requests?"

"Because you once loved him, too," Charlotte whispered. "Because you once called him brother. And that should be worth something."

Douglas stilled.

"Please."

"Mercy?" He sounded doubtful but intrigued.

"Yes, mercy," she said. "A noble nature can be merciful."

"All right." He grabbed her other wrist, wrenching it, too, behind her back. Then with a sound of contempt, he pushed her forward so that she stood within reach of Dand. She met his eyes, leaning forward, ignoring the pull of her arms in their sockets, bringing her lips gently against his. She kissed him with all the tenderness and hope in her heart.

"I love you," she whispered against his mouth and hooking her ankle behind Douglas's foot, pitched herself forward.

Her left shoulder popped. Agony speared through her arm and she was tumbling forward, Douglas falling after her, twisting, swearing, trying to regain his balance. She heard Dand, his voice raw with effort, then a roar of triumph and the clatter of chains and then Douglas was snatched away from her.

She landed on her knees and rolled, scrambling backward and turning to see what had happened.

Dand stood behind and over Douglas, the chain that had bound his right arm twisted tight around Douglas's throat, his other hand still manacled to the wall. Douglas was gasping for air, clawing at the metal links digging into his flesh. Dand twisted harder, his face terrifying, feral in its cold ferocity. He pulled up and back. Douglas's heels drummed uselessly against the floor as he sought and failed to find his footing. His arms beat less urgently now, the life draining from him.

"Dand! Let him go! You're killing him!"

"He was going to kill you!" he roared.

She winced, cradling her arm as she stumbled to her feet. "Let him go! You're not the murderer! *He is!*"

Dand's lips drew back in a snarl, his teeth bared. But awareness slowly seeped in his eyes as a panoply of emotions flickered across his face. He jerked one last time on the chain and Douglas went limp. With a growl, he suddenly loosened his hold and stepped back, breathing heavily.

"Are you hurt?" Concern etched his face.

"I'll be fine," she lied. Her shoulder ached abominably.

"There's an iron bar behind the door. Can you get it?"

"Yes," she answered, suiting action to words as she found the iron rod. She turned. "It's only my—Dand!"

She was too late. Douglas, if he had ever been unconscious, was conscious now. He threw himself across the room, well out of Dand's reach and scrambled up onto the north window's sill, his eyes wild and his smile maniacal. "You couldn't kill me any more than I could kill you. It's the bond, you see. The brotherhood. It won't be gainsaid."

"If you make one movement toward her, I swear I will rip you to shreds, Douglas," Dand said as he yanked savagely at the one chain still holding him.

"More hubris, Dand?" Douglas asked, eyeing her and the weapon she held, clearly trying to decide whether he could wrest it from her without further injury. She wasn't certain he couldn't.

She had been courageous enough. She could not be courageous any longer. Without thinking, she flew across the room and into the shelter of Dand's arms. They enfolded her tightly. He made a gesture of invitation toward Douglas with his free hand. "Try me."

"I think not. Not now," Douglas said. "You're too formidable. And I am not quite up to snuff, you see."

He was babbling, his eyes darting about the room, edging backward. "Something will have to be done. About all of you. I just can't think what right now. I have to make plans. Make preparations—"

He looked down. What he saw made him smile. He looked back at Dand. "Remember the ivy vines we used to climb at the old castle, Dand?" For a second his voice was eager, a friend reminiscing about the best of times. "Remember how it was? What a foursome we were! How valiant! How worthy!"

And without any further word, he threw his leg over the casement and disappeared.

Charlotte didn't give a tinker's damn. She was here, in Dand's arms, and they were both alive. Against all odds, they had lived. She started weeping and then sobbing, and finally buried her face against his broad, bloodied chest and burst into full-blown tears.

"What is this, Lottie?" She heard him murmur tenderly into the crown of her head. "Why, I do begin to suspect you aren't so tough after all."

His gentle teasing brought her back to herself.

She was Charlotte Nash, one of Society's most coming chits, as fly to the time of day as a woman twice her age, a fluent temptress, a naughty wench, and an acknowledged heartbreaker. She lifted her face and drew Dand's poor abused mouth down to hers, meeting it in a deep and lush kiss. If it hurt him he didn't seem to mind, his untethered arm tightened about her lifting her up, crushing her to him.

After a long moment, she drew back, a little breathless, a little dazed.

"Lest you are uncertain about what that was, what *this* is," she said in a triumphant voice, "let me make it clear for you. You are mine. *Mine.*"

"My love," he answered. "I never doubted it."

It was exactly like when they were boys and had escaped the abbey to play in the old castle ruins on the moors. The same type of stone, the same sturdy thick vines to grapple and swing from. The same sense of freedom and adventure and *rightness*. Except . . . there would be no other lads waiting for him at the bottom. No long companionable journey back under the star-splashed skies. Nothing.

All he had ever wanted was to go home. For things to be as they once were. Was that too much to ask?

He groped for a foothold on the heavy vine and slipped, catching himself at the last moment and that is when he saw it. Improbable. No, *impossible*, but there it was, just above him and a few feet over, shining in the early dawn light with all the grace and beauty of his long-lost boyhood, a yellow rose, a little dew trembling like a tear on one tenderly curving petal. With a sigh of wonder, he pulled himself up, stretching to reach it and felt the vine beneath him crack. He didn't care.

He strained further out, his fingertips brushing the

velvety bloom, stretching, stretching . . . He seized it and the thorns hidden beneath the glossy leaves plunged deep into the meat of his palm. With a gasp he snatched his hand back, having captured his prize.

It was beautiful. The one utterly perfect thing in a world of regret and disappointment—

With a sound like a sob, the vine beneath his feet gave way completely.

He never felt himself hit the ground.

Kit and Ram burst through the door, pistol and sword drawn. They found themselves in an empty room. Except for Dand, who was holding Charlotte as though he would never let her go. And kissing her.

Kit lowered his pistol and cleared his throat.

The manacled man raised his head. "You're late," he said tersely. "Charlotte could have been killed waiting for you two to make your appearance."

Ram was the first to recover. He strolled into the room and looked around. "Sorry about that. We had the matter of some thirty of St. Lyon's men to attend to, as well as the comte who, by the way, claims he knows nothing of any letter. Although there was a mysterious scrap of paper in his library fireplace. His guests, some of whom I suspect are on this soil without the proper documents, are fleeing in droves."

"Good," Dand said.

"You are, I suppose, Charlotte's paramour, the mysterious Monsieur Rousse?" Kit asked.

"Yes," Dand answered. "Now, if you would be so kind, I believe the keys to my shackles are on a hook outside the door."

It was Kit who did the honors, returning with the key and unlocking the cuffs, obliging Charlotte to disentangle herself from him during the process. Freed, Dand grimaced slightly at the aches he was beginning to feel and feared he would feel a great deal more in the days to come.

"Better?" Kit asked consolingly.

Dand nodded.

"Good," Kit said, smiling, and promptly knocked him out cold.

EPILOGUE

"You're a seer, Brother Martin. A bona fide mystic." Brother Fidelis, beaming with pleasure, clapped the wizened old herbalist on the shoulder.

Brother Martin, in the middle of tying a little silk bag filled with various herbs and flower petals, slapped away the rotund and benevolent monk's hand. "I don't know what you're blathering about."

"Well, you said that if we kept having weddings at the abbey we would end up having christenings and here we are today, about to have our very first christening! Isn't it wonderful?"

"Fabulous," the old crabbed monk snickered, but there was not much venom in his sarcasm. "Now, if you don't mind, I promised this tisane for the baby."

"Poor little wretch," Fidelis said. "She must have an upset tummy."

"She has," Brother Martin declared, "her father's disposition and her mother's temper. I always said Dand Ross, or Andre Rousse, or Sir Ross, or whoever he's fancying himself these days, was a limb of Satan and now his daughter is proving to be a twig from that same branch."

It sat hard with Brother Martin that the boy they'd sheltered as an orphan might be some sort of Bourbon royal, though by his own words he admitted he could never prove it. What was certain is that he'd been knighted for his work on behalf of His Royal Majesty.

"The babe is perfectly beautiful," sighed the smitten Brother Fidelis.

"Aye, she is that," Brother Martin allowed with a little grunt. "Looks like her aunt Kate what with all that ebony fluff on her head." Brother Martin had always had a soft spot for the handsome Kate MacNeill. "But with such parents the world had best beware. Now, come along before the little witch screams the rafters down."

The two monks left Brother Martin's herbalist shed, passing through the walled rose garden as they went. It was a fine day. The deep blue sky above their remote little valley sparkled, kissed with warmth. Around them the first blooms of spring were just beginning to show, little hints of color trembling on the tips of vines and canes sheathed in fresh green down, like deer antlers in velvet. The crusader's yellow rose, the only one of its kind in all of Scotland, had not yet set its blossoms, but the promise was there in verdant new growth and glossy green leaves.

At the wall, Brothers Martin and Fidelis ducked beneath the low arched doorway and headed across the common. Even from here they could hear Dand's brat squalling. She didn't sound as if she was in pain. She sounded angry.

They hurried into the chapel where thirty pairs of eyes turned around. The boys and monks kneeling in the back relaxed. Lizette Barnes and Ginny Mulgrew, sharing a pew as well as Ginny's carriage on the long trip up during which Lizette had learned Many Fascinating Things, breathed audible sighs of relief. The Baron and Baroness Welton, both wearing the superior look of those who have bet everything on a long shot and somehow managed to have been right, smiled weakly. The Marchioness of Cottrell, as swollen with child as a tick and as alarmed by the baby's yelps as a rabbit by a dog's keening, cast a desperately anxious look at her sophisticated and urbane husband, who answered her unspoken plea with murmured assurance that their anticipated darling, "would know from the beginning how to conduct himself. Herself. Theirselves." And Colonel and Mrs. MacNeill traded moist-eyed romantic gazes, Mrs. MacNeill having just last week been certain enough to reveal to her brawny husband that they, too, were soon to be parents.

In the front-most pew, Charlotte sat with her howling red-faced baby on her lap, looking completely at ease while beside her, in direct contrast, hovered her husband, Dand Ross, looking completely nonplussed. For whatever reason, this afforded Brother Martin a great deal of satisfaction. He supposed he would be obliged to confess it later. Father Tarkin, most impressive in his clerical garb, stood at the foot of the altar beside a basin of holy water.

"Thank you, God!" the abbot muttered and motioned them forward.

Brother Martin, shadowed by Brother Fidelis, stomped down the center aisle decorated with nosegays of spring snowdrops and spring ephemerals. He made Charlotte's side and without ceremony thrust the little bag of herbs under the baby's nose. The baby inhaled deeply . . . deeply . . . deeply . . . and sneezed. Then, fixing Brother Martin with her mother's gold-shot eyes, she wailed even louder.

"The poor little angel!" Brother Fidelis muttered, edging Brother Martin out of the way. "The poor little darling! There now, sweetling."

The baby unlocked her basilisk gaze from Brother Martin and turned her attention to Brother Fidelis. Her face, screwed up in a tight little knot of discontent, relaxed. She gave a cursory wail and held out her tiny arms.

Brother Fidelis held out his.

With a look of surprise, first at her daughter and then at the round monk, Charlotte lifted the baby into his waiting arms. At once, the baby settled in with a last little grumble.

"Oh, my dearest," crooned Brother Fidelis, bowing over his precious bundle. "None of these people understands, do they? There now. She only wanted a little cuddle."

And the little girl, having pegged her first male conquest in what would prove a very long list of them indeed, sighed and closed her eyes.

Blowing out a deep sigh of relief, Father Tarkin motioned the parents—along with Brother Fidelis—forward to stand before the baptismal font.

"Now then, we are gathered here today to welcome into the Lord's family this child. Have you a name for her?"

"Yes," Dand and Charlotte replied in unison.

"And what is it?"

"Rose."

AUTHOR'S NOTE

There are Catholic monasteries in Scotland. After all, Scotland was a Catholic country for centuries. And after the French Revolution, many priests, remembering those old ties, in fleeing France sought sanctuary on Scottish shores. Many returned to France after the Concordant was signed, but many did not.

Napoleon's wife, Josephine, maintained the largest collection of roses in the world, many brought to her by diplomats, adventurers, and toadies.

There were no yellow roses in England in 1800. However, the first yellow roses were probably from Persia and so the notion that a crusader brought one back from his travels is not so very far-fetched.

The street and place names in this book are all real and depicted as close to reality as my imagination and research allowed.

There are many people who made their talents and research and friendship available to me throughout the writing of this series. Chris, Mary, Terri, Liz, and Lisa, the applause continues. Susie and Merry, thanks for having my back.

Not sure what to read next?

Visit Pocket Books online at
www.SimonSays.com

Reading suggestions for
you and your reading group

New release news

Author appearances

Online chats with your favorite writers

Special offers

And much, much more!

POCKET BOOKS
A Division of Simon & Schuster
A VIACOM COMPANY

POCKET
STAR BOOKS
A Division of Simon & Schuster
A VIACOM COMPANY

10421